DREA DAMARA

THE
WEEPING
BOOKS
OF
BLINNEY
LANE

A NOVEL

HAPPY
WANDERER
PRESS

Cover, interior book design,
and eBook design by Blue Harvest Creative
www.blueharvestcreative.com

Edited by Sarah Logan Loomis

THE WEEPING BOOKS OF BLINNEY LANE

Published by
Happy Wanderer Press

ISBN-13: 978-0692445990
ISBN-10: 0692445994

Visit the author at:

Website: *www.bhcauthors.com*

Facebook: *drea.damara*

Twitter: *@DreaDamara*

Goodreads: *Drea Damara*

Blog: *dreadamara.wordpress.com*

Visit the author's blog by scanning the QR code.

for those who dare to dream

THE
WEEPING
BOOKS
OF
BLINNEY
LANE

CHAPTER

ONE

O F ALL the comforting objects in this world, few things are as reassuring and accepting as books. Books keep and reciprocate our secrets, dreams, regrets, and hopes better than any friend in the world. Sarah Allister took comfort in this thought as she walked past the shelves of books in her shop, countless stories she knew by heart. Each one marked a different time in her life, a different mood — they were forever linked in her mind by the days she'd read them. Living alone wasn't so lonely when you were surrounded by that much history.

Sarah sidled up to a stool behind the old mahogany store counter and settled onto the seat. She leaned against the upholstered leather back and glanced across the shop at two customers, a young couple. They were nestled into the oversized padded chairs by the window, looking cozy with their newly purchased books, sipping on some coffee they'd likely purchased across the street. Sarah couldn't help but feel they looked out of place amidst the 1940s-era ambiance of her shop in their Massachusetts tourist t-shirts.

Sarah then shifted her gaze to the other customer in the store, an old man in his late seventies. Mr. Wexton was busy as usual; precariously lingering over the out-of-print poetry section just in case he'd missed an edition he hadn't seen before or one that Sarah had somehow forgotten to mention she had in stock. She sighed, seeing her shoppers were content, and shifted her gaze down to the mail on the counter.

Bill. Bill. Junk. Membership renewal. Sarah flipped the unwanted envelopes into an old wooden milk crate on the floor that served as her recycle bin and tossed the bills into the narrowly divided banker slots of the antique bureau behind her. As she swiveled her chair back around to face the rest of her mail she noticed movement beyond the letters of her shop window.

From the back of the painted cream letters outlined in burgundy, Allister's Books, Sarah smiled at the sight of Francis Doltman hurrying across the cobblestone street of Blinney Lane from her own shop, just opposite to Sarah's. Francis, or "Franci" as all the shop owners on Blinney Lane called her, always wore long high-necked black dresses and her hair atop her head in the same tightly bound bun for as long as Sarah could remember.

At the moment, Franci ran on tiptoe towards Sarah's door with two to-go cups of coffee in her hands. Sarah chuckled at the sight of her. Franci's tall thin stature and spindly arms held high with a container in each hand, clad in her black attire, made her look like one of the old street light poles on Blinney Lane.

Sarah got up and went to the door just as Franci bounded up the two little stone steps to *Allister's*. The jangle of the old store bells attached to the door hinge let out their clanking chimes as Sarah pulled the heavy door open for Franci's entrance and smiled at her old friend.

"Good Moooorning!" Franci cooed in her high sing-song voice. "Fresh from the pot!" She smiled and handed one of the white paper cups to Sarah. The young couple looked up from their books upon hearing the disruptive tone of Franci's unique voice and nodded at her with their cups held up. "Oh! Hello, again!" Franci smiled and nodded back at them as she walked around to the edge of Sarah's store counter. Sarah followed and returned back to her stool behind the counter where she sniffed the aroma coming from the coffee cup.

"What have we got today, Franci?" Sarah paused in thought as she sniffed. Franci leaned against the edge of the counter, her bright white teeth beaming through thin lips and peered over her round bifocals at Sarah. It amazed Sarah that Franci appeared more like an old schoolmarm or librarian rather than herself, when Sarah was the one who dealt in books. Franci ran Spices and Stems across the street, specializing in variety of herbs and flowers that she mainly grew herself in a greenhouse and small garden behind the shop. Franci prided herself, however, on her medicinal and mood inspiring specialty teas and coffees. Sarah had been her guinea pig for such concoctions over the years. "I've got it... Cinnamon, clove, and...something else."

"Lavender...and...well, a little something else," Franci smiled mischievously.

Sarah raised a brow at Franci's comment and pursed her lips. "Okay. What's the deal? I know your premonitions for this mix and please don't tell me it's Blinney's lavender," Sarah referred to the special qualities of the lavender that grew in the dirt on Blinney Lane.

"It's Monday," Franci shrugged and took a sip of her own coffee.

"Just like it is every day after Sunday, Franci," Sarah shook her head in confusion.

"I saw Henry Teager down the street making his deliveries," Franci gestured to the window annoyed that Sarah didn't already know the significance of Monday. Sarah tried to hide her frustration as Franci jabbered on. "Did you notice he always wears the uniform pants on Mondays, but then if he stops later in the week sometimes he wears blue jeans? Seems to get more casual as the week goes on."

"Mmm hmm," Sarah muttered unenthused. She flipped through the stack of mail.

Franci leaned on the counter with one arm and rested her chin to a fist. She looked dreamily out the window. "It's like he's saying he's ready to let loose the closer it gets to the end of the week, you know, when our true selves come out. I can't decide though what I like better, the uniform slacks or the jeans." Sarah usually didn't mind that Franci did most of the talking, as Sarah was naturally quiet and non-talkative herself, but today the subject matter was disconcerting. Still, Franci continued on incessantly, unconcerned with the reaction of the recipient of her conversation. "The grey uniform slacks are so tight in the buttocks because he has to wear the belt and it sort of…cinches everything up, you know? The jeans, though, well…you know how jeans sort of rumple up in the front area? Always makes me wonder just how much is going on down there."

Sarah was intoxicated by the inviting scent of Franci's coffee concoction today and breathed in the steam as she raised the cup to her lips. Publisher's Clearing House. Electric bill. She took another sip of the coffee to involve herself in one more action that made her feel she wasn't a part of Franci's Henry-monologue, but instantly felt a flutter in her stomach when Franci made mention of Henry's butt. Sarah imagined Henry strolling gracefully down Blinney Lane, pushing his hand truck full of heavy boxes. Tanned biceps trying to breath under the restraint of elastic on his polo shirt sleeves. Long solid thighs effortlessly guiding the heavy load closer and closer to *her* shop door. Sarah's cheeks felt flushed and she was sure that the pale skin there now matched the hue of her long deep-auburn hair. Damn it, Franci!

"Franci! Really? Come on now! He's not a piece of meat," Sarah shocked herself with the velocity in which she scolded Franci. She noticed the young couple look up at them and heard the woman customer giggle. Franci remained unabashed from where she rested her pointy elbows on the counter. Sarah lowered her voice and looked at her friend, "Why do you always do this? Is this what the lavender was for? Damn it." She turned and spat some coffee flavored saliva into the garbage can between them, then firmly set her coffee cup down on the counter, releasing her grip on it.

Sarah eased back against her chair, gazed out the shop window, and folded her arms across her chest. She could feel moisture on her hands from the perspiration that seeped through her thin blouse under her arms. Yuck! She was sweating. A dull burning began to dwell at the base of her sternum and she pressed the fabric of her tank top inward between her C-cups to apply pressure to the pain. "Ugh, I think you gave me heart burn," she groaned and wondered if the coffee had been meant to encourage hot-bloodedness.

"Oh, come on Sare. Its powerful stuff, but coffee or not you can't deny the pull towards a man like Henry Teager. You two have danced around each other like school children for years," Franci added matter-of-factly and laid a knowing stare on her petite friend.

Sarah rubbed at the discomfort in her chest and sighed. "Franci," she started with a more loving and softer tone than before, "nothing changes here in our little part of the world. We both know that. I'm not going to insult years of friendship by denying that there's...there's..."

"Yeees?"

"Ugh…okay, *some*…kind of *pull*, but you and I both know it's not that. It's…it's just that I…I choose to ignore it. I *have to* ignore it. And we both know why," Sarah ended more firmly with the last sentence. At that, Franci scowled, slumped her shoulders, and looked down at her coffee. She said nothing for a moment and picked at the plastic lid.

"A girl can dream can't she?" Franci muttered dejectedly.

The sound of her friend's jolt back to reality made Sarah chuckle a little in sympathy. She shook her head as Franci clearly pouted. Franci was thirty-eight and had lived alone her whole life with her widowed mother above their shop across the street. Sarah pitied her plain yet hot-blooded friend more than most of the other shop owners on Blinney Lane. However, anything Franci lacked in beauty she made up for in compassion towards others. Luckily Franci survived on the passing smiles and occasional compliments from a few of the nerdy male tourists who happened through Spice and Stems and found her old-fashioned mannerisms appealing.

Sarah was grateful that she had never longed for companionship, lust, love, or whatever it was that Franci so desperately wanted. She was only two years behind Franci in age at thirty-six, but she never thought of herself as a doomed spinster. Sarah was perfectly content with her solitary lot in life, unlike her friend. Well, content — except for the occasions when Franci would vocalize her observations about Henry Teager. Sarah chided herself at the thought. In spite of having to ignore Henry Teager's charm, kindness, and abundant sexuality because she would never be able to divulge the secrets of Blinney Lane to him, she had other reasons.

Sarah had loved once in her life, maybe twice if she were honest. The first time had ended in tragedy and heartache which was responsible for her present serious and guarded demeanor. The second time, she knew that the love hadn't been as powerful as the first, but she sure remembered how good it had felt for a while. She'd fallen for a handsome cus-tomer who frequented her shop and loved the same books as much as she had, but as time passed he grew less and less patient with her refusal to ever wander very far from Blinney Lane. She knew she could never explain to him why she couldn't take vacations or go out for dinner more than three blocks away from her shop. He would have thought she was insane if she had. Worse yet, he likely would have went insane himself had she showed him the proof of why she couldn't leave.

The silence that sat between her and Franci as they both stared out the shop window lost in their thoughts made Sarah more uncomfortable. She shifted her attention back to her mail and stared at the next letter. It was from her brother Richard, from New York City. "That's odd," she didn't mean to say out loud.

"Hmm?" Franci peered over at the letter. "From Richard?"

"Yeah. We usually just talk on the phone every couple of months. The only time I get a card from him is on my birthday or at Christmas." Sarah sliced the letter opener through the top of the envelope and pulled out two sheets of paper that bore the unmistakable penmanship of her brother.

Franci stared out the window, waiting for Sarah to divulge the contents of Richard's letter. She tried to appear inconspic-uous as she searched through the passing shoppers for a sight of Henry Teager and his delivery cart, but after a few moments with no sign of him and silence from Sarah, she returned her attention back to her friend. Sarah's pale complexion had gone almost white against the backwash of her dark hair and light yellow blouse. Her hand was back up against her chest and her mouth hung open as she stared at the letter in her hand.

"Sarah? Well, whatever's the matter, dear?" Franci straightened up and laid one of her thin, long-fingered hands on Sarah's shoulder.

"He's…he's sending my nephew…Ricky…here," Sarah said in almost a whisper.

"Oh! Well, how nice! He hasn't been here in a few years now. It'll be nice to visit with him. How long's he staying?"

"Franci! He's sending him *here*…to stay with *me*…for the whole summer. By himself," Sarah met Franci's eyes with a stern tone.

"The whole summer?" Franci gasped, "but…but that's too long! Doesn't Richard remember anything? He should know that's too dangerous…too long for an Allister to be here."

Sarah dropped the letter and let it fall to the counter. "He *should* know," she added with scorn, "but apparently he seems to think Ricky will be safe."

"Safe? Hrmph, what a fool. Men are just as susceptible to the curse of Agatha Bl…"

"Franci!" Sarah snapped to prevent Franci from uttering the name every shop owner on Blinney Lane feared to mention on the chance it would evoke any dormant lurking energy of the curse that so tightly confined their lives already.

Franci slapped her pale hand over her mouth, eyes wide. "Sorry," she gasped. "Men are just as susceptible to…to the curse as women. How old is Ricky now?"

"Seventeen," Sarah sighed.

"Almost a man. Oh, dear lord," Franci reached for the phone on the counter and shoved it at Sarah. "Call him. Call that silly brother of yours and tell him he can't do this to his own son."

"I can't."

"What do you mean you can't? What's the number? I'll call him myself! That Richard, what an idiot!"

"He arrives tomorrow, and Richard apparently has to go overseas on business."

"Well…well…" Franci adjusted her bifocals several times and then chewed on her thumb nail. She was an easy one to fluster. "Well, what about Allison? Does Ricky ever see his mother anymore?"

"No. Not for the last four years and she wasn't much of a mother to begin with." Now Sarah actually felt some pity towards the situation her brother had described in his letter and less of the anger upon first reading it. He really didn't have much choice but to send Ricky to Salem.

"Surely, they have friends in New York he could stay with or…or Richard could take Ricky with him on his trip." Franci began to pace at a predicament that wasn't even her own.

Sarah picked the letter back up, full-well knowing what it said. "Richard will be gone for three months, six different countries, with the CEOs. And Ricky," she sighed. "My dear little nephew seems to have thought car theft and joy-riding were rites of passage amongst his friends. "*Court-ordered familial supervision and community service.*" I guess leaving the country for the next few months with all the work he has to do would limit Richard's ability to properly 'supervise' him. It sounds like Richard really didn't have any other options. He told the judge I agreed to let Ricky work *here* and stay with *me.*"

"Oh, no! Without your actual consent first? Well, that's… that's just illegal!"

Sarah slumped back into her chair and ran her hands through her thick hair. Then she rested her elbows on the counter and plopped her face in her hands. "Ugh, I hope to hell nothing happens to him."

"Sarah," Franci patted her on the back. "We'll help you take care of it. I'll whip up the best protection blends I have and…let me see. Mary! Mary will do the same with her masking soaps. I'll go ask her myself."

"Would you mind?" Sarah looked up with some hope in her eyes.

"No, no. Not at all. And we'll get Ricky out of the shop as often as we can."

"Ha! So he can go lift cars downtown? How am I supposed to bail him out if I can barely make it to the jail?" Sarah lifted her wrist up to Franci's face and shook a wide cuff charm bracelet. The little trinkets, charms, and key that dangled from it rattled together. Franci frowned and looked down at Sarah's other wrist, covered up by the collar of her long sleeved blouse. Franci reached up to the high collar of her black dress and rubbed at her neck, a far-off look of fear crept into her eyes. Sarah pulled Franci's hand away, feeling guilty for the sensations she knew the woman was remembering. "I'm sorry, Franci."

"Oh, it's not your fault," Franci stated with a firm look. "I'd better go before mom reorganizes the entire inventory," she said a little flustered.

"Okay," Sarah smiled.

"I'll let you know what Mary comes up with," Franci said as she started towards the door.

"Thanks. And thanks for the coffee," Sarah smiled reassuringly, picked up the cup, and fanned herself with one hand in a swooning manner. Franci forced a laugh, but the two knew this was no time for lightheartedness, especially with the reminder the rattling of the charms on Sarah's wrist made with the motion.

Sarah set the cup down as soon as Franci was out the door and seriousness washed over her. She rotated the bracelet around her wrist. She wondered if she imagined the tinge of pain she felt across the scars under the thick leather band that she had worn every day since the summer she turned eighteen.

CHAPTER
TWO

NEW YORK CITY

RICHARD ALLISTER paced back to the suitcase on his bed with a stack of undershirts in his hand. He tucked them down into the space he'd saved for them and then stared blankly at the contents as he fidgeted with his tie. He knew he had everything he needed for the trip and was just avoiding the obvious by meticulously going over what he'd packed and repacked three times already. Sarah was going to hate him.

Richard couldn't turn down the overseas trip to meet with the new investors. He was the lead financial manager in his company and the new international corporate clients were critical to taking his firm from a multi-million dollar level to a multi-billion dollar level. He stood and looked at himself in the mirror and could see the worry on his face. He hadn't slept well since the verdict on Ricky's grand theft auto joyride. There were dark circles under his eyes and the black five o'clock shadow stubble that matched the thick hair on his head made his corporate appearance seem disheveled just now. Damn it, Alison, why couldn't you have been more of a mother, Richard thought to himself as he looked at the reflection of a haggard over-worked single father. He sighed, knowing that if he'd chosen a better spouse, one less materialistic, his life might not have ended up the way it had, nor would he have had to bombard his little sister with the sneaky way he'd duped her into doing him a favor.

Richard slumped down to sit on the end of his bed as he looked around the obscenely impersonal look of his fifth floor penthouse bedroom. He stared blankly at the awful monstrosity of a large, red, steel blob-like structure that hung on the wall opposite his bed. Alison had insisted that it helped balance the lines in the room, which still made no sense to him. He didn't even feel comfortable in his own home, not that he was ever there much. How had that happened?

Sarah still lived on the second floor apartment they had grown up in, above the book store. He used to feel guilty that she was the one who was stuck there. As time went on, however, sometimes Richard now envied her the coziness, the quaintness, and the history of Blinney Lane in that forgotten sleepy part of Salem. Richard pushed up off of the bed. Okay, maybe not all of the history, he chided himself. He hadn't forgotten everything about the peculiar place he grew up in. He hadn't forgotten how every word and every action seemed to have a repercussion, especially for his sister. She was so tense and worrisome, but Richard still knew that things had never been so severe for him on Blinney Lane. He was convinced he'd made the right decision about Ricky.

No one, in the time he could remember before he left home, had ever fully figured out all of the quirks of Agatha Blinney's curse, but Richard still believed that the men were affected less than the women. For certain, he was also convinced that once Agatha Blinney's curse took hold of at least one family member of each of the shops on Blinney Lane, it usually left the rest of the family free to leave Blinney Lane. The curse only seemed to claim more than one family member if someone was getting on in age, as though it sensed a replacement would be needed soon. After Sarah was chosen to replace their father, Richard thought he was able to leave without being pulled back, without being bound to serve on that eerie street through the resurfacing of Agatha Blinney's wounds on whomever she deemed her chosen victim.

Marks started to appear on Sarah's wrists when they were just teenagers. Richard assumed that his sister had read too many of the cursed books in the shop, or said the name of Agatha Blinney too many times. Sarah used to cry and swear she'd done nothing wrong when their mother interrogated her about the marks, not wanting to see her bound to the shop. Finally, it had become apparent that the curse of Blinney Lane had taken hold on Sarah and she was doomed to stay there for the rest of her life. The curse had chosen Sarah, and not Richard, who remained unmarred.

Richard remembered how he felt guilt and relief at the same time. He'd long worried he'd be stuck on that niche little tourist strip, which consisted of twelve shops on a dead end street. He didn't even like books and hadn't wanted to disappoint his father by not taking over the family business. Richard had wanted to see the world, meet normal people, and to fall asleep without worrying what unnatural thing would occur in the night. Thank the stars the curse never got him.

You never believed all that hogwash, Rich, he told himself as he sat down by his suitcase. So then what's eating at you? To be honest, Richard had forced himself to forget any of the abnormalities he had witnessed on his home street. As the years passed he'd almost completely forgotten them except for the occasional dream. Sitting in his dimly lit, bachelor's cell of a room that so deeply contrasted the home he grew up in, and facing the reality that he was sending his son to his childhood home, made Richard recall one memory with perfect clarity — Deronda. There was no fancying Deronda a mere dream amongst his mix of memories. As unreal as she was, Deronda had been very real.

Sarah and Richard only spoke every few months by phone and Richard had only visited her about four times since he'd moved away after college. Her coming to New York City had of course been out of the question — she could never leave Blinney Lane, just like the rest of the poor souls who were stuck there. During phone calls and visits, however, neither Sarah nor Richard had ever mentioned Deronda's name. The time he'd spent with Deronda hadn't been a dream. Richard was just afraid to remember it or he would go mad. What Richard did remember as he reflected for the first time with such clarity about the place he grew up in, was that his little sister had saved his life and sacrificed so much for him.

"Ugh," he moaned and pressed his fingers to his eyes. He felt the burning sensation of tears in them. Guilt. What he was feeling now was definitely guilt. Richard knew he hadn't avoided Blinney Lane or Sarah because he was afraid of the hocus pocus that went on there. He'd avoided them because there was nothing he could do to help Sarah. Now you've gone and probably thrown her in a tizzy over Ricky coming there, he thought. Way to go, asshole.

Richard stood up at the thought of the word "asshole." It was something he'd been called recently and the term quickly reminded him of his dear teenage son who was supposed to be packing for Salem in the next room. Richard walked down the hallway and the rock music from Ricky's room became louder as he approached the doorway.

There was a bright yellow metal hazardous sign on the door and several *New York Giants* stickers. The bright colors sure messed up the lines of the plain white walls of the penthouse, Richard mused as he knocked on the door and smirked in spite of himself. "Ricky?"

The squealing guitar solo and chainsaw bass sound continued to emanate through the door, but no sound of Ricky's acknowledgement. "Ricky!" Richard pounded on the door.

The door jerked open and a topless, ripple-chested teenage boy stared hostilely up the five inches that his father still towered over him. Richard took in the look of his son, the same thick black hair spiked stupidly upwards and canted to the side, the shadow of stubble on his more youthful skin, the light grey eyes. How can he look so much like me and hate me so much? He's a teenager, he hates everything.

"What?" Ricky belted in a deflated tone that clearly warned his time and privacy were being invaded.

"Are you packed?" Richard matched Ricky's annoyance with his own.

Ricky sighed, turned his back, and retreated further into his hovel of a room. "Yeee-ah," came his snotty reply.

"We went over this, *Mr. Gone In Sixty Seconds*! This is your own fault and I'm sure not happy with the situation, but I can't cart you all over Europe and Asia with my bosses. You want to go stay with your mother?" Richard added the last line as a threat.

Ricky spun back around, "Why? If we knew where she was do you think she'd actually want me there?"

Richard sighed at his poor choice of words. "All right. All right. Easy *Earnhardt*." Ricky scowled at the name calling his father had picked up since Ricky's joy-riding incident. "Look, don't give your aunt any grief. You hear me? Turn that crap down!" Ricky hit the volume button on his stereo and stared out the window, hands on hips. "She's got a business to run! It's a quiet little place not used to teenagers."

"More like a retirement home," Ricky muttered.

"What?"

Ricky just shook his head and crossed his arms over his chest. "Yeah. I got it."

Richard ran his hand through his hair. "Just try to help her out as much as you can, will you? Keep your nose clean and don't cause her any problems. She's doing both of us a favor with this."

Ricky didn't like the sound of being someone's favor like he was a burden people had to put up with. He'd felt like that most of his life, always in the way. The only time someone noticed he was around was if he did something they didn't like. He'd never done what Mom wanted him to do with her Ivy League etiquette and demeanor. He wouldn't mind Dad hollering at him when he did do the occasional stupid thing like hot-wire Gerry Wrenly's sweet-ass Camaro, the stupid hotshot prick, but Dad was never around enough to do anything else but scold him. Didn't he know he couldn't have love and respect if he didn't take the time to say "good job" for the things Ricky ever did that were a good job? Now I'm being sent off to Colonial Days USA with the weirdo tourist theme-shop players to make caramel apples and sell postcards, Ricky griped in his mind. This is such bullshit!

"Ricky, are you listening to me?"

"Yeah," Ricky lowered his defenses...just a little. "I heard you. Play nice with Aunt Sarah. Smile at the old ladies. Read a book. Got it."

As Richard started to close the door he stared at his defiant son for a moment. For once he didn't mind Ricky's sarcasm. He knew his son didn't like to read and right now he was actually grateful for it. "No one expects you to read any books, son. Just do what you're told."

CHAPTER
THREE

AFTER FRANCI had gone back to her own shop, Sarah began to make a list of things she might need for Ricky. She'd never had an outsider stay in the flat above the shop, nor had her parents from what she could remember. Ricky was family, but that didn't really make him an insider. She had enough linens for him. She could add a little more meat to the grocery order, but being a teenager maybe Ricky would prefer to go out in town and devour some junk food. At least that would get him away from the book shop for a while.

Sarah made a note to add more manly magazines to her next order in the hopes they would keep Ricky entertained and out of trouble when he was in the shop. She couldn't let him wander around the city by himself all the time, especially after what Richard had said he'd done to get into trouble. Trouble. Great. Would Ricky be trouble? Was he no longer the sweet little boy who used to love listening to her stories? Locks. Maybe I should get some more padlocks, Sarah thought. She wrote the word down just before she sighed and dropped her head into her hands.

The scrape sound of footsteps against the wood floor approached and Sarah heard the phlegmy garbled voice of Mr. Wexton as he passed by the counter. "Nothing new. Let me know if you get anything new in Sarah," he said dejectedly followed by the jingle of the shop doorbell as he opened it to leave.

Without looking up, Sarah yelled through her hands, "Will do, Mr. Wexton." She heard the shop door slam shut and let out a long loud sigh now that the shop was free of customers. "What did I do to deserve this?"

"It's Monday," came a deep wholesome voice that she would know anywhere, causing the tiny hairs on the back of her neck to stand up.

Sarah slowly lifted her head from her hands and peered first at a black leather belt on grey uniform slacks, then up a wide and solid chest pressed firmly to the green polo shirt which covered it. She tilted her eyes up the rest of the way, past the Adam's apple in the center of a tanned muscular neck, to the firm square jaw and supple lower lip of the most handsome smile she'd ever seen. Sarah locked eyes with the light green ones above Henry Teager's very masculine and seemingly unbreakable nose. How can his nose even seem muscular, she thought.

Henry's dark brown hair was cut close at the sides. The length on top was long enough that it arched just slightly from the part above one eye over to where it lulled on his head above the other. He had that all-American boyish look, minus any of the overzealous grease a teenager would glob through such beautiful hair. Henry smiled down at her, the corner of his mouth higher on one side, always in the shape of a happy, innocent smirk.

"Hello, Henry." Sarah wondered why her voice suddenly sounded like that of a little girl's and cleared her throat.

"Rough day already? It's only eleven."

"Ha, tell me about it."

Henry lifted a clipboard off the top box of the pile stacked on his hand truck and set in on the counter for Sarah to sign. She looked around the counter for her pen. "How are you today, Henry?"

"I'm great. Beautiful weather. Not too hot yet." Easy for you to say, you didn't have Franci's coffee, Sarah thought as she scribbled her name on the invoice. "And I'm on my favorite street on my route, so I can't complain."

Sarah chuckled and glanced up at him for a brief moment, until she saw his eyes were still looking directly at her. "What did we do to receive that honor?"

Henry leaned on the hand truck and propped one of his thick legs up on the foot rest. The stance made Sarah worry that he wouldn't be leaving any time soon and in her current emotional state she didn't think she could quite handle Henry's presence for as long as he usually stayed in the shop. "I love Blinney Lane. You know that. The people are so friendly, some of the best people you'll ever meet," Henry smiled and glanced out the window then back to Sarah. She smiled at that comment thinking of her friends on Blinney Lane. "I get the most unique orders here due to the specialty shops. It sure breaks up the monotony of my day from the basic office material delivery type of supplies. Heck, the distributor I work for sells stuff I didn't know we could get or even existed if it weren't for the Blinney shops. I don't know. I think I just love how nothing seems to change here. You can always count on Blinney Lane even though the rest of the world moves on around it."

"Hrmph," Sarah scoffed lightly at her private opinions on why Blinney Lane couldn't change. Henry was an outsider. What did he know? However, Sarah wouldn't have it any other way. Henry was her dream of the joy of the outside world — the one book she had never read, but could write and rewrite as she wanted. "Well, change is coming tomorrow, whether we're ready for it or not."

Henry looked at her quizzically. "Barnes and Noble moving in?"

She smiled, "No. Worse, I think. My teenage nephew is coming to stay with me for the summer."

"Richard's boy?"

"Yeah. Little Ricky. Well, I guess he's not that little any more. Gosh, I haven't seen him in three years. He's seventeen now," she winced at the proclamation.

Henry let out a deep chuckle. "Yeah, that could be worse. I can't imagine being seventeen and spending my summer in a bookstore."

"Hey, what happened to loving this place?"

Henry blushed. A man who blushes, wow. How could someone so machismo in appearance be so shy and kind, Sarah wondered. She let herself stare directly at his face then for the first time since he had walked into the store.

"Oh, I didn't mean any disrespect. I just meant I spent my summers outside playing ball and swimming. If I hadn't been so busy dreaming about being a pro-athlete I probably would have been hanging around in here throwing glances at Richard's little sister," he ended with a wink. Sarah cast her eyes quickly back down to the clipboard at the comment. "I guess I didn't do anything very productive…is what I meant to say," Henry's tone softened as he cleared his throat. Sarah let out a soft laugh in response.

Henry brought his foot back to the floor from the hand truck and grabbed the clip board. He wheeled the hand truck to the end of the counter and slid the stack of boxes onto the floor, leaving enough room for Sarah when she needed to get by. He looked at her for a moment, neither of them saying anything, and then he swallowed. "Well, uh, need me to order anything for Ricky?"

"Yes, actually," Sarah grabbed her list.

"Some *Playboys* and Def Leppard albums?" Henry smirked and reached for the list.

"Def Leppard? What do kids even listen to now? God, you just made us sound old, I think," Sarah turned towards him with her list. She couldn't help but wonder if the graze of his fingers on hers as he took her note was deliberate.

"We're not *that* old, Sarah," the softness in his voice was simply cruel combined with his looks.

He shouldn't be allowed around women, she noted to herself. Sarah's breath caught in her throat, not knowing what to do or say when he acted in this peculiar way. Henry was consistently friendly and complimentary by nature, but every so often Sarah got the impression his compliments were specifically intended to remind her that she was a woman, and he was a man. As if I need that reminder, she swallowed a lump in her throat. The shop bell chimed like a savior.

"Hi Sarah!" A thin, blue-eyed teenage girl with dirty-blonde hair waved with one hand, the other gripping her embroidered back pack. She had a ruffled jean skirt on and bright horizontally striped knee socks to further contrast her ever-cute little Boho appearance.

"Good morning, Shelby," Sarah smiled in relief at the distraction. The slim little gal walked happily by with a bounce over to one of the chairs where the young couple had been earlier, and tossed her book bag down with familiarity. Shelby dropped down into the chair and let her striped-clad legs bounce up in the air with the motion, and then her Converse shoes tapped back to the floor. Sarah looked back at Henry, who had also seen Shelby walk in.

Henry looked back from Shelby to Sarah and muttered with seriousness, "Okay, scratch the *Playboys*. Good luck."

"Hrmph, that girl's sixteen going on P.H.D. I doubt she'll even notice him."

LATER THAT night, Sarah locked the door to the shop behind Mary Millville and Franci after they came over from across the street upon locking up their own shops. They settled themselves down onto the old, olive toned sofa in the reading nook as Sarah pulled the window shades of the shop down and turned out the main lights. She walked over and sat in one of the chairs across from the ladies, eyeing the basket Mary held in her lap. "Okay, what've you got?"

Mary Millville was a former blonde, going grey in spite of the age-defying concoctions she could whip up at her own shop, Scents and Suds. Mary claimed she let it go grey since she didn't have the face or figure a fifty-something woman would need to still look good as a blonde.

Mary was also convinced that the historical dresses she wore to cater towards the theme of Blinney Lane's shops went well with her gracefully aging appearance. She opined that grey hair indicated wisdom, and thus customers were more likely to trust her and her products. She sat on Sarah's couch now in one of her ruffle-collared dresses with an empire waist, which was hidden under the large barrel shape of her bulky bosom. The long billowy skirt of Mary's dress was covered in the front by a traditional linen apron with a large bow tied in the back above her big rump. Her lace-up black boots peeked out from under the dress hem along with her underskirts. That's got to be hot as hell in the summer, Sarah thought.

There wasn't any type of written or spoken agreement amongst the shop owners on Blinney Lane in regards to uniforms. Those who chose to dress in garb reminiscent of the past did as they chose. Sarah preferred the Marlene Dietrich look of suspenders and long-sleeved dress shirts with slacks.

She felt it held up the 1930s era for the district and gave her a clerk-like appearance, as Allister's was originally a print shop when her first ancestor built the place. She was just grateful they could get away wearing unusual clothing since many of the shop owner's on the little cul-de-sac had physical abnormalities they'd rather hide. Mary for instance, would never be caught wearing an open-back anything. The marks on her back were far too prominent for her to feel comfortable revealing them in public, thus the reason she likely stuck with her full-backed haughty old colonial style gowns.

"Sarah, first off, I have to say…and without any disrespect to you of course, my dear, but your brother is being most irresponsible with his son," Mary frowned and gestured with a halting sign of her hand to accentuate her point. Here it comes, Sarah thought. Mary was a loud woman with plump cheeks and jowls that made her face appear similar to that of a bulldog, ironically fitting her personality. Springy curls bounced around her face as she nodded with each point she firmly made. Mary was a thoughtful voice of reason and wisdom in the district and knew the history of Blinney Lane the best of all its residents with the exception of maybe Franci. When she spoke everyone listened, even if they'd heard it before. The dignity with which Mary carried herself was a way of the old, and her gracefulness and propriety commanded an audience. "To come and put this on you and the community is simply inconsiderate to the very fabric of…of," she paused to look at a nervous Franci beside her. Franci just nodded in anticipation for what Mary would come up with. "of our society here."

"I know that Mary," Sarah offered delicately.

"And I know you know that, Sarah, which is why I would never consider *you* had anything to do with this…this unfortunate arrangement," Mary added compassionately. Franci just smiled and nodded at Sarah.

In spite of being some twenty-plus years Mary's junior, Mary treated Sarah with the utmost respect. Sarah assumed this was due, in part, to the responsible way she had always carried herself, and the rest to Mary's respect for the part the Allister family had played in the history of Blinney Lane. As Mary fretted on about the impending arrival of Ricky, Sarah silently reminisced on the story of her ancestors.

During the late 17th century, as a witchcraft-mania swept through Salem, a young woman named Agatha Blinney was condemned to death by the local villagers who lived on what was now called "Blinney Lane." The villagers discovered that Agatha had become the lover of their local cobbler, Nathan Nurscher, who happened to be a married man. The only plausible explanation for a married man with four children to behave so sinfully at that time was that the uncommonly beautiful Agatha must have used witchcraft to lure him under her spell. It didn't help that several other wives in the village were quite jealous of the young lady as well as having husbands who were dismayed to find they hadn't been chosen as the object of the woman's designs.

Controlled by their enraged hysteria, Agatha's neighbors pulled her from her home, where they subdued her wrists and ankles with rope. The party of angered men and women grew as they dragged her down the street, all the while screaming their accusation that she was a witch for "seducing" a married man. Agatha cried out denials to the charge, as the villagers brought her to the end of the street in front of Nurscher's cobbler shop, where a lone tree stood. They tied her to the trunk and someone began to whip her as the sky cracked thunder and a heavy rain began to fall, taking Agatha's streaming blood down the street with the flooding water. When the local magistrate finally arrived, he knew there was no turning back the incensed crowd and he approved the girl's execution. Agatha was untied briefly enough to allow a rope to be thrown over a branch of the tree and to speak her last words as a noose was placed around her neck.

Agatha eyed the villagers coldly, as she shivered from the pain of her wounds being stung by the pouring rain. "My only sin was giving my love to a man who took it, but wouldn't claim it. Take from me my soul, but I leave you my heartache!" She cried out before the stool was kicked out from under her feet causing her to fall and her neck to snap.

The next morning, weeping and wailing could be heard from within many of the buildings on Blinney Lane as inhabitants awoke to find people dead in their beds. It was later determined that anyone who had walked through the rainwater, tainted with Agatha's blood, did not awake the next day. Other peculiar things began to happen and the villagers soon realized they had not damned Agatha Blinney, but rather had damned themselves with the curse she left behind.

Nathan Nurscher saw the untimely death of his wife and three daughters in the months after Agatha's hanging. One day, a woman ran screaming from his shop that she felt like nails were being driven into her feet after trying on a new pair of shoes. Nurscher suggested the villagers hold a festival to honor Blinney's memory hoping the tribute would help to change his foul luck. He even made a new pair of boots to wear for the occasion. That night, as the fiddlers played, the neighbors couldn't believe their eyes as the usually serious and stoic Nurscher spun, twirled, and kicked in time with the music. "It's not me! I'm not doing it! It's *her*. It must be her!" Nathan had cried. Sometimes at night, that same pair of old boots are still known to dance on their own. At his wits' end with the surprises of the curse, Nurscher made a proposition to the Allister family who had also been as plagued by the curse as him.

When the rain had washed down the street the day Agatha Blinney died, it pooled in a low spot right outside

Allister's print shop where the cul-de-sac met the main road. No one doubted that this was the reason why the Allisters were plagued with so many more peculiar phenomenon in their shop than others on the little street. The Allisters agreed to Nathan Nurscher's proposition that their daughter marry his son, Wilbur, when the two came of age. The union was arranged in the hopes that the pledged faithfulness of the pair would serve to honor Agatha Blinney and luckily diminish the strength of the curse. Durley Allister had already lost one child to the bloodied waters and was willing to try anything to protect what remained of his family.

Sarah shuddered at the thought of having to live during those early days of the curse. How had the residents endured unexplainable deaths, books that suddenly came to life, and all the other occurrences that had been documented once the Blinney Council was formed? While living on Blinney Lane was precarious, at least now it was fairly peaceful and free of violent circumstances if the "rules" were followed. Sarah sighed, "The rules." Another Allister showing up on Blinney Lane didn't seem like playing safely by the rules. It had bothered her all day and sent her mind worrying if Ricky's arrival would shift the curse off-balance. Acknowledging this, Sarah didn't begrudge how Mary sat nervously before her now, delicately warning her of her shared concerns.

"In order to respect the...*history* of Blinney Lane, we want to avoid any blundering that an uneducated outsider might unintentionally bring." Mary raised her voice at the word "unintentionally," and Sarah had to try not to laugh. She knew Mary was trying to address Agatha directly, the curse, or what-have you that if Ricky did something wrong it wouldn't be a deliberate attempt to invoke Agatha's wrath. "Which is why, Sarah, I've brought you something as Francis has requested of me."

"Yes, Mary, thank you," Sarah waited patiently, hands between her knees and watched to see what Mary would retrieve from the old wicker basket on her lap.

Mary pulled out a large glass jar that contained a dark creamy liquid and handed it to her. Sarah studied the jar and shifted it gently back and forth. She'd seen jars explode in Mary's shop before if they weren't handled carefully. Luckily, effects like that usually only occurred in the presence of Blinney Lane residents and not the unsuspecting public.

"Have him wash his hair with that and he can use it like a body soap as well. You should be able to funnel it into a less conspicuous bottle when he's not looking," Mary dug through the basket as she spoke.

"Mary, is there any way you can make it...not so brown looking?" Sarah hesitated.

Mary frowned, knowingly, "No, dear. Believe me, I've tried. Just tell him it's some new expensive exotic thing from... oh, who's that fellow? Calvin Clean or something?"

"Klein," Franci smiled.

"What?"

"Klein. It's Calvin Klein."

"Yes. Yes, that's what I said," Mary waved Franci off with her hand and squinted at the label on a small salve tube she pulled from her basket. "It'll protect him from any harm as best we can hope. Now this," she handed the tube to Sarah, "is for his teeth. Being a teenager and foreign to our ways here, we can just assume he'll probably say something...well, things that might be unpleasant to...to say in such a place as this." Mary, frustrated for words, just nodded to Sarah hoping she understood her meaning.

"Yes, I understand." Sarah started to open the cap, "May I?" She knew little of potions and pastes or their power; books were her specialty. She wasn't sure if this particular creation was harmful to anyone that it wasn't intended for, and wanted to make sure Mary approved.

"Yes. Yes, you can open it. These are both safe to you, Sarah. I made sure of that."

Sarah unscrewed the cap and sniffed the paste. "Oohf, it smells like citronella." The paste was yellow and waxy in consistency.

Franci giggled, but stopped when Mary shot her a dark look. "Well, it won't keep the mosquitoes away if that's what you're thinking," Mary arched a brow.

Sarah grazed her index finger across the top of the tube to catch a small dab of the paste. She tapped her tongue with that finger and then grimaced. "Ugh! Mary…it *tastes* like citronella."

"Hrmph. You *know* what citronella tastes like?" Mary straightened up her proud back.

"I do," Franci peered knowingly over her bifocals. At that, Mary rolled her eyes.

"Don't you have something to offer, Miss Know-it-all?" Mary asked Franci.

Franci reached into her pocket and pulled out a cellophane baggie of grey powder. She tossed it at Sarah and it landed in her lap. "Just mix that up like an Arab or Greek coffee. Remember how to make those?" Sarah nodded. "It'll make him feel a little warm, which is the downside since it's getting hotter out, but the heat means its working because it's giving off protection."

Sarah opened the cellophane baggie and sniffed the powder. She sneezed immediately and eyes burned. Good lord, she thought, it's like cayenne pepper!

"Got a bit of a kick to it, doesn't it?" Franci grinned and swung her arm in front of her, fist clenched.

"Mary. Franci. I'm so grateful to the both of you for doing this for me, but…I mean, what if I can't get him to use any of this stuff. No offense," she held her hand out to accentuate her gratitude, "I mean, he's a teenager. I'm not his mother and he hasn't seen me in three years. I can't make him use poop-brown shampoo, citronella toothpaste, and drink...jalapeno tea."

Mary's features softened and she stood up, smoothing down the wrinkles of her dress. She smiled and approached Sarah, where she cupped the young woman's chin lovingly in her soft hand. In spite of all Mary's displays of strict serious-ness, she was all heart. She was like a protective old aunt to Sarah, and had been since Sarah's mother died some fifteen years ago. "Sarah, you're right. He *is* a teenager. Which means *you're* the adult, so just remind him of that. You're the boss."

Sarah forced a smiled and squeezed Mary's hand as she looked up into her dark brown eyes. That was easy for Mary to say. Mary had a daughter, Valerie. The two argued often, but when Mary wanted something done or had a point to make, she got that motherly tone and Valerie inevitably complied. Mary had years of practice. Valerie was twenty-six years old. Sarah had never commanded children in her life, only play-fully entertained the children of customers who came into her shop. "What if he doesn't want a boss, Mary?"

Mary let her hand drop from Sarah's chin and readjusted the basket handle in the crook of her arm. "Well, then we go with plan B." Mary nodded to Franci that it was time to leave and they headed towards the door.

"What's plan B?" Sarah asked as she unlocked the shop door.

Mary studied her descent of the stairs as she stood in the doorway. Everyone on the street knew the Allister's shop had received the plethora of the curse's power due to that dark red pool that had seeped into the ground out front so long ago. To this day, Mary was so superstitious of the thought that she gathered up her skirts to bound over the front steps each time she passed. Mary took that very action just then.

She jumped and steadied herself on the cobblestone street at the bottom of the steps and wheezed. Mary primped her curls and called over her shoulder, "We give him an acne outbreak and tell him that stuff is the only cure."

Sarah locked the door after Franci and Mary left. She flipped the switch for the remaining lights to the shop, and then walked past the elbow-high shelves towards the back of the store.

The shop had a split-level structure and there was a wide set of three stairs leading to the upper level against the wall just beyond the store counter. An ornate wooden balcony rail jutted out to the left of the stairs and stopped at a dividing wall that hid the majority of this level from the customers. The front side of the wall served as more book display shelving, while the back side of this partition held yet another set of book-filled shelves. Beyond that were even more ceiling-high shelves in rows. This portion of the shop looked like an archaic library, all of its shelves filled with antique and out-of-print books and manuscripts. Very few customers were ever allowed back here.

Sarah stood on the landing at the top of the three stairs and looked up the next staircase that led to her living quarters, the place she had lived her entire life like many Allisters before her. Just as she reached to place her hand on the next stair railing, she stopped and turned her head towards the last row of book shelves, where a glowing light emitted through the darkness of the room.

Sarah walked slowly around the stair case and past the other four bookshelves until she reached the final shelf against the back wall of the building. She felt a damp coolness waft against her face like a chilly night breeze and acknowledged the feeling of an internal pull. It made her feel as though her insides were aching to lunge forward.

There on the last shelf, behind iron padlocked bars, behind thick glass cabinet doors, five thick, leather bound books appeared to glow under the light of the yellow lamps. Each sat slanted back on display stands, basking ominously under the light.

Sarah stared at the books and watched as a drop of water slowly fell from the bottom of one of them and ran down the base of the inside of the cabinet. She heard a thin trickle sound and she noticed a tiny thread of water along the bottom crevice of the cabinet shelf. The water slowly dribbled towards the center of the shelf, which angled slightly downward in the center to a small silver drain hole. A knot formed in Sarah's throat as she gazed over the books and she noted with her discerning eye the minuscule bits of dew which clung to their seams.

"You know he's coming, don't you?" She whispered to the glass.

Sarah listened to her breath and the trickle of the drain. The lights in the case were heat lamps, intended to dry the weeping books as much as possible, but all Sarah could feel was a cold chill emanating from the cabinet.

"Please don't hurt him. Don't take him. You *have me*," she pleaded and looked at the books. Just then, Sarah heard a clink noise and felt something brush against the skin on her hand just above her wrist.

Sarah looked down at the leather cuff bracelet. All of the charms attached to it dangled in their usual places, except for one — one that wasn't really a charm, but rather an old metal key. It flipped upward against Sarah's arm and shook, then came down and stopped perpendicular to where her arm hung limply at her side like it was pointing at the case. The key pointed in the direction of the book farthest to the right. Sarah looked from the key to the fading words across the book's cover, *The Lands of Farwin Wood*. "No," she whispered forcefully and pushed the key back down with her other hand. "I told you. I'm *never* coming back."

A large drop of water seeped out between the page bottoms of *The Lands of Farwin Wood* and landed on the metal base of the bookshelf with an echoing *plop*, and then another. Sarah pursed her lips. She knew it wasn't Agatha Blinney answering her plea. It was simply the devious power of Agatha's curse at work. It had a mind of its own. The curse certainly knew something was coming. It sensed the impending presence of another Allister, one of the descendants of the first villagers. The curse had to feed something with this new burst of extra energy, unfortunately for Sarah it appeared to be feeding the "Weeping Books," as her family had come to call them. She should have suspected this would happen. It was her brother's son who was coming after all. Why wouldn't the book that had nearly killed Richard awaken with the arrival of his only child?

CHAPTER

FOUR

JUST LET me out here, man," Ricky called over the seat to the taxi driver who had already circled the block twice.

"Sorry, kid. I don't see no Blinney Lane. You sure you know where you're going?"

"Yeah. I think I remember now." The cabbie pulled over and got out to lug Ricky's suitcase from the trunk. Ricky pulled a twenty out of the wad of bills in his wallet, courtesy of his absent father. The sight of his full wallet just made him more pissed off.

From what Ricky remembered, there wasn't anywhere he'd even want to spend money in this part of Salem. The area where his eccentric Aunt Sarah lived was full of historical Salem stuff that he'd seen the last few times he'd been here with his parents. His last trip had been only with his father, shortly after Ricky's mother had abandoned them. He'd been in too much of a slump during that trip to enjoy anything, not that his mother had ever been a joy to be around. Ricky's dad had taken him out of the district to a ball game and a movie, but the rest of the time hadn't seemed as fulfilling as when he'd visited as a younger child. There had been nothing about Blinney Lane to awe a pissed-off fourteen-year-old, and he doubted his opinion would change now that three years had passed.

The cabbie slung the large suitcase up on the curb and took his hat off to wipe the sweat from his balding head. Ricky handed him the twenty and then closed his wallet up to tuck it back into his jeans pocket.

"That's a lot of dough for a kid you're age," the guy nodded and smiled at the sight of Ricky waving away the offer of change for the cab fare.

"Paternal guilt," Ricky said flatly and tugged his baggie pants up a little higher on his slender hips.

"Well, try to have a nice summer, kid," he tipped his hat and got back into his cab.

Ricky looked up and down the street to familiarize himself with his surroundings. He knew his aunt's cul-de-sac was along this road somewhere. It was one of those old narrow roads with the original cobblestone, so contrite and historic that it was blocked off to wheeled vehicle traffic by two black posts bolted into the ground just before the intersection where it met the busy main drag.

"Harold, I tell you he said it was just up here past a barber shop. 'Blinney Lane' or something, the man said," a loud female voice came from behind Ricky. He turned around and saw a short chubby man and woman in their sixties, both wearing matching sun visors on their heads. The woman toted an over-sized bag that read *Come see historic Salem!* on the side of it. The man, obviously Harold, followed unenthusiastically behind the woman as though each step pained him. He looked weighed down by the shopping bags he held in the crook of each of his arms and held a tourist map limply in one of his hands.

"Eileen, you don't have to buy something from every damned shop in Salem!" the man called after her as she kept scurrying onward. Ricky smirked at the sight of the pair, happy to see that someone was at least more miserable than he felt. He looked beyond the woman and saw a spiral barber shop sign. He remembered it from his last trip to Aunt Sarah's, so he followed in step behind Harold with the same amount of enthusiasm.

"Yes, but he said they're supposed to have all this organic type stuff over there. And they've got all this stuff from the olden days and a book store. You like books. You can go sit in the bookstore while I just have a gander," Eileen chirped and squinted to read shop names across the street as she walked.

"I'm sitting my ass down on a bench is what I'm doing," Harold muttered. "Eileen, I don't even see any Blinney anything on the map. Come on, this is enough for one day!" Just then Eileen reached the barber shop. She stopped and turned to Harold.

"Ooh! See! Here it is!"

Harold stopped too, and Ricky swerved to avoid running into him. "Great," Harold and Ricky both sighed at the same time. Harold glanced over at Ricky as he passed by him. "Hey kid," he called.

Ricky stopped by the two metal posts that sat just before an ivy-covered metal archway that marked the entrance of Blinney Lane, and looked back at the stout little man. "Yeah?"

"Don't ever get married."

Ricky forced a smirk and wheeled his suitcase under the archway. He heard the footsteps of the old tourist couple behind him as he pulled his suitcase up to the first tree planter that sat in the middle of the little street. It was encased by wooden timbers, as were several others in line with it all the way down Blinney Lane. He peered down the street at the shop fronts, knowing his three months of book store prison time would start as soon as he arrived at Aunt Sarah's. Ricky sighed and took in the change of scenery. Old gaslight-style street lamps lined the sidewalks and intricately-carved alcoves and buttresses adorned the shop awnings and roofs.

"Oh, isn't this just charming, Harold?" Eileen had stopped next to Ricky to also take in the splendor, although her reaction was much more appreciative than his. She looked down at his suitcase. "Excuse me, young man," she said too loudly for her proximity, "but is there a little B and B to stay at somewhere down here?"

"Um," Ricky glanced at his suit case. "No. I'm staying with my aunt. She owns a shop here."

"Oh," Eileen took in the information like it was a wonder. "Do they let rooms above any of the shops? Wouldn't this just be the most darling place to stay, Harold?" Harold just grunted behind her and adjusted the plastic shopping bags sticking to the perspiration in the crevice of his arm.

Great, a chatter box, Ricky thought. I'm going to have to talk to tourists like this all summer. Ugh! Dad, I hate you! Ricky decided that walking and talking would be the quickest way to escape Eileen and began to pull his suitcase down Blinney Lane with the couple following along beside him.

"No. There's no place that rents rooms here that I remember. All the shop owners live here on Blinney Lane, though. On this side, the side that connects with…well, with the rest of the city, the shops all have apartments above them." Eileen shifted her gaze in the directions Ricky pointed, taking in her guided tour. "And on this side there's like a big courtyard behind the length of the shops that the owners all sort of share as a community yard or garden. Their houses sit on the other side of that, sort of hidden behind the last couple of shops on the main drag out front. Then there's just a wash way and open space between that and the highway."

Ricky stopped just before Allister's Books, almost grateful to actually have arrived at his destination, hoping it would let him end his ad hoc tour guide session. "Well, this is me," Ricky pointed behind him.

"Oh!" Eileen chirped and smacked Harold with one hand. "See Harold. I told you they had a bookshop!"

"I'm going for an ice cream," Harold twitched his nose at the scent coming from the little bakery next to Allister's.

"Well, you have a nice time with your aunt, young man," Eileen smiled and continued down the street.

"I'll try," Ricky muttered as he faced the bookshop window. He lugged his suitcase up the stone steps and dragged it through the doorway. As soon as he entered, his eyes were drawn toward the sight of his aunt. Aunt Sarah was hard to miss with her hourglass figure, and the way her dark reddish-brown hair looked so vibrant against her light complexion.

Sarah wore grey checkered pants and a pair of black suspenders held them snugly to her backside. Her long-sleeved blouse puffed out around where the suspender straps pressed against her back. Her collar outstretched in a casual manner from the top where two of her shirt buttons sat opened. At least she doesn't dress as goofy as the rest of the freaks around here, Ricky thought. He remembered Franci and Mary from his prior visits and how he'd never seen them in anything other than frumpy historical garb. Just then Sarah turned away from the customer she was speaking with at the sound of the shop bell.

"Ricky," she smiled after looking at him for a moment.

Great, she's not happy about this either, Ricky swallowed at the pause she'd taken. From what he remembered of Aunt Sarah, she'd always seemed loving and happy to see him, but that had only been several times in his life when he was younger and for much shorter durations of time. Was three months too long for her too, he wondered.

"Look how big you are!" She eyed him up and down as she walked over, arms outstretched for a hug. "I hardly recognized you."

"You look...the same," Ricky smiled. Minus my friends probably thinking you're a MILF, he scoffed mentally, acknowledging how beautiful his aunt was for the first time in his life. Well, okay, a cougar, she's not a mom. Why didn't she ever get married? Maybe she's a lesbian or something.

"Well, nothing changes around here. Come on, let's get you settled in," Sarah smiled after a silence settled between them.

RICKY CAME out of the spare bedroom after stowing his suitcase in his room and washing his face off in the small adjoining bathroom. I hope she doesn't put me to work right away, he sighed to himself.

Sarah was in the kitchen putting away some dishes. She turned and smiled upon hearing the floor creak as Ricky walked into the room, hands stuffed into his pockets. They both stood in an awkward silence for a moment, both visibly uncomfortable to each other's notice.

"So I get the feeling you probably don't want to be here," Sarah started softly, non-threatening.

Ricky grimaced. Had he made it that obvious? "No. I don't mind. I mean, thank you for everything and letting me stay with you." He didn't want to be here, but he knew he had to be somewhere with an adult family member. It was probably better to be with Aunt Sarah in the bookshop than arguing with his Dad all summer in hotel rooms. Ricky just hoped she was still as cool as he remembered her being.

"Look, I don't know how we're supposed to do this. I mean, I know what your Dad wants—for you to not wander around Salem all by yourself all summer long and to slave away in my shop." *Be the adult*, Sarah thought of Mary's words. "I haven't seen you in three years, so I don't expect you're still the little kid excited by the limited ambiance of Blinney Lane and the fairy tale adventures I used to tell you." At that, Ricky genuinely managed a little grin as he listened and looked down at the floor. "I've got a business to run and I'd love the help if you'll put your enthusiasm into it. I don't have time to get out much, but you're welcome to go out around town for lunch. However, I will need you back at the same time each day. I'm too old and too busy to have to worry about where you are. Just be where you say you're gonna be, and be back when you should be, and the summer should fly by for you. I can live with that if you can."

Ricky chewed the inside of his lower lip. He knew she wasn't scolding him, just covering her ass with the initial ground rules. She looked scared to have to keep track of him. What? Did she think he was going to go out every night and tag the sides of buildings? Ricky looked up at her, nodded, and even managed a smile. "I won't be a pain in the ass, I promise."

"Hrmph," Sarah smirked. "I never said that, Ricky," she said softly and headed towards the door that opened to the staircase down to the shop. "I've got to get back downstairs, but you go ahead and make yourself at home."

Ricky looked around awkwardly and then watched as she neared the door. "Uh…Aunt Sarah?"

"Yeah?"

"Uh, am I supposed to come downstairs later or something?"

She smirked, "No, you don't have to. A kid's got to have some kind of relaxation during the summer." Awesome, Ricky thought, she's still pretty cool. "You dive in whenever you feel like it, but I imagine it'll start to get boring up here after a few days, so just let me know when I can put you to work."

"Yeah, sure. Thanks," he looked around. "Uh, do you have Wi-Fi up here?"

A guilty look crossed her face, "Nooo, sorry. I spend all day downstairs, so I keep the computer down there, but you're welcome to use it all you want."

"Thanks," Ricky tried to sound grateful, but knew the lack of privacy in her shop would likely curtail any internet surfing. That meant gaming and video chat was probably out for the next three months. He could still chat with his two good buddies back home, Matt and Dweezil. "Well, maybe I will be down...later," he called as Sarah headed out the door.

Sarah hid a smirk, her back to Ricky. She knew that meant his boredom would likely set-in much quicker than she thought. Damn it. He'd better find something to keep himself occupied. I don't want him nosing around the shop all summer, or worse. With that thought, Sarah peered back through the door, just as she was about to close it. "Oh, and Ricky?"

"Yeah?"

"I don't have a car...let's keep it that way, okay?" The door closed and she was gone.

"Damn it," Ricky muttered as he stared at the door. "There just went some cool points," he sighed into his hands and groaned in the frustration he knew was going to last the whole summer.

CHAPTER
FIVE

SARAH SAT on the old swivel stool behind the store counter, knees tucked up to her chest, feet resting against her butt on the seat of the chair. She pressed her teeth up and down on the end of the pen she held in her mouth and tapped her finger on the counter as she rested her other arm across her leg. The charms of her bracelet made an incessant, clink, clink, clink noise.

She glanced at the door as Shelby walked in. "Hi Shelby," she muttered and then returned her aimless stare back out the window. Clink, clink, clink.

Shelby dusted her soft feathery bangs across her forehead with one finger as she stared at Sarah. She usually got a more observant greeting from the woman than this. "You all right, Sarah?"

Sarah inhaled and looked back at the girl, "Yeah. Just thinking." She continued to tap her finger on the counter and looked down at another list she had begun. *The Weeping Books. Bad Language. Shampoo.* She was trying to think of things she needed to warn Ricky about and things she had to get done without garnering his notice. It was easy to tell a little kid not to do something. You just told them and they listened without question. Teenagers though had an annoying word in their vocabulary: Why? It was a lot harder to sell a lie to a teenager.

"Want me to put some stock away for you or something?" Shelby smiled and approached the counter where she crossed her arms and leaned forward.

The tapping stopped and Sarah quickly palmed the note, crumpling it up into a ball. She dropped her feet back to the footstool of her chair and sat upright. "No. No, that's all right. Eh, hem," she tossed the note into the old milk crate and shifted around her business card holder. "My, uh, nephew is here for the summer to help me, so I'll have him do that," she glanced up the stairs and sighed, "whenever he decides to come down."

Shelby followed her gaze up the stairs and then glanced back at Sarah who still hadn't made eye contact with her. "Oh," she let out a little dejectedly. "Sooo, you probably won't need my help anymore."

Shelby loved Allister's Books and Sarah. She stopped by as often as possible, usually spending most of her school evenings studying in one of the cushy old chairs by the window. In the summers, she often spent most of her days there curled up reading or pricing new books for Sarah. Shelby took pride in the unofficial job as though she were a valued and knowledgeable member of the store, even though Sarah had no staff. She fulfilled all her family obligations, held straight A's in school, and excelled at everything she did, so her busy parents never concerned themselves with her frequent trips to Sarah's store. At least they knew where they could find her. They felt lucky to have such a stellar, responsible daughter, even though she seemed unusually knowledgeable and serious for her tender years.

Sarah finally looked up at Shelby, whom she noticed was frowning a bit dejectedly and tracing the details of the counter trim. "Oh, Shelby, no. I didn't mean it like that." She instantly realized she'd made the poor girl feel unwanted. "I would never fire you, sweetie."

Shelby looked up and grinned at that. "So I *do* work here, huh?"

"Ha! I wouldn't call a few hours a week in exchange for some free books a job, but...but sure! You're the only real employee I've ever had, if you want to call it that. You're my unofficial right hand." Shelby never wanted money from Sarah when she manned the cash register, so Sarah went out of her way to find some rare books she knew the dear girl would enjoy. Sometimes that was difficult, since the only person who had read as many books as she had was Shelby. "Besides," Sarah patted Shelby's hand, "I doubt my nephew will be as enthused to help around here as you are."

"Hmph. Well, he's a boy. What do you expect?" Shelby turned to take her favorite spot—the plush chair by the front window.

Sarah opened a box that still sat where Henry had left it the day before. She stopped herself and closed it again, just as she had the day before. This was getting frustrating. Usually she just put the new inventory away as soon as it came in, but she had to force herself to leave something for Ricky to do. She looked around the store and then at the shop counter. Sarah remembered she'd put Mary's shampoo concoctions in one of the bottom cabinets. She grabbed one of the brown paper bags she used for customers and threw the toothpaste and shampoo jar in it.

"Shelby?"

A loud bubble from Shelby's gum popped and she laced her tongue around it to pull the remnants of the pink substance back into her mouth as she looked over her shoulder at Sarah. "Yeah?"

"Can you watch the store for a minute? I need to go over to Mary's."

Shelby unslung her legs from across the arm of the chair and hopped up. "Sure."

"Thanks."

Sarah picked up the bag and went across the street to Scents and Suds. The interior of the shop was sided with plain old barn-style wood and the same gray wood planks lined the floor, which creaked under Sarah's steps as she walked up to the side of the counter where Mary stood.

As she waited for Mary to finish up with a customer, Sarah looked around at the glass bottles of creams and paper wrapped soap bars that lined the shelves. Mary had done a nice job of maintaining the original ambiance of her building. In the middle of the store sat an old crock with a large pestle displaying an old crushing technique for grinding down flowers and herbs before adding them to medicinal creams and soaps. Likely it had been in Mary's family for years. Even the best historical film sets couldn't compare with the feel of Mary's little beauty product shop.

"Hey Sarah," a large-breasted young woman with a nose piercing called as she passed Sarah and walked to the back toting a box of soap bars.

Sarah stared at the ends of the girl's thick midnight-black dyed hair that stuck up in the air at all angles from where the rest was pinned at the back of her head. She wore a low-cut, bright orange tank top, blue jean mini skirt, and deep purple tights with tiny purple dots on them. "Hi, Valerie," Sarah smiled. She noticed Mary glance over at Valerie's appearance with almost a scowl, ignoring the customer in front of her who

50

praised the effects of her last purchase. Sarah stifled a chuckle at Mary's apparent embarrassment of the contrasting appearance of her daughter in her refined and orderly store.

"Oh, Mrs. Millville, I'll be back. Again, thank you! I can't tell you how much I love this stuff!"

"Good day!" Mary smiled and waved at the customer's back as she exited the shop. Mary then reached for the paper bag from Sarah. "Valerie!"

"Yeah!" Valerie yelled from the back in as loud of a voice as her mother's.

"Did you get that shampoo I asked you about?"

Valerie swung her hips as she walked to the front. What little excess she had on her body, jiggled with every step. Mary sighed and closed her eyes as her daughter approached with a dark plastic Calvin Klein bottle. "Straight from the real world, Ma," Valeria winked and shook the bottle back and forth.

"Here," Mary shoved the bag at Valerie. "Go dump that out and funnel this into it for Sarah, will you?"

Valerie peered into the bag quizzically. "Oooh! Ricky's special blend, huh?" She looked up and smiled at Sarah.

"Just take it in the back quickly, will you? I don't want anyone thinking I'm stealing Calvin's stuff and re-bottling it," Mary snapped.

Valerie snatched the bag away and looked at her mother with a serious expression. She whispered, "Let's just hope old Calv never finds out about this." Then she chuckled and sauntered into the back room.

"Ugh," Mary threw her hands up in the air as Valerie walked away. "Sarah, you're lucky you never had children, I tell you! Twenty-six and she's still as incorrigible as a teenager!"

Across the street, Ricky Allister stared into the refrigerator for the third time that afternoon. I'm not even hungry, he thought as he let the door shut. He walked back to the living room and clicked the remote. Click. Click. She doesn't even have good cable channels, he thought. He sighed, turned the TV off and walked back to the kitchen. He glanced at the door leading to the shop down below and grumbled, "All right, let's get this over with."

Ricky watched his black sneakers land on each of the old wooden steps as he descended down into the shop. He heard the crank and ding of the old-fashioned cash register at the counter where his aunt was probably collecting a purchase from someone. He used to like that noise when he was a kid. The big, shiny brass cash register with its little round buttons and crank lever on the side had fascinated him. Ricky remembered sitting on Aunt Sarah's lap and how she had let him pull that crank lever down to pop the drawer open. Somehow the appeal didn't seem to be there for him anymore and he already dreaded hearing that sound for the next three months. He looked up from his feet to where he could see the base of the counter now from his descent, and noticed a pair of brown Converse sneakers swinging back and forth below the chair where his aunt usually sat.

As Ricky continued down the staircase his view of the shop floor expanded and he noticed a pair of purple and white striped stocking-clad legs attached to those sneakers. "That's a new look," he mumbled to himself thinking of his aunt's usual apparel. Then he saw a hint of pale thighs and the ruffle of a khaki skirt, a slim waist, and an olive green corduroy vest over a thin white t-shirt. There was a big purple and yellow glitter flower on the front of the t-shirt. As the wearer swung her thin legs underneath the chair, the chair swiveled slightly from side to side as did the two small mounds behind the top of the flower image.

A long blond ponytail dusted the back of the olive vest as the girl ricocheted from side to side on Sarah's chair. Her defined little jaw angled to a soft round chin, which moved as she chewed her gum. She had a little button nose that curved up at the end slightly, and it too moved a bit with each chew. Blond bangs hung down over two light colored, Barbie-perfect eyebrows where long lashes sat on the lids below them. Ricky felt himself swallow as he stopped on the bottom step just before the landing to the lower level of the shop. The girl stared down at an open book and smiled in thought as she read. Her mouth then curled up at the corner and a tiny dimple formed on her creamy skin.

Ricky heard the air finally escape his lungs after he realized he'd been holding his breath. The girl must have heard it too because her head jerked up and she looked over at him with bright blue eyes. He waited for her to say something, but she just continued to stare.

"Hi," Ricky let out as he took a hesitant step onto the landing. Still, nothing. The brief smile was gone from her face and had changed to a quizzical expression. "Uh," he started slowly down the three steps towards the counter and then stopped behind the stack of boxes between him and the vibrantly dressed little blonde. "I'm Ricky. Sarah's nephew."

"I know," the girl said flatly and continued to stare at him as though she were waiting for some other explanation.

"Oh," Ricky glanced around the store, but saw no sign of his aunt.

"She had to run across the street for a minute," the girl said and then turned her head back to her book. Her jaw clenched and a large pink bubble appeared in front of her pursed lips.

"Do you, uh...work here?"

Pop! The bubble burst onto the girl's lower lip. She sucked it back into her mouth, still looking down at her book. "I help," she said matter-of-factly.

Ricky felt awkward then as the girl seemed to have no interest in him. At home, the girls in Ricky's class swooned after him and he didn't hesitate to take off his sweaty shirt after soccer practice when a feminine audience was present in the bleachers. He decided to change his tone to purely conversational and less intrigued, "You go to school around here?"

The girl looked over at him and again stared for a moment blankly as she said nothing. "It's summer," she finally stated flatly.

All Ricky could come up with as his cheeks flushed was, "yeah." Why did he suddenly feel so stupid? That should have been a normal question to ask someone. Maybe she wasn't normal.

She's probably one of those know-it-all bookworm types, Ricky thought. He sighed and glanced around the store again, then took the last step that would leave him standing right up against the boxes. He looked at the dainty blonde again and felt another round of tightness in his throat. It was cute how she nonchalantly swung her slender legs back and forth, twiddling a strand of her pony tail with one finger, lost in her book. She was way too cute to be a nerd, he thought. Maybe this summer won't be as boring as I had imagined.

Ricky leaned onto the stack of boxes. He pressed his ribcage up against the sides of his triceps so the bulges there would be forced to protrude out in an effort to further emasculate his appearance. Just as he opened his mouth to say something he thought would sound clever, the top box gave way and slid forward from the pressure of his weight. "Shit!" was the clever word which escaped his mouth as he lunged forward awkwardly, ass sticking out, arms outstretched over the remaining boxes to catch the one he'd shoved forward towards the girl. He stood stupidly bent over, grasping the front edges of the heavy box with his fingertips digging into the cardboard.

The girl looked up and sighed in what sounded to Ricky like exasperation. She slapped her book shut and hopped down from the stool as Ricky tried to rock his butt backwards so the momentum would help to lug the box back onto the stack. He wasn't able to muster enough force, however, and remained in his precarious, bent-over position.

Chin resting on the top of the box, Ricky gasped, afraid to lift his head for fear the box would tumble down against the girl's feet. Then he saw her blue eyes in line with his, and they seemed to narrow at the corners as he felt the weight of the box lessen. She lifted the bottom on her side and helped him slide it back on the stack as she said, "if you need help, maybe you should just ask next time."

"I..." Ricky didn't know how to respond as he adjusted the box once they set it back on top of the others.

The door chime clattered and Sarah walked in with a paper bag in her hand. She smiled over at them. "Oh, hi. I see you've met Shelby."

Ricky thought he saw Shelby roll her eyes just before she turned and waltzed back to the counter. She grabbed her book and took it over to a big green chair by the window where she jumped onto the cushion and let her legs fall over the arm.

"Yee..ah," Ricky drawled out.

"Well, I got this new promotional shampoo from Mary across the street, but of course she has no interest in selling this name brand stuff, so I thought maybe you'd like it." Sarah pulled a bottle of Calvin Klein shampoo from the bag so Ricky could see the label, then dropped it back in.

"Oh. Thanks."

"I'll just go put it upstairs. Be back in a second," Sarah patted his shoulder on her way past him.

"Okay," Ricky stood by the counter awkwardly for a moment. He looked over at Shelby who sat chin to chest staring at her book, chewing her gum. Her eyes shifted over to him momentarily, and one of her light brows arched briefly downward in an annoyed quizzical expression until she looked back at her book.

Ricky scraped his feet along the floor and sat behind the counter to wait for Aunt Sarah. Little did he know, that upstairs, she had just tossed his toothpaste into the garbage can and set a new bottle of shampoo in his shower next to the one he'd brought from home.

Ricky chewed on the cuticle of his thumb as he stared out the shop window feeling out of place. He tried not to look over at Shelby, but the vividly striped knee socks bouncing up and down against the green chair was an eye-catching distraction against the more muted color tones of the other furniture and dark mahogany floor. He sighed in relief when he heard Sarah's footsteps coming down the stairs.

Sarah smiled hopefully, "Well, ready to get started?"

"Yup," Ricky forced as much enthusiasm into the word as he could muster.

For the next hour Sarah showed Ricky how to run the cash register, how to zero it out at the end of the day, and how to take credit card payments on the much newer device that sat next to it. She explained where the daily deposit went and when it was picked up by the bank, how she manually inventoried all the book sales, and more mundane tasks. Ricky tried to absorb all of the information, but occasionally looked up at the bouncing purple and white socks on the green chair. Each time he did, he seemed to be met with an angrier and angrier glare. This last glance he stole as his aunt chatted on about special orders; Shelby sighed and slammed her book shut. She hopped up out of the chair and tucked the book into a backpack with embroidered flowers all over it.

Sarah noticed Ricky's eyes were focused on Shelby and also that Shelby was walking to the door. "I'll see you later, Sarah," Shelby smiled less pleasant than usual.

"Okay," Sarah smiled back in wonder as to what seemed to be wrong with her young friend. She looked back at Ricky who was staring out the window after Shelby, which caused her brow to rise. Ricky finally brought his eyes back to the paper in front of him and looked up at Sarah when he realized she had stopped speaking.

"What?"

"Don't they have girls where you live?" She smirked.

He sassed an unimpressed, "Yeah."

"Well, be nice. She comes in here a lot and I really like her."

"What's to like?" Ricky muttered and picked up a pencil. Sarah chuckled knowing the two kids must have had words in the brief time she had left the store.

Sarah walked around the store explaining where each genre of books was located. She glanced to the upper-level beyond the balcony rail several times. Each time she did, Ricky followed her gaze instinctively, but then she'd turn and go back to some shelf on the lower level she'd just told him about.

"Aunt Sarah, I think you've pretty much covered everything down here already," Ricky tried not to sound impatient but he was becoming bored to death by the repetition.

Sarah thought for a moment and glanced around at the book displays. She muttered different genre names under her breath and pointed at their corresponding shelves. Then she sighed and scratched her head. "Oh, the geography section is on this lower shelf here," she pointed to a round shelf in the middle of the room.

"Yeah. You covered that one already," Ricky stuffed his hands into his jeans pockets and rocked back on his heels.

"I did?" Sarah asked more to herself. Then she looked beyond the balcony railing again and stared at the shelves on the upper-level of the shop.

"Yeah. You've repeated yourself like three times already," Ricky smiled. He followed her gaze to the upper level. "We haven't gone back there yet," Ricky nodded. "You still keep all the old books back there?"

Sarah looked at him for a moment, in thought. She rubbed her hand across the back of her neck and then pursed her lips. "Umm, yeah. You remember that?" She smiled at the thought Ricky remembered anything she'd told him as a child.

"Yeah. You used to yell at me if I'd run around and play back there," he laughed.

Sarah put her hands on her hips. "Well...they're old, Ricky, like you said. A lot of them are worth a lot of money. Plus, I didn't want you knocking some shelf over on top of yourself and getting squashed."

Ricky turned and started up the three stairs to the upper level. "Well, I promise I won't run any more. Come on, tell me what I'm supposed to do with these," he called over his shoulder as he started towards the first shelf behind the partition that hid much of the back room from the lower floor.

Sarah felt her heart beat increase in frequency as she watched him near the antique book collection. She quickly jolted up the three stairs after him and came to stand next to the second towering bookshelf in the room. She leaned and placed the palm of her hand on the aisle side of the shelf to form a barrier between herself and the back of the room. Ricky peered over the rows of book bindings from floor to ceiling on the three shelves that surrounded him.

"Does anyone ever buy these or borrow these or whatever? How's that work?" Ricky tilted one book back by the top of its binding and pulled it out from its place on the shelf.

"Well, yes, sometimes, but it depends," she watched him nervously. There was an old wooden podium next to the end of the first shelf with a padded stool in front of it. Sarah nodded towards it, "if someone wants to look at something for research, they have to do it there. None of the books back here ever go up front, unless I sell them to someone. No food or drinks back here, ever."

"So how do I know which ones are for sale?" Ricky slapped the book shut and shoved it back into its place on the shelf.

"Careful!" Sarah held a hand out and jumped at the slap sound the book made after Ricky's quick action.

Ricky jumped slightly himself, "Geesh, sorry." He stuffed his hands in his pockets after he put the book back, afraid to touch anything in fear that his aunt would freak out.

"Well, just…go easy with them," Sarah softened her tone. Ricky walked underneath her outstretched arm to the next row of shelves.

"Got it," he muttered. "So…how do I know which ones are for sale?" Ricky stopped in between the second and third rows to gaze across the lines of books again as he had done at the first set of shelves.

Sarah moved quickly around him and stretched her arm out again. She leaned against the shelf in front of Ricky. Sarah placed her other hand on her hip. She tried to jut her elbow out as far as she could in the other direction to form an obstruction between Ricky and the final row of books behind her.

"Well, I don't want you selling anything from back here for now," she said gently.

Ricky rolled his eyes. "I know there's a lot of them, but I'm not an idiot. I can learn if you just tell me. What am I supposed to do if a customer wants to buy one and you're not here?"

"Just tell them nothing is for sale back here unless I'm here. Sometimes I don't even know if I want to sell one of these. It depends on what the current value of the book is, how much the person is willing to pay, and other things. And Ricky," her tone softened, "I don't think you're an idiot."

Ricky grimaced in guilt at his choice of words. He kicked his foot to skid a sneaker across the floor underneath him. "Dad does," he muttered.

Sarah smiled, "Well, then prove him wrong. I did when I was your age."

Ricky smirked, "he busted your chops too?"

"He tried," she rolled her eyes. Just then Ricky ducked his head under her outstretched arm and walked to the final row of shelves behind her. Sarah spun quickly around and reached out to grab a handful of his shirt sleeve. Ricky looked over his shoulder at her with a smile and she quickly pulled her hand back and acted like she was adjusting the bracelet on her wrist.

"Are these those goofy books you used to tell me about when I was a kid?"

"Uhh," Sarah didn't know what to say.

"You know the ones you used to tell me...crazy stories about mythical lands and weird animals. How you and Dad used to pretend when you were kids that you were in these weird worlds," Ricky laughed. "What a dork Dad was."

"Oh, I don't...remember. Maybe. Why don't we go back up front now?"

Ricky stepped closer to the glass and read the titles of the five books that sat on pedestals behind the bars and doors. "Farwin...yeah, that was the one I liked. Remember?" Ricky looked back with a big grin on his face. "What were those things you told me about that I liked so much?" Ricky looked at the floor and thought.

Sarah breathed rapidly and swallowed. Her body was half-turned towards the front of the store, ready to retreat in the hopes Ricky would instinctively follow. She grabbed him gently by one shoulder and nudged it for him to turn in her direction.

"Stroom...stroom-something," Ricky muttered. "Come on. You remember, don't you?" His expression almost seemed hurt that she didn't remember the stories he must have so lovingly attached significance to as a bond between them.

"Uh...stroomphblutels?"

"Yes! That's it! Man, I wanted to get a stroomphblutel so bad after that," he laughed and looked back at the books. "Why do you keep them in that case all locked up? They look damp."

"It's...it's a moisture system so...so the leather doesn't crack. They're very delicate," Sarah stated quickly and took a step towards the front of the store. She gestured an impatient come-hither motion for him to follow.

"Oh," Ricky acknowledged, but his expression still seemed curious.

"Those are never for sale, never to be touched. Understood?"

Ricky looked at Aunt Sarah's back as she hurried towards the front of the store ahead of him. He arched an eyebrow in offense, "Oooo-kay. It's locked, how the hell can anyone touch them?"

Sarah stopped and rested a hand on the railing post to the lower level. She turned to look back over her shoulder, her expression stern. "It's always locked and it stays that way, got it?"

Ricky scoffed at her hostile tone. "Got it," he retorted in a tone he reserved for his father. God, they're just books! What's she throwing such a fit about? I'm trying to be helpful! Old people can be such assholes, Ricky thought as he stomped back down the steps.

CHAPTER
SIX

RICKY SPENT the next day manning the cash register. His butt was asleep and sweaty by noon. Luckily, Sarah let him take off for a long lunch. There was a Jimmy Burgers down the street on the main drag and Ricky took his sweet time in the air conditioned fast-food joint. He half-heartedly followed a rugby match on the television that was mounted to the wall. Finally, he crumpled up the wrappers from his burgers and walked back to the book shop. He took his time lingering past the shops on the main drag before reached the entrance to Blinney Lane. By late Thursday morning, Ricky was already tired of faking smiles for the customers and tourists that entered the shop.

He kicked his feet up on the counter and leaned back in the swivel stool while he played solitaire on the desktop computer that sat in front of him. The door chimed and a big, burly looking delivery guy strode in pushing a hand truck with some boxes stacked up on it. Ricky's mouth gaped open slightly as he looked up and down at the man, who smiled at him. Holy linebacker, Batman, Ricky thought.

"Ricky, get your feet off the counter," Sarah called from across the room. Ricky sighed and let his feet fall to the ground.

"So, you're Ricky." The man reached over the boxes with his hand outstretched. "Hi. I'm Henry...local distributor."

"Hey," Ricky forced a smile and shook the iron-like hand. He slumped back in the chair and peered down at his own physique after Henry turned his attention to Sarah. Ricky noted how puny he looked compared to this guy. Man, I hope I'm that ripped when I'm older.

"Miss Allister, how are we doing today?" Henry watched Sarah approach from across the room. She stopped on the other side of the boxes and he heard the familiar jingle sound of her bracelet as she reached up to grasp her arm in her usual shyness.

"Hi, Henry. We're fine. Just fine," she said softly, much friendlier than she'd spoken to Ricky the other day, he thought. Ricky looked at the two standing in front of him on the other side of the counter. Neither Henry nor Aunt Sarah said anything for a moment. Henry smiled down at Ricky's petite little aunt and stared. Sarah looked up at Henry and then quickly down at her shoes.

Ricky wanted to laugh out loud. Clearly this wasn't a typical neighborhood Mr. McFeely friendship like on *Mr. Rogers' Neighborhood*. It was amusing to see his aunt act...well, flustered was probably the right word. Ricky leaned forward and rested his chin on a balled fist, smiling up at the couple. It was like having a personal live soap opera performance.

"I...I was just reorganizing some things since Ricky here's been such a help taking over the cashier duties."

Henry glanced at Ricky and smiled, then quickly turned back to Sarah, "Well, good. I'm glad you've got a helper." Sarah didn't notice the smile and was busy studying the clipboard Henry held out for her. He turned his head back to Ricky after no more words came from Sarah. "How you liking your summer employment so far?"

"It's great," Ricky smirked and thought he actually sounded sincere due to his amusement with the awkwardness between the adults. "You don't get to stroll around downtown with a hand truck, but who needs all that when you've got a world of knowledge at your fingertips." Okay, now that was sarcastic.

"Ricky," Sarah warned with a glance up from the clipboard. Her eyes met Henry's and she averted her own back to Ricky.

Henry chuckled. "Well, you could probably come out on my route with me one day if you want. That is...," he stammered and looked at Sarah, "I mean if it's all right with you... if he gets too cooped up in here."

"Uh..." Sarah started.

Ricky curled his lip up to one side when they weren't looking. I don't even know this dude. I don't want to be stuck in a truck with him all day long. "Well, I'd hate to leave Aunt Sarah here to do all the work when I'm supposed to be helping her out."

"Wow. Responsible," Henry smiled. He looked back to Sarah, "you can't always find that in kids these days. I think you got lucky here, Sarah."

Sarah let out a half-chuckle and smiled at the comment as she fidgeted with the clipboard. "Well, that was nice of you to offer though, Henry. Thank you."

"Yeah. Thanks," Ricky added sincerely. More awkward silence between the two adults. "I bet I don't end up as ripped as you though by the end of the summer after working here," Ricky nodded slightly at Henry to break the silence. Ricky swore Aunt Sarah's cheeks went red.

64

Henry laughed and glanced down at himself. "Well, I think a lot of that is just residual from my youth. I was always a bigger guy."

"Uh…Henry used to play football," Sarah diverted her gaze again to Ricky. "He played for USC and then some Arena ball…I think."

"Yeah," Henry nodded and grinned shyly at her apt knowledge of his past.

"No shit?" Ricky exclaimed.

"Ricky," Sarah warned again.

"You play?" Henry queried. "You look like you're in good shape."

"Yeah. Receiver. I'm a striker too on the soccer team or… well, I was. Just graduated."

"Well, hey Ricky, I still play sometimes. I help coach a local football team's summer practice if you want to come down sometime. I'm sure the guys would love to have you."

"Oh, Henry, you don't," Sarah started.

"Yeah? You don't mind?" Ricky perked up at the thought of smelling turf again. Seeing sunshine, kicking a ball, anything that was permitted far away from the store to help break up the monotony of the rest of the summer.

"No. Not at all, but that's up to you of course," Henry glanced back down at Sarah.

Sarah saw the pleading look on Ricky's face, and then she saw the look of hesitation in Henry's. She wanted to trust Ricky and didn't want to offend Henry by appearing to not trust his supervision skills. "Oh, I…guess, it's all right."

"Sweet! Thanks, Aunt Sarah," Ricky leaned forward and gently patted her on the shoulder. She let out a little smile.

After Henry had deposited the boxes by the side of the counter, he wheeled his hand truck back over to where Sarah remained standing. Ricky had since gone back to clicking the solitaire cards with a pleasant smile on his face, knowing he'd successfully secured at least one day of freedom a week.

"I can pick him up on Saturday morning, if that works for you?"

"Sure, if you don't mind."

"Yeah. It's over at Baker Field if you ever want to come… and watch," Henry added cordially.

"Oh. Well, I'd love to, but I'll have to be here, so," she shrugged.

"Oh. Yeah," Henry frowned a little and looked down. "Well, I'll bring him back for you, so no worries. See you Saturday, Ricky?"

"Yeah. Great, man. Thanks!" Ricky smiled.

"Thanks, Henry," Sarah opened the door for him.

Sarah flashed the kind of unrestrained smile that Henry so often tried to form on her face. At the sight of it, he felt his breath catch in his throat as the sunlight beamed in to reflect on her hair. "Sarah," he swallowed and nodded once before heading out the door.

Sarah stood with the door open and watched Henry guide his hand truck back down to the end of Blinney Lane to where his delivery truck sat idling. Lost in the view, she jumped as she heard the snide sound of Ricky's voice call from behind her, "Romeo's gone, Juliet!"

Sarah let the door slam shut and didn't even bother to make eye contact with her nephew as she started towards the back of the store. "Like you ever even read that book," she muttered.

"I saw the movie," Ricky smirked.

The rest of the day seemed to drag on for Ricky after the little spectacle between his aunt and Henry had occurred. Aunt Sarah showed him how to lock up the shop about three times, as she had done the night before. Ricky tried to hold his tongue as each repetitive instruction made him feel belittled and incompetent. By the time they went upstairs for the night, Ricky didn't feel like having any idle chitchat. He hopped in the shower and tried the Calvin Klein stuff Aunt Sarah had given him. He figured it was something simple he could do to appear to be an appreciative nephew.

"That's disgusting," Ricky said to himself as he stood in the shower and watched the snot quality brown goo ooze out of the bottle. "Maybe it's gone bad or something."

A little while later, after hearing some rattling noises from Ricky's bathroom, Sarah heard his feet pounding across the floor into the living room, where she sat watching the news. "Aunt Sarah?"

"Yeah," she glanced back and saw that Ricky was standing in the doorway to his room with just a towel around his waist. She quickly snapped her head back to face the television. She didn't want to see her little nephew half-clothed. Blech.

"Did you see my toothpaste?"

"No, bud. I haven't been in there since you got here," Sarah grimaced at the lie.

"Damn it," Ricky muttered.

"Um, check in the medicine cabinet. I've got some in there from Mary's. It's just a plain white tube," Sarah added sweetly.

"Thanks." Sarah heard Ricky's feet stomp back into his room.

"Ugh! This stuff looks like ear wax!" Ricky's muffled voice came from within his room.

"That's it!" Sarah called back.

Ricky appeared at his doorway again, tooth brush in his mouth. Sarah glanced over at the brushing noises. Ricky had a sour look on his face as the foam built up around the tooth-brush pressed between his lips. "Man, this stuff tastes like," he coughed, "gross."

Sarah turned back to the TV and smiled. Maybe it was working already. Ricky's choice of word usually would have been something like "shit." "Well, it works," Sarah said happily and heard him disappear again back into his room. She sighed. The less vulgar he was, the less likely he was to instigate the intensity of the curse's potential. It had been two days and Ricky had remained unharmed so far. Sarah was happy with that outcome, but still worried about the many days to come. Nothing else seemed out of the ordinary yet, except for the minor activity by the books the other night when she'd stood before them. That, however, wasn't out of the ordinary.

Sarah was an Allister. Her genetic makeup caused a natural stir in the power the curse had given those books. Plus, once an Allister had been inside of a book's world, the power of the book was always more aware of their nearby presence. If Sarah had known that when she was younger, she wouldn't have made so many trips into *The Lands of Farwin Wood*. She shook the thought away with the changing of the channel.

CHAPTER
SEVEN

OEDHER VILLAGE, FARWIN WOOD
18 YEARS EARLIER

"SARAH...SARAH," she heard her voice called like it were far off in a dream. Sarah slowly opened her eyes to see a chirping bird pass by the bright blue sky above her where she lay in the grass. Instantly she smelled the sweetness of daphne flowers around her and knew that she was in Farwin Wood. She felt something nudge her shoulder and looked over to see her brother, Richard, leaning down by her side. He was clad in his brown leather Robin Hood-like costume. "Wondered how long it was going to take you," he complained.

"I'm here," Sarah called groggily as she sat up and looked around the small glen, where they had just awoken.

A light breeze rustled the vibrant green leaves of the many trees that towered over them and blew a strand of her auburn hair into her young face. She reached up to swipe it out of the way and felt the soft linen sleeve of the emerald green gown she'd changed into before she drank the sleeping tea and fell asleep on the old book. I'm really here again, she thought.

Sarah loved Farwin Wood. She and Richard had so many adventures there growing up when they'd escape into the magical book one of their ancestors had written. Durley Allister had penned a few tales in his reign over Allister's Books and liked to brew his own ink. After working late one night and falling asleep on one of his manuscripts, Durley soon found that he awoke in the very story he had penned. Once he realized this occurrence could happen only on pages written by an Allister, with ink that was created from ingredients found in different shops on Blinney Lane, he got an idea; something to make the burden of living on Blinney Lane more bearable for his children.

Durley penned a special story for his children, entitled, *The Lands of Farwin Wood*. He gave it to them as an escape from the narrow view of life on Blinney Lane. There, in the peaceful tranquility of the world he had created, full of kind and generous people, wondrous creatures and extraordinary scenery, he knew his children and future descendants would be able to take the closest thing to a vacation anyone indentured to Blinney Lane ever could. If they could never leave Salem and see the world, he was grateful he had found a way to bring a new and exquisite world to them.

The tradition had followed with his grandchildren, their spouses, and their children. Sarah and Richard's parents used to take them for picnics to this very glen on Sundays when the shop was closed. They would all excitedly run around the flat getting ready in medieval looking costumes that they'd special ordered from Mather's Dress Shop down the street. Then they would sit down to the kitchen table with some special sleeping tea from Spices and Stems with *The Lands of Farwin Wood* open on the center of the table in front of them. Gradually each of them would drift off to sleep, and the next time they awoke they were in Farwin Wood. Whatever was on their person would arrive with them when they awoke in the land that Durley Allister had created on paper so many years before.

Getting back from Farwin Wood was the difficult part, something Durley Allister had wished he could have made easier. He'd been terrified the first time he woke up in a manuscript he'd written—a violent battle story of the Revolutionary War. Durley had done all he could to escape death and battle, but it took him weeks in the war-torn New England setting he'd created before he was able to return to Blinney Lane. During an accidental run-in with a British soldier he battled in a creek bed, the last thing Durley remembered was his head being held under the water, forced to swallow gulps of it. As he blacked out, the next thing he remembered was waking up in his bed with his worried wife by his side. She informed him that he had been in a cold, sweaty state for the last several weeks and had been sure death would have been the final outcome.

After that, Durley decided to write a story free of any violence to see if the phenomenon would occur again. When he awoke in Farwin Wood for the first time he was elated with the discovery, knowing that the first episode in his Revolutionary War tale hadn't been the result of a fever or subsequent bout of delirium. He wandered around in Farwin Wood long enough to ascertain that things were just as he had written them, then he found the River Duke that he wrote about and dove in. He let himself sink to the bottom and held his breath until he thought he could bear it no more. Moments later he awoke in his basement study, staring down at the very work he had penned and just departed. Durley was able to convince his wife of his discovery and the world he'd created. She traveled into Farwin Wood with him and was so pleased with the escape he had created from Blinney Lane that they began to take regular trips into the land of the book.

"I can't believe you haven't been back here in four years! If I still lived at home, I'd come here every weekend!" Richard looked around excitedly and adjusted the leather belt around his waist that held a small sword in a holster. He reached down to help Sarah up.

"It wasn't the same without you," Sarah followed sadly. "We always came here together and after you left for college, well, it just didn't seem right to go alone."

"Ahh, you could've gone without me. I would have!" He smirked.

"Gee, thanks," she smacked him. "Richard," her tone softened again, "you know Dad hasn't gone since his heart attack either. Mom's afraid the trip back in would kill him or that the sleeping tea would be just as dangerous."

Richard looked at his little sister with a bit more seriousness then, "Yeah. I know." He didn't want to think about his father's failing state and the ultimatum of who would run the book shop. On this trip home, he'd learned that Sarah had started to get the marks of Agatha Blinney's rope burns around her wrists. This meant the curse had likely chosen her to be the next Allister who would stay bound to the book shop for life. Learning of Sarah's misfortune, and still seemingly free of any physical pull from Blinney Lane himself, left Richard feeling guilty for being able to freely go off to college and travel beyond Salem unfettered.

Richard decided one last trip with his sister into Farwin Wood, while he was home to visit after graduating college, would cheer the both of them up. With enough prodding, Sarah had finally agreed to the "best damned summer vacation" they'd ever have as he'd prophesied it. Their parents had agreed not to disturb their sleeping and let them go for as long as they liked—a gift to Sarah for having just turned eighteen. Knowing Sarah was now branded with Agatha Blinney's scars had also factored into their decision—they knew their dear daughter would never get to see the world.

Sarah sighed upon seeing she'd caused her brother to feel badly. She glanced down to make sure that the bell shaped sleeves of her gown were covering the little marks that had started to form on her wrists that spring, in an effort to not remind him that she'd been chosen. "Well, shall we do this?" she smiled.

Richard looked up and grinned again, "Lady Allister," he held out his elbow for her to grasp. Sarah laughed and shook her head at her brother's enthusiasm. "House of Allister awaits us, I do believe," Richard strutted forward in a silly noble gait.

"Just behave yourself, Richard. You're twenty-two years old now. Our little childhood friends might look at you differently this time," Sarah scolded him.

"What do you mean? Everyone's always been ridiculously friendly and welcoming here, no matter what we say or do." Richard steered them out of the woods and onto a dirt road under the canopy of an endless expanse of forest.

"I meeeean...you're a man now. Come on, I know what goes on at college!"

"Ooooh, I'm a big scary man!" Richard laughed. "Don't worry. I won't throw any beetleburry keggers at the house." Richard referred to the stone villa they were enroute to that Durley Allister had built years before, come to be known in the land as House of Allister.

"Just don't go getting cocky if the girls start looking at you silly and the boys start getting jealous. I don't want any trouble, kind-hearted locals or not. I assume jealousy exists everywhere...in every world."

Richard reached over and tapped Sarah's nose with his finger. "You worry too much, squirt."

A half an hour later, the young Allisters reached the edge of Oedher Village. People milled around the widening expanse of the dirt street and as Richard and Sarah continued forward. Some stopped what they were doing to stare, while several leaned to each other and whispered. Finally someone smiled and waved. Richard and Sarah elegantly raised their hands and waved back, both smiling at the familiar faces. People began to move closer towards them upon recognizing that the Allister children had returned to Oedher Village.

None of the villagers had ever been to Blinney, where the Allisters originally hailed from, but knew that it was far away to the North and was the reason they did not often visit. However, it was always a nice addition to have them in the village when they did make the long journey from the "North."

Richard and Sarah were met with a warm greeting at House of Allister by the watchman, Dergus, who manned the villa gate and oversaw the few stable workers and groundskeepers that maintained the villa, ever keeping it prepared for when an Allister may arrive.

Miss Netta French encompassed both of the children in her strong, beefy arms after she'd ran squealing in glee down the stairs of the main hall. "Oh, my little dears! How you've both grown!" she beamed from ear to ear, her rosy cheeks flushed with the excitement. "Look at you, Master Richard! What a fine young man you've become! And Sarah," Netta's tone softened and she gingerly took one of Sarah's hands in her own sweaty calloused one, still covered in flour from working in the kitchen. "Sarah if you're not now one of the most beautiful maidens in all of Farwin Wood, then I don't know beetleburry from muckas milk," the woman admired motherly.

Sarah glanced at Richard to see him chuckling in excitement at the references to Farwin Wood plant life and animals that he'd obviously missed so much during his days away at college. He loved the royal treatment they received in Oedher

Village as their family had come to be known somewhat as nobility in this world.

Sarah cast her eyes back to Netta, a woman several years older than her mother, who kept the villa clean, did all the cooking, and made sure the interior remained impeccable for whenever the beloved Allisters arrived. Sarah broke the sad news that her parents would likely not make the long journey from the North anymore due to her father's health, which saddened the poor woman immensely. Sarah was much more responsible in considering the feelings of these people than her brother. He seemed to think of Oedher Village and the rest of Farwin Wood as his play-land and not what it actually was—a real world with real people who had real emotions.

The Allisters spent the next few days receiving local visitors and feasting with them in the villa's great dining hall. They sat by the massive fireplace at night and Sarah listened to Richard's stories from college, while she updated him on the silly happenings of Blinney Lane. One day, after the cabin fever of the villa had started to set in, Richard and Sarah saddled up some stroomphblutels to take a leisurely ride out through the other villages in Farwin Wood.

The big, furry beasts lumbered along down the dirt roadway through the forest, their wide-hipped, bear-like backsides shifting with each step. Richard reached down to scratch behind the furry, floppy ears of the stroomphblutel he rode. "Grroooah," it purred in a deep throaty howl at the sensation. Richard laughed as the stroomphblutel's big pink tongue came out to lick its black nose.

The beasts, when full grown, stood about six feet high. They had heads like giant Saint Bernard dogs with grizzly bear bodies. Their backsides were without tails, and at the bottom of their massively wide legs were thick beefy paws with slightly dull claws. Sarah's was all white with chocolate brown spots over its eyes, while Richard's was a calico mix of grays, browns, and black. "I love these things," he beamed.

They steered their beasts off the path towards a stream to let them drink. Sarah's popped its slobbery mouth up from the water at a crackling sound within the woods ahead of them, and let out a soft growl. Richard and Sarah looked at each other in silence to see if the other had heard the same noise. Just then a musical sound of feminine laughter floated through the air.

"Hello?" Richard called out. More sticks cracked, and on the other side of the stream two young women appeared between the trees, carrying baskets.

Richard held his breath as he stared at the taller of the two young women. The beauty before him had long, wavy blonde hair that cascaded down her light blue cloak, which matched her sparkling eyes. Her thick lush lips sat parted returning the surprise of seeing them before her.

"Deronda?" Sarah called.

The heavenly blonde finally breathed herself, while the shorter, plain brunette stood behind her, curiously looking at Sarah and Richard. Deronda laughed and flashed a beautiful white-toothed smile in their direction. "Sarah! Richard!" She gracefully descended the small bank, lifting a hint of her elegant embroidered grey gown as she did.

"Careful, Lady Deronda," the brunette called from behind her, and lifted Deronda's cloak to keep it from dragging in the dirt.

Richard left his stroomphblutel by the side of the bank and hurried into the stream. He hopped from one rock to another until he was just two feet away from where Deronda peered down into the stream to find her own rock to step on. He stretched out his arm and offered her his hand. Deronda noticed it, placed her delicate fingers in his, and looked up at his face.

They gazed upon each other for a moment and she wistfully let out, "Richard…I hardly would have known you."

A heavy amount of saliva had somehow formed in Richard's mouth at the sight of their old childhood friend. He swallowed as he stepped back to carefully guide Deronda to the next stone. "Nor I you."

His last visit to Farwin Wood had been before he left for college four years prior. He hadn't even seen Deronda on that visit, having spent all his time horsing around with the Wortwart brothers in Oedher Village. He'd have spent less time with them doing archery and playing "Knick Knack," a drinking dice game popular in the local pub, if he'd known what a beauty Deronda would turn out to be.

Once across the bank, Deronda and Sarah lunged at each other with equal force for a long and tight hug. Richard helped the brunette across; who he surmised was Deronda's handmaiden, now that she had come of age as a true Lady of the Daundecorts. Durley Allister had penned two simple social classes in his world—a few ruling noble families, and everyone else. Deronda was of the upper class minority, her ancestors being the leading characters in Durley's original tale.

The group walked in the direction Richard and Sarah had arrived, and rested on the forest floor in an open area. They visited and laughed, recalling the fun they had all had as children whenever the Allisters had visited Farwin Wood.

Deronda lived an hour's ride to the east in Daundecort Hall (a large castle structure that was in itself a fortress), surrounded by many houses that made up Daundecort Town, and all were safely nestled within a brick wall perimeter. Therein lived many families that looked to the governing Daundecort family for management of everyday life's necessities. There wasn't much that required ruling anywhere in Farwin Wood, as all of the people were generally peaceful in nature, however Durley Allister had written this family as the equal of nobility whom everyone loved to see at a festival, feast, or simple walk through the outlying grounds of Daundecort Hall.

Sarah and Richard's parents had taken them to Daundecort Hall to meet their friends Lord Clennon Daundecort and Lady Rella Daundecort on one of the children's visits to Farwin Wood when they were but six and ten years old, respectively. There Sarah remembered playing with the fancy toys in Deronda's play room, so strange from her own things at home on Blinney Lane. They would run through the elaborate garden maze of flowers and shrubs that filled the expanse behind Daundecort Hall, and get lost amongst the colorful insects and flowers for hours at time.

Short on many girl friends, Deronda had wholeheartedly accepted Sarah, just two years younger than she, each time Sarah visited. Deronda loved Sarah like a little sister, and when she was old enough to ride out alone, she'd venture over to Oedher Village to see her little friend whenever she knew the Allisters were there.

Richard recounted the many jousting sessions he'd had with Deronda's older brother of four years, Vasimus. While the girls used to run through the gardens, Richard would try to not get the tar beat out of him by Vasimus' impeccable fencing skills in one of the shaded side courts of Daundecort Hall. "Vasimus was a good half-foot taller than me the last time I saw him and the advantage left me on my backside quite a few times," Richard feigned a complaint, at which the girls laughed.

"Well, I believe he still is, if not more," Deronda added proudly.

"From what I remember, dear brother, I think Vasimus was equipped with much larger muscles than yours," Sarah grinned.

"Hey," Richard whined and looked down at his arms.

"He always looked so serious, having to stand next to your father at the court or striding along with him in long steps. I have to admit Deronda, I was a bit intimidated by him," Sarah told her friend.

"Oh, Sarah. Vasimus would never harm a soul unless provoked and never a woman," Deronda patted Sarah's hand. The handmaiden next to Deronda giggled. Sarah glanced at her in question. Deronda looked from the girl back to Sarah, "And as our Richard here," Richard smiled at the sound being called *hers*, "so gloriously recounted, Vasimus as you can imagine has only grown in size. This of course has made him quite pleasing to see by the ladies of the land."

"Quite," the handmaiden added with a blush.

"How is that *less* intimidating?" Sarah laughed.

"Well, my sweet little old friend, while my brother still bounds off to hunt wickrits every chance he can get, he is nothing to be feared. He merely takes his role as future lord quite seriously. He'd never be one to disappoint our father. He doesn't disappoint anyone for that matter, and is as dear a friend to me as he is my brother, so fear not." Deronda assured her.

"Maybe he could teach Richard a few things then," Sarah laughed.

"Hey, I'm not hunting wickrits all day if that's what you want," Richard complained recalling the huge horse-like beasts with their rhinoceros shaped heads. Each had long, sharp talons on their four feet, two sharp fangs that protruded from the fronts of their mouths, and snorted like pigs. They left people alone, but when startled in herds, everyone knew to stay out of the way of wickrits. Such ferocity, physical prowess, and their skittish nature made them a worthwhile hunting target of the men in the land, who killed them for skins, meat, and the right to prove their own machismo.

Deronda laughed at the brother and sister who sat before her. "Oh, you two have always made me laugh! It's been so good to see you. Will you come to the hall and join us tomorrow? I'll tell my father you are here. He'll be so happy to see you again. He's a bit gloomier since mother is gone now."

"We'd love to," Richard responded in an instant. Sarah didn't like the eagerness in which he replied after noticing the long glances he'd given Deronda over the last hour. It was apparent that he approved of what a beauty she'd become, and Sarah wasn't sure she trusted his carefree manner of the last few days to not get them in to trouble.

"Wonderful," Deronda smiled as Richard helped her up. He even helped to gently dust some leaves from the skirt of her dress. Oh brother, Sarah thought as she looked on. "We'll have a feast in honor of your return to Farwin Wood!"

THE NEXT day, Sarah emerged from Allister Hall in the fine golden gown that Netta had laid out for her. When she came down from her room, she found Richard already saddled and waiting out front with another stroomphblutel next to him. He tossed her the reins and called down, "Geez, it's not the prom. What took you so long?"

Sarah huffed and put her hands on her hips. "Richard Allister, I can smell you from here! Don't think I don't know you were upstairs dousing yourself in lampy root oil. And what's with your hair?" Sarah grabbed the horn of her saddle and hoisted herself up onto the beast.

"What?" Richard gently tapped his palm to his slicked back hair.

Sarah rolled her eyes. "You look like Reggie Nurscher. It's creepy."

"Gee, thanks," Richard huffed and nudged his stroomphblutel to head out the villa gate once Sarah was saddled.

"Who are you trying to impress?"

"Uh...well, no one apparently, if I look like Reggie Nurscher," he scoffed at the thought of their socially awkward neighbor and distant cousin back home that Sarah loathed for always putting the moves on her. Richard waved to the Wortwart brothers as they passed them on the street. The redheaded twins beamed back, their attentions fixated more on his sister than himself.

"Ugh, you know good and well what I mean. I saw how you were looking at Dcronda yesterday. She's not some frat girl, Richard. College is over, remember?"

"What's your problem?" Richard whined. "Geez, this is supposed to be a summer vacation for us. When has anything we've ever done here been a problem?"

"It's a vacation for *us*, not for *them*. We've never had more than friendships with anyone here. Aren't you worried about what could happen?"

Richard raised an eyebrow at her and the corner of his mouth turned up on one side. "Define *friendship*."

Sarah gasped, "Huh! Who? When?"

"Lorney Wortwart," Richard laughed. "Last time I was here."

"Ew! She looks just like her brothers," Sarah grimaced.

"It was dark. We were in the barn," Richard shrugged.

"Hrmph. Well that's what you get when you play too much Knick Knack at the pub," Sarah stuck her chin a little higher in the air.

"Oh, come on! No one died. No one mysteriously emerged back on Blinney Lane with us. A dark cloud didn't descend over the house," Richard flailed his arms this way and that while Sarah stared stubbornly ahead down the road. "You're the one always telling me these are *real* people. Not that this is the kind of thing I feel like talking about with my little sister, but haven't you ever seen anyone here that you might have thought about...*you know,*" he didn't feel like finishing the sentence.

"Not the way you imply!" Sarah barked back at him.

"Pfft, well, fine. Stay up there on your high-stroomphblutel."

Sarah rolled her eyes at Richard's play on words. "You're an idiot."

"Maybe you're the idiot for not realizing we've grown up."

They rode along in silence for the rest of the trip. Richard thought about Deronda's pouty lips and big blue eyes. Sarah forgot about her brother's stupidity and looked around at the general splendor of the scenery. The road out of Oedher Village cut through a thick forest of wide knobby-trunked, towering trees, and a plethora of vibrant green undergrowth. She wasn't sure how big the world in Farwin Wood was, but the giant leaves of every type of foliage made her imagine it was vast.

The road eventually came to a clearing and Daundecort Hall could be seen on the top of a hill beyond the windy road ahead. They ascended through the curves on their frumpy beasts until they finally reached the apex of the hill and passed under the wide stone archway that was the entrance to the Daundecort fortress.

Two valets dressed in tights and knee-length overshirts came running over. Each man wore a blue sash across his chest that had a wavy pattern and an image of a purple daphne flower on it, the mark of the Daundecort family. The men took hold of the reins from Richard's and Sarah's stroomphblutels and guided them further into the Daundecorts fortress town.

Many of the passersby were elegantly dressed, not near as much as Sarah and Richard in their best finery, but more so than the residents of Oedher Village. Sarah liked that Durley Allister had settled the family's 'vacation home' in Oedher Village rather than at Daundecort Town. It seemed to her that it would have been quite presumptuous to surround them by a high-ranking place such as this. There were less people in

Oedher Village as well. Perhaps that was why he'd chosen the place to build Allister Hall—less people to ask them questions. She hoped there wasn't something Durley had known that she didn't, but sighed away her worry as they continued towards the center of the fortress, knowing her parents never would have brought her there as a child were it not safe.

Richard and his valet strode ahead of Sarah and slowed as they approached another grand stone archway in a lower wall that encircled the main Daundecort Hall. A well-built man stood in front of two heavy wooden doors that blocked the view beyond the archway. Sarah heard Richard's valet announced them to the man, "Lord Richard Allister and Lady Sarah Allister of Blinney and Oedher Village." With that the man rapped on the door and the wood squeaked as they were opened from within.

Sarah looked around shyly at the small crowd of town residents who had gathered around to watch their arrival. She smiled and nodded, then turned her attention back to the gate. She could see an enormous, pure-white stroomphblutel ahead of Richard inside the courtyard of Daundecort Hall, but its rider had already dismounted and she could not see who had come to greet them. She wondered if it would be Lord Clennon as he always had in the past. She hoped he was in better health than her father. It would sadden her to hear of any further changes beyond the sorrow Deronda had relayed in the passing of her mother, Lady Rella. It seemed the tradition for a family member to greet their distinguished guests personally at the gate, and Sarah would hate to vex Lord Clennon if he was not getting on well in years.

Richard's head lowered and he stretched down an arm. Sarah tried to peer around his back from where she sat some ten feet behind him, but couldn't see with whom he was speaking. "Richard! Welcome, welcome! So good to see you again," she heard a husky deep voice from beyond Richard's riding beast. Richard then slipped off his stroomphblutel to the side where the voice had come from, and Sarah saw whom their host was — Vasimus Daundecort.

The dark black shadow of whiskers around the lower half of Vasimus' face made his perfect teeth appear radiantly white as he smiled a large, wide grin at Richard, their hands clasped. Vasimus' black hair was wavy with little tufts curved outward along the ends of it which stopped just above his shoulders. He had to look slightly downward to smile at Richard, and Sarah could see his strong fingers clasped on Richard's shoulder as he slapped him there in a brotherly greeting. The gesture caused the thin, smoky blue fabric of his loose shirt to rest upon his upper arms and Sarah saw the undeniable curve of his muscles there. There were even chords in his neck that bulged in the same manner as he smiled at her brother, indicating the amount of strength that ran throughout him. Sarah swallowed at the sight of him — he *was* still intimidating, she thought, but somehow...in a different way. The long, blue cloak that was attached to his wide shoulders with two silver daphne flower medallions made him look like a superhero as it billowed out behind his massive height in the light breeze.

"You remember my sister, Sarah, don't you?" Sarah thought she heard Richard say and suddenly the two men turned to look in her direction.

The strong, square jaw with dark whiskers softened from the creases of its smile into a more blank expression, lips parted. A line across Vasimus' forehead that had formed with his previous smile also disappeared behind several short strands of black hair that dangled down over his bronze forehead. His eyes...Sarah felt her breath stop while the water blue orbs stared directly at her while she sat numb atop her ride. She felt nothing. Not the many pins Netta had pushed against her scalp to keep her long hair in delicate little swirls at the back of her head, not the fur of the stroomphblutel against her hands, nothing but a warmth in her stomach and a tingling sensation everywhere else.

"Sarah," Vasimus' voice proclaimed slowly like it was a new word he wanted to learn correctly.

Enamored by this strange, new reaction to whom she once thought of as a dark and serious looking boy she had only encountered several times as a child, Sarah didn't notice Richard's outstretched arm by her side. All she could see was that Vasimus was looking at her, just as she was looking at him.

Richard realized his sister didn't even see him waiting to help her down off her ride. He glanced in the direction of her gaze. When he saw that Vasimus (who also stood unflinching and dumbstruck), was the object which had affixed her attention so acutely, Richard smirked. He rapped his arm against Sarah's leg and whispered, "Looks like someone just got knocked off her stroomphblutel."

CHAPTER
EIGHT

ALLISTER'S BOOKS–PRESENT DAY

SARAH MOANED as she drew her heavy eyelids open. She felt chilled by a light layer of sweat which covered her body. Her mouth felt unpleasantly dry. She let out a long breath and shook the images from her mind that still resonated from her dream. She threw her legs over the side of the bed and looked at the clock on her night stand. Ten o'clock! Oh my word, I've never slept this late, she mentally screamed and jumped up off the bed. Damn it!

Sarah scrubbed her body voraciously under the hot steamy water in the shower. She thought of stroomphblutels and staring down at Vasimus the day of their welcome feast. Dang it, Ricky! Why did you ever have to mention those things to me, she thought as she got out of the shower and dried herself off. She must have sunk into a memory-filled dream last night which caused her to oversleep. Sarah hadn't thought of the people and the strange creatures in *The Lands of Far-win Wood* so intently in such a long time. She must have lost control of her subconscious in her sleep. With the presence of a second Allister now on the premise, the pull on her mind into that mythical world must be stronger than ever. Certain books were something of a temptress, and Agatha Blinney's curse allowed them to beckon those they wished would come visit them. It was the reason why some of the books wept, as though they were longing for the return of the Allisters. Sarah would have to get something from Franci to help keep her mind clear if this continued.

"Ricky!" Sarah hopped as she shoved a leg into her pants. She called again down the hallway for her nephew. "Ricky! Get up! We overslept!" Still no answer. Sarah stopped bouncing once she had both legs in her pants and listened. She yanked the zipper up and then hurried to Ricky's door. A knock. "Ricky?" Still nothing. She opened the door, but there was no one in the mussed up bed covers. Sarah raced to the bathroom. Empty. She ran to the kitchen. No one. "Oh my, God!"

Sarah dashed to the door and hurried down the stairs in her bare feet. She heard the zip and ding of the cash register and let out a long exhale as she stared at Ricky. He handed an old woman some change and then turned to look up at her. His eyebrows went up and then he smirked, "Slept in, huh?"

Sarah closed her eyes and felt her wet hair drip down her back. She sighed in relief and then opened her eyes again to see Ricky still looking at her. "God. I thought you were gone."

"Don't worry. I got it covered," he called offensively. "Geesh."

Sarah turned and stomped back up the stairs, hand held to her chest. She was sure that was the closest she'd ever come to having a heart attack. Her nerves gradually calmed, but for the rest of the day she remained on edge. Ricky's some-what humorous, uncaring and smart-ass comments got on her nerves, and when she wasn't acting mute, she snapped at him. Finally, he just quit speaking to her.

Shelby came in a little after lunch and Ricky sensed that even she thought Sarah didn't seem herself. He had wondered when the cute little blonde would come back in the store, even though he was sure he bombed with her during his first impression. Today, however, he noticed that her expressions toward him seemed more sympathetic rather than annoyed like the last time he saw her. Unfortunately, he assumed the cause of the new reaction was because Shelby had heard his Aunt Sarah's sharp tone directed at him several times.

Ricky aimlessly walked around trying to remember where certain books went as he stocked shelves. He was grateful to get his butt out of the chair behind the counter after Sarah had finally come down from upstairs with dry hair, several hours after the normal eight o'clock opening time. He thought she would have acted grateful that he'd taken the initiative to get up and open the shop for her, but boy was he wrong. Every half hour or so, she would call out, "Over there, remember?" in a stern tone. Or, "by the poetry," dryly. Ricky felt a little dumber every time she said something like this, and even more so when he'd see Shelby peering over her book at him from the green chair.

As Ricky, hands filled with books, walked along one wall of the store gawking at titles, he didn't notice the corner of a short book tower on his other side. *Thump!* The top of his pelvic bone jarred into the sharp corner and he doubled over, dropping the stack of books in his arm to the floor. "Ah! Son of a bitch!" he hollered and grabbed his hip.

"Ricky!" Sarah looked up from her chair.

Ricky pursed his lips against the breath of air he held in from the pain. He let it out finally and threw his hands up, red-faced. "That's it! I've gotta get out of here!" He did his best to not hobble as he marched to the door and jerked it open.

"Wait! Where are you going?" Sarah stood up behind the counter.

"For a walk!" Ricky yelled as he let the door slam behind him.

Sarah sighed and looked over at Shelby, who quickly lifted her book up to hide her widened eyes. The girl was smart enough to know when not to get involved. Sarah blushed and dropped her butt back into her seat. She gazed out the window and saw that Ricky was headed further down Blinney Lane at least, and not out towards Salem.

Ricky shoved his hands in his pockets once he reached the sidewalk in front of the store. He stood there for a moment and looked down the street, not focusing on anything in particular. Some shoppers strolled towards him and then around him. He started down the street to avoid being a spectacle. He really didn't feel like talking to anyone right now. If he stood outside the store, someone might think he worked there and be open to giving out tourist information.

A sweet smell from the Blinney Lane Bakery next door caught Ricky's attention, and he went inside. He perused the sweets and deli sandwiches behind the glass as he waited in line. He wasn't sure he really wanted anything. He couldn't remember ever having to think of so many ways to keep himself occupied. Getting back home to his old life, his old routine, seemed more heavenly each passing second. Is that why Dad sent me here? Does he think I'm going to return a "Mr. Please and Thank You" kind of kid, grateful to get out of Mayberry? Ha! He'll be sorry, Ricky thought as he eyed a bistro sandwich.

Ricky paid Walter Freedhof, the fat, bald, old baker. He took the sandwich and soft drink, happy the man didn't know who he was. He didn't want to hear Aunt Sarah's name right now or be told how 'lovely' it was that he was there helping her out for the summer. He shoved the door open with his knee and walked back out onto the cobblestone street.

Ricky sipped on the soda as he looked at the storefronts across the street. He could see that weird old Mary Millville in her big puffy dress at the soap store. A flash of color appeared by the window and Ricky stopped sipping as he gazed at the ginormous boobs of Valerie Millville as she bent over forward. "Helloooo," Ricky cooed quietly and smiled. Valerie stood up and looked across the street through the glass at him. She smiled knowingly and waved with just her fingertips. Ricky looked back and forth, but realized he'd been caught, so he just smirked and waved. Then he moved on before she saw him blush.

Ricky sipped the soda again as he shifted his eyes to the next shop window, Spices and Stems. Just as he was reading the store sign he saw a bean pole of a woman, all in black, wave excitedly to him from inside. Her head moved back and forth with a bun on top of it as she happily mouthed, "Hello!" through the glass. Ricky forced his mouth into a smile and raised his soft drink up a notch in her direction then quickly turned his head and continued forward. "Freak," he muttered between his teeth. He passed an old-fashioned blacksmith shop next to the bakery and watched a sinewy, goliath of a man in a leather apron sweating and hammering down on a glowing piece of metal as some tourists stood cooing in amazement. Man, that's got to suck in this heat, Ricky thought.

Ricky bit into the sandwich as he passed one of the potted trees that sat in the center of the street. He chewed and walked and checked out the strange shops that hadn't seemed to change since the last time he'd visited Blinney Lane. At the end of the street ahead, he spied a big bronze statue. There was a little fountain pool around it that sprayed mist up every few seconds, and flowers around the edges of the base. He noticed a bench underneath a tree in front of it, and decided it was a good place to sit in silence and enjoy his meal.

The statue was of a thin woman, and had stood for as long as he could remember. Ricky studied it as he sat down on the bench. Her arms were stretched out to her sides and a little behind her; each wrist appeared to have a strand of rope around them, but the ends that hung down ceased abruptly and were likely left to the imagination. The woman's glazed-over bronze eyes were eerie. Her lips were parted as she gazed upwards in what seemed to be appeal to someone or something. There was another strand of rope around her neck and behind her back was a bronze cast of what looked like a twisted tree trunk, but the tree statue ended just above her head. The woman depicted looked young. Her long hair flowed down around her and out to the sides as though she were crying into the wind. "Creepy," Ricky muttered through a mouthful of sandwich.

This is that chick the place is named after, Ricky thought to himself and glanced around for some type of sign. At the base of the statue was a plaque canted backwards. He leaned forward and squinted to read the words. *The people of this quarter hereby decree this statue and surrounding properties in memory of Agatha Blinney, who unjustly met her death on the 23rd day of May in the year 1694, by the hands of her own neighbors.*

"Geesh," Ricky scoffed and looked back up at the statue. "I know how you feel." He swallowed his bite of sandwich and stared at the bronze woman's gaping mouth. "So you're the reason this place is so freaking weird?" Ricky took another bite, but stopped chewing at the sour taste forming in his mouth. The taste spread across his tongue and suddenly his entire mouth tasted bitter, like strong lemon, vinegar, and nail polish. "Ptoooah!!" Ricky spat chunks of sandwich out onto the ground and drops of spit. "Blech!! What the hell was that?" Ricky looked between the sandwich bread, but saw nothing but chicken, lettuce, and tomato. "Shit," he grumbled and took a big draw from his drink.

Ricky jumped at a scraping sound on the cobblestone next to him and saw a pair of black shiny shoes. As his gaze shifted up the legs covered by rust-colored polyester slacks, he thought to himself, 1974 called and they want their pants back. He looked at the wearer, a gaunt-faced man with black hair slicked down firmly across his head.

The guy looked to be around the same age as his aunt and had the same pale skin most everyone did on Blinney Lane, except for the overcooked blacksmith. The man's well-groomed hair indicated that he tediously parted and greased it down each day. His shoulders sat back as he stared at Ricky, hairy wrists showing above his hands that were stuffed into his tight pants. His pecs looked a little bulky beneath the snug, dorky sweater vest that covered a cream, short sleeve button-up shirt. Ricky raised an eyebrow at the smug and cocky look on the stranger's face. The man's dark eyes looked down at Ricky while he kept his long tipped nose in the air as though his neck was permanently fixed in one position.

"Watch where you're spittin', kid," the man drawled in a low, lazy, nasal tone.

"Sorry," Ricky scoffed in his defense, "there was...something bad in that sandwich, I think." Ricky dusted some crumbs and slobber off of his lap.

Mister Rusty Pants reached behind himself and pulled a pack of cigarettes from his back pocket. He tapped the end of the pack slowly in his hand. His dark brown eyes glanced up at the statue and then back to Ricky. He lifted one of his dark hairy arms and lit a cigarette. Then he reached back behind him and the cigarette pack was gone. How the hell does he fit anything in those pants, Ricky thought.

The guy took a long drag and stared with his dull brown eyes and emotionless face at Ricky. He brought one hand up and ran it across his slick hair. "You Rich's boy?"

"Yeah," Ricky looked at the shop behind the creepy guy. The sign on it read, Nurscher's. Ricky could see shoes and boots on display through the window. "You the *shoe guy?*" Ricky shot back at him dryly.

The man nodded once slowly and took another drag, still training his eyes on Ricky. "Regis. Regis Nurscher. Everybody calls me Reggie," the smoke seeped out of his mouth. Reggie held the hand he'd just run across his hair out to Ricky. *Gross!* Ricky limply shook Reggie's hand in spite of himself. "How's Sarah?" Reggie flicked an ash into the hand he just shook Ricky's with. Double gross!

"Uh...probably hating my annoying teenage guts right now," Ricky grumbled.

Reggie snickered at that, "Mine too. Don't worry." His slow calm voice was discomforting. Reggie turned his head finally and looked down the street.

"Oh, yeah...why's that?" Ricky ventured. He followed Reggie's gaze and saw two slender young women wearing big sunglasses and high heels approaching Reggie's shop.

"Ladies!" Reggie called to them and held up his hand with the cigarette. Ricky saw one of the women whisper to the other and then they giggled. Reggie watched them as they walked into his store, then he turned back to Ricky. "Some women can't handle a man about town," he flicked another ash into his palm with the response to Ricky's question, and then nodded at him. "Duty calls, son." He turned and walked back to his store, dumping the ashes in his hand into a garbage can by the doorway.

"Pfft, yeah. Good luck with that, buddy," Ricky laughed to himself as Reggie walked like a prowling peacock into his store after the women. Ricky tossed his sandwich into a trash can next to the bench along with the soda and then winced. "Ah!" He slapped his arm over his shoulder onto his back. He forced the elbow with his other arm to get more leverage. "Shit!" he cried, feeling a quick, sharp pain in one of his shoulder blades. It felt like something stung him, and with that, he decided the comfort of the a/c at the book shop was better than lingering outside by the creepy statue with the creepy locals.

CHAPTER
NINE

RICKY WALKED back into Allister's Books and saw Shelby still sat nestled in her big green chair, nose in a book. He stopped at the counter where Sarah sat, and locked eyes with her. Neither of them said anything for a pause, and then Ricky broke the ice with, "Your friend Reggie sends his regards."

"Pfft," Sarah rolled her eyes and looked back down at a book catalogue in front of her. Ricky looked over to where he'd dropped the books on the floor earlier, noticing that they were now gone. He walked over to the last box by the counter and opened it. "That guy looks like a pedophile gigolo." He thought he heard a giggle come from the direction where Shelby sat.

"Pedophile—no. Gigolo...maybe," Sarah stated flatly without looking up.

Ricky was happy to see Sarah acknowledged his presence and wasn't yelling, even if she didn't make eye contact. He figured he was forgiven, or in the least his outburst had been forgotten. He spent the next hour putting away the rest of the books in the box, and then came over to lean on the counter by his aunt. "All right, what else do I have to do?"

Sarah hated his choice of words sometimes. "Have to do," not "What can I do?" She hoped the toothpaste would work a little better in the coming days. If not, she'd have to have Mary or Valerie whip up something stronger. Whenever someone spoke disrespectfully, it seemed to help fuel the curse. Sarah looked up from the computer and sighed. She tugged open a drawer and pulled out an old dirty cloth and can of dust polish. "Here," she handed him the rag and set the can on the counter. "Why don't you dust the shelves?"

Ricky spent the next hour taking books down and dusting their shelves. He'd made it all the way across the top of the first shelf that ran along the wall opposite the cash register and halfway down the second when he heard his aunt's voice again. "Ricky, I have to go to a meeting across the street. Would you mind watching the register for the last hour and starting what closing work that you can? I'll duck out of the meeting as quick as I can."

Shelby let her book fall into her lap. She suddenly felt left out, "I'll help him close up, Sarah."

"You don't mind?"

"No. I've done it before," Shelby smiled, finally happy to have some of her former duties relinquished back to her.

Ricky rolled his eyes and turned back to his monotonous dusting duty, now that he was forgotten. He heard a rattle from behind the counter and then saw Sarah's head pop back up from the cabinet below it with a thick journal in her hand. She looked at him and uttered, "Well, I'll just be over at Franci's if you two need anything." Ricky nodded once in comprehension and then turned back to the shelves.

The door clanked shut and Ricky and Shelby looked at each other for a second. They both broke eye contact at the same time and Ricky heard her soft steps walk up to the upper level. He glanced over his shoulder, but didn't see her. "Shelby?"

"Yeah?" she called from back where the old books were.

"I don't think she wants anyone back there," Ricky warned. Shelby re-emerged by the railing with a broom and dust pan in her hands.

"I was just getting the broom. She lets me go back here all the time," Shelby looked at him oddly and then skipped down the steps.

"Figures," Ricky muttered. Trust Miss Precocious, but not your own flesh and blood. He listened to the quiet of the shop, the sound of the spray from the dust polish can, and the swish of the broom where Shelby swept behind him. The swishing stopped next to him some minutes later and he looked down from the ladder he stood on.

"What did you do?" Shelby looked up at him.

"What do you mean?" He wondered if his aunt had blabbed about the trouble he'd gotten into at home.

"I mean...to make her mad. She *never* gets mad."

"I don't know," Ricky shrugged and wiped the shelf.

"Well, why does she have you doing busy-work?"

"Busy-work?" Ricky stopped dusting.

"Yeah, you know...*busy-work*, like dusting shelves that she just dusted a few days ago," Shelby added smartly and gestured up to him as she leaned on the broom.

Ricky glared back at the shelf in front of him and now noticed just how little dust was on the shelves he hadn't cleaned yet. He grumbled and shoved a stack of books back into the empty space on the shelf. "I stole a car. Well...not really stole it. Borrowed it...from a friend," Ricky felt the urge to smirk. He tossed the rag down to the floor and started to descend the ladder. "This is my...community service I guess, while my Dad's out of town for work."

"Oh," Shelby let out. Her mouth remained agape. Ricky looked at her, waiting for judgment. He barely knew the girl, but assumed she'd have something to say about the matter. "Well, that sounds like a stupid thing to do."

"Maybe," Ricky muttered and pushed the rolling ladder to the end of the wall. "It seemed like fun at the time."

"Where's your mom?"

"What?"

"Your mom. You said your dad's out of town. Why couldn't your mom watch…supervise your community service?" Shelby kicked the broom to act like she wasn't that committed to the conversation. It made her feel less nosy.

"I don't know. She left a while ago," Ricky frowned and picked up the dust rag and can, then carted them back over to the counter.

"Oh," Shelby's voice sounded soft and low as she watched him walk away. "Was…was your dad pissed off?" She added hesitantly, not sure how much she could intrude, but still eager to know. She'd never stolen anything in her life and couldn't imagine what her parents' reaction would be.

Ricky looked up at her, "Uh, yeah. He's pretty much pissed off at me about something every time I see him."

Shelby looked down and kicked the broom again, "Oh, bummer."

Ricky folded his arms and leaned against the old bureau desk behind the counter. "Yeah, bummer," he mumbled. "What about you? What are your parents like?"

"Mmm, normal, I guess."

"Normal?" Ricky leaned forward for an explanation from her.

"No, I…I didn't mean you weren't normal. I just, well, I don't know. They're the only parents I have. They work a lot. My mom does women's club things. They do these stupid barbecues with the neighbors sometimes and laugh about things that I don't think are funny to anyone. I don't know," Shelby shrugged.

Ricky's expression softened. Clearly she didn't connect with her parents very well either, especially if she spent the majority of her summer in the bookshop. "They don't care that you come down here all the time?"

"I'm not here *all* the time," she sassed and started sweeping again. After a few strokes she added softly, "No. They don't care. I'd probably have to steal a car for them to care."

Ricky rolled his eyes at what he thought was a dig at his confession. "Poor you," he sneered and plopped down onto the counter stool. She's probably never been yelled at a day in her life. Spoiled brat, he thought.

"You know what? You don't know me! Don't judge me. You asked," Shelby scowled, one hand on the waist of her skirt.

"Easy, cheerleader," Ricky taunted.

"Spare me, stupid jock!"

"You know what? Why don't you just run on home? You don't *have* to be here like some of us," Ricky sneered from behind the counter.

"Hrmph, now who's throwing themselves the pity party? Besides, I was here long before you ever showed up," Shelby's head annoyingly bobbed back and forth with the words.

"Tsk," Ricky clicked on the solitaire game on the computer to avoid eye contact with his new nemesis. "Whatever," he muttered and stared at the screen until it was time to close.

ACROSS THE street, Sarah sat at a small bistro style table in Franci's shop. The shades on the front windows were drawn and the lights were dim. Across from her sat Regis Nurscher. Mary sat to her left, and Franci was on her right. In between Mary and Regis sat the very wide Walter Freedhof. A cup and saucer sat on the table before each of them and in front of Sarah sat the journal she'd brought with her from the bookshop.

"Sorry we couldn't have the meeting at my place. As you know my nephew's in town and the longer he knows nothing, the better," she said to the group.

"I think that must have been him in my shop today," Walter said and tugged at his thick grey mustache. "Came in for a sandwich just after lunch time. Looked just like Richard when you guys were kids."

"Yeah, that was him," Reggie added and lit a cigarette.

"Oh, Reggie! Do you really have to smoke every second of the day?" Mary fanned the air in front of her face.

Reggie ignored Mary's complaint and inhaled another drag, "Saw him over looking at the statue by my place."

"You did?" Sarah seemed startled. "Well, keep him away from there if you can."

Reggie just shrugged innocently. "What am I supposed to do? He's a kid."

"Please, Reggie."

Reggie curved his thin lips into a smile as Sarah's intent gaze held him. She rarely made an effort to look at him unless she was forced to at one of these council meetings each month. "Sure thing, babe."

Ugh, he's disgusting, Sarah thought to herself and averted her eyes to her journal. "All right. What new business...other than the obvious." Sarah jotted a note down in the book. *Arrival of Richard Allister Jr. to Blinney Lane, intended stay – 3 months.*

Each member of the group pulled out a list they'd brought with them. They went around the table taking turns to report any "happenings" that had occurred on Blinney Lane during the past month. As each of them read their list about the activity from their shops or from the shops that other business owners had reported to them who weren't on the council, Sarah noted the activity in the log book. *Nurscher's/dancing boots – 4 occurrences. Freedhof's/bloating bread – 2 occurrences.* Sarah continued to write until they'd gone around the circle and ended with Franci's inputs.

"All right. What about your end, Sarah?" Mary queried before sipping her tea.

"A book snapped twice on someone when Ricky swore in the store or made a smart-ass comment," her voice sounded guilty.

"Did you give him the toothpaste?" Mary's brow creased.

"Yes…and he used it."

"Well," Mary sighed, "just make sure he keeps using it."

"The books," Sarah paused for a moment, but felt the eyes on her waiting to finish, "the books seemed to weep a little more this past week."

"How much more?" Reggie's voice was stern.

"Shh," Walter's fat hand pushed Reggie back in his chair. "Let her finish."

Reggie shakily took a drag from his fifth cigarette. He hated this damned curse more than any of them. He didn't care if this stupid kid was around, as long as it didn't start to cause him problems.

"Just…just a little bit more," Sarah added in a reassuring tone.

"Well, keep an eye on it Sarah. *Everyone* keep an eye out," Mary warned as she looked around the table. "We don't know how this will play out yet." They all nodded quietly, and Sarah closed the journal. "Until next month," Mary added as they all stood up to leave.

When Sarah reached the steps of her shop, she felt exhausted. She knew she'd spent the day worrying ever since waking up late and finding Ricky gone. Her dream of the summer she and Richard had spent in Farwin Wood had also weighed on her mind. She hated the task of logging all the Blinney happenings, but it had to be done. Hearing about them now that Ricky was in town only troubled her further. She wanted to let her head hit her pillow and fall into an oblivious sleep—free of any Farwin Wood memories.

Sarah opened the door to the shop to see that the lights were already dimmed except for the glow coming from the computer where Ricky sat playing his card game. Shelby immediately walked past Sarah.

"I've got to get home. Goodnight, Sarah," she hurried out the door without looking at either Allister.

"Thank you!" Sarah called after her as Shelby rushed down the steps. When Sarah turned around she saw that the computer was shutting down and Ricky was already headed upstairs. "Uh…goodnight!" she called up after him.

"Night," he mumbled flatly.

Sarah locked the door and then let her head thump against it. She closed her eyes and let out a long breath to relax the tension in her neck. "Teenagers," she whispered. "Just what I need…a curse *and* teenage hormones."

CHAPTER
TEN

SATURDAY MORNING, Ricky waited anxiously on the couch by the window peering over the back of it for a sight of Henry. Sarah looked over at him several times during that first hour Allister's Books was open, surprised at just how much he seemed to be longing for the promise of football. She wondered if it was because he wanted to get away from her, the shop, both, or just because he liked sports that much. The thoughts made her wish she knew her nephew better; made her wish they were still as close as they had been when he was just a little boy. Ricky yelled, "There he is!" causing Sarah to jump and an elderly woman browsing the cook book section to gasp and place her hand over her heart.

Ricky bounded up off the couch and out the door so quickly, the bright yellow basketball shorts he wore seemed to move in a flash. Sarah watched him high five Henry out on the sidewalk. Henry looked up through the shop window and gave her a wave. He wore a tight white t-shirt just like Ricky had on. Why do men wear light colors when they go out to get dirty, she wondered.

Henry walked into the store and Sarah was able to see the rest of his attire. The t-shirt made his frame seem more triangular from his wide shoulders down to his waist. He was wearing some bright green shimmery sports pants, which caused his thick thighs to look even bigger. Sarah pulled her eyes back up to his face and hoped she didn't look like she was gawking at his casual appearance. She wasn't used to seeing him out of uniform.

"I'll have him back around one. That okay?"

"Yeah, sure. Uh," Sarah grabbed a sticky note and scribbled some phone numbers down on it. "I guess I should give you my cell phone number, just in case...something happens. And here's the shop number too," she pointed with the pen on the note as Henry took it from her.

"See," Henry held up the note and smiled, "you're a natural."

"Huh, no. I'm just terrified," she laughed.

"Like I said...a natural," Henry winked and went out the door.

SEVERAL HOURS later the boys emerged through the door. Both had grass stains all over their once white shirts. Ricky's had considerably more stains than Henry's. "Are you limping?" Sarah asked Ricky. Henry seemed to hobble a step after Ricky as well. "Are *you* limping?"

"My muscles are just sore. I haven't worked out in a few weeks," Ricky winced and wiped some sweat from his forehead with the sweatshirt slung over his shoulder.

"It's just my old ankle injury acting up," Henry breathed a bit more heavily than usual too. He stood with his hands on his hips and he and Ricky smiled at each other.

"Good game, Henry. Thanks," Ricky slapped him on the shoulder then he turned and hobbled towards the stairs. "I'm gonna go shower," he called over his shoulder to Sarah without looking at her.

"He's still pissed off at me, I think," Sarah shook her head as she watched Ricky climb the stairs.

"Well, I hope I took some of the steam out of him. I was throwing him some long passes after practice got over. Had him running up and down the field quite a bit," Henry said as he took a deep breath and wiped some sweat from his brow.

Sarah smiled up at him and noticed that Henry had obviously paid a price for the effort. It was nice to know he wasn't invincible. Sarah was naturally slender, but she often felt out of shape and self-conscious standing next to Henry and all of his muscles. "Well, don't die on me Henry." She followed him to the doorway. "I'll have to find a new delivery man."

"Huh," he laughed and hobbled down the steps catering to his good leg. He turned back to look at her from the sidewalk and fanned himself by tugging at the front of his shirt a few times.

"Does it make you wish you were seventeen again?" Sarah called down from the doorway.

Henry glanced down at his sweaty clothes and then back up at her light grey eyes. Her white teeth were showing in one of the beautiful rare big smiles he so loved. "Nah. Forty's just fine with me." He watched her laugh and wondered if she knew that she was the reason he preferred being forty rather than seventeen. He hadn't known her when they were teenagers. If getting to know Sarah meant he had to be forty, he was content with his age.

Later that afternoon, Ricky sat taking his turn at the cash register. It was fairly busy that day, which helped pass the time. Sarah came over and leaned on the counter to take some of the weight off her feet. She'd been walking around the shop guiding customers most of the afternoon since he'd got back with Henry.

Sarah looked up at the scratching sound she heard coming from Ricky. His head was down as he annotated some sales on a spreadsheet with one hand. His other hand was slung over his back scratching roughly through the fabric of his shirt.

"What's wrong?" She nodded to him.

"Hmm?"

"Your back. You've been picking at it all afternoon."

"I got tackled a few times. Think I must have got grass burned once or twice," Ricky said, still scratching.

"Well, don't scratch it. You'll make it worse." He stopped writing and scratching and looked up at her with a perturbed expression. "Maybe try some of that shampoo on it that I gave you. It'll…help clean it out if it's infected."

"Yeah, sure," he mumbled and went back to his writing. Screw that, Ricky thought. He tried that already when he showered after practice and it burned like hell. It'd been itching a lot more since then. That slimy brown stuff from Mary made his hair feel greasy, too. The first thing he was going to do each night was dump some of it down the drain when he was in the bathroom. That way, he wouldn't hurt Sarah's feelings if she thought he wasn't using it. The second thing he was going to do was dispose of the earwax toothpaste in the same way. Disgusting. Thank goodness he'd gotten Henry to stop at a store on the way home and picked up some normal toothpaste, small enough to hide in his sweatshirt pocket. See, I can be the perfect nephew, Ricky smiled to himself. "You want to sit down for a while?"

Sarah looked around the shop at the few customers in it, two with whom she'd spoken to already. The third sat in the chair that Shelby usually occupied. Where was that girl today? It was unlike her to miss a Saturday in the summer. "What are you going to do?"

Ricky yanked the top counter drawer open and pulled out the rag and dust polish can. "I...am going to go dust shelves," he hopped up off the stool and walked past her. Perfect nephew, done. Why do old people make you play games and lie to them?

Later that day, Franci stopped by to ask if Sarah and Ricky would be coming to the neighborhood cookout. The Blinney Lane residents all got together for a cookout most Saturday nights throughout the summer in the courtyard behind Franci's side of the street. Sarah liked going over there and seeing the grass, smelling meat on the grill, and having a few drinks with the whole crew, but she thought with moody Ricky in tow it wasn't a good idea.

"I...think we'll pass this week," Sarah said as she watched Ricky shove the dust rag back into the drawer beside her.

Ricky shook his head as he walked towards the couch. Doesn't want to take me around her weirdo friends? Or does she think I need a babysitter? "You can go if you want. I'll go watch some TV," he called to her.

"No. I've been to enough of them," she hollered over Franci's shoulder. Once she saw that Ricky's attention was turned to the magazine stand next to the couch, she whispered to Franci. "I don't think it's a good idea. What if something weird happens? You know how it is when we're all together."

"Yeah," Franci adjusted her spectacles. "Well, good. Then I can call Reggie and tell him he can still bring the dancing boots and get drunk."

"Great. So sad I'll miss that again," Sarah rolled her eyes.

"Oh, Sarah. *That* never gets old," Franci beamed and went back across the street.

Sarah and Ricky sat in awkward silence on the couch in her living room that night as the TV played. She finally went to bed when she could no longer stand feeling like a jailer due to the bored expression on her nephew's face.

THE NEXT day, the only day of the week the shop was closed; Sarah spent most of her time in the basement rebinding old books that customers had brought in for restoration. She even rebound some from her own collection, long since neglected, until she was too bored with the process. When she finally came back upstairs to her flat, she found Ricky gone and a note on the table. *Went to Jimmy Burgers, back by 7.*

When eight o'clock rolled around, Sarah was livid and sick with worry. She went downstairs through the closed shop and started down Blinney Lane towards the metal archway that led to the street.

"Damn it, Ricky," she muttered and took a deep breath as she passed under the metal arch. "Ah!" she gasped and clenched her fists, then leaned forward and pulled them both close to her stomach. Her wrists burned and ached instantly and she chided herself for the angry outburst. Agatha Blinney's curse did not permit foul utterances without repercussion, perhaps because those were some of the words the woman had last heard from the townsfolk before they killed her. Yet the combination of Sarah's swearing and stepping one foot outside of Blinney Lane was enough of a blast for the scars on her wrists to flare up.

Sarah let out a breath when the burning subsided. She turned and headed towards *Jimmy Burgers*. Closed. "Are you freaking kidding me?" Sarah blurted out and felt stupid standing before the unlit restaurant. "Aaahh!" She shoved her hands underneath her armpits and groaned aloud. "I'm sorry. I'm sorry," she whispered aloud. Sarah darted her eyes up and down the street for any sign of Ricky. She should have given him her cell phone. She should have injected a tracking device in his scrawny little neck. She stopped the negative thoughts at the reminder of the pain in her wrists.

Up ahead, she spotted Ricky leaning against the movie theater talking to a couple teenage boys. His back was turned to her. "Ricky! Ricky!" Finally, one of the kids tapped him and he turned around and saw her. Sarah didn't have the courage to take a step closer in his direction. She didn't want to get any further away from Blinney Lane. She waved silently, beckoning him to come back in her direction. She thought she saw him mouth the words, "Oh shit," before he nodded and turned back to say goodbye to the two kids.

"Ugh," Sarah grumbled, hands tucked back under her arms where she stood until she saw Ricky start to head towards her. When his eyes met hers she scowled at him, then turned and headed back to the flat.

Ricky turned the key in the shop door that Sarah had left in the lock for him. He went upstairs slowly, looking around each corner like a hunted thing, but didn't see her. He could see a light on from underneath the door to her bedroom. Ricky tapped softly on the door. "Aunt Sarah?" She said nothing. "I'm sorry. I lost track of time," he called loudly at the door in front of his face.

"Just go to bed, Ricky," a sour muffled voice came as her reply. Ricky sighed and walked to his room. Great.

Inside her room, Sarah got up from where she sat on the bed waiting for the sound of her nephew's return. Once she knew he was back, she went to her bathroom and shut the door.

Sarah opened the cold water faucet to the sink and started to unfasten the thick bracelet on her wrist. Sarah winced as she pulled the leather away from her skin and felt a bubble of flesh beneath it stick for a moment. She groaned as she looked down at the vivid red mark around her wrist. There were a few blisters along the radial bone. She reached over and rolled up the sleeve of her blouse to see the same marks on the other wrist. Then she leaned forward and held both hands under the cool water of the faucet and closed her eyes. The key on the bracelet rattled up and down against the shelf where she'd laid it. She didn't see it, but she knew that's what the sound was. She kept her eyes closed as the water flowed over her blisters.

After a while, Sarah breathed deeply as the pain subsided and hoped that Ricky wouldn't react negatively tomorrow to her cold shouldered reaction on the street. She'd hid in her room, too afraid that if she saw him face to face when she was upset she might say something harsh. The result would be her doubling over in pain in front of him, which he wouldn't understand.

When the throbbing in her wrists stopped, Sarah took some ointment out of the medicine cabinet and rubbed it over the marks and blisters. She wrapped a thin gauze bandage around each of them and taped the bandages in place. Then she picked up the bracelet with the rattling key, which had settled down a bit, and fastened it back to her wrist. She chucked her shirt on the floor beside her bed and let herself fall down onto the bed and into her pillow. Sarah stared at the bracelet on her wrist as her hand lay next to her face on the pillow. Too exhausted to worry about the curse, without a thought in her mind, she closed her eyes and fell asleep.

CHAPTER

ELEVEN

THE NEXT day, neither Ricky nor Sarah said but two words to each other. Henry sensed the discomfort between Sarah and her nephew. He omitted most of what little small talk he could come up with for the day and left disappointed, without a single smile from Sarah.

Shelby brazenly came in that afternoon, determined to show Ricky that his haughty comments from the week prior hadn't dampened her spirits. She intended to defiantly sit in her chair all day and prove she had just as much right to be at the bookshop as he did, yet found she didn't enjoy the show of force as much as she thought she would. Clearly Ricky wouldn't notice it, as he seemed distracted by casting more angry glances at his aunt then at her. Sarah wasn't her friendly self with Shelby either.

On Wednesday, Shelby came back in to find that neither Allisters' temperament had improved, nor did the two seem to wish to speak to each other. Ricky busied himself as much as he could without asking for direction. Sarah kept her nose buried in spreadsheets, catalogues, and mail at the counter. Finally, Sarah got up and announced she was going over to Franci's.

Ricky dropped down on the couch across from Shelby with a magazine in his lap and sighed. He flicked the cover open, and then batted another page away. Shelby avoided looking at him and kept her eyes glued to her book. After their last conversation and his current mood, she didn't feel like asking him what had caused the trouble between him and his aunt.

"You still mad at me too?" Ricky finally asked her.

Shelby glanced over the top of her book. "I wasn't *that* mad," she lied to be kind.

They both looked back to their reading materials. Ricky smacked at another page and then looked back up at Shelby. He desperately wanted someone to talk to after two days of silence from Aunt Sarah.

"What are you reading?"

"Do you really care?" Shelby inquired.

"I read. Just not as much as you," he leaned forward and tossed the magazine onto the couch.

"It's about…knights and demons," Shelby added dryly.

"You like that kind of stuff?" Ricky smirked.

Shelby sighed in exasperation. "You asked."

"I'm not making fun of you," Ricky added with as much sincerity as he could.

"It's hard to tell sometimes."

"My aunt used to read me stuff like that when I visited as a kid. It was pretty cool."

"Oh." Shelby did something Ricky hadn't seen her do yet since he met her. She closed the book, set it down in her lap, and made eye contact with him. Him…instead of a book.

"I didn't think *you'd* like stuff like that," she half-smiled.

"I did...I just haven't read anything like that since I was a kid. Okay, I haven't read much since I was a kid. It just kind of lost its appeal where I live. It was nicer to get out of my house and go run around outside. Pretending stuff just...I don't know, made me think about how I couldn't change anything at home no matter how much I pretended."

Wow, a God's honest truth answer from Mr. Know-it-all, Shelby thought. She smiled then and offered, "Maybe that's why I like them. I still hope." Ricky let out a soft chuckle.

"Well, what's your favorite?" he nodded to the book she'd discarded.

"Hmmm," Shelby brought her sparkly painted fingernails up to her lips and tapped on them with her fingertips while she peered at the bookshelves.

Dang, she's cute when she's not glaring at me, Ricky thought. He watched her hop out of the chair and skip over to the fantasy section of books on the wall. He knew it was the fantasy section because he'd dusted it three times already in the past week. She came back toting a small hard bound book and handed it to him. "Probably this one," she smiled as he took it from her.

Ricky read the back cover as Shelby came back around the sofa and sat next to him. He looked over, surprised at the proximity in which she sat to him. She didn't notice as she leaned over to point at a picture on the back cover. "It's got a lot of action in it, so it makes it kind of manly," she looked up to see him watching her. "Um, and it's short, so if you don't like it..." she started quietly.

"No," he swallowed and held the book up. "I'll try it out," he smiled and leaned back against the sofa and opened the book to the first page. Shelby sat for a moment with her hands on her knees, pleased with herself.

"Good," she nodded. She leaned forward and grabbed her book off the chair where she'd left it and then scooted back into the couch, leaving a little more distance between them. Both of them sat with the slightest smile on their faces, oblivious to that of the other.

Sarah came back in and received just a cursory glance of acknowledgment from the both of them before they turned their gazes back to their books. Sarah, however, stood and stared at the sight of the two of them on the same couch. More shocking was the sight of Ricky with a book in his hand that was open, eyes directed to the actual words on the page. She shook her head in confusion and went back behind the counter without question.

When Shelby entered the shop the next morning, Ricky greeted her from behind the counter. Sarah yawned and waved from further in the shop, turning her head away from one of the first customers of the day so she didn't appeared disinterested. Shelby propped her elbows on the counter after Sarah turned back to the customer. "So? What did you think?"

"I liked it," Ricky smiled.

"Really?" Shelby demanded.

"Yeah, really! I surprised even myself," he laughed. "Do you know anything else like that one?"

"Of course," Shelby grinned proudly and trotted over to her favorite chair to deposit her book bag before she went to the shelves to search for another novel to intrigue Ricky's new-found hobby. She came back a few moments later with another book, this one a little bigger than the one from the day before. "You can do it. I know you can," she winked.

For a wink like that, I'll do anything, Ricky thought. He actually did like the book she'd given him the day before, but he was glad his friends would never find out about it. Ricky flipped the book over to read the cover and enjoyed the light scent of flowery perfume coming from Shelby as she watched him read.

"Ricky? I'm going to go get a coffee from Franci's and some breakfast from Freedhof's. You guys want anything?" Sarah's query broke Ricky's thoughts.

"Uh...no thanks," he muttered softly. At least she'd spoken to him. He reached to his back and scratched at his shoulder blades without looking up from the book. "That guy's sandwiches aren't anything to brag about," Ricky thought of the disaster by the statue several days prior.

"Suit yourself," Sarah said dryly at Ricky's expected negative comment. "Are you still scratching at that...that grass burn from the other day?"

"It's nothing." It itched like hell and burned a little too, but he wasn't going to tell her that and have her treat him like a baby in front of Shelby.

"Have you been cleaning it with the shampoo like I told you?" Sarah's tone turned to concern.

"Yes. And I put underwear on today too, Mom," Ricky finally looked up at her. "It's a scab, it'll go away."

Sarah frowned and jerked the shop door open. Ricky sighed after she'd disappeared. "Sorry," he muttered to Shelby. "I think she tries too hard and it just gets a little annoying."

"Yeah, I can kind of see that," Shelby offered.

Ricky sat at the counter and delved into the new book Shelby had retrieved for him. He set it down only if a customer needed to pay for a purchase and then found himself hurrying to pick it back up. He looked up once and caught Shelby smiling at him from her chair. Ricky just smirked and shook his head, knowing she could sense his renewed love of reading. By six o'clock he'd finished the book and was surprised to see how late it was. He got up and put it back on the shelf and then went around to sit down on the couch. Just before he did though, he playfully smacked Shelby's feet off the armrest of her chair.

"Hey," she laughed.

Sarah emerged from the second level, both of her sleeves rolled down and carting her bracelet in her hand. She'd been down in the basement most of the day, rebinding books and the pressure against the thick leather cuff was irritating a new round of rope burn that had flared up after her frustration with Ricky that morning. She walked over to the counter and set the cuff down by the computer. Ricky looked over at hearing the jangle of the charms touch the wood.

"I need to go see Mary across the street. You guys all right?"

"Yeah," Shelby smiled. Ricky just nodded. He didn't know why she always felt the need to add, "across the street." Aunt Sarah never went anywhere else but across the street, no wonder she was so moody all the time. He was also really sick of how insulting it was to ask if he was all right while she went, "just across the street." I'm not a freaking baby, he wanted to say to her, but he held his tongue since Shelby didn't seem to like seeing the two of them argue.

Sarah fidgeted with her sleeves, tugging them both down a little closer to her hands, then she walked outside. She wanted to get a protective ointment for herself from Mary and didn't want to take any of what little had remained in Ricky's bottle. She'd snuck upstairs earlier to check if he'd in fact been using it, only embarrassed to find that the bottle was almost empty. Even the citronella smelling toothpaste seemed depleted from what she'd first given him. She hadn't heard him swear in several days now that she thought about it, just some brief comments in an angry tone. Apparently Mary's remedies were working for him. Sarah chided herself that perhaps she needed to worry less about Ricky's behavior and more about her own, since she was the one whose scars kept flaring up.

"Okay, I trust you now," Ricky smiled at Shelby once Sarah had gone. "Get me something different, something really out there that you like. Like that knights and demons book you were reading."

"Wow, what have I done to you," Shelby feigned pity. Ricky watched her squeeze past him between the couch and magazine rack. Suddenly he realized he felt like a puppy, getting treats for doing tricks. He wanted to contribute to this kinship somehow, but didn't think inviting her to watch him run around on the football field would sound enjoyable to her. He didn't want to fall on his face and have her laugh at him. No, Ricky wanted to prove to her that they truly did share this interest. He got the impression she was the type of girl more impressed by brains than brawn. Got it, he thought, as he went over to the counter.

Ricky leaned over the counter and peeked through the letters on the shop window. He saw Sarah go into Mary's shop, then he looked back to the counter where he'd seen her leave her bracelet. Once he spotted it sitting just below the computer monitor, he snatched it up and hurried to the second level of the shop. He glanced over at Shelby who was standing on tip toe searching through book titles on the wall.

Ricky took long strides to the back of the upper level until he stood in front of the iron bars of the glass display cabinet. He looked down at the leather bracelet under the soft glow of the cabinet lighting and flicked charms out of the way to find what he wanted. Ricky rotated the cuff and saw a flowery gold ring shift out of the way, and then he spotted the little silver key his aunt said unlocked the cabinet.

Ricky careened his head around the shelf behind him and squinted to see that his aunt wasn't coming back across the street. Good, she'll probably be over there with that old lady and Big Jugs for a while, Ricky snickered at the thought. In the nearly two weeks that Ricky had been at the store, he'd only seen his aunt look at any of the shelves in the back part of the store once, and it hadn't even been this well guarded display where his favorite childhood story sat like some relic. If she wanted to treat him like a little kid, he might as well get to do something that actually was wrong. Although, he didn't really see what was wrong with loaning a book to someone like Shelby. Shelby went gaga for books more than anyone he'd ever met. She truly loved them, while Aunt Sarah seemed possessive and overprotective of them. Shelby devoured books and could finish this big story in a night or two, then safely return it to the store.

Ricky inserted the little key into the padlock and clicked it open. He carefully opened the glass doors and let the lock hang in its place. He picked up *The Lands of Farwin Wood* and couldn't help, but notice how cold and damp it felt. Staring at the massive book he worried for a moment that if his meticulous aunt did happen to pass the case she'd definitely notice the empty space where it had sat. Ricky glanced behind him at the other shelves and spied a book of similar girth on the bottom row behind him. He tugged it out with his free hand and set it on the little wooden pedestal where the other had been. Quickly he refastened the padlock, retrieved the key, and hurried back to the front of the store. Ricky tossed the bracelet back onto the counter and then walked over to where Shelby sat on the couch.

"Did you find something else?" Shelby looked up at him with a book in her hand that she'd obviously selected for him.

"Nooo," he grinned. "This one's for you."

"For me?"

"Yeah. I used to read this all the time when I was a kid," Ricky reached for Shelby's book bag and dragged it over to his feet as he held the book in his lap. Okay, that was kind of a lie, he thought. Aunt Sarah read it, I listened — same thing. Ricky took the new little book out of her hand that she had for him and set *The Lands of Farwin Wood* in her lap.

Shelby ran her fingers gently across the cover. "It looks old, Ricky. Did you get this from the back?"

"Don't worry where I got it. Just do me a favor though, and don't read it in here," he glanced out the window and then picked the book up from her lap to shove it into her book bag.

"Ricky, if this is one of Sarah's antiques I don't want to take it out of the store without her permission," Shelby warned and grabbed his wrist. When he looked at her, she let go quickly.

Ricky let the book slide the rest of the way into Shelby's backpack and then sat back up. "Listen. Do you take good care of books?"

"Yes, but..."

"Has she ever loaned you an antique book before?"

"Yes, Ricky, but..."

"Do you promise to bring it *right* back to me?"

"Sure! I'll give it back right now," Shelby started to reach for the book, flustered by Ricky's peer pressure.

Ricky crossed his arms. "It's not like you're stealing a car, don't worry. You're bringing it back. I just think it's a shame that the only people who've probably ever read it have been my family. I just wanted to share a story with you that I think you'd like since you've been giving me some good ones," Ricky tried to sound hurt.

Shelby stopped tugging on the book and looked at him. She sat back on the couch. "What if she finds out?"

"She won't," he shook his head. "I know this place like the back of my hand already." Ricky rotated his hand and smirked. Shelby rolled her eyes and laughed. "Trust me, you'll love it. It's got these cool creatures in it that are like half bear, half dog."

Shelby giggled. "All right, but just so you know," she cinched her bag shut, "I don't like being your accomplice."

"You will once you read about stroomphblutels," he exclaimed confidently and followed her to the door.

"Stroomph-what?"

"Blutels," Ricky declared. "What's the matter? Making your escape before she gets back?"

Shelby quickly looked across the street, but Sarah was still nowhere to be seen. She exhaled and turned back to face Ricky, whom she firmly smacked in his solid chest.

"You know, you're pretty cute for a law-breaker," Ricky winked at her.

Shelby blushed and descended the shop steps, laughing off the insult mixed with a compliment. "I'll be back tomorrow," she sassed over her shoulder with an eyebrow raised. She gave a smile and a silly wave that she instantly regretted as it was not consistent with her usual behavior towards boys.

As Shelby walked the four blocks home to her house, she took each step with a chipper feeling inside bouncing from heel to toe. She had to admit, she was starting to warm up to Ricky. He wasn't quite the knuckle-dragger she'd first assumed him to be. Sure, he tried to show off to her, but she kind of liked it now that he'd brought it down a notch and let his guard down. She never would have imagined such a good-looking athletic guy like Ricky would be recommending a book to her. She was impressed.

"Stroom...stroomph...blutel," Shelby sounded out the word and laughed. When she reached the fence gate to her house, she flung it open and ran to the door. "Hi Mom! Hi Dad!" She yelled over her shoulder as she darted up the stairs to her room. "Hi, sweetie! Did you have a nice day?" Her mother called from below.

Once inside her room, Shelby took the book out and set it carefully on her pillow. She kicked her sneakers off and flung them across the room then flopped down onto the bed. She smiled down at the title, and traced her finger around an image of a golden flower.

"The Lands of Farwin Wood by Durley Allister," Shelby read the cover aloud softly. "Hmm," she wondered if the author was a relative of Ricky and Sarah's. Gently she opened the book and the first protective page. She mumbled the words on the next, handwritten in a dark green ink, *"To my beloved children – a place far beyond, but forever yours and near.* Aw," Shelby cooed at the sentiment and turned the page. Again, the words on the following page were all handwritten in the same dark green ink. It was then Shelby realized that she was about to read her first ever handwritten book. What a rarity! "Cool," she whispered and began the first line of the chapter.

CHAPTER
TWELVE

DAUNDECORT HALL, FARWIN WOOD
18 YEARS EARLIER

AFTER SARAH finally noticed her brother Richard standing below her, she forced her eyes away from Vasimus and dismounted her stroomphblutel. She quickly smoothed the fabric of her dress skirt and could feel a hint of sweat on her palms. Hundreds of tiny pearls were carefully sewn up and down the front and sides of the skirt, across a lace section of her bodice, and throughout the billowy sleeves. They rustled at the motion with muted clacking noises and Sarah imagined the goose bumps on her arms coming out to meet the tiny orbs in her nervousness. She looked up at the back of the long green and gold vest of her brother to see if he was ready to take her arm as was appropriate. However, he was standing hands on hips admiring the view of the courtyard. She then realized she was once again the object of Vasimus' apt attention.

Vasimus held his arm out. Sarah slowly brought a hand up to clasp the inside of his bicep. His parted lips and intent stare, watching her minutest motion, made him appear to be wholly consumed with this simple action. Once her hand was in place, his lips came together and he held her gaze as he brought his free hand down, pausing just for a second, before it lightly clasped over hers.

Sarah felt almost nauseous with the unexplainable discomfort she felt by his close presence. Her bodice wasn't too tight and it wasn't warm out on this lovely cool day, but she felt flush, feverish, and her knees trembled.

Vasimus gave a cursory glance to his hand over hers then quickly looked towards the hall door and began to walk without a further acknowledgment to Sarah. "The festivities are waiting for your arrival. Shall we?" Vasimus spoke quickly to Richard.

"Lead on, my dear man," Richard cheerfully followed in step with them. He was eager to see Deronda and see the good old-fashioned feast. Richard mentally applauded himself for the idea to 'summer vacation' in Farwin Wood while he walked, chest puffed out in as stately a manner he could assume.

Sarah urged her feet onward to keep up with Vasimus' long-legged strides. The less she did, the more her little hand was forced to make more substantial contact with his rock hard bicep where it lay in the crook of his arm. A glance up at the side of his face showed tension his jaw, his eyes straight ahead of him on the high wooden door they approached.

On the wide stone landing before this entrance door to Daundecort Hall, they stopped. Sarah noticed frigidity in Vasimus' movements as he briefly turned his head to look at Richard and slightly raise Sarah's arm without even looking at her. "Richard," he muttered flatly with a nod.

"Huh? Oh yeah, right," Richard took Sarah's hand from Vasimus and slapped it around his own much smaller bicep. "Ready, kid?" he whispered.

Vasimus stepped ahead of them, and with a lunge he swiftly sent the heavy doors careening open. Revealed below them was the grand expanse of the Daundecort Hall great room. A long, light blue carpet lie on the stone floor before them all the way to the end of the room where Sarah could see an elderly but solid man dressed in similar clothing to Vasimus' — Lord Clennon Daundecort. To Lord Clennon's right stood the petite yet shapely figure of Lady Deronda Daundecort. Richard must have spied her location at the same time as Sarah because she thought she heard him inhale at the sight of her. Before Lord Clennon and Lady Deronda, sat a thick wooden table with three empty chairs awaiting the rest of the honored party. To the right and left of the carpet pathway were countless other tables, each filled with guests of the Daundecorts eagerly looking on at the arrival of the Allisters.

Vasimus swiftly descended the three stairs from the doorway down into the great room and strode down the carpet towards his father and sister. Sarah jumped at the loud call of a man beside her as his voice echoed through the silent masses, "The Lord Richard Allister and Lady Sarah Allister of Allister Hall, Oedher Village and Blinney of the North."

"I guess that's us," Richard muttered, and then added, "Smile," as he tugged his sister forward.

Sarah let out a nervous chuckle and did her best to smile pleasantly. She made a conscious effort to cast refined glances back and forth across the expanse of guests. She felt herself finally breathe again when they reached the Daundecort's table at the end of the room.

Lord Clennon with his leathery, wrinkled but kind face, smiled before them at the head of the table where he faced the room. The salt and pepper hair he had on Sarah's last trip was now much greyer, yet his blue eyes, handsome face, and the lively color of his skin still indicated years of life to come in the aging man. "Welcome, Allisters! Welcome back to Farwin Wood!" Lord Clennon outstretched both of his arms, palms open, to indicate the empty chairs on each side of the table.

Vasimus stood behind the chair immediately to Lord Clennon's left, while Deronda stood behind the one to his right. Next to the brother and sister were the intended chairs of their guests; prime seating for viewing the festivities that would take place throughout the evening. Just as Sarah realized the chair before her was the one next to Vasimus, she let go of Richard's arm and took a panicked step to the left in an effort to snag the place next to Deronda. However, as soon as his arm was free from her grasp, Richard departed in the same direction. Vasimus pulled out the empty chair by him and gazed at Sarah with a questioning look.

Sarah felt her cheeks flush with color, yet as everyone was busy being seated no one seemed to notice her blunder or flustered state—no one except Vasimus. He backed slowly away from the chair, mouth parted, eyes on the demure brunette, and shifted with a step into his own chair. Sarah quickly slid into the seat to avoid being the last person standing. Just as her backside touched the wood, she felt the seat slide forward underneath of her. With an outstretched arm, eyes on Richard and Deronda, Vasimus slid Sarah and the heavy chair she sat on into place with one easy motion. Lord Clennon then gave a nod to an attendant who scurried away and disappeared through a side doorway off the great room.

The next hour easily passed with happy conversation full of inquiries from Lord Clennon on the welfare of the elder Allisters, and stories of Farwin Wood since Richard and Sarah's last visits. Richard was jovial and carefree, refilling everyone's goblets with beetleburry ale, recounting childhood memories of his visits as well as ad-libbing his studies and adventures from their far off "northern homeland" of Blinney.

The feast brought out to their table and the numerous others was nothing short of exquisite. A massive wickrit leg hock was placed in the center of the Daundecort's table for their party, and the tender meat easily fell away from the giant bone. Servers continued on with muckas milk pudding, baked kierberts (which looked like a lime green potato and had the taste of almonds), and tierumpt stew. Tierumpts were tiny birds that swooped up and down when they flew, making a call that sounded like their names.

Musical players ran into the room with the onset of the meal and began to dance around and play kerryorts, a triangular stringed instrument that created haunting chime melodies when strummed. Other players gaily followed amidst them with their dillidumps. Dillidumps consisted of a pair of grated wooden sticks with large rectangular blocks on the ends, either making cricket noises or knocking sounds to add to the musical array.

A short stodgy man in colorful clothing threw daphne flowers about the room as he enthusiastically recited a poem about the details of a hunt where Lord Vasimus killed a wickrit in honor of the Allisters for the feast. When the man finished, the players started again and Sarah took her first glance at Vasimus since being seated. He firmly held his goblet with one hand, still giving his attention to his father and the couple across the table from him. His other hand sat clenched in a fist atop of his leg closest to Sarah's, his elbow out behind him.

Sarah could barely hear Richard or Deronda now as the players grew ever louder and the guests began to mill about the room. She couldn't eat anymore, and sat with her hands pressed against the textured base of her goblet on the table before her. Lord Clennon excused himself to mingle amongst the other guests and Sarah instantly felt the void of the visual distraction. She shifted her eyes to the movement of guests about the room. Richard and Deronda were clearly immersed in giggling conversation, which was now down to whispers between the two of them. They seemed to enjoy being forced to carefully lean in and speak directly into each other's ear amidst the noise of the room.

While the room grew in temperature from the body heat of the dancing guests, Sarah noticed the bulk of the warm sensation she felt seemed to come from behind her. Occasionally she would glance back from the crowd to Richard and Deronda out of cordiality, although she had clearly been forgotten. Sarah made an effort to half turn her face towards Vasimus to also acknowledge his presence, although he had not spoken but two words to her since they sat down. She couldn't help but feel that his eyes were back on her without a second's relief.

"Have you enjoyed your time in Farwin Wood thus far Lady Sarah?" His deep voice eroded through the noise.

Sarah whipped her head back around to realize her assumption had been correct. Vasimus' intense expression was affixed on her. "I have always enjoyed my time here, thank you," Sarah tried to match the old-fashioned propriety of speaking common in Farwin Wood.

"Pardon?" Vasimus leaned slightly forward. He grabbed the base of his chair between his legs and shifted it to angle towards her. "Forgive me, but the guests have grown loud."

Sarah repeated herself with more force but felt her voice come out in nearly a squeak forcing Vasimus to lean in even closer. Heavens, it's getting warm in here, Sarah thought. She took another sip of her ale and waited with eyes down on the brew, sure Vasimus would soon be bored with entertaining her and leave. She still hadn't resided herself to feeling comfortable about visiting Farwin Wood or its peoples since she no longer felt like a child, nor were the children she remembered there clearly children anymore!

"I am pleased to hear this." Vasimus watched her for a moment, and then took a drink from his own goblet. Surely, he'll get up soon to go talk about hunting and fencing with some of the men here, Sarah told herself. Just a few more minutes of awkwardness. "What do you do to enjoy your time here?"

Sarah thought on the question for a moment. Her answers would likely sound silly to him and she wondered if the things she bemused herself with previously would still hold enjoyment now that she was older. "Well…in the past I would often come to Farwin Wood with my family, and we would travel through Oedher Village visiting with the townsfolk. I enjoyed walking through the forest around the village and of course my visits here to see Deronda. I suppose even without my parents now, Richard and I will just continue to do the same."

"Have you not seen beyond Oedher Village in your travels here?" Vasimus almost sounded appalled. The arm of his clenched fist came up and he rested it across the back of her chair.

Sarah tried not to go stiff as a reaction to his movement. What was this feeling of discomfort that had come over her upon their arrival? She sipped some more of her beetleburry and then stared at it wondering how much was too much. "Well, no I suppose I haven't."

"Perhaps you would let me escort you to see more of the countryside," the muscles in Vasimus' face had seemed to soften. Sarah parted her lips trying to think of a polite protest, but her reply was not quick enough as Vasimus continued. "There is much more to see than Oedher Village has likely afforded you, and I would hate for you to leave with a droll opinion of our land."

"Oh, no!" Sarah exclaimed and turned her eyes to him now with the courage of an overcoming beetleburry numbness. "I would never think that! Not with how much I enjoy riding stroomphblutels! Um," she stumbled for a moment to think of an explanation, "you see we don't have stroomphblutels in the North." He watched her with a growing fascination. "But there are other things I will treasure in Oedher Village as well…like all of the lively games of Knick Knack I've played."

"Knick Knack?" Vasimus canted his head.

"Yes, it's a game with these dice…or stones rather, that you jump and grab depending upon how they land…"

"Yes, yes, I know what Knick Knack is," Vasimus laughed thunderously from his chest. Sarah instantly felt stupid. "I've never met a lady, however, who played Knick Knack," Vasimus let his laughter subside into a smile and the ominous look of his dark brow was gone.

The embarrassment Sarah felt over partaking in something she didn't know was not lady-like was diluted by the awe she felt in the view of his smile. He was beautiful. His transformation from ominous to gorgeous with just one laugh and smile was something as magical to behold as how she'd come to Farwin Wood. "Oh. I'm sorry. No one ever told me I shouldn't."

Vasimus' brows softened even further into a kind arch. He lowered his voice and leaned in closer. "I promise not to tell…just as long as you promise to play a round with me."

It was Sarah's turn to laugh now. She was grateful for it because it lightened the weight of discomfort caused by the tension of her muscles and stiff posture. She finally closed the half-inch of space that had kept her back from the chair and leaned into it now, taking another long draw of her ale. Smiling to herself, she ran a thumb over the patina on a daphne flower imprint at the base of the goblet.

"Do you know this flower, Lady Sarah?"

"Hmm? Oh, please, just Sarah. Lady Sarah sounds so... well, makes me feel like my mother," she smiled meekly.

"Sarah," his husky voice came softly.

"Oh, yes. Of course. The daphne flower. I think they're beautiful. We...have something a little similar," Sarah thought of the much smaller pansies that grew behind her friend Franci's house.

"This is the flower of my family — they are said to symbolize strength and compassion," Vasimus rested his own goblet and hand on the table, turning the cup to find the same imprint.

"One isn't worthy without the other," she added softly.

Vasimus looked at her thoughtfully. "How did the little girl who played dolls with my sister while I fought with her brother grow to be such a wise woman?"

Sarah smiled at the accolade of being declared a "woman" after living so long in her parents' shop where she was ever-viewed as their "child." "Well...we must have had some very wise dolls," she raised her glass slightly. Vasimus chuckled and tapped his glass to hers.

The players switched to a livelier tune just then. Couples came together throughout the room and joined hands. As the melody hit higher notes and trills, the couples quickly spun and twirled. The men's arms would come down around the women's waists, and then back over their heads. Everyone seemed to be smiling and laughing at the delight of the pace and motions. Sarah watched with fascination, never having seen this before nor remembering ever reading about it in the book. Was it possible Farwin Wood took on a life of its own in some aspects? People whooped and yelped loud boisterous cries along with the music, and Sarah found herself laughing at the sheer pleasure of everyone's delight.

A stray strand of hair tickled her ear and a warmth touched her neck as she felt Vasimus' breath close to her skin. "Do you know this dance?"

"No. No, I've never seen it."

"Would you like to try?"

Sarah turned her head towards the voice and had the urge to lean the few inches closer that would let Vasimus' face touch hers. "I…don't know how," she mumbled.

"Nor do I, hardly," he said softly.

"I…I think people would end up laughing at me," she offered, still captured by their proximity.

She felt strong fingers slip under hers, pulling them away from her goblet, "That's impossible. I won't let them."

Vasimus came around Sarah's chair and guided her to a place on the floor in front of the table. He gently grasped both of her hands and stood before her, then smiled just before glancing to see when the other couples would turn next. Sarah quickly looked over at Richard, who sat with one arm behind Deronda's chair and saw them both gazing upon her and Vasimus with surprised smiles.

Before Sarah could look back to Vasimus and voice further protest, he had lifted her arms above their heads and she felt herself shifted to his side, then still facing him she shifted to the other. Next, an about-face spin, then back to face his handsome smile. Okay, this isn't so bad, she thought.

Their clasped hands left her arm being pulled gently down behind his back and his behind hers where they rotated, pivoting in a circular motion like one entity. She quickly saw there was no rhyme or reason to how each couple spun. They just bobbed slightly up and down by bending at the knee in time with the beat, every second in some sort of spin or twirl with their partner. Sarah's sensations focused to each new touch as Vasimus' arm would press gently across her back or her own arm. With each new smile she saw from him as she turned, she felt her own growing across her face and soon they were laughing and spinning faster and faster.

To their side, Sarah soon saw Deronda and Richard join in and as she turned, the flash of their own smiles passed by her face. Soon a portion of the crowd had backed away to give more room around the two couples and a steady clapping arose. Whoops and hollers floated up from the happy crowd as they cheered on the two young couples. Richard tried new spins and goose steps to impress them, which led way to friendly competition.

Sarah then found herself sprightly lifted into the air about the waist by Vasimus who rapidly turned them in time with the climax of the melody. Sarah laughed heartily at the whir of the room about her, breathless and almost relieved once the music ceased. Amidst the roar of applause, she slid down the solid expanse of Vasimus' chest as he lowered her to the ground. His arm now firmly around her waist, she looked up panting from the exertion and could feel his breaths do the same from where her hands rested gently against the front of his shirt. Lips parted, he gazed down at her as they breathed.

The melded feeling of his closeness to her was disturbed when she felt the grasp of Deronda's hand around her arm. Her friend pulled her in close for a tight hug as she laughed. Sarah pulled her mind away from the intoxication of her dance partner and grasped Deronda's arms. "Oh, what fun that was!"

Deronda laughed again, "Yes, we haven't had so much dancing in quite some time. And you dance so well!"

"I hardly knew what I was doing. Luckily, Vasimus did!" Sarah laughed.

"Yes, Sarah, what have you done to my brother?" Sarah was confused by the inquiry. "He never dances! And here he was twirling you about the place," Deronda laughed.

"Shall we try another?" Sarah saw Richard beaming down by Deronda's side.

"Oh," Deronda gasped and wiped her brow, "I think your brother has taken a liking to our dancing!" Deronda then sidled up to Richard as a slower melody floated about them.

Sarah exhaled as she watched them begin to step. "I think I'll step outside for some air." Deronda gave her a nod before she disappeared as Richard shifted them about the floor. Sarah took a step and then felt someone lightly touch her elbow.

"Sarah do you feel faint? Did I spin you too quickly?" Vasimus bent down with a look of concern.

"Oh," she brought her hand to her chest at the surprise. "No. No, it's just a bit warm in here and...I think your ale might have been a little strong."

"Here. Come with me," his expression turned serious and she felt his arm rest delicately about her waist. He steered her through the crowd, his other arm extended protectively to keep people from bumping into them. Sarah smelled a hint of something sweet and cinnamon in nature from the proximity to his clothing. A gentle breeze watted through a small open archway near the back of the room and Vasimus guided her up the single step where they emerged onto an open terrace aligned with cut stone and ivy covered archways. They slowed their steps and Vasimus continued to guide them towards a half wall at the edge of the terrace that looked down upon the gardens and the River Duke beyond.

The moonlight illuminated the greenery of the gardens and cast shadows down from the higher shrubbery. Sarah inhaled the cool night air and basked in its cleanliness compared to the stuffy bookstore. She gathered her skirt in one hand and held onto her waist across her front with the other as she looked out into the radiated night.

"There. Is that better?" Vasimus' voice came quietly.

"Mmm, yes. Thank you," she managed a smile. She numbly walked beside him until she felt overheated no more. The sound of her thoughts in the silence began to wear on her now that the noisy couldn't drown them out. With the next step Sarah broke away from the solid arm that was still about her waist and walked over to the terrace wall. She laid her sweaty palms on the damp stones of the wall top and looked down at the garden grounds.

The soft scrape of Vasimus' boots let her know he had followed behind her and the location where he stopped was only a few feet away. She sighed, content with the mix of solitude and the knowledge that he was still close by. "It's so beautiful here," she thought aloud.

"What is Blinney like?"

Sarah hid her smile at the question. "It's...much less green, mostly...buildings," she wasn't sure how else to describe the little stretch of street she knew as home.

"Then I see now why your family likes to come here," Vasimus remarked thoughtfully. "I suppose we do not fully appreciate our lush surroundings."

"Yes, Blinney can be...a bit stifling," Sarah added flatly. That was an understatement.

"Sarah?" Vasimus' voice neared to her side. She turned her head to see him come to rest his hands on the wall a few feet to her side.

"Yes?"

"Will you let me then...show you all Farwin Wood has to offer while you are here for the summer? Before...before you go back to the confines of Blinney?"

Why does he look nervous, as though I'll disappoint him if I refuse, she wondered at his expression. "I...I would like that. But...you don't need to show me *all* of Farwin Wood."

Sarah thought she heard him exhale. He smiled then, "Well...we'll start with just some of it."

"I'm sure you have more serious things to do than to make sure I'm happy," Sarah added.

Vasimus turned to face her directly then. "On the contrary. I think making you happy should be taken very seriously."

Sarah let out a nervous little laugh, "Oh! Well, not too serious, I hope. Where would be the fun in that?" She brought her arms up around her as the breeze chilled her perspiring skin causing a shudder.

"Are you cold? Shall we go back inside?"

"Yes. I think I'll go up to the room now though. Will I offend your father if I leave the party early?"

Vasimus laughed, "My father is probably asleep already. Think nothing of it. Here," he extended his arm to her. "I'll escort you."

They walked off the terrace to an entrance that opened into a hallway behind the kitchen. Vasimus led them up two flights of stairs to a wide corridor lined with several doors and banners hanging on the wall space between them. He stopped in front of an entrance to a room she remembered staying in during her childhood visits. "Here you are. I believe they brought your things into the room upon your arrival."

"Thank you."

"I'll let Richard know you've retired for the night."

"I don't think he'll notice that I am gone. He seemed to be enjoying himself," she smiled.

"And did you?"

"Yes, yes I had a wonderful time," she assured him

"Well, tomorrow morning? Shall we start our adventures then?"

Sarah smiled. She couldn't tell him what she wanted to say — that she was already on an adventure. "I'll be ready."

Vasimus lightly picked up her hand and paused as he noticed the marks on her wrist when her dress sleeve drew back. "Are you hurt?"

Sarah pulled her hand quickly away, ashamed of her Agatha Blinney scars. "No! I...I mean...yes. I was. A long time ago. It's just scarred now and looks…awful. I try to keep it covered, but…as you can see that's not always easy to do."

Vasimus said nothing for a moment and just looked at how flushed her cheeks had become at his observation. "Well, until tomorrow, Sarah." He did not take her hand again and instead leaned forward and placed a soft kiss on her cheek.

"Goodnight," came her quiet reply.

Sarah went inside after Vasimus strode back down the hallway. She tugged herself out of the elaborate dress and donned a long ruffled sleeping gown that Netta had placed in the wardrobe her stroomphblutel had hauled on his back. She let out a soothing moan against the plush pillow of the oversized bed in the room and looked out through the open balcony doors at the twinkling stars in the Farwin Wood sky. She didn't know if she still felt like she was spinning on the dance floor from the beetleburry ale or if she was reliving the sensation as she looked out the window. Whichever it was made her feel giddy and she found it difficult to fall asleep.

Several minutes went by and then Sarah heard the scrape of boots she knew to be familiar out in the hallway nearing her door. They sounded like they stopped in front of the room across from hers and there was silence for a moment before she heard the door open and the steps go inside. He didn't stay at the party, Sarah thought when she realized it was Vasimus retiring to his room after informing Richard she'd gone to bed. She felt a comfort in his nearness and a soothing warmth moved over her. As she closed her eyes, Sarah smiled at the memory of his words: *On the contrary, I think making you happy should be taken very seriously.*

CHAPTER
THIRTEEN

ALLISTER'S BOOKS
PRESENT DAY

SARAH SAT up in her bed as the morning light crept through the window. She brought her hands up to rub her eyes and stopped to peek under the bandages on her wrists. The skin there still felt raw. Peering under one bandage, she noticed the tiny blisters hadn't dried in the slightest. This meant the ones on the wrist where she wore her bracelet would have healed even less in the night, the bracelet keeping the air from touching her skin. She wished she could take it off, but she didn't dare while Ricky was under her care. The last time Richard had visited and Sarah took off the bracelet before bed, she'd awoke to find it across the floor ramming slowly against the door from the pull of the curse beckoning it towards the book. She shouldn't have even taken it off yesterday for those few moments, but her skin had been so irritated.

As she became more alert and the sleepiness left her, Sarah felt queasy to her stomach and pressure in her chest. She exhaled wondering if her thoughts were already vexing her this early in the morning. She felt almost…afraid. As she looked down at her other wrist, she realized why. The last thought she'd had before awakening from her dream had been about Vasimus and the day he gave her the bracelet. Oh, no. I really *did* have that dream, she sighed.

Sarah ripped the covers away from her and forcefully got out of bed. She stomped into her bathroom to reapply the cream Mary had given her, determined to not revisit her thoughts of the night. She wouldn't let the book taunt her with the memories she'd forced away for almost the last twenty years. Not now.

Sarah ran cool water over her wrists and tried to humor herself, anything to keep a clear mind. At least the villagers hadn't given Agatha Blinney black eyes, she thought. I could be walking around with two black eyes all day. Vasimus' eyes…he had beautiful eyes… Damn it!

Why had her mind wandered in her sleep to that unforgettable summer? Was Agatha Blinney so cruel that she sought to torment every villager's ancestor for all eternity? Did all pleasant memories have to have a repercussion? Shoot! Sarah looked down to realize she'd put her underwear on inside out. Oh, yeah, the curse made you put your underwear on the wrong way, she chided herself. Sarah sighed, "I'm losing my mind."

In the room down the hallway, Ricky slapped the whiny alarm clock and groaned. Another day on the pages of boring history, he thought sarcastically as he rolled to get out of bed. "Ah! Crap!"

A sharp pain sliced through Ricky's shoulders and he slapped an arm around to his back instinctively. The skin there felt welted and he lightly touched his fingers across the places he could reach, detecting the size and length of the raised flesh. "What the?"

Ricky stumbled groggily into the bathroom and flipped on the light. He squinted into the mirror, but saw no marks of mosquito bites on his face. He thought maybe something had bitten him while he slept. Turning around to inspect his back in the mirror, Ricky gasped at the sight of his upper back.

Five long, maroon colored welts about a half-inch in diameter stretched from the top of his shoulder blades in various angles down to the middle of his back. "Holy cow! That's no grass burn," he muttered. Ricky didn't know if he was having an allergic reaction to something or if the few times he'd been tackled several days ago had just now residually surfaced their impressions. He took a chance with the stinky shampoo his aunt had given him (what little bit he had not yet dumped down the drain), and let the suds run down his back in the shower. If her oddball remedy didn't help reduce his irritation by tomorrow, he decided he might have to ask her to check out whatever was going on back there.

A minute feeling of relief came over the tender skin when Ricky got out of the shower. He hoped that was a sign the brown goo actually had some antibiotic effect. He found the loosest fitting shirt he'd packed and decided that would alleviate any unwanted chaffing throughout the long day ahead of him in the bookshop. Ugh, the bookshop.

Ricky stared at himself in the mirror once he couldn't think of any other excuse to avoid going downstairs. "I'm too young to waste away in a place like this," he sighed at his reflection. Ooh, wait a minute! Shelby. Shelby might be back today and she just might have some praise for the guy who recommended such a good book to her! Ricky hurried out of the room in his new-found enthusiasm to head down and open up the shop.

Ricky was grateful that Aunt Sarah had assumed counter duty for the day. He was too anxious glancing out the window so he could see the look on Shelby's face when she arrived. He burned off his excitement by moving around the shop pricing new books, straightening displays, and any other task that kept him active. Why on a day when he had so much energy did his aunt seem to be so inattentive? It was already noon and she had spent most of the day staring out the window and fidgeting with that stupid bracelet she always wore.

Sarah looked out at the heat of the summer day, the sweaty tourists walking down Blinney Lane, the glare of the warmth rising up in the air. A woman strolled slowly by the shop window, her large hairy dog lumbering along on its leash, tongue drooped out to the side. It stopped, turned its head, and looked directly at Sarah. It was a Saint Bernard. The sight of it instantly delved her back into the thoughts she'd been having all morning, thoughts of Farwin Wood. She ran her finger over the floral ring attached to her bracelet and felt as though her heart would burst.

Vasimus had given her the bracelet that ring was affixed to on the second day he took her on their "adventure" as he called it. They'd ridden out to the east of Daundecort Hall that day where the land flattened out into a vast plateau, littered with fields and cottages. They took their stroomphblutels down one of the passes to the plateau and road among the village roads where Sarah saw a new kind of creature she'd never known existed in Farwin Wood — roomples.

Roomples looked like sheep with not as much wool, were reddish in color, and had no visible legs. When they lumbered slowly forward their entire bodies rippled similar to caterpillars. Because of their slow progress, roomples were a domesticated farm animal that depended upon the farmers to feed them. Each time they passed a pen full of roomples, Sarah looked on at them until she was sure she had observed all there was to see. Vasimus seemed delighted that he'd found something new to fascinate her. They stopped at a small tavern for lunch, where he then teased her for not having the heart to try roast roomple.

When they returned to Daundecort Hall that afternoon, where Sarah and Richard had both ended up staying on longer than planned, Vasimus gave her the leather bracelet. "I see that I may have embarrassed you the other night," he started with soft hesitation. "I have watched you...and can tell you do not like for anyone to see your wrists, so I made this for you. It's from the wickrit we had at the feast for you and your brother." Sarah watched as he gently put the intricately braided leather band on her wrist. Later that summer, Vasimus gave her something she held even more dear — the small, golden, floral ring that hung on that very bracelet today.

"Excuse me? Miss?" A man impatiently cleared his throat on the other side of the counter from where Sarah sat. She abruptly sat up straight, ashamed of her daydreaming.

"Yes? Sorry."

"Do you have any nautical books? About sailing?" Sarah directed the man to the travel and sport sections, then walked back to the counter to find something productive to pass the time.

About ten minutes later the man she helped slowly walked to the door, empty-handed. Sarah looked up at the scraping sound of his feet against the wood floor. "Did you find what you were looking for?" He didn't reply, only stood with one arm across his stomach. His skin looked paler than before and Sarah thought she saw the gleam of sweat across his forehead. "Sir? Are you all right?"

"Wha... Yes. Yes, I...I just feel a bit ill all of a sudden," he mumbled.

"Would you like me to get you a glass of water?"

"Water? No! No, I'll..." The man glanced back over his shoulder to where he'd been perusing books. "I'll be fine. Think I'll go home and lie down." He went out the door as quickly. His steps seemed wide in stance, as though he were trying to keep his balance.

"Strange," Sarah muttered.

"Aunt Sarah, I'm going to lunch," Ricky called as he also headed to the door. "I'll give Freedhof's one last try. You want anything?"

"No. Thank you." Sarah smiled, happy he'd spoken a full sentence to her.

Ricky rubbed at his back as soon as he was out of the view from his aunt. His back was starting to sting again and the stifling heat of the day irritated it further. He walked into Freedhof's and waited behind the last customer in line.

Several people were sitting at the tables that lined the wall. He heard some of them laughing as he peered around the customer to inspect the day's baked goods. A man walked past him, holding a hand up to his mouth, chuckling. Ricky looked back at the seated customers and noticed everyone in the store seemed to be laughing to some degree.

The man stopped beside Ricky to throw his paper bag in the trash can. "What's so funny?" Ricky nodded to him.

"Huh? Well...nothing really." The man chuckled again and left the bakery.

Ricky shook his head, not understanding what he was missing. When it was his turn at the counter he quickly saw that Mr. Freedhof wasn't laughing. The baker's plump cheeks looked more rosy than usual and his thick mustache was curved downward indicating his displeasure.

"What do you want son?" He asked a bit gruffly. While Ricky hemmed and hawed over the items behind the glass, he noticed Mr. Freedhof nervously cast his eyes towards the customers who were eating.

"What's so funny?" Ricky asked.

"Hmm? Nothing. Nothing," Mr. Freedhof grumbled. "Well, what'll it be?"

Ricky spotted a tray of pastries on the counter behind Mr. Freedhof. They were glazed on top with a drizzle of white icing and in their centers was a crimson goo. He felt his mouth water and nodded to Mr. Freedhof, "How about two of those things."

"What?" Mr. Freedhof didn't even turn around to look.

"Those pastry things behind you. I'll take two of those."

"They're no good. Pick something else," Mr. Freedhof glanced back at the customers.

Ricky arched an eyebrow. He glanced over to see that several customers were eating the very pastries he wanted. He didn't see a look of dissatisfaction on any of their faces. "Come on, Mr. Freedhof. Everyone else is eating them. I'm sure they're as good as they look," Ricky assured the old man. Ricky heard a woman cackle loudly at one of the tables.

Mr. Freedhof's eyes narrowed on Ricky. He turned and grabbed the baking sheet with the pastries on it, walked over to a large, open garbage can beside the back counter, and dumped the pastries into it. He stomped back over to where Ricky stood in awe. "We just sold out!"

"What the...hell? I would have eaten those! Why'd you do that?"

"I told you, boy! They're no good! Now do you want something else or not?"

Two young men brushed behind Ricky on their way out of the store, both doubled over, giggling. "Geesh," Ricky scoffed at Freedhof's grouchiness. "I don't care. Just give me something."

Ricky let the door to Allister's slam behind with the sandwich Freedhof had finally given him in hand. He looked over at Sarah with a perturbed look on his face, "People around here are so weird." Then he walked over and sagged into the couch to eat his lunch. Freedhof's tone and the fact that Shelby still hadn't shown up yet had put a damper on his spirits.

"Ricky, I have to go over and help Franci for a while. Will you watch the shop?" Sarah called to him and he acknowledged her with a cursory wave of the hand.

ACROSS THE street Franci was in a tizzy. She chattered more quickly than usual and paced aimlessly around her shop fidgeting with products. "Sarah, I'm worried. I have ants all over the non-remedy teas, all of my pansies in my greenhouse were wilted to death's door this morning, and did you hear about Genie?"

Sarah felt a lump in her throat on hearing about the state of the pansies. They uncomfortably reminded her of the daphne flowers in Farwin Wood and she felt a sense of guilt for thinking about her ring earlier, wondering if she'd caused Franci's flowers to whither. "Uh, no. What happened with Genie?" Sarah started to take down the normal teas that had no special spices or powers from the Blinney curse.

Genie Mathers owned a dress shop next to Freedhof's. She did alterations for people, but also made Blinney Lane more niche for its tourist appeal due to the period-themed attire she crafted. Renaissance players, actors, local theatre groups, and many locals around Halloween would come from miles to buy costumes from Genie's shop.

"She said she was helping a woman into a corset and the woman started to complain it was too tight. When Genie went to loosen it, it wouldn't budge. The next thing she knew, the woman was hollering for Genie to help her get it off," Franci paced around flailing her arms up in the excitement of the story. "Well, Genie looks down then and the drawstrings had broken and they weren't even tied! The corset was just

144

pulling itself inward and here this poor woman is about to pass out and Genie's trying to pry her fingers into it to get her out! I mean, my word! What else is going to happen?" Franci pressed a hand to her stomach and breathed rapidly.

Sarah shook some ants off her hand that had crawled from a tea box to her skin. "Now, Franci," she soothed her shaken friend, "you know Genie drinks a lot."

"Well, yes that's true, but I doubt she imagined all of that. And what about all these ants?" Franci waved a hand at her infested shelves.

"I don't know, but don't worry. I'll look around. Maybe someone spilled something and it's just attracting them," Sarah patted her friend on the shoulder. Franci sighed and patted a nervous hand over the bun on her head.

"Well, I hope you're right. Thank you," she managed a smile.

After about three hours of calming Franci down, squashing ants, and inspecting all of Franci's stock for unwanted inhabitants, Sarah felt she'd done all she could for one day in Franci's shop. She gave her friend a firm hug and tried to make a few parting jokes to cheer up Franci before she left to get back to the bookshop.

SARAH LEANED against her shop door once she'd closed it behind her and relaxed in the cool feel of the air conditioning. It was blessed hot out and she was grateful for the frigid feel of the bookshop, yet as she stood there basking in it she realized it felt a bit too arctic. She shivered and walked over to inspect the thermostat. Seventy-five? That's odd, Sarah thought. She tapped at the dial, but the needle stayed in place.

"Is it cold in here, Ricky?" She called to her nephew who sat in the counter stool, legs pulled up to his chest, arms tucked behind them.

"I'm freezing," he muttered from behind the computer screen.

"Great," Sarah grimaced. *Just what I need, an air conditioning repair on top of the utility bill.* She walked over to a little table by the couch and grabbed some discarded magazines to put back in their rack. Sarah noticed a glare catch her eye caused by a small puddle of water on the floor in front of the travel book rack. Ugh. "Ricky, toss me that rag in the drawer, will you?"

Sarah caught the dirty rag that Ricky had put dusting miles on and walked over to the puddle. She squatted down by the shelf and soaked up the water. *At least I hope it's water,* she thought. As she was about to stand up she noticed a single book out of place, sitting on top of the others on the travel bookshelf. She picked it up to tuck back onto the shelf and felt some beads of water on it. "Ugh, great," Sarah muttered and dried the water with the rag. She set the rag down and opened the book to see if there was any damage to the pages. *Sailing the Aegean.*

There were no water stains or damp pages as Sarah fanned through them. She stopped when she saw motion and turned the few pages back to a double page image of a small yacht on the open sea. Before her eyes, Sarah saw the image of the deep blue sea on the page begin to ripple up and then down. The little yacht rocked with the undulating motion of the waves. Sarah caught her breath and her mouth hung open as she watched the picture come to life.

The waves picked up and the yacht moved closer to the edge of the page, closer towards her, arching its bow upward from the force of the windblown sea. As it bashed back down into the water Sarah thought she heard the spray of water and felt a mist shoot out and spatter her face. She gasped and fell to her backside letting the book fall and slam shut on the floor.

"You all right?" She heard Ricky call with little enthusiasm from the counter. She couldn't see him from behind the shelf as she sat on the floor, the book between her feet.

"Fine," Sarah's breathless call came out. She panted several breaths and remained on the floor for a moment, absorbing what had just occurred. No. This can't be happening! What else? What else is going on? Don't panic, Sarah. Don't panic, she thought.

Sarah finally got up from the floor. She nudged the sailing book back into its place and then began to walk around the shop. Arms across her chest, hands tucked under her armpits, she slowly paced beside the shelves looking at the books. She watched, listened, and even smelled for a sign of anything unusual. As she rounded the line of shelves to where they ended by the overlooking balcony, she noticed Ricky digging his fingernails forcefully into his back.

"Ricky, stop that!" Her agitation level was at its peak.

"Geez, sorry. It itches," he grumbled and let his hand drop to his lap.

Sarah decided to take a walk past the book shelves in the back. She needed to know what the extent was of the peculiar events that were occurring in the shop. With Franci's ant infestation and pansy crop failure, Genie's killer corset, her own agitated wrists, and now a normal book coming to life, Sarah worried that what could be overzealous reactions of her nervousness were in fact indications of a heightening in the curse's power.

Scanning the rows of books on the second level, Sarah began to feel calmer. Nothing seemed out of the ordinary. Hopefully the worst of what would happen had already occurred.

"You need some help with anything?" Sarah heard Ricky call from the floor below.

"No, I'm fine," Sarah said, eyes still scanning for anything unusual. She'd have to start getting Ricky to go out in town more. Maybe getting him away from the shop a little longer each day would alleviate the peculiarities from happening. Sarah rounded the last shelf to the back row. From ceiling to floor, the rows of books seemed just what they were—old books, sitting diligently on a shelf. Sarah let a deep breath out.

Through the glass, Sarah stared at the cover of Durley Allister's book on the Revolutionary War, the first in the like of weeping books behind the bars and glass cabinet doors of the illuminated case. There were no drops of dew about the bottom pages of the book and that's when Sarah felt a final wave of relief.

Those books were the most susceptible to acting up when the curse gained strength, and if the books weren't weeping in full force now, then she was satisfied there wasn't cause to overreact. She stared at the book for a moment, wondering what Durley Allister must have gone through on his first encounter inside his own creation. The thought that she hadn't been the one to bear the brunt of fear that Agatha Blinney's curse could instill comforted her. She hadn't been the one to pin down and determine all the strange activities that occurred in her shop. What to do. What not to do. What to avoid. How to get out of a book! Sarah gave a grateful smile as she started to walk out of that last cubby of shelves.

At the end of the shelves, she stopped. Something caught her eye...or rather didn't. She took a step back to look at the last book on the inside of the cabinet and her heart felt like it dropped into her stomach.

Each time she had ever passed *The Lands of Farwin Wood*, she would distinctly see the slightest glint of light on the foil embossed letters and images of daphne flowers adorning the book's cover. Standing before the thick book now, there was no glint. There were no flowers. Sarah stepped forward and pressed her fingers against the glass. There...where *The Lands of Farwin Wood* had sat untouched for nearly the last twenty years, sat a very early edition of *The Canterbury Tales*. She slowly turned to glance behind her and couldn't happen but notice that Ricky's head quickly shifted from casting his eyes in her direction, back to the computer screen.

"Agatha…don't stop me until I've had enough time to kill him," Sarah growled under her breath with each steady stride towards the counter.

CHAPTER

FOURTEEN

FARWIN WOOD
18 YEARS EARLIER

SARAH SPENT an entire week at Daundecort Hall after the feast, at the insistence of Vasimus, Deronda, and even Richard who seemed to be enjoying his time immensely. She traveled out into the surrounding countryside each day with Vasimus, leisurely strolling along on their stroomphblutels. Each day they would stop to relax and either eat at an inn or from a basket of goods Vasimus had brought from the hall.

On the morning she had gotten Richard to agree upon returning to Allister Hall, Sarah packed her things with a bubbly and nervous feeling throughout her entire body. The afternoon before, by the base of the great mountains to the north of Daundecort Hall, where Sarah claimed she and Richard lived far beyond, Vasimus had kissed her. As wonderful as the moment had been, Sarah now felt a sudden urge to flee back to the motherly comfort of Netta and the safety of Allister Hall, a place that reminded her more of home, more of the reality she had to go back to once the summer ended.

The Daundecort brother and sister promised to come and visit Richard and Sarah at Allister Hall to return the company that had been bestowed upon them. Vasimus watched Sarah with curious eyes as they parted. In spite of her nervousness over her first kiss with a fictional character, she couldn't help but smile at him each time he looked at her. Sarah noticed she was the first to mount her stroomphblutel and saw that Richard stood intimately close to Deronda, whispering something in her ear. Deronda looked up at him with a familiar dreamy look on her face; it was one Sarah had seen on her own in the mirror just that morning.

"Sarah? May we continue on beyond Oedher Village when I come to visit you?" Vasimus queried hopefully, referring to their rides throughout Farwin Wood.

"Yes, I'd like that," the words came out without thought. Wait! Is this a good idea?

"I'll count the days," he smiled.

As they rode down the long windy road away from Daundecort Hall, both Richard and Sarah cast occasional glances back to the place they had just departed. Neither of them said anything for a long while, each lost in their own thoughts and melancholy from parting their hosts. Finally Richard let out a long satisfied sigh, "Ah, Sarah...I think I'm in love."

"What?" She snapped her head around at him so quickly she nearly fell off her stroomphblutel who also jolted at the cry. Richard's shifted a few paces away from hers as quickly as it could and he soothingly patted the poor beast.

"Easy! What's with the hostility?" Richard frowned at her.

"Hostility! Try *reason*!" Sarah's mind reeled as she recollected all the times during the past week she'd seen her brother and Deronda together...and worse, all the times she hadn't seen them at all because she was off with Vasimus! What ever had happened?

"Would you lower your voice, please?" Richard tried again to steady his mount.

"Richard, how would that work? Are you going to stay here and remain in a coma like sleep back on Blinney Lane for the rest of your life? And what if she wants to see Blinney? Our land in the 'North.' What then?" Sarah tried to keep her composure.

Richard seemed unaffected by his sister's worries. He sat erect, confidently gazing forward as they strode down the dirt road towards Oedher Village. "Well, maybe I'll tell her."

"Tell her! What? You can't do that. What...what if everyone finds out. What if telling her means you can't go back again? What if..."

"What if, *what*? You don't know. Do you?" Richard scoffed.

"Well, no, but that's the point I'm trying to make. You *don't* know what could happen, Richard."

"Sarah, I hate to break this to you, but that's life...no matter where you are," Richard remarked calmly.

Sarah was irritated by his calmness and the idea that her nonsensical brother might make more sense than her for once in his life. How can he be older than I am, when he's usually such a carefree idiot? "So...what? Are you not going to start working somewhere after the summer now? I thought you got an internship in New York?" Sarah started again with less severity.

"Sarah," Richard sighed. "I don't know. We'll see where it goes...how she feels about me. I don't know, but...but I'm happy. I've never been so happy," he let out a laugh. "I've never met anyone like her before, Sarah. She's kind and beautiful, funny and generous, and she's not pretentious like these girls at school were."

"What is there to be pretentious about here, Richard? Who has the bigger stroomphblutel?" Sarah scoffed.

"You know what? I'm sorry I told you. I thought I could talk to you, but I guess you're just not mature enough to deal have a serious conversation. You're the one who always wants to be serious anyways. Maybe you're just afraid. Is that what all this is about?" Richard scowled at her now.

"Afraid? Afraid of what?"

"Don't give me that! I saw how you and Vasimus were checking each other out; staring at each other like fools all week, smiling and laughing, going off all day on rides. I was happy for you, but now maybe I should just pity the poor guy. You're going to be the one who's the heart breaker, not me," Richard stared ahead as he ranted in a sour tone.

Sarah didn't like the observations he'd made about her and Vasimus when she was just coming to terms with them on her own. "I don't know what you're talking about. Vasimus and I...well, he's just proud of their lands and was showing me around. I was just being polite. What? Was I supposed to say 'no'? Don't read too much into it," Sarah avoided his eyes after her haughty reply.

"Oh yeah? Nice bracelet," Richard smirked.

Sarah scoffed and tugged her sleeve down over the bracelet. "It...it was from the wickrit from our feast! He was just being nice," she stammered defensively.

A short silence followed and Sarah looked over to find her brother holding back a grin. He sputtered out a laugh which continued to grow with intensity.

"Ugh, I hate you," she muttered. A few moments later she found herself smirking and the desire to knock Richard off his stroomphblutel began to gradually subside.

Not two days later, Vasimus and Deronda arrived at Allister Hall to stay with their old friends. Both apologized for the brevity between their last parting, inquiring if they had come too soon and were imposing upon the Allisters. However, it was apparent amongst the four of them that no one was dismayed by the reunion.

Netta was happy to have more mouths to feed in the Allisters' great room, much smaller in size to the one at Daundecort Hall. The house grew quite droll during the long absences of the Allister family. Netta was overjoyed by how well the young couples got on together and hoped it proved that new unions were promised in their futures, well at least for Sarah. Lady Deronda, as everyone else in the land knew, was promised to marry Ranthrop Groslivo of the Southern Lowlands. Netta, however, was still happy the young lady seemed to be enjoying her time with Sarah and Richard before the impending marriage next spring.

For the next two weeks, the Daundecorts and Allisters rode out together each day from Oedher Village in a new direction. They were happy times, the four of them laughing at Richard's jokes, old stories of their youth, and tales of Farwin and the North.

Sarah found several moments to steal off behind a tree or bush when they would dismount to rest, where she could enjoy more of Vasimus' wonderful kisses. She noticed how happy Deronda also seemed, as her friend often rode close alongside her brother. Sarah truly started to feel happy for them and felt some guilt in how she'd scolded Richard when he'd first professed his feelings for Deronda. Now, well...now she didn't disagree that she could get very used to a life in Farwin Wood, even if she too didn't know what would happen. She was only grateful their bodies, back in her room on Blinney Lane, never seemed to deteriorate no matter how long they slept once inside of a weeping book. Could she stay asleep forever? Had Sleeping Beauty been as lucky to have traveled to a beautiful place with a man she cared for while she slept, she wondered.

The third week, Vasimus had all but forgotten his sister and Richard, as had Sarah. Each couple eagerly agreed to their own sets of plans for the day and the next. And so it went for the next week. The days grew much more intimate between Sarah and Vasimus with their rides much shorter and their time basking in the shade of a glen much longer. By the end of that week, the Daundecorts knew they needed to return home before their father grew too lonely back in the great hall by himself. They returned home, but a few days later, Deronda wrote and invited Sarah to come stay at the hall. She added in her letter how eager her brother was to see Sarah.

"You don't mind if I go?" Sarah felt bad now for leaving her brother after she'd put up such an initial fuss over his accusations about her and Vasimus.

"No. No, not at all," Richard assured her.

"But what will you do now that Deronda's had to go back home? I suppose it might start to look a little too intrusive if we both went and I'm spending more time with Vasimus than you are in front of their father. How does that work anyways? Would you have to ask his permission to court her or something?" Sarah giggled.

Richard's laugh almost seemed nervous. "Maybe I have to slay a wickrit or something," he smiled. "No, I'll come along a little later. I need to win some troogies back from the Wort-wart brothers after that last bout of Knick Knack," Richard referred to the means of coin used for purchases in Farwin Wood. "Just invite me for dinner or something after a while so I have an excuse."

Sarah hugged her brother. She was glad he'd planned this trip into Farwin Wood. It had given them a chance to grow closer together as young adults. She enjoyed being able to talk to someone who knew about their peculiar past; who she could unabashedly tell whatever she wanted. As she rode out from Allister Hall and waved goodbye to Richard and Netta, she felt guilt for Richard having to stay behind out of propriety while she knew he longed to see Deronda, but also glee in anticipation of reaching Daundecort Hall to see Vasimus. She urged her stroomphblutel on as quickly as it could muster, and promised to herself that she would talk about her brother as much as she could to her dear friend.

Behind her on the road, Richard felt a hint of relief at seeing his little sister leave. He was grateful she didn't seem to know about Deronda's engagement to Ranthrop Groslivo yet. If she found out, he'd never hear the end of it. As of then, any of his behavior that Sarah had seen would have looked innocent. Luckily she and Vasimus would disappear long enough for them to forget about him and Deronda. He wondered if they had been as intimate as he and Deronda had by now. Ugh, he thought, at the image of his sister being physically romantic with someone. He was happy she was able to go off and live for a change, free from Blinney Lane. Moreover, he was happy he could now sneak off on his own without question to meet Deronda in a quiet glen not far from the Daundecort gardens, where they had agreed to rendezvous before she'd left.

At Daundecort Hall, Sarah saw little of Deronda. They spent the mornings together, but Deronda always seemed to excuse herself to tend to some task — designing new draperies for the hall, planning the evening meal, visiting sick villagers. Vasimus always quickly volunteered to find some occupation for Sarah when his sister was called away, although that usually resulted with the two of them spending time together. Sarah was grateful that Deronda made these excuses to give them privacy and that she seemed genuinely ecstatic that Sarah was smitten with her brother. "We could finally be sisters some day," Deronda had gushed to her one morning.

Sarah, blushing, couldn't deny the truth to her response, "Nothing could make me happier."

A week into her stay, Richard arrived to spend the day with her and the Daundecorts. Sarah and Vasimus had little opportunity to speak to each other amongst the added company, and both did their best to avoid showing their affection in front of anyone else.

Lord Clennon joined them for lunch and then took Richard and Vasimus out on a hunt, leaving the girls behind. Deronda and Sarah both bound out of the garden smiling and holding hands as they heard the men return on their stroomphblutels that evening. Sarah tried to linger at the dinner table after Deronda and Richard left, but she felt awkward in the presence of a nobleman who sat at the end of the table visiting with Lord Clennon. She cast a longing glance at Vasimus and then retired to her room.

Vasimus regretfully watched her go slowly up the stairs and then excused himself to his occupied father and the nobleman. Once he was sure they could no longer see him on the stairs he bound up them two at a time. In the darkness of the hallway he glimpsed the green skirt of Sarah's dress just as she had opened the door to her room. "Psst!" He whispered through the darkness to catch her before she disappeared into her room for the night. He knew he would dream about her while he slept, as he had each night since the day she'd first arrived at the feast, but if he had the opportunity to just speak to her in the flesh for a few more seconds, he would steal them. Sarah turned her head and flashed him a radiant smile. She paused by her open doorway and waited as he hurried towards her.

They glanced up and down the hallway in silence, and then Vasimus encircled her waist with his sinewy arms to pull her into him for a hungry kiss. Sarah clasped her hands on his face and felt the soft bristle of his short dark whiskers against her palms. His hand came up her back and she leaned further into him, yearning to close the distance of the gap his absence during the day had filled her with. They both froze at the sound of footsteps on the stairwell and Sarah grasped his hand. Without a second thought she pulled him through her open doorway.

Vasimus steadied the door with one hand applying pressure so it wouldn't creak, and slowly shut it with the other. He carefully set the latch down in place and listened as the steps faded down the opposite end of the hallway. Still breathing heavily from Sarah's kisses and the excitement of being discovered, he turned to find her standing behind him. The bright grey moonlight flooded through her open balcony window and laid a soft glow on everything it touched within her room — the floor, the top of her head, her light skin. She looked radiant and majestic in the light, smiling softly up at him.

Realizing he was now locked in her room, in the place where his captivating Sarah slept, he knew he should go. She had a pull on him that was like nothing he'd ever experienced before. He liked beetleburry ale, but could stop drinking it. He loved to ride through the woods on stroomphblutels, but would walk the rest of his life if he had to. But to stop thinking about, talking to, looking at, or touching Sarah whenever she was near...well, these were things he didn't think were possible. "I'm sorry. I only meant to say goodnight," he whispered.

Sarah's grey eyes sparkled in the light as she smiled up at him, "Well, then...say goodnight," she whispered and took a step closer to him. She brought her hands up and gently placed them on his chest. He could feel the edge of the leather bracelet against him and his heart beat at the knowledge she'd worn it each day since he gave it to her.

Vasimus brought a hand up to clasp the side of her face. He let out a breath at the feel of her soft hair on his finger tips. They leaned into each other and Vasimus gave his best effort to say goodnight with his lips against hers. Her fingers gripped small handfuls of his shirt front and her mouth opened, welcoming him for more. He drew her even closer with his other arm and held her to him, his widespread fingers across her back.

Sarah felt her skin tingle all the way to her toes. She didn't know if she was being too eager or not eager enough, or who was thirstier for the kisses. She unconsciously tugged at the front of his shirt and the laced portion across his chest loosened to reveal his velvety warm skin. Their lips parted for a breath of air and she inhaled the sweet aroma of his skin and gazed longingly at the sight of his bare chest before her. She felt his heavy breath against her temple, then against her hair. Sarah thought she would be dizzy if she looked at the thick cords in his neck any longer without touching them. She brought her lips to the skin there and brushed it with slow kisses.

The sensations that rocked through Vasimus were maddening as his delicate little Sarah tortured him with her new discovery of his body. He tried not to knead his fingers too deeply into her back as she awakened more and more desire in him. Her hands began to explore the exposed skin of his chest and then crept underneath his shirt. He found his own hand sliding down her back and pulling her backside closer to him and he let out a low groan. As soon as the sound escaped his throat he regretted it in fear that he sounded like a starving beast. He brought his head back to look at her and heard a small gasp of her own. When he stared down at her he saw that her eyes seemed as glazed with wanting as his did, and her lips parted as she breathed.

"Sarah," his voice came out in a hoarse whisper. "I should go. I haven't even had a chance to ask your father for you," he said painfully. "I would ride to the North tomorrow if I knew he would say yes."

Sarah's heart stopped at the sound of his decree. She brought her fingers lovingly to his jaw. "There's no need for that," she smiled at the delight of looking into his eyes. "In Blinney a woman doesn't need permission. She chooses herself."

Vasimus continued to labor under his bated breaths looking down at her. He processed her words and their meaning. "Sarah, would you...would you ever choose me?"

Sarah wanted to laugh at the question. Where was this formality back in the real world? The control. The sexiness of self-denial. As he looked at her in hope, Sarah realized she needed to reply. She didn't want to lie to him, but she'd never said something so deeply committal aloud to anyone before. She hoped she didn't misconstrue his look as one of hope, were it really one of fear that she would declare her precious feelings. "Vasimus, I already have," the words came faintly out. She felt his arms crush around her and he hoisted her up in the air against him. He spun them around several times and let out a laugh.

When he brought her back down he grasped her face with both hands and placed kiss after kiss on her face. If she'd known the words would have given him so much joy she would have said them sooner. She didn't want to think about consequences now, only revel in the shared happiness. As his kisses softened and directed back to her lips, she pushed the unknown of the future from her mind and focused on the very real present.

Sarah brought her hands up to run through his silky black hair, delighting in the reality of him. He was real. He felt real. He and everything else in Farwin Wood had been real. All she wanted in that moment was to prove how every inch of him was real and how everything that had passed between them that summer had been too

Vasimus struggled to hold back his excitement for concern his sheer size and strength would crush his little love in his abounding joy. She made him laugh. She was afraid of nothing. She loved to discover every sight and sound of Far-win Wood and took interest in things ladies never seemed to care about. He didn't know such a person could exist, nor one that wanted him as much as he wanted her.

Vasimus felt another groan escape him as Sarah pulled his gaping shirt open even further and let her fingers slip across his ribs. Without thinking, he brought his own hand up to the laces on the front of her bodice as their mouths remained united. With a light tug on the silky strings, he paused for a moment to look down at her. She'd "chosen" him, but he didn't know if she truly had chosen…well, what they weren't doing yet.

Sarah pulled her eyes away from his for a brief glance down at the fingers which held her bodice string. She looked back up at him and pulled him back for a kiss and Vasimus felt her hand come up and wrap over the top of his, where she gently urged it to pull on the laces. Knowing she had just committed to the action, he slowly tugged the strings loose, afraid that any haste would frighten her into losing this delightful eagerness.

When Sarah's overskirt and bodice had dropped to the floor, Vasimus held his breath, afraid to touch her for reasons he did not know. Never in his life had he been nervous around a woman. But Sarah, just recently blossoming into womanhood, standing so angelically and non-threatening in front of him, somehow terrified him. He worried if he touched her again she might disappear. When he saw the hint of self-consciousness cross her face, he felt her insecurity pull on him. Ashamed that he'd offended her by ceasing his caresses at the sight of her revealing chemise, his own fears vanished immediately.

Vasimus pulled her to him again with one arm and shed his shirt with the other to make himself appear as vulnerable with his bared skin. Soon she was back to grazing her fingers across his body and they traveled further along the muscles over the expanse of his back. The pair, entangled in each other's arms, moved slowly towards her bed. Vasimus reached down, picked Sarah up in his arms and threw back the bulky bed cover. He lowered her slowly to the bed as their lips still explored each other's and he followed her onto the soft blankets, lying down on his stomach next to her.

Sarah reveled under the pressure of Vasimus as the weight of his chest gently settled onto hers. Her skin felt like goose flesh when one of his strong hands came down to grasp her waist against the thin fabric of her chemise. One of her legs instinctively came up and bent at the knee, and she leaned it against his hip where it felt like it belonged. She tried to concentrate on a path line for her kisses and her hands against his back and his ribs, but the distraction of his warm breath against her neck was maddening. Her palms started to sweat at the thought of anatomy. She'd never done this before and although she had an idea of what men on television and in magazines looked like, she wondered if Durley had penned his Farwin peoples in the same manner? Was it so simplistic that the stroke of the pen could cast them as equals to the humans in her world? In the same regard, would Vasimus find everything under what remained of her thin clothing to be what he was expecting?

Sarah nervously let her hand slide down Vasimus' stomach to where his form-fitting pants were laced. She skirted her hand around the laces slowly and eased it further to where she had felt a bulge press against her earlier. Vasimus moaned in her ear and his hand slid down her canted leg to grasp the flesh of her backside as he pulled her closer to his own waist. Sarah's lips parted and her own throaty groan came out in reply at the feel of his fingers on her bare skin so close to her most delicate parts.

Okay, everything seems…normal, she thought remembering the brief make-out session she'd had with a kid named Joey Warner behind the bleachers during her last semester of high school. Vasimus' strong fingers slid up to cover her stomach pulling her shift up with it, and Sarah breathed wistfully between deep kisses at the sensations it gave her. Joey never made me feel like *that,* she thought somewhere in the back of her mind.

Vasimus did his best to be gentle and fight the urge to devour Sarah with the force of his passion. He caught her hand on one of its circling passes near the laces of his pants and guided it back to the place that would free him. As he slowly nibbled and teased her lip, he forged his free hand closer to trace the curves of her breasts. Each whine and whimper he expelled from her delighted him further, encouraging him to take his time and he soon felt a wanting tug of her fingers as she pulled at his pant laces. Her hand freed the confines of the laces and he could bear it no longer when he felt her hand slide through the open flap to touch him.

Vasimus shifted his weight over her and pressed down onto her own waist to bring the firmness of what she'd made him feel closer to her own place of wanting. He kissed her deeply as she moaned at the pressure. Then he tugged her shift up over her arms and tossed it to the side. As he gazed down upon her nakedness, he whispered, "You are the most beautiful thing I have ever seen." Lowering his head, he softly kissed her breasts causing her to claw her fingers through his wavy hair. She nudged his pants downward with her free hand and legs, and delighted at the feel of his warm silky buttocks against the skin of her calves.

Surprised by her own boldness, Sarah urged Vasimus back up towards her with her feet against his backside as the kisses he scattered across her stomach and the soft caresses of her breasts drove her crazy. He slid back up her body slowly with a hesitant look in his eyes and stroked a strand of hair away from her face. Sarah traced his cheekbone and breathed huskily at the feel of his skin against her thighs. She welcomed the slow deep kiss he lowered his head to give her and grasped on to his hips. He delicately lowered himself into her, and moved ever so slowly until he knew her initial pain was gone, replaced by the pleasured wanting she indicated by her pawing.

Sarah lay content with Vasimus' arms around her after the waves of their urgencies had rippled through them, finally relieved by their bodies rocking together as one. Whatever pretense of insecurity she had felt before was completely gone now, as she lay with her naked back pressed firmly against his chest, their hands clasped together against her breasts. If she had to die while asleep on Blinney Lane, she hoped this is what it would feel like.

ALLISTER'S BOOKS
PRESENT DAY

RICKY PEERED nervously around the computer screen as Sarah inched dangerously closer to the enclosed book-shelf in the back of the upper level of the shop. His mouth suddenly felt dry and he swallowed to urge some salivation. What the heck does she need to be doing back there, Ricky thought. There's no one even in the store right now. Sarah's head whipped back around and her eyes fixed on him. Ricky averted his eyes quickly back to the solitaire game on the computer screen, hoping she hadn't noticed anything amiss.

The sound of the steady footsteps on the wood floor grew louder and nearer to the front of the shop. Ricky heard the creak of the balcony steps and the next thing he knew his aunt was standing, hands on hips at the end of the counter. He felt her eyes on him, but remained his ruse of ignorance.

"Ricky?" The solid tone touched his ears.

"Yeah?" Ricky mumbled, eyes still forced towards the computer.

"Did you take my book?"

"Hmm?"

"Ricky!" He thought he heard her stamp one of her feet with the second calling of his name.

Great. Here we go. Ricky slowly looked up at her and forced himself not to swallow a lump in his throat at the sight of her wide wild eyes. "What? What book?"

"Ricky...I think you know what book I'm talking about," she gritted the words out slowly.

"How the heck would I know? You know how many books you have here?" Ricky shrugged.

"Yes! Yes, I do! I know exactly how many books I have here, which is why I know exactly which one is missing. It's one of the only five that are kept locked behind bars in a thick glass cabinet. One of the only five I specifically told you never to touch!"

"Well, what the hell makes you think I touched it? Why does it have to automatically be me? 'Cause I'm the bad guy? I'm trouble? Is that why?" Ricky tried to lay the guilt on in his own panic.

Sarah raised her bracelet-clad wrist as she spoke, "because you're the only one who knew where the key was and how to get it."

"Wh...what? Well, maybe you left it lying around some-where!" Ricky waved his arms hoping that somehow the motion would distract her rant.

"Ricky, I never take this off. Just tell me where the book is, please," Sarah tried to calm her voice and her nerves.

"Well, what if...like when you left it on the counter the other day? Maybe you take it off more than you know."

Sarah narrowed her eyes on him. "How ironic that you remember that with such clarity." She said nothing else and placed one hand on the counter and the other on the bureau desk to her left, pinning him in behind the counter space.

"What's the big deal? It's just a book. I mean, if someone took it, I'm sure they'll bring it back. Who'd want to steal an old book anyways?"

"Ricky...where...is...it?"

Ricky squirmed in the stool. "This is such bullshit! Just because I got into a little bit of trouble, you assume it's me. Ah!" Ricky winced and slapped his hand to his back. His skin stung where he'd found the marks that morning.

"What's wrong with your back?"

"Oh...*now* you're worried about me?" Ricky rubbed and scratched.

Sarah thought for a moment. "No. I just want to know if I need to tell the police to take any special care of you when I call them to report your second theft," she replied with perfect calm.

"What? Are you kidding me?"

"Ricky...just tell me where it is so I can get it back. Now!"

Ricky's worry had turned to discomfort and agitation as he scratched his back and now contemplated if his aunt's threat was real. "All right! I didn't tell you because I knew you'd freak out!" He gestured at her with his free hand. "I didn't think it was a big deal because....because it's safe. I loaned it to someone who'd take good care of it...just to read, then bring back."

Sarah's mouth hung open, trying not to scream at what he'd done so she could learn the book's location. "Who did you give it to?" Her voice was a terrified whisper.

"You have to promise me you won't yell at her. It was my idea. It's my fault!"

"This is no time to be noble, Ricky! Who?"

Ricky frowned and swallowed. "Shelby. I gave it to her yesterday."

Sarah dropped her head and pinched her eyes shut. "Oh my word," she gasped. "Not her."

"What? Come on! Who takes better care of books besides you and me than she does?" Sarah looked up and glared at him. "Okay…besides you."

"You need to go over there right now and bring it back here," Sarah looked out the window in thought. "Immediately."

Ricky grimaced at the thought of having to admit to Shelby that he'd been caught. "Can't I just call her or something?"

"Ricky, it's probably too late for that. Just get your butt moving and get over there. I'll write the address down for you." Sarah scribbled Shelby's address down on a notepad.

"It's like three o'clock," Ricky looked up at the clock in confusion. "I'm sure she's awake."

Sarah arched a brow as she looked up at him, "You'd better hope so!" With that thought, Sarah became ill. "You gave this to her yesterday?"

"Yeah," he admitted again under his breath.

"Just wait a minute," she handed him the note with the address. "I'm going to call first, but you're still going over there."

"Oh, come on," Ricky objected. Sarah looked at him in question for his change of heart about the phone call. "I…I mean what are you going to say? You're…you're not going to embarrass me are you?"

"That's the least of your worries," she snapped as she picked up the phone and dialed Shelby's number. "Yes, Mrs. Dannovan? This is Sarah Allister at the book store. Is Shelby there?" Ricky watched his aunt as they both waited anxiously through the pauses. "Oh. No, she hasn't been in today, so yes… maybe she is up in her room. Look, I'm sending my nephew over there to get a book from her if that's all right. He loaned her one of my old books and I…found a buyer who's coming in for it later, so Ricky will be over to get it. She'll know the one. Okay, thank you Mrs. Dannovan." Sarah set the phone down with a shaking hand.

Ricky sighed and smiled a little, "Thanks."

"For what?"

"For...not ratting me out."

"I didn't do that for you," she said icily. I did that not to freak her mother out, Sarah thought. "Listen to me very carefully, Ricky." Ricky took an awkward step back as his aunt approached him and set both of her hands on his shoulders. "You go over there right now and no matter what happens...no matter what you see, you get that book. Do you understand?"

"Uh...yeah," Ricky looked from her hands back to her pointed stare.

Sarah shook him once, "Ricky! I'm serious! Whatever happens! If she's sleeping, don't wake her up, but still get that book. If her mother says she's sleeping and to come back later, get that book! Tell me you'll come back here with the book!"

"Yeah! Yeah! I got it already. Geez! You're acting kind of weird. I'm sorry already," Ricky brushed her hands off and took the chance to escape from behind the counter.

"Ricky. Don't be sorry, just..."

"Get that book. Yeah, I got it!" Ricky ran out the door before she could scold him any further. Man! She is crazy about her damned books! Ricky hurried down Blinney Lane and was never happier to be out on the main road. He glanced behind him a few times, paranoid his aunt might come out to check that he was actually going. He'd never seen her act so intense before. Aunt Sarah was usually cool. Well, at least the coolest family member he had. Okay, so he didn't have many family members, but still, she was the least likely to freak out compared to his Dad and from what he remembered of his mother.

Ricky glanced down at the paper with Shelby's address. He wondered if he could take his time once he got to her house, not that he'd feel like staying if it got awkward and Shelby became upset that they'd been found out. It'd be a nice distraction from his angry aunt though, if he could spend a few sane minutes with the cute little bookworm instead.

Shelby's house was only about five blocks from the book shop. He knew the street as it crossed the main drag he'd walked down so many times that summer to escape for lunch outside of Blinney Lane. As he turned onto Elm Street he noticed a reflection of light on the street sign. Ricky reached to his stinging back and scratched as he looked down the street. There was an ambulance parked a block down with its blue and red lights flashing. He started down Elm and glanced back and forth at the house numbers. 101. 102. He needed to get to 203 Elm. Ricky looked up at where the ambulance sat with its back doors open, no one inside, as he neared the end of the first hundred block. It looked to be pretty close to where he needed to go. Ricky began to walk faster and only paused to check the side traffic as he crossed the intersection.

As Ricky walked down the sidewalk up behind where the ambulance was parked next to the curb he looked at the number on the house to his left: 201. Wait, Ricky thought. That means 203 is next. Ricky stepped slowly between the ambulance and the gate of a white picket fence in front of a large two story house with a wide porch. Three numbers were affixed to the open gate of the fenced-in yard. 2-0-3. He looked up at the house where the lights of the ambulance reflected off the windows. The front door was wide open. "This can't be right," Ricky said under his breath. He started up the walk with a bit of a jog and stopped at the open door.

Ricky peered inside and tapped gently on the open door. "Hello?" He peered to the right and saw an empty dining room, to the left an empty living room. Ricky heard voices upstairs and stepped in over the threshold to the entryway which lay before a wide staircase. He peered up the stairs and saw a man with light brown hair holding on tightly to the shoulders of a well-dressed blonde woman in front of him who looked a lot like Shelby. She stood with one arm crossed over her waist, the other propped on it with a hand held up to her mouth, tears in her eyes. The man and woman stood in the doorway to a room at the top of the steps and stared in worry. Ricky didn't like the look of this and his legs willed him boldly, but slowly up the stairs towards these two strangers.

"Mister and Misses Dannovan?" Ricky said hesitantly as he ascended the steps closer to them.

The man turned his head, but the woman was obviously too distracted to have registered the intrusion. The man's dazed eyes just stared at him in question.

"Mr. Dannovan? I...I'm Ricky. A friend of Shelby's." Ricky said slowly as he came up to the step below them. "Is... is everything all right?"

The woman noticed him now, but her reaction was the same as her husband's had been — unable to speak, staring with an open mouth. "I'm Shelby's friend from the bookshop, Ricky. Is..."

"Oh, Ricky," the woman gasped. She leaned down to grab his hand and then guided him to the other side of her husband. Ricky tried to glance into the room at what the Dannovan's were so clearly fixated on, but he couldn't see with them blocking his view. "You can't go in there now... they're, well..."

"What's wrong? Is Shelby okay?" Ricky heard the worry in his own voice now. What the hell's going on?

"Son, Shelby's... She won't," Mr. Dannovan grasped Ricky's shoulder but he choked up before his words could come out.

Mrs. Dannovan now stood behind Ricky with her hands on his shoulders, just as her husband had done to her a moment ago. Ricky felt the pressure from her hands as she clutched onto him tightly in the comfort one wouldn't normally give to a stranger. "Ricky, I tried to wake her up, but... but she just wouldn't...wake up. I didn't know she was still up in her room until your aunt called and then I went up to check on her and...well, I thought she was sleeping," Mrs. Dannovan said in clipped breaths. Ricky tried peering into the room to see what was going on as Mrs. Dannovan spoke, but all he could see was an empty bed and heard muffled voices inside the room that had garnered so much attention.

A paramedic came to the door and pulled it open the rest of the way. He gave a brief glance at Ricky and then at Shelby's parents. "Folks, if you could just back up now, we're bringing her out."

Ricky felt Mrs. Dannovan urge him backwards. What? What do they mean "bringing her out"? Bringing her out dead or alive? Ricky needed to know the answer immediately! "What? Is she dead?" Ricky didn't mean to blurt the words out so forcefully, but he felt like he was going to swallow his own heart. He felt Mrs. Dannovan's arms come around his shoulders and she began to weep. Now Mr. Dannovan grasped his shoulder with one hand.

"No. No," he said softly and broken, "they think she's in a coma, but we don't know why."

Ricky heard a creak and the paramedic at the door turned his back on them and began to step backwards towards them slowly. Ricky saw the shiny metal and white sheets of the stretcher mattress approach them. The first paramedic turned on the landing, swinging the stretcher towards the stairs.

"Oh! My baby!" Mrs. Dannovan gasped and went around Ricky to stand as near to the stretcher as she could.

Ricky stared dumbly as he saw Shelby's pale face, eyes closed, head lying back on the pillow. There was an oxygen mask covering her mouth over her ruby lips. She looked lifeless. This girl that he knew to be incredibly full of life, now looked like a wax figure, peaceful and pale.

The paramedics slowly lowered the stretcher down the staircase as Mrs. Dannovan sidestepped along side of it with one hand on top of her daughter's. Mr. Dannovan waited for the last paramedic to go down a few stairs until he started to follow. He stopped and turned back to Ricky who still stood staring, dumbfounded.

"Uh…" Mr. Dannovan hesitated for words looking at Ricky.

"Ricky," Ricky muttered his own name pathetically.

"Ricky. I'm sorry. We have to go to the hospital now. We'll…we'll call you and…your aunt when we know some thing," his words came out in a hoarse voice.

Ricky nodded curtly. "I'll…I'll lock up for you," he offered.

"Thank you," Mr. Dannovan managed a pained smiled and then hurried down the steps after the paramedics.

The lights from the ambulance rotated their reflection into the house and the scene before Ricky felt like it played out in slow motion. Finally, the stretcher with Shelby on it was shoved out the door and whisked down the sidewalk, her parents in tow. He continued to stare at the open door for a moment as the red and blue lights still flashed onto the polished wood floor below, stunned by what had just occurred.

Ricky felt ill. He'd never seen anyone lifeless before, nor had he ever imagined seeing anyone so young and vibrant look so helpless. Deep down inside of him, he had a guilty feeling that this was somehow his fault. His aunt's words crept back to him then. What had she meant by it being *too late*? And why had she hoped that Shelby wouldn't be sleeping? The irony of her peculiar behavior confounded him. He'd been so shocked by her behavior, yet it now seemed like she had known something terrible was bound to happen.

Ricky glanced back at Shelby's room. He walked inside slowly, thinking he might find a clue as to why Shelby had been forced into such a sudden vegetative-looking state. There was no indication that anything violent had happened in the room. Everything had the resemblance of a typical teenage girl's bedroom.

There was a thick white comforter pulled back on the bed and ruffled throw pillows. A lamp with flowers sat on the nightstand next to the bed along with some of the beaded necklaces and bracelets Shelby often wore. Ricky walked over to it and saw an open pack of the gum she was always chewing. He wanted to both smile and cry at the sight of it. His foot hit something hard as he stepped closer to the nightstand and he almost jumped, feeling eerie that he was the only one left in a house where a tragedy had just occurred.

Ricky looked down and saw *The Lands of Farwin Wood* lying on the floor half under the bed. That stupid book, he thought, and reached down to pick it up. He wondered if she'd even had a chance to read it, and now felt like he was stealing from a dead person. God, don't say that, he told himself. Suddenly, Ricky wanted to be as far away from Shelby's room as possible.

Ricky hurried down the stairs and stopped by the door. He looked around not sure what to do. He went into the living room and turned the television off, and then came back into the foyer. He found the light switch for that room on the wall and turned it off as well, then locked the front door. As he grabbed the knob to pull it shut on his way out, he glanced back up the stairs and shuddered. "You'd better be all right," he whispered into the air and shut the door.

Shelby was the only friend Ricky had made that summer, Ricky thought as he hurried back to Blinney Lane with the thick book under his arm. Why was life so cruel? Why had he been forced to come here? Why was the only thing good that had happened since his arrival being ripped away? It wasn't fair. Someone like him deserved to end up in a coma, maybe, but not someone like Shelby. What did she do to deserve something like that? The poor girl barely had a life! All she did was read books all day or try to help his aunt! Ricky felt sick to his stomach and his eyes were burning. Damn it, he wasn't going to cry!

Ricky reached Blinney Lane without even thinking about how he'd arrived back there, lost in his thoughts. He sighed as he saw the ivy covered archway to Blinney Lane and started down the cobblestone street. Aunt Sarah better not give me any more grief about this stupid book after this, he thought. He wasn't in the mood to hear it right now, no matter what he'd done wrong.

As Ricky walked up the steps to Allister's he saw his aunt sitting at the counter, peering out the window like a hawk. She jumped up out of her seat as she saw him opening the door and came around the counter. The sight of her eagerness made him angry. All she cared about was her stupid books.

"Oh, thank goodness," she sighed and took the book from him. She turned it over to inspect it and flipped through the pages. Then she turned her back on him and started walking towards the stairs.

"Aunt Sarah," Ricky called, upset she hadn't asked about Shelby, even though he knew deep down she couldn't have known anything was wrong.

"What?" She stopped and turned back to look at him.

Ricky tried to speak, but a lump in his throat prevented his words from coming out. He shoved his hands in his pockets and looked away, blinking to ease the burning in his eyes.

"Something's wrong, isn't it?" She stated flatly.

Ricky looked back at her with his mouth agape. "Yeah," the word came out as a croak.

Sarah looked intently at Ricky, "It's Shelby...what's happened?"

"She…" Ricky didn't understand how she seemed to know something was wrong with Shelby, "she's in a coma. I got there and an ambulance was out front. They took her out of her room and wheeled her out," Ricky stopped to swallow. Sarah watched him, every muscle in her face alert. "Her parents thought she was sleeping. I mean…who knows how long she lay there like that!" Ricky was becoming upset the more he had to think about Shelby.

"Oh no," Sarah muttered and put her free hand to her stomach. Her eyes dropped to the floor, affixed on nothing in particular. "I was worried this would happen."

"What are you talking about? Why do you keep saying stuff like that?"

"Ricky," Sarah looked up at her already distraught nephew and wondered if what she needed to tell him would send him over the edge. "There's something I need to tell you."

"What?"

Sarah moved around Ricky to lock the door. Then she pulled the window blinds down.

"You know why this happened to her, don't you?" Ricky felt fear, like he was about to discover something devious. He didn't want to, but his aunt was acting so peculiar it made him feel like he was watching a murderer covering her tracks. Sarah said nothing and just glanced at him, then she walked over to the other window and pulled its blind down. "What the hell's going on? What did you do?"

Once Sarah had locked up the shop to ensure they wouldn't be disturbed, she walked over to the couch with the book still in her hands and sat down. Sarah sighed and motioned for Ricky to join her. He walked hesitantly with each step, watching her like prey watches a predator. "Would you please say something!" Ricky demanded once he was near enough to Shelby's chair that it gave him a chill.

"It's the book, Ricky," Sarah held it in both hands and stared up at him.

"What about the book?"

"The book. *This* book…is the reason why Shelby appears to be in a coma," Sarah said slowly as she studied her nephew's face.

"What?" Ricky's face contorted in confusion and he flopped down in Shelby's chair, dumbfounded by his aunt. "What are you talking about? What? Like because I did something bad, something bad happened?"

"Sort of…but it's more complicated than that," Sarah truly didn't know how to have this conversation. She'd never had to explain the curse to anyone before.

Ricky shook his head and held his hands up, "Look, Aunt Sarah, if you have weird superstitions about karma or whatever, I'm not going to argue with you, but it's not going to make me feel any better and it's certainly not going to help Shelby. And if you're trying to make me feel bad about what I did, congratulations! I already do, so I don't need another guilt trip. But I absolutely don't think that me loaning her a book put her in a coma for crying out loud."

"It's not that you loaned her the book, it's that she had the book in her possession. It's…the book. It's…cursed. That's why I didn't want you to ever touch it." Sarah knew she sounded like a lunatic, but she had to tell him.

Ricky snorted a laugh, "Uh…yeah, sure. The book is cursed. Does that make you feel better now?" Ricky chewed on his lower lip and raised an eyebrow. He couldn't hold back his sarcasm any longer, "You think because you believe this…curse, that it somehow puts me at fault or…no, ahhhh, I get it now! You feel guilty that you didn't do a better job of keeping the book away from me! Is that it?" Ricky felt proud of himself.

Sarah sighed and dropped her head in her hands. Why did she have to have such a smart-ass for a nephew? She was going to have to ask the others for help with this. There was no other way to go about it. He wasn't going to believe her.

Ricky laughed now for the first time since he'd gotten back to the store. He got up and patted his aunt on the shoulder. "Aunt Sarah, it's okay," he said with true sincerity. "Look, you believe what you want. I promise I won't tease you about it."

"Ricky?"

Ricky chuckled once more, "What?"

"Do you believe in magic? No wise cracks, just give me a yes or no answer."

Ricky sighed, "Uh…that'd be a no for me."

"What if I can prove to you that you're wrong?"

Ricky arched his brow again and stuffed his hands back into his pockets. He was about to smirk again, but now he was starting to think his aunt was a level of freak he'd never met before. He sighed instead, "And how would you plan to do that?"

Sarah stood up, and without any emotion on her face looked Ricky in the eyes and said, "By taking you to Farwin Wood with me to rescue your little girlfriend." Sarah walked over to the counter and picked up the phone.

Ricky looked around the shop, realizing it was closed. The door was locked. He was now locked inside with his…with his crazy aunt? Did his dad know she was this weird? Dad! Maybe Dad can talk some sense into her, Ricky thought. "Aunt Sarah, maybe we should call my Dad, you know? I mean, you look like you could use someone to talk to right now."

"Ha! Ha ha, that's a good one. Your father would kill you if he knew what you'd just done," Sarah laughed over her shoulder as she dialed a number.

"Pfft," Ricky scoffed, "it's not like it was a car."

"No, it's so much worse than that," Sarah stared at him with a serious expression. Into the phone she said, "Yes, Franci? Yeah. I hate to do this to you, but I need to call an emergency council meeting. Ricky loaned one of the weeping books to Shelby, that girl that's always in my shop. Yeah... well now she's been taken into the book. I know. Can you have the others meet me over here in about an hour? Okay, thanks." Sarah set the phone down and then started towards the back of the store. "Come with me," she barked over her shoulder to Ricky who stood flabbergasted from the phone conversation he'd just heard.

CHAPTER
SIXTEEN

RICKY FOLLOWED after Sarah and caught up with her as she opened the door to the basement, back by the shelf where he'd taken the infamous book. She flipped on the light and started down the stairs. "Come on," she called dryly.

Ricky wanted to protest but thought better of it from the tone of her voice. She was acting nuts, for sure, but if he could at least avoid getting yelled at maybe she'd snap out of it and come back to "Normal Land."

They walked past some large tables in the basement where Sarah kept book binding materials and tools. Ricky looked around the musty basement, but his aunt moved so quickly he didn't have much time to dawdle. He swerved around some old furniture and wooden barrels and saw Sarah open a wooden plank door to a small closet. She flipped another light on once the door was open and Ricky could see old clothes hanging up.

Sarah flipped through the clothes, pushing things to the side and inspecting them. Then she'd shove another outfit out of the way and look at something else. She held up a pair of grey wool leotard pants and shoved them at Ricky. "Here."

Ricky grabbed the hanger of the pants without wanting to and lifted it to inspect the strange article. What the hell are we doing down here, he wondered.

Sarah held out another hanger. This one had a long brown leather vest and belt on it. She held it up to Ricky's chest and he tried to back away from the musty smell of it.

"Hold still, will you?" Sarah scoffed and eyed him up and down. "That'll have to work. Here. Take it," she shoved it's hanger into his chest. Ricky dumbly grasped onto the unusual smock and tights as Sarah went back to digging through the closet.

"Um...are we going to a Medieval festival or something?" Ricky watched Sarah hold a long dress with wispy bell sleeves up to herself.

"I doubt they'll be having any festivals where we're going," she muttered and shoved the dress at Ricky.

"Wherever the heck you're planning on taking me, I'm not wearing a dress...or these tights for that matter," Ricky held up the pants she'd given him.

"The dress is for me since you've dragged me into this. The tights...are considered pants in Farwin Wood and your father never complained about wearing them," Sarah's muffled voice came out of the closet where her head was buried, shifting through the outfits it contained.

"Farwin Wood. Yeah...right. And I can't ever see my Dad wearing tights," Ricky muttered. He sighed hoping he'd soon figure out what his aunt had planned.

"Ricky, just don't talk, okay? Don't say anything funny, anything sarcastic. Just...just stand there and do what I say, and remember anything you possibly can of what I told you about Farwin Wood when you were little. Can you do that?" Sarah finally looked back at him, her gaze intense.

"Yeah...sure." Sure...and call you a doctor as soon as I get out of here! Ricky was getting agitated serving as a human clothes rack. He decided if she was going to continue being crazy, he could at least humor her to pass the time. "So... what's this council meeting for?"

Sarah tossed a long puffy-sleeved cream colored shirt at Ricky. It hit him in the face and he sputtered. "Your pile, I presume?" He held it up like a dead rat.

"No. Yours," she called, head and arms still in the closet.

"Of course," he muttered.

"Ricky? What did I say?"

"Okay! Fine!" Ricky tossed the ancient looking shirt over his left shoulder with the tights. "So, what's the council meeting for?"

"Blinney Lane has a council. I'm one of the members. We meet once a month to report any strange activity that occurs on Blinney Lane."

"Strange activity?" Like *this*, he wanted to add.

"A woman who the original settlers of Blinney Lane believed to be a witch was executed for witchcraft at the end of the street over three hundred years ago. Ever since then, all of the shops on Blinney Lane have been cursed. Strange things still happen here all the time. Usually we know what they are, but sometimes things happen that we've never witnessed before, so we have meetings to document the activity." Sarah chucked a leather sword holster over her shoulder at Ricky. He caught it in his hand and held it up to the light.

"Yeah! Now we're talking," Ricky beamed.

"You'd better *pray* we don't need that," Sarah grumbled. She hunkered down to the floor then and dug in the closet underneath the hanging items. "What size shoes do you wear?"

"Ten," Ricky said without stopping to think about how weird this activity was anymore. He was so lost in determining what his aunt was up to that he didn't care what they were doing as long as she wasn't griping at him. He was definitely calling his dad as soon as he got a chance. Ricky held up the leather sword holster to his waist and wondered if it would fit him. *Is this for me or her, I wonder?* "So… these meetings. Well, you called this an emergency meeting. What's the emergency?"

"I'm glad you finally asked," Sarah started to shove her foot into a light brown calf-high leather boot. "Shelby's the emergency," she huffed out a breath once the boot was on and looked up at Ricky. "There are a few books in my shop that are very susceptible to the curse. If you fall asleep in close proximity to one of these books while they're open, well…you wake up inside the book." Sarah started to pull the boot off.

"*Inside* the book?"

"Well, not *inside it*, inside it. You go to the land that's in the book. And Shelby, being the book lover that she is, probably was reading the book and fell asleep. When you fall asleep and wake up in one of the books, your body stays where you fell asleep, but you just look like you're sleeping. You can't wake up though. Nothing will wake you up on the outside — on Blinney Lane. You have to wake up from *inside* the book."

"Uh…what?" Ricky didn't know what to ask. He had comments, but didn't want to say them. Ricky didn't know what to think, say, or feel.

Sarah tossed the boot and its partner over on the floor by Ricky. She sat cross-legged and looked back up at him with a gentle smile. "Ricky, I don't expect you to believe me. I know it sounds insane or like some silly story. You probably think I'm losing my mind, but you're just going to have to trust me. We need to get some things first, but then…as much as I don't want to," Sarah grimaced, "you and I are going *into* the book; into *The Lands of Farwin Wood* to rescue Shelby and bring her back out."

Ricky blinked at her with his mouth still agape. "And... and how do we go into this book exactly?"

"I told you already. We need to fall asleep with the book open next to us," Sarah couldn't stand the shocked expressions on his face and turned back to the closet to find some of Richard's old boots for him.

"Yeah. Okay...soooo, then what happens to us? Our minds like dream we're in the story? What if we wake up thinking we're still in the story or...I mean, what if I act different when I wake up like..." Ricky couldn't finish his sentence or take it back.

"Like me?" Sarah shot him a look.

"I didn't mean anything like that, I just... Look, Aunt Sarah, seriously, I really think we should call my Dad. I don't care if he knows I took one of your books. I think you should talk to him," Ricky couldn't keep humoring her. He was really afraid for her now. She truly appeared to believe all the things she was telling him.

"Ricky, your Dad knows all about the curse, and all about the books. He used to love going to Farwin Wood when we were kids. Those are the clothes he used to wear there when we were teenagers," Sarah gestured at the outfit Ricky had slung over his shoulder. She turned back to the closet and pulled out another pair of boots. These were a little taller and bigger than the last pair. "Here, try these on."

Ricky, covered in clothing slung over each shoulder looked down at the boots she'd thrown at his feet. "Seriously, my Dad would never wear this shit. Is this like role playing? Are you one of those role players, like Dungeons and Dragons sort of stuff?"

"Ricky, I'm going to slap the shit out you, I swear," Sarah grabbed her hair in tight fists and exhaled a long breath.

Just then the floor above them creaked. Ricky jumped and dropped the dress that was slung on his shoulder. "I thought you locked the shop! What's that?" He gasped looking at the ceiling above him.

"It's probably Franci and the others. She has a key. Come on. Pick this stuff up and help me upstairs with it," Sarah gathered up the boots and shut the closet. She had to physically turn Ricky around and point him in the direction of the stairs.

"Helloooo!" Sarah heard Franci's voice coo from the stairwell.

"We'll be right up!" Sarah started through the basement.

"Are they coming with us?"

"To where?" Sarah was happy Ricky couldn't see her smirk.

"To...to Farwin Wood?"

"Heavens, no," this time she was perfectly serious. "I'm not wasting a perfectly good stroomphblutel on Reggie Nurscher."

As Ricky emerged from the cellar door with his theatrical wardrobe hanging over both shoulders, he saw some of the local shop owners milling around the lower level of the shop. He followed Sarah as she carted the rigid boots with her down to where the other shop owners waited for them with anxious eyes. As Sarah descended the steps to the lower level, Ricky noticed all the stares coming from the shop owners in his direction seemed contemptuous.

"Thank you for coming on such short notice. Could you just take a seat over there and I'll be with you in a minute," Sarah waved them over to the couch and chairs by the drawn windows. "You too, Ricky."

Ricky felt awkward given the company. Present were: Mary Millville, Regis "Reggie" Nurscher, Franci Doltman, and Walter Freedhof. So this is the council, he thought. Ricky set the stinky clothes down over a book rack and then began to slowly pace back and forth between them and where his aunt was at the counter talking to someone on the phone.

"Yes. Like the one you made for Richard the last time we went in, but maybe with some blood grooves and a compartment in the handle for protection aides. Okay, thank you. We'll be here," Sarah hung up the phone and walked over to where Ricky stood.

Reggie Nurscher looked around for a place to ash his cigarette. Franci fidgeted nervously, but each time she looked at Ricky she forced a polite smile. Mary Millville sat with her back rigid, hands folded in her lap, head held high with vacant serious eyes cast in the Allisters' direction. Walter Freedhof sat with his hands folded over his large stomach staring down at his feet, if he could see them, and would occasionally shake his head and sigh.

"All right, let's get started," Sarah exhaled and placed a hand on Ricky's shoulder. "I believe by now you all know my nephew, Ricky." Mr. Freedhof grunted softly. If Sarah heard him, she pretended otherwise. "And in case Franci left out any details, I'll explain the situation."

Ricky could feel himself sweating as the adults sat, looking so serious in their ridiculous clothing, yet he wondered would they think his aunt was the ridiculous one once she started talking about Farwin Wood and curses?

"So as you know, Ricky was completely ignorant of the curse of Blinney Lane when he came here. He took one of the weeping books, *The Lands of Farwin Wood*, without my knowledge and loaned it to a friend of his and mine, Shelby Dannovan, a sixteen-year-old whom I'm sure you've seen around here from time to time. When I found out the book was gone, I had Ricky go over to her house immediately to retrieve it. When Ricky arrived, Shelby was being taken away in an ambulance because her parents had said she'd slipped into a coma."

Mary gasped and shook her head. Franci rang her hands. Mr. Freedhof still stared at the floor shaking his head. Reggie stared at Ricky and looked to be cleaning his teeth with his tongue behind closed lips.

Sarah continued on, "I think she's been gone most of the day and maybe as long as last night. Ricky was able to get the book and bring it back, so I'll go to Farwin Wood with Ricky, find her and bring her back."

Yep, here we go. She's giving them the full nutso version, Ricky thought. He shifted his eyes to the ground and started to chew on his thumb nail. He couldn't bear to make eye contact with these people now that they would know how insane his aunt was.

"Sarah, are you sure that's a good idea taking Ricky in with you?" Mr. Freedhof finally looked up.

"I have no choice. I don't want to leave him here for the bookshop to feed off of him. I think we can all agree that within the last few days strange things have been happening, and it's most likely due to more villager descendant blood being in town. If I leave him with one of you, then that could just cause more trouble at your own shops," Sarah sounded concerned.

"He ain't going anywhere near my shop," Reggie harped.

"Regis, who asked you?" Mary quipped.

"I'm just saying, Mary. You want him in your place? Let him go with her. At least the blood won't stew things up in the book," Reggie gestured with his free hand.

"Yes, but Sarah..." Franci started.

"What is it, Franci?" Sarah urged her on.

"Well, forgive me, Ricky," Franci smiled nervously. For-give what, Ricky wondered. You're *all* insane apparently! "I don't know what you've told the boy...about his father and... well, you know, the last time you were in Farwin Wood."

Ricky looked from Franci to his Aunt Sarah. Sarah paled and stared down in thought. She dropped her hand from his shoulder and toyed with the bracelet on her wrist. What about my father? And why is everyone so convinced this is some kind of magical book?

"No, Franci. It's all right. You make a very good point," Sarah finally muttered softly.

"Yes, an excellent point, I'd say. What about the last time…and the trouble there?" Mary piped in.

"What trouble?" Ricky heard his own voice now.

"Oh, now you want to believe me?" Sarah was happy for the distraction and put her hands on her hips.

"No, I don't believe any of this nonsense. I don't know what in the hell any of you are talking about!" Ricky threw his hands in the air.

"Has the boy been marked, Sarah?" Walter asked.

"I…I don't know. I don't think so," Sarah stared at Ricky with worry.

"Marked? What do you mean marked?"

Mary stood from her place on the couch and took a few steps towards Ricky. "Ricky. I know this all must seem very strange, but do you want to help your friend?"

"Of course, but I don't see how," Ricky started.

Mary held up a commanding hand. "That's all we need to know. You have a chance to help her if you go with your aunt. And while I don't think it's a good idea for *anyone* to go to Farwin Wood after what occurred there last time," Mary glanced at Sarah, "I still don't like the idea of your aunt going there alone." She placed her hands on the boy's shoulders. "Ricky, we're counting on you to help your aunt and save your friend. We're all here to help you, but you have to trust us. You don't have to try and understand it, but you do need to believe it. This curse…it's very real, Ricky. If you don't *believe*, you'll become so overwhelmed with all of it, that you won't be much help to Sarah in there. Can you do that for us?"

"I…I don't know. I'm sorry, but I don't see how anything is cursed. All I know is I took something I wasn't supposed to and it was wrong, okay. And my friend is in a coma…for some reason," Ricky held his hands out pleading.

"Show him," Walter spoke plainly, almost in defeat, from his place on the couch. "Here, I'll go first." Walter began to pull his pant legs up and stretched his legs out. Reggie started laughing a wheezy, smoked-filled laugh at the sight. "Oh, shut your trap Reggie! It's not my fault I have big ankles."

"Yeah, kid. The curse gives you cankles! You see that?" Reggie laughed some more.

Sarah sighed and slapped a hand to her head. Mr. Freedhof had scars around his ankles similar to the ones that she had on her wrists, but they were not visible due to the girth of his massive calves oozing down over his puffy ankles and fat feet.

"Ricky," Sarah spoke gently at his side. "When Agatha Blinney," she started.

"Don't say that name!" Reggie barked and pointed his cigarette at her, eyes wide.

"Once isn't going to do anymore harm," Mary snapped at him and then turned back to Ricky. "Saying the woman's name whom our ancestors murdered seems to...encourage the power of the curse, so we avoid it at all costs."

Sarah continued to her wide-eyed open-mouthed nephew. "Ricky...when they dragged her from her home, they tied rope around her neck, wrists, and ankles. They threw stones at her and they flogged her. Anywhere she had marks from this...torture, people who are relatives of those villagers end up with similar marks on their bodies for no explainable reason. It usually happens when they turn seventeen. She usually only takes one family member from each household to claim. That person, after their scars form, can't ever leave Blinney Lane. They can go out about a three block radius from here at best, but then it becomes too painful. Their scars hurt as though they are experiencing the pain she felt the day she was killed. Do you remember the day I had to find you on the street?"

Ricky just nodded. Sarah rolled up her sleeve and then started to take off her bracelet. "Ooh, Sarah!" Mary gasped at the sight of the rawness of her scars and the blisters on them. Ricky looked down in horror at his aunt's wrist and then the other once she'd taken off her bracelet. What in the world?

"I couldn't go after you Ricky. I was in so much pain from these marks flaring up like I was having rope burn, just like Agatha did when she was dragged down the street. I got these when I was seventeen. Your father never got any marks. The curse only chose me. That's why he got to leave and go to New York, and that's why I stayed to run the book-shop," Sarah's voice was almost sympathetic as she watched for Ricky's reaction.

Ricky had no words. He just looked from Sarah's wrists to her intent expression and then to the others who looked on somberly. He shifted his gaze when he saw Franci stand up from her chair and move towards him.

"Ricky," she spoke while reaching behind her neck to unfasten her collar, "I too got my marks when I was seven-teen. You think I wear these high-necked dresses because I like them?" She smiled kindly and lowered the front of her dress just enough to see the dark purplish red marks that twisted all the way around her pale, slender neck.

"Yeah, but I mean those could have been accidents or...I mean some people...do that stuff...to themselves," Ricky didn't know how to phrase it without offending them.

Reggie burst out of his chair, eyes wild, and came right up to Ricky as he ferociously tugged his undershirt out from his pants. "You think I wanted to do this to myself?" Reggie hoisted his shirt up to reveal long burgundy colored scars across his chest. The lines went every which way, all curving slightly at the ends in a wide arch like those made by a whip.

Ricky instinctively brought a hand up to his shoulder. He wanted to reach his fingers over his shoulder and inspect the strange welts he'd gotten on his back over the last week.

Mary's eyes caught the motion and she locked eyes with him. Ricky quickly looked away. "You have them now too, don't you?" Mary whispered sympathetically.

"No! No, I just have a scrape or rash or something," Rick panicked.

"Ricky, let me see," Sarah tried to reach for the back of his shirt, but he brushed her hand away. "Why didn't you tell me? Didn't you use that stuff I gave you?"

"It stinks! I dumped it out," he whined and wrapped his arms tightly around his chest.

Frustrated, Mary looked at Sarah and then turned to Franci. "Francis, help me would you?" Mary turned her back to Franci and brought her hands up to the back of her own gown collar.

Franci fastened the neck of her own dress back up and came over to help Mary. She started to unbutton the back of Mary's dress from the top.

"Oh, come on! I don't want to see this either," Reggie grumbled as he walked back to the chair stuffing his shirt back into his pants.

"Yeah, seriously. What…are you all going to get naked until I believe you?" Ricky fidgeted.

"Ricky, I don't know how else to explain it to you. We're not making this up. The sooner you believe us, the more of a chance we have at saving Shelby. Things have probably changed in the book since the last time I was there. I really could use your help," she pleaded.

Mary held the front of her loosened dress to her as she looked at Ricky. "Ricky, I'm guessing whatever has happened to your back," she turned around slowly, "looks a lot like this."

Ricky gasped and stepped backwards, fumbling into his aunt as he stared at the long reddish welts across Mary Millville's back. She had the same number of lines that had appeared across his shoulder blades, in the same pattern. He felt his aunt's hand against his back where the marks were. Ricky pulled away.

"I can feel them, Ricky. I know you have them too now," she looked like she would cry. "I'm sorry. I never wanted this to happen to you. That's why I was so upset your father sent you here. He was convinced it wouldn't happen to you. He thinks women are more susceptible to the curse." There was nothing joking in her tone of voice.

A knock came at the door and Mary quickly gestured for Franci to help button her dress. Sarah walked over and peeked behind the blind on the door. It was Alexander Rainsford, who owned the blacksmith shop down the street. Sarah opened the door for him then locked it again once he was inside.

Alexander filled the crowded storefront even more with his six-foot-six stature. His wide shoulders were rounded with large muscles from years of pounding out metal over the anvil in his shop. He wore a dirty, sweaty, white tank top underneath his leather apron and there was a shimmer of sweat on his sinewy arms. His thin brown hair appeared damp with sweat and looked like it had been brushed back with his fingers to keep it out of his green eyes. At thirty-five, this brute of a man put Ricky's own father to shame and possibly even Henry. "Here it is. I hope this works for you," Alexander held out a long object wrapped in a piece of burlap.

Sarah pulled the cloth back and revealed a narrow sword about arm's length within the fabric. It had a thick grip that was bound tightly by leather chord. Sarah inspected it. "Thanks, Alex. Where's the capsule?"

"It's here," Alexander pulled the base of the hilt with a tug and it came out, leaving an opening where the grip was bound by the leather.

Franci and Mary moved back to their chairs and each grabbed their purses. They both returned to Sarah and Alexander with them in their hands. Mary pulled out a small glass bottle filled with two small white clay looking rocks. She handed them to Sarah who tucked them down inside of the grip.

"This will help to keep you safe," Franci smiled at Ricky reassuringly, and handed Sarah a small cellophane packet with a black grainy powder in it. Ricky watched as Alexander held the sword and Sarah funneled the substance into the hollowed hilt. Alexander then shoved the hilt base back in its place and then handed the sword to Ricky.

"Here you go, son," he smiled proudly, "one of the best I've made on such short notice."

Ricky looked down at the sword Alexander held out to him. He noticed Alexander wore two wide leather cuffs around his wrists, much like blacksmith's did in the old days. Ricky had previously thought the man wore them at an attempt to look the part of a village blacksmith, but now he wasn't so sure. Ricky hesitantly wrapped his hand around the sword hilt and looked up at Alexander. "Can I...can I see your wrists?"

Alexander's brow went up. He looked at Sarah and then the others. Mary glanced at Ricky and then nodded to Alexander. The man unfastened one cuff and Ricky could see the wiry jagged scars that encircled the man's thick wrists. The skin there was pale compared to the rest of his bronzed arm, except for the color of the brownish-purple scars. Alexander started to unfasten the cuff on his other hand, but Ricky held a hand up to stop him. "It's all right."

As much as Ricky wanted this to be a joke, he worried that something horrible had happened to these people, something that may actually give their stories merit. Now that he thought about it, what worried him the most was that he'd never seen any of these shop owners leave Blinney Lane while he'd been there. "Are you saying...that I can't leave Blinney Lane now that," Ricky sighed and set the sword down. He tugged at the top of his shirt to hike it up over his back, "now that I have these?"

Ricky heard someone gasp from behind him, likely Franci. He felt the cold fingers of his aunt as she lightly touched them to the marks across his back.

"They're still new, Ricky. Still forming. If we get you out of here, you might be safe," Sarah called from behind him.

"Might be?" Ricky pulled his shirt back down and turned to her with wild eyes.

"If you go into the book with me, you'll be safe from the curse claiming you, in case..."

"In case what?"

"In case something that happens while we're inside the book strengthens the curse," Sarah pursed her lips.

"Well, what would happen inside of it? Are we going to get hurt doing this...this...whatever it is?"

"Ricky, Farwin Wood is probably not the same as the last time I was there with Richard. Your father got into some trouble there, and because of it...we've never gone back. I don't know how the people there will react to seeing me," Sarah swallowed.

"Well, screw that. If you're afraid to go, what makes you think I want to go with you, if this even is possible?" Ricky flapped his arms up once in his excitement.

"Because if you don't go, kid," Reggie sneered, "your little girlfriend will never wake up."

Ricky stared at Reggie with his mouth open, and then he wheeled around to look at his aunt. She had her hand up to her mouth and her eyebrows were canted down in worry.

"Is that true?"

"Yes, I'm afraid so," Sarah let out.

"Well...what about us? Who will wake us up?" Ricky raised his voice.

"I will. I know how to...from inside the book?"

"How?" Ricky demanded, but she said nothing. "How?"

Sarah sighed, "I'll tell you when we get there. Come on," she called looking up to Franci and then Mary. They nodded and helped her pick up the clothing that Ricky had discarded. Sarah started towards the stairs that led up to her flat.

"Ricky, bring the book," Sarah called to him. Ricky gaped after her wanting to know what it was she wasn't telling him. He grumbled and fetched the book. As he walked past Alexander, the man grasped one of his strong hands around Ricky's arms.

"Don't forget this," Alexander looked at him knowingly and handed him the sword again.

"I hope you're all just crazy," Ricky muttered as he took the sword from Alexander and followed his aunt and the women upstairs. From behind him he heard Alexander's deep laughter.

CHAPTER
SEVENTEEN

UPSTAIRS IN Sarah's apartment, Ricky found Mary cleaning off the kitchen table. The pants and shirts his aunt had thrown at him were hanging over one of the chairs, the high-legged boots sat together on the floor.

Franci stood at the stove where she'd started a pot of water to boil. She turned to shuffle through her purse and pulled out another cellophane packet. This one contained dried leaves in a light-green, grainy powder.

Ricky heard his aunt walk through the living room and turned to see her clad in the floor-length, light grey dress she'd recovered from the basement closet. The dress had a wide dark grey belt with shimmery stitching across it and was firmly cinched across his aunt's slender waist with the long ends hanging down to one side. Tucked underneath the belt against her stomach was a slim needle sword, much smaller than the one Alexander had given him, but equally as threatening. Around Sarah's wrist, Ricky could see that she'd reattached her brace-let with the silver key on it. As Sarah walked into the kitchen,

Ricky could see the toes of the light brown boots she'd tried on poke out from under the gown's hem.

"Ricky, you need to go change now," Sarah took the book from him and glanced at the clothing slung over the chair.

"Change?" Ricky looked down at the clothes.

Sarah let out an exasperated sigh as she took the sword from Ricky and laid it on the table. She picked the clothes up and forced them at Ricky's chest, "Do you want to help Shelby?"

Ricky sighed, "Yes, but I still don't understand how this…" Ricky looked back over his shoulder and saw Franci stirring something in the pot on the stove. She smiled at him, "Run along now, you'll see soon enough." Ricky shook his head and grasped onto the bundle of clothing. He started for his room wondering what would come next.

As Ricky changed in his room he thought about how grateful he was that none of his friends could see him right now. The long puff-sleeved shirt hung down to his knees over the scratchy man-tights and he sighed as he looked in the mirror on the wall.

"I look like Meatloaf," he muttered thinking of the elaborate shirts the rock singer used to wear. Ricky gathered the shirt up and tucked it into the tight pants. He let enough hang out not only to cover the bulge the formfitting pants created around his groin, but also over his butt where the fabric clung equally close against his cheeks. "This is so gay," he moaned.

Ricky picked the leather vest up off the bed and put it on, happy to see that it covered his tightly clad butt. The vest had leather laces on the front flap and he tied them together then looked around. He spied the wide sword holster belt and hoped he would look less ridiculous by donning that last item. He threw it around his waist and caught the end, which he fastened and tightened around the leather vest. The empty rectangle flap hung down against his leg and tapped the top of the knee high boots his aunt had given him. Ricky sighed at his appearance and grudgingly walked out of his room. As he approached the kitchen, Ricky felt insecure and held his hands together over his crotch, walking slowly as the leather creaked with each movement.

The women in the kitchen saw him and Mary held a hand to her chest, "Oh, how dear."

Ricky shot her an icy glare and felt his cheeks grow warm. He practically waddled, shuffling his feet as he approached the table. Sarah chuckled and Ricky turned his angry glance in her direction.

"Consider that your punishment for taking the book," she smirked and nodded at his outfit as she brought a steaming cup up to her mouth where she sat. The book sat in the middle of the cleared table and Ricky took the chair where his clothes had hung earlier. The sword flap bent uncomfortably beneath him and he flipped the end of it out to hang towards the ground as he took a seat.

"Ha, ha, funny, funny," Ricky grumbled and shoved the sword into its sheath.

"Here you go," Franci whispered as she set a steaming tea cup down in front of him.

"I…I'm not thirsty, thank you," Ricky curled his lip up at the licorice smell of the dark brew in the cup.

"Well, you have to drink it, dear. It'll help put you to sleep," Franci smiled.

"What? Are you guys going to knock me out now?" Ricky exclaimed and looked wide eyed at his aunt who sat sipping on her own cup of the fowl smelling tea.

"Ricky, it's how we'll get to Farwin Wood…to Shelby. Just trust me. I won't let anything bad happen to you. Now chug it," she added sternly.

Ricky sighed and looked down at the cup. He picked it up and brought it halfway to his mouth with a grimace on his face. He peered up to see Mary and Franci standing next to each other looking down at him with anxiousness in their expressions. "I swear, if you guys are drugging me and do anything weird to me," he looked over at his aunt, "relative or not, I'm going to the police when this is over."

"Bottoms up," Sarah called flatly from across the table. Ricky grumbled and looked down at the cup then brought it to his lips. He swallowed until he couldn't stand anymore.

"Ugh! That...is disgusting," he gasped as he set the empty cup back down to the table and wiped his mouth. "Blech!" Sarah watched him from where she sat as Ricky looked around to see what would happen next. "Well, what about you? Aren't you going to down yours?"

"This is my second cup, Robin Hood," she took another sip.

Mary stepped forward and opened the book where it sat in the middle of the table, then she stepped back and leaned against the counter with Franci.

"I need to go in first so I'm there for you when you arrive," Sarah yawned. She finished her cup and set it back down on the table. "Ricky, just let yourself relax and fall asleep. Everything will be fine." Sarah brought her arms in front of her to rest on the table. She set her chin down against her arms and peered at him over the book.

Ricky still sat erect and alert looking from his aunt to the two onlookers who studied him. "Maybe he needs another cup, Sarah. He is younger than you," Franci said watching Ricky.

"No! No, I'm fine. Really, I'll...I'll just rest my head down," Ricky assured her and took a position similar to his aunt's even though he didn't feel like sleeping.

As Ricky looked across the book at his aunt she spoke about Farwin Wood, things he remembered from the stories she told him as a child. She described the scenery of the land, Oedher Village, and some woman named Netta. "When we get there, just outside of Oedher Village, we'll walk to where,"

Sarah yawned, "where our family has had a house for years, Allister Hall."

"Allister Hall?" Ricky felt himself say lazily. He was starting to feel relaxed, but he didn't know if it was out of the boredom of humoring his aunt. Sarah went on to explain how one of their ancestors had built it. Next she started slowly describing different animals—stroomphblutels, wickrits, roomples, teirumpts, and muckas, until her speech was so slurred and low he could barely understand her anymore.

Ricky felt his head lowering into his arms and he jerked it back up, but the weight of it found him lowering it back to his arms. He stared at his aunt who sounded like she was whistling the quietest snores, her head now buried in her arms. Ricky blinked as his vision blurred when he looked at the book before him. He slowly turned his head, eyes closing, and made out the blurry image of Mary and Franci leaning forward to peer down at him. "What...what did you... do to me?" Ricky let his eyes close again and felt himself drift off to sleep.

There was blackness for a while and the next sensation Ricky felt was a cool breeze against his skin. Eyes still closed, he slowly sensed his weight come back to him. He felt pressed against the earth. Dampness invaded the fabric of his shirt and the back of his pants. Far off and muffled he heard a long shrill noise that sounded like, "tierrrrrumpt!" He felt his shoulder move when something nudged him and he heard a warbled, "Ricky?" He slowly pulled his eyelids apart and saw a hazy darkness with dim light creeping through. "Ricky?" His aunt's voice called to him from somewhere. "Get up. Are you there?"

"Yeah," Ricky heard himself mutter through the taste of licorice in his mouth. He sat up and felt his legs stretched out in front of him on the ground. He blinked and rubbed his eyes as he focused on his feet. Ricky saw the toes of his boots and noticed his feet were resting on dried, muddied grass. He looked up beyond them where the sound of water trickled. Ahead, as his vision cleared, through a dim dawn light he saw trees and a stream. Ricky jumped at the feel of a hand on his shoulder.

"Are you all right?" Sarah whispered sharply.

Ricky turned to look at her and saw they were surrounded by towering trees, many of them dead or charred. A bright yellow bird with a fat body and long beak swooped down past them. Its cry rang out, "Tieerrrrumpt!" Ricky jerked his feet under him and staggered woozily as he stood up. "Ah! What the hell was that?"

"Shhh!" Sarah pressed her hands against his chest. "It's a tierumpt."

"Wha...wha... What? Where are we? Where did you take me?"

Sarah steadied Ricky with her hands on his shoulders and turned him to look directly at her. "Ricky, we're in Farwin Wood."

As Ricky looked around at the eerie woods surrounding him and dying grass below him, he started to feel the sensations of his body. His back was damp like he'd been lying on the ground for a while. He lifted a foot and heard the mud below it suction to his boot. A branch cracked in the darkness beyond the stream and Ricky jumped. "What was that?" he gasped.

Sarah, still holding on to Ricky, was silent as she peered into the woods. A muffled horse-like sputter and then a grunting noise sounded from within in the dark woods ahead of them. Ricky heard his aunt gasp and pull on his arm as she backed away. "Oh no, it's a wickrit," she whispered. "Come on."

Ricky turned toward her as she pulled his arm and started into the woods behind them. He took a confused step and looked behind him towards the sound of more wood breaking. "A what?" Ricky stopped to stare at the movement in the darkness of the trees. Something moved. Something big. The tree branches shifted well above his own height as he squinted through the fading daylight to see what was making the animal sounds.

"Ricky! Let's go!" His aunt's harsh whisper cut through the chilly air, but Ricky remained fixed in his place on the woods floor, waiting to see what emerged.

Another grunt, louder than the first, came through the darkness and Ricky saw a long, hefty, horse-like leg step out from the woods behind the stream and into the dim skylight that peered down through the treetops. Four sharp, curved claws jutted out from the hoof and their pointy ends sank into the ground. A massive horn on a slimy snout shoved past a leafy branch as the creature stepped with gradual force towards the stream. "What...the?" Ricky gasped. The beast's back was at least six feet high with a massive and muscular girth to its dark brown body and leathery skin.

Sarah tiptoed back and grabbed Ricky's arm. She tugged on it. "Ricky, move! Now!" She rasped in his ear. Ricky watched as the animal jerked its enormous head up into the air. Its skull was as wide as on oven, its eyes red, and the cool damp air showed the animal's power as two clouds of steam burst out of its large nostrils with each massive breath it took. It grunted and swung its head from left to right, its crimson eyes scanning the woods.

"Holy shit," Ricky muttered. "It's a..."

The beast snapped its head and eyes forward. The wide red orbs fixed on Ricky. It grunted a snort and its entire body went rigid. Its chest puffed up with air making it appear even larger than before. Its leathery lips parted, revealing a row of jagged yellow teeth with two longer fangs on each side of its jaw. It let out a piercing snarl as it reared up on its hind legs.

"Wickriiiiiit!!" Ricky screamed and finally felt his body shift as he spun around and moved his legs toward his aunt. Her eyes were wide as she held her hand outstretched behind her and motioned for him to follow her. A loud splash sounded behind them from the wickrit's weighty clawed hooves hammering the ground.

"Run, Ricky! Run!" Sarah yelled as she darted through the woods ahead of them. She ran wildly through the trees, jumping over dead ones, and pulling herself forward zigging and zagging between tree trunks. Ricky followed, heart pounding, pressing his sword against his leg so as not to snag it on any of the brush.

The wickrit charged ferociously, butting its solid skull at branches. Ricky glanced back and saw it heave a downed branch up into the air by hooking its horned snout under the thick log, then flung the timber effortlessly to the side. The wickrit let out another grumbling snarl as it locked eyes with him. Ricky bounced against a tree and winced at the pain in his shoulder. He caught himself from falling and zipped through the forest, keeping his eyes on the light grey flash of his aunt's dress up ahead of him.

"Here!" Sarah yelled and pointed to some thick entangled vines ahead of them. She ducked underneath where the vines clung tangled to a wide-trunked tree and squeezed through the space. She turned and pulled the vine up for Ricky to crawl under. "Come on! Come on!"

"I'm coming!" Ricky yelled wildly and scurried on all fours under the vine. Sarah helped him up and they dashed further into the woods, hand in fearfully-gripped hand. As they ran, Ricky heard a crash and crack behind him. Another wild snarling growl came from the beast and he turned back to see it thrashing on its hind legs, one front leg caught within the maze of vines.

"Ha! Take that, asshole!" Ricky called, slowing for a moment.

"Ricky!" Sarah ran back and jerked his arm forward. Ricky started back into a run to keep up with his aunt. He snapped his head back and forth to see in between the trees of the forest as they raced on, looking for any other predators.

"Was…was that thing real?" He gasped as they pounded the mucky ground below them.

"What do you think?" Sarah wheezed sourly. The snarls behind them slowly died down and eventually could be heard no more. Sarah slowed her running to a fast walk and gasped for air. "All right…all right," she wheezed. "We're close now," she brought one hand up to her hip and took deep breaths.

Ricky came up beside her and rested a hand on the hilt of his sword. He didn't want to let it go after seeing the wickrit. He panted as he peered around them and squinted through the fading light up ahead where the forest thinned. In the distance he could see rows of buildings with light from their windows illuminating places on an open dirt road between them.

"Close to what?" Ricky decided whispering like his aunt might be a good idea after all.

"To Oedher Village and to Allister Hall."

Ricky balked at her and then back in the direction where they'd encountered the wickrit. He didn't want to believe it, but the wickrit had looked just as his aunt had described to him when she'd told him stories of Farwin Wood as a child. He followed her as they stepped through the woods to the forest's edge. She stopped in the tree line and peered around with hesitation, a look of worry on her face.

"If this is Farwin Wood like you said, why…why do you look worried? I mean, you described it as a happy place and a," Ricky looked around at the dead and gloomy surroundings, "a lush, green world. I don't get it."

"It's not the Farwin Wood I remember, Ricky," she looked at him with fear in her eyes. "Something has happened here since the last time I came."

"Well...when was that?"

Sarah looked down and then pursed her lips. She started towards the road that led into Oedher Village, past a decrepit village sign that hung down to the ground by one hinge. "Almost twenty years ago. Your father and I came here for summer vacation after I graduated high school and he graduated college. He wanted us to have one last adventure before he went off to New York."

As difficult as all this was to believe, Ricky was starting to accept a little of it after seeing the wickrit and waking up in the woods. Imagining his father believed in this sort of thing, however, still seemed unfathomable to him. "Well, do you remember anything that might have happened to change things? I mean, how did this place get so creepy looking?"

Sarah swallowed. "I remember everything, Ricky. And yes, something happened. Something horrible."

CHAPTER

EIGHTEEN

FARWIN WOOD
18 YEARS EARLIER

SARAH TRAVELED back to Allister Hall with Richard two days after the night she'd spent with Vasimus. That was also the night Vasimus had told her about his sister Deronda's engagement to Ranthrop Groslivo. Sarah wanted to leave the day after learning that information, but everyone seemed to protest. The last night she was there, Vasimus met her in her room when everyone had retired for the evening.

Vasimus walked up to Sarah and knelt down before her. He pulled out a small golden ring with tiny daphne flower imprints on it from his waist belt and held it up to her. "Sarah, you have honored me with your choice and I want to honor you with mine," his husky voice floated up to her. Sarah felt herself swallow as she looked down at the candlelight glinting off of the little ring. "I would like for you

206

to join my family, to join my life...my future—a future we could share together."

There was a large part of Sarah's being that wanted to throw her arms around his neck and resound a loud "yes" through the room. However, the small part of her that nagged at the thought and reality of going back home to Blinney Lane, and her fear over what would occur between Richard and Deronda, made her hesitate enough to dampen her glee. She stared at the ring near her folded hands in front of her and couldn't bring herself to speak as she realized how complicated a future the ring signified.

"Forgive me. I thought you had chosen me. Have I spoken too soon?" Vasimus looked up, softening his voice. He grasped one of her hands gently, "I know we have only come to know each other well these past few weeks, but Sarah...I have never felt such steadfast conviction in a belief as I do in my feelings for you, which is so great that I know they will not change."

"You...you do not speak hastily, in my opinion," Sarah managed a smile. "It is only that I worry for our...," she had to stop herself before she said "future." "Well, we live so far apart and I would not always be able to be here."

"I will come to Blinney with you. I can leave Farwin Wood from time to time," Vasimus assured her with a kind smile.

"No," Sarah shook her head. "I...it's just that I don't think I could take you away from here...for as long as it takes to get to Blinney. I mean, since you are to lead Daundecort one day. Your people need you here."

"Sarah, my people will survive without me a few months of the year if they must." Vasimus stood, still holding the ring between his thumb and index finger. Sarah felt more under inspection now that he towered over her looking down.

"Vasimus," Sarah looked down and tried not to let the ring fall upon her line of view. "Blinney is very different from

Farwin Wood. I don't think that you would like it, but I must return there often."

"Are you afraid I would not let you go? Sarah, do not look at this ring as a sign that I would be master over your decisions. I only meant that I would go wherever you must go for as often as I can. I will like Blinney as long as you are there beside me," he urged her chin up to look at him with his hand.

"I don't know how to say this, but...you cannot go to Blinney." Sarah swallowed at his confused look. She couldn't possibly tell him the truth, yet she didn't want to lie to this man she cared for so much. "Outsiders are not allowed in Blinney. It's...it's always been this way and will remain so forever, I fear."

"Would I still be an outsider if we were to marry?" Vasimus' expression was quite quizzical.

"Yes. That's why it hurts me to tell you this," Sarah cast her eyes down again and then looked away so she wouldn't have to see the token of a dream she could not have.

Vasimus exhaled in disappointment. He turned the ring over between his thumb and finger, staring at it in thought. "Sarah? Is this your only objection? That you would say 'no' because I cannot come to Blinney?"

Sarah looked back at him with teary eyes. "Well, yes, I suppose. And that...and that I would have to leave you for a part of the year," she swallowed at the thought of how she could make that possible. Perhaps when she had to take over the store she could hire someone. Maybe someone else on Blinney Lane had a relative who wouldn't mind filling in for a few months each year.

"Then worry not. I can accept this objection. It would only serve our love more for the anticipation our happy reunions will bring," he smiled thoughtfully. "I promise to wait eagerly by when you must go. And when you return...to your other home of Daundecort Hall, I will be here. Always."

"You could live like that?"

"I do not think living without you could be easily done now that I have come to know you. I hope that you will accept this so it means you will always return to me. Let it serve as a reminder that I am always with you, no matter how far away you must go," Vasimus held the ring up a little higher to Sarah.

Sarah wanted to cry realizing that a thought she'd only pondered over the last several weeks and shrewdly pushed aside had now become a reality. In spite of what she told Vasimus about a woman choosing, her situation was a little more complex than that. At the end of the summer she would have to speak to her parents about how often and how long she could be allowed to leave her responsibilities in the store and return to Farwin Woods. Aside from that, if everyone else were not sleeping at the present moment in Daundecort Hall, Sarah would have yelled her response, "Yes! Yes. Oh, thank you!" She clasped her hands around his that held the ring and reached up on her tip toes to kiss him.

Vasimus grasped his arms around her waist as he kissed her in return. He spun her around once and then set her back to the ground. Laughing he began, "Why do you thank me? It is you who came back to Farwin Wood and changed my world forever."

"Don't thank me," Sarah laughed. "Thank Richard. He's the one who urged me to take this trip." The thought of Richard soured her elation. Richard and Deronda. What would become of their growing feelings for each other? How deep were their affections already? It had only taken several weeks for Sarah and Vasimus to come to the current situation. What would happen should Vasimus and Lord Clennon find out about the two of them? Sarah's mind began to reel with all of the negative possibilities.

"Well, thank you Richard!" Vasimus laughed again. "Here, let me," he said and grasped her hand to place the ring on her finger.

Sarah caught her breath at the thought of Richard and Deronda seeing the ring on her finger. She didn't want to look like a hypocrite to her brother or cause Deronda any more perplexed thoughts at the sign of marriage.

"No, wait," Sarah gently tugged her hand back. "Will it be all right if I don't wear it, just yet?" Vasimus looked at her with confusion. "I'd rather speak to my parents before my brother knows. It...it would be the proper thing to do. You know how Richard can't hold anything back," she smiled.

Vasimus seemed quite satisfied with her explanation. He smiled reassuringly and clasped his hand over hers. "I think that would be best since I may not go inform them myself." Sarah sighed with relief. "However, you will keep this until then, won't you?"

"Yes, of course," she smiled and finally touched the little gold ring for the first time. Sarah spotted her bracelet as she took the ring from Vasimus. "Perhaps I can put it on this bracelet someone made for me," she smiled up at him.

When Sarah and Richard returned to Allister Hall the next day, Sarah tried to inquire about his level of interest in Deronda. He angrily repeated that what he felt for Vasimus' sister was not a mere fancy and was quite an earnest love. Sarah avoided any mention of her previous argument—that loving and living in Farwin Wood was impossible. Instead, she carefully reminded him that Deronda was already spoken for, and about the repercussions that could happen should he continue his relationship with her. Richard assured his sister that he wouldn't continue to pursue Deronda, but his huffy manner unsettled her belief in his conviction.

After another four days alone together at Allister Hall, Sarah yearned to see Vasimus again. She'd gone out riding with Richard whose mood remained much sourer than when they first returned to their own hall. They'd spent time with the Wortwarts and some of the villagers during the day. In the evenings they invited Netta and the hall's watchman, Dergus, to dine with them. Vasimus arrived in Oedher Village on the fifth day, after Sarah replied to his message that he was welcome to come visit them again. Richard appeared grateful for the extra company, but still seemed distracted. Sarah felt guilty for having Vasimus there after she'd scolded Richard to stay away from Deronda. She had a moment to speak with Richard privately on the second day of Vasimus' visit, after breakfast as he prepared to go out without them.

"Richard, you can go out riding with us again if you'd like. I promise not to act silly around him and make you uncomfortable. I don't want to be a hypocrite since I know you can't... can't see," Sarah didn't want to say her friend's name.

"No, I know. Don't worry. I discovered the next village over and have plans to take some archery lessons from a hunter there," Richard donned his vest and slung a bow over his shoulder as he walked to mount his stroomphblutel.

"Are you mad at me?"

"Sarah," Richard warned. "Come on. Are you going to make me say it? I know you're right this time, okay?"

That wasn't what Sarah wanted to hear. She accepted that his anger wasn't directed at her, but rather circumstance. "I'm sorry. I really wanted us both to have a good summer."

Richard smiled down at her "Oh, I'll still have a good summer. Don't you worry about me. Now leave me be and go entertain your guest, will you?"

Sarah smirked in spite of herself. She felt relieved after the rub about Vasimus, how he'd referred to him as "her" guest, and his sincere insistence that he was still enjoying their summer.

The two weeks that Vasimus spent at Allister Hall went by too quickly. He and Sarah spent each day and night together, and every one left her feeling more and more content, loved, and blissfully happy.

Richard went out each day and returned in the early evening. His mood improved with each passing day, which made Sarah happy that he was finding a way to enjoy his time while she was distracted with Vasimus.

On Vasimus' last day at Allister Hall before he had to once again return to Daundecort Hall, he sat by the fire with Richard and Sarah playing Knick Knack and drinking Netta's special recipe of beetleburry ale. Richard yawned and got up to leave them after three or four hands. "Well, Vasimus. Happy travels and we'll see you again, I presume," he shook his hand.

"Oh, Richard you don't have to go just yet," Sarah didn't want her brother to think she needed more privacy than what she'd already had during the last two weeks. "I've seen so little of you lately."

"Ah, well I'm sorry but I'm headed out tomorrow as well to test out my new archery skills. I've rallied the Wortwart brothers to go with me in case I'm not as adept with the bow as I hope to be," he raised his glass once more and finished the last swallow.

"Your brother's becoming quite the woodsman," Vasimus smiled.

"Yes, yes he is," Sarah shot a surprised look at Richard before he left to head upstairs.

Vasimus left Sarah in the morning with the promise to come see her later in the week and the hope that she would again return to Daundecort Hall for another stay the week following. Sarah caught her breath as Netta walked through the room and saw them embracing in a kiss by the door. The old woman just smiled and continued on into the kitchen. Sarah should have expected Netta to have figured out by now that she and Vasimus had feelings for each other. Nothing eluded her mother's dear old friend, but Sarah didn't want to publicly flaunt her affections. Vasimus departed and she watched him ride through the small courtyard in front of the hall until Dergus had closed the gate of the outer wall behind him.

Sarah went back inside and into the kitchen. With Richard gone again for the day and after the two lazy weeks she'd just spent with Vasimus, she felt like doing something productive. She used to embroider fabric with her mother when they had no visitors at the hall during their former visits to Farwin Wood. Her mother would take them to a dressmaker in Oedher Village and sell them to add to the household funds of troogies. What extra milk they got from their three Muckas they kept in the barn behind the hall, they also sold or Netta would make a cheese-like substance that would fetch a higher price.

In the kitchen, Netta busied herself about cleaning bowls from the breakfast meal. She turned upon noticing Sarah enter the room and smiled. "Has your young fellow gone then now?"

Sarah wasn't going to lie to Netta. She just couldn't do it. She knew the question was an innocent inquiry as only Netta could manage. "Yes, he has. He'll be back later in the week, just for a day."

"Of course he will, dear," Netta's smile widened before she directed her attention back to the dishes.

Sarah shook her head and smiled into her hand as she watched Netta secretly delight in approval of the young romance. "Netta, I'm going to take some of the fabric I've been working on to the market and I think some of my old dresses that don't fit me anymore. Do you have anything you'd like me to sell or do we need anything for the hall?"

Netta wiped her hands on her apron and started towards another doorway at the back of the room that led to a store room. "Yes, I have more cheese than we know what to do with. And if you could pick up some more candles? We're a bit low."

Sarah carted the large basket of goods under her arm as she walked to the gate. "Good morning Dergus. How are you today?"

"Very well, Lady Sarah. Off to the market?"

"Yes," she smiled as Dergus opened the gate for her. "I'll bring you back some of Riley's beetleburry."

"Ah, we have beetleburry. No need to do that," the rugged man called as he closed the gate.

"I know you don't like Netta's brew," Sarah winked over her shoulder. Dergus chuckled softly and waved.

Sarah walked up the street with her basket to the dress shop and sold the fabric and old frocks. Then she went down to Riley's, Oedher Village's form of an all-purpose store. She spoke with Riley about the cheese she'd toted from the hall and he happily agreed to take it off her hands. "Wonderful, I'll just get a few things and then be back up for the difference."

Sarah walked around the shop looking at Riley's wares. She grabbed two bundles of candles and a small bottle of the beetleburry ale that Riley brewed in a little distillery behind his shop. She picked up some colored threads for her and Netta to embroider with that would contrast nicely with some new plain fabric bolts she also found. Sarah carted the armful of items back up to the wood plank counter and set them down.

"Well, Lady Sarah, let's see what we have today. I'll give you twenty troogies for the cheese," Riley inspected the pile of Sarah's purchases. The door creaked open and they both turned their heads to see two large men enter the shop.

Both men were clad in black tunics with a deep red over-laying smock. Each man wore a black sash that fell down across his chest to where it connected to his sword holster. Their matching black head covers were each drawn up and they peered around the shop with stony expressions.

"I'll be right with you men as soon as I finish with the Lady here," Riley nodded and went back to counting Sarah's purchases. The men took a turn around the inside of the shop and peeked out any door or window in the store before they came back to the place they had entered. Sarah watched them curiously as they methodically strode through the store. They didn't seem to look at any of the items in Riley's shop, but just the shop in its entirety, like they were searching for something large that would appear obvious to them upon sight.

As the men walked past Sarah again on their way to the door, the lead man glanced at her. His mouth was set in a tight line. His square jaw line seemed tense and his eyes had a cold hostility to them. Sarah almost shuddered at the sight of him. She'd never seen anyone so unsettling in all of Farwin Wood. Durley Allister had only written about people possessing a kind and warm-hearted demeanor, or at least she thought so until she saw that man. There was something about his expression that hinted at hostility. The men walked out and let the door slam shut behind them.

Riley looked up at the sound of the door, but when he saw no one enter he glanced around the shop and then back to Sarah. "Huh, did they leave?"

"Yes. Riley, who were those men?"

"Ah, looked to be Ranthrop Groslivo's colors. We've been seeing more of them around the village as of late, what with his engagement to Lady Deronda Daundecort. The union will unite the northern lands and the southern swamps. It promises to bring an increase in agricultural partnerships and improve the commerce of the entire region," Riley went on as he tallied up Sarah's total.

"Unite" the lands, Sarah thought. How silly. What was there to unite when no one in Farwin Wood seemed to quarrel about anything? Another thought on the look of the two serious men that had just breezed through the shop had Sarah hoping that for Deronda's sake, Ranthrop Groslivo was a much more pleasant looking and amiable man than his soldiers.

Sarah returned to the hall with her purchases and the troogies she'd obtained from her fabric sales. She delivered the basket to Netta and stored the coins in a locked chest in the cellar. Not in the mood to hunker down and embroider, Sarah had Dergus saddle up her stroomphblutel to take out for a ride. She headed north out of the village, comforted by the distance it would reduce between her and Vasimus.

About a half hour down the road from Oedher Village, Sarah steered her ride off into the woods. She knew there to be a stream just a short distance ahead and decided it would be a peaceful place to sit and enjoy the splendor of the beautiful breezy day. Her stroomphblutel snorted as it ascended a small grassy incline. She urged the reins against its neck to continue up the little hill, but it nudged its head against them and started in a clumsy sprint off to the left of the hill back into the woods.

"What in the world has gotten into you, girl?" Sarah let the furry beast lumber closer to the woods where it seemed intent to take her. As they rounded the base of the little hill she heard some more snorting sounds off in the distance.

Up ahead, Sarah could see Richard's stroomphblutel rubbing its side against a tree where its reins were tied. "Ahh, found your boyfriend, did you?" Sarah patted her furry beast's side as it waddled closer to Richard's. As they neared where it stood next to some brush, Sarah saw yet another stroomphblutel on the other side of the bushes. Well, that's not one of the Wortwarts', she thought. Sarah inhaled once she could see the other animal in full. It was Deronda's. She was sure of it. "Oh, no," she muttered.

Sarah dismounted her ride and tied its reins to the tree where its mate was. She peered around the opening in the woods and across the stream, but saw no sign of Richard or Deronda. She started along the stream, walking towards where it curved. Up ahead, the water was hidden by a ridge that jutted into the stream.

In the distance, Sarah heard muffled voices. She couldn't make out the words, but the pitch was sharp enough to indicate they were tones of distress. "Richard?"

"Sarah!" she heard a woman's voice call out from beyond the hill. Sarah hiked up her skirt so she could move faster and ran to the top of the hill. She heard a swoosh, then a whirring and thunk noise. The motion of an arrow's fletching wobbling as it stuck into a tree at the base of the hill caught Sarah's eye. She gasped, worried it may have come from Richard. Perhaps he didn't see her and was still hunting, although clearly not with the Wortwart brothers. Worse yet, maybe he and Deronda had come across some wickrits. Sarah quickly surveyed the glen below and the winding stream through the open portion of the woods. She spotted Richard and Deronda. They were both running at full speed, hand in hand.

"Richard!" Sarah called down to them, seeing he did not have his bow drawn, but was urging Deronda ahead of him. He stopped at the sound of her voice and looked up to locate her on the hill above them.

"Run, Sarah!" Richard's eyes were wide and his usually jovial face was stricken with fear.

Deronda's face was filled with terror as she also locked eyes with Sarah. Suddenly she stopped and her eyes widened further. She turned back around at the sound of Richard's voice and ran to him with her hand stretched out, ensuring he wouldn't be left behind to face whatever they were running from. Just as Richard put his hands up to stop her approach, Deronda's movement halted abruptly like she hit a wall.

Sarah watched in utter confusion and horror as Deronda's arms went out to her sides and her chest arched backwards. Sarah gasped and brought her hands to her mouth when she spotted an arrow protruding from Deronda's chest.

"Nooooo!" Richard's scream curdled through the air over the soft trickle of the stream.

In the wood line on the other side of the stream came the cracking sound of breaking twigs. Sarah looked up and instantly spotted the bright red smock of the lead soldier she'd seen in Riley's. His arm was outstretched, bow in hand, but slowly lowered as he gazed upon Deronda limply falling to her knees.

Deronda slumped forward. One hand went to the ground while she held the other at the place where her chest had been pierced. Richard fell to the ground and wildly crawled over to her. He wrapped his arms around the light grey of her dress, where a deep crimson began to appear in front. Sarah's mouth gaped open as she absorbed the scene.

The second soldier ran up behind the first and stopped abruptly as he saw Deronda. Sarah locked eyes with the lead soldier then, her jaw agape in question at what he'd just done. The look of intensity and anger she'd seen on his face at Riley's was no longer present. His brow sagged, his jaw draped open, and his eyes looked up to her in pain and horror at what he'd just done.

"You hit Lady Daundecort!" the other man cried and held his hand to the top of his head, his eyes equally glazed in horror. Sarah knew instantly that the arrow had been meant for her brother. She tore her eyes away from the soldiers who fumbled back into the woods. She ran down the slope to where Richard cradled Deronda in his arms.

Sarah panted as her heart pounded in her chest. She dropped to the grass beside Deronda where Richard cradled her limp body in his arms. Richard wept as he tightly grasped one of her pale slender hands in his. He cupped her shoulder with his other hand and rubbed his thumb against her arm. Deronda's lips sat parted. Each breath she took caused her to jolt as her chest visibly rose with the difficulty of the effort. She turned her heavy-lidded, blue eyes away from Richard to Sarah and the motion seemed to take her some time. "Oh, Deronda," Sarah whispered. She didn't know what to say on seeing her friend like this, possibly at her end.

"Sarah," Deronda's voice came out as a whisper and the corner of her mouth turned up slightly to the side.

"Don't leave me, Deronda. Hang on!" Richard squeezed her and her eyes lazily shifted back to him. She tried to bring her free hand upward to his face, but halfway through the motion it dropped back down into her lap. Sarah caught her breath in her throat and bit her lip. "Deronda! Deronda! No! No, don't go! Come on!" Richard shook her in his arms as he screamed. Sarah slapped her hands to cover her face and felt the pressure in her throat cause her to sputter for air as she watched her brother's heartache before her and the lifelessness of her friend.

"Richard! Richard, stop!" Sarah could take it no longer and tugged at her brother's sleeve until he stopped jolting Deronda in his arms. He looked over at Sarah, tears in his eyes as all of the tension in his face sagged out. "Richard...she's dead," Sarah uttered the wrenching statement as both brother and sister stared at each other in a horrific silence.

CHAPTER
NINETEEN

FARWIN WOOD
PRESENT DAY

WHILE ENSURING he stayed in stride next to Sarah, Ricky took in his surroundings as they walked along the edge of the roadway into Oedher Village. Ricky pondered the possibility that Sarah, Mary, and Francis had kidnapped him and moved his body to the woods outside of Salem after he'd fallen asleep, but the more they walked the less sure he was of that notion. The wickrit had been his first reason to doubt that theory. He found no explanation for how they would have managed such an enormous and violent beast. It certainly didn't seem robotic. As they entered the village, Ricky eyed the thatched roofs of the little cottages. He noticed scents and smells he'd never experienced before, and people stopped to look at them. The people wore clothing similar to his and his aunt's, but the villagers' seemed shabbier, dirtier, and more threadbare. The people they passed looked thin and hungry.

They pointed and whispered, freely ogling the sight of Sarah and Ricky.

Several of the buildings behind the people had holes in the roofs covered by ramshackle patchwork. Some buildings had sections of stone missing and charred black smudges along the outside of the walls as though they'd been burned at one time and never fully repaired.

"Eyes ahead, Ricky," Sarah muttered under her breath. "The more you gawk at them the more they'll gawk at us."

"What happened here?" He hurried back up to her side.

Sarah walked with her head pointed forward, but peered her eyes out at the town as she spoke, "I...don't know, but I'm guessing there's been a war."

Ricky looked back down the street and saw that the stragglers in the street still stared after them. Sarah slowed in front of him and Ricky followed her gaze to a high stone wall at the end of the street that came to an arch in the center. Under the stone archway were two large wooden doors.

In the shadows under the archway a leathery skinned old man sat on a little wooden stool. His salt and pepper hair curled up at the ends dangling down to his shoulders. His face was covered with the same color whiskers. He held a sword firmly in his knobby grip, the tip of the blade stuck in the dirt at his feet. As they neared him, Sarah approached slowly. Ricky watched her go towards the man and saw that he was squinting through the darkness at her with intent curiosity.

"What are you about, missy?" The man's growly voice pierced through the dark.

"Dergus? Is it you?" Sarah stopped a few feet in front of the man.

The man stood up rigidly and Ricky heard his joints pop and crack with the motion. The old man took a rigid step closer to Sarah and stared. Ricky swallowed. He wondered if they would be met by as much threat as the wickrit had posed. Even though the man looked to be in his late fifties, there were still signs of chorded muscles to his thin physique where the fabric of his grey tunic pressed against his arms. He wore a cream colored smock over the tunic with a grey belt across his chest attached to the holster at his hip. He looked to be the guard of this place with his sword out of the holster on as ready as an aging man could have it, Ricky thought.

The tension in the man's faced went lax suddenly and his narrowed eyes widened as he reached for Sarah's face with his weathered fingers. Ricky gripped the hilt of his sword, although he didn't know how to use it.

"It can't be," the man whispered. "Lady Sarah..."

Sarah reached up and grasped the man's hand. She pressed it to her face and sighed with her eyes pinched shut. "It's me, old friend," she whispered back.

Half weeping, half laughing, Dergus pulled her to him by the shoulder and grasped onto her tightly. "Oh, heavens, we thought you were dead! All this time!" He grasped her face in his hands and smiled, now not looking as lethal as when Ricky first saw him. Ricky sighed with relief and stepped to get a better look beyond the wall, but he could not see much through the darkness. "Richard?" Ricky heard the phlegmy voice of the old man call, and he turned his head upon hearing his formal name.

"Yes?" Ricky mustered a smile.

"It can't be. You haven't aged at all," Dergus grasped Ricky's arm and eyed him up and down.

"Oh, no, Dergus. This is...this is Richard's son, Ricky... short for...Richard the second," Sarah patted the old man's hand. Ricky arched his brow at Sarah and rolled his eyes.

"Well, that explains the similarity," Dergus chuckled. "My...just like your father, it's uncanny. We'd better get him inside then, Sarah," Dergus' expression became serious again.

Just then the wooden doors screeched open causing Ricky and Sarah to jump.

Two large men both in long sleeved blue shirts with blue smocks over top their undershirts stood by each door. Their serious expressions didn't seem to match the feminine look of the large flowers that were embroidered at the tops of each of their smocks by their shoulders, Ricky thought as he studied them.

Dergus grunted at the sight of them and walked through the gate. "We've had some...company these last twenty years. Vasimus' men," Dergus gestured at the two men who eyed Sarah and Ricky as they walked through the gate.

"Dergus," one of the men called in a stern tone. Dergus continued to hobble through the courtyard as the other man closed the gates. The man who had addressed Dergus followed after him and called again, "Master Dergus, who are these two persons?" Sarah and Ricky looked at each other. Clearly she didn't know the meaning of his inquiry either.

Dergus stopped and sighed a haggard breath. He turned back around and looked from the man to Sarah. "I suppose after coming through the village everyone will know by sunup anyways, m'Lady," Dergus grimaced at her and then glared back at the man whose impatience with him was evident.

"Lady?" the man questioned.

Sarah took a step towards the man. "I am Lady Sarah Allister of House of Allister," she spoke with finesse. Ricky felt a smirk at the condescending tone she used.

"Lady...Lady..." the man stammered and eyed her up and down.

"Sarah Allister," Dergus barked and took Sarah's arm. "And as this is still Allister Hall and she's still in charge, I suggest you scamper off!" Ricky watched the man's mouth drop open as Sarah took Dergus' arm and continued on through an open court yard to the hall.

The man looked at Ricky and swallowed. "Your Lord...I apologize," he bowed his head. Ricky wasn't sure what to do and inhaled a breath to puff his chest up a little.

"Carry on," he waved with a hand and turned to hurry after his aunt and Dergus.

The towering doorways to the hall opened up into a sizable great room. It looked as though it had the potential to be elegant and perhaps had been in its day, yet its present condition was far from impressive. A dusty table sat in the center of the room with two benches on each side, one of them newer and more make-shift than the other, likely a replacement from the original. At the end of the room was an expansive fireplace with a stone chimney that ran up the length of the wall to the ceiling. Two chairs sat before the fireplace and another smaller wooden table about knee-high. On the wall opposite the entrance door was a set of wide stone stairs that ascended further up into the house. Ricky jumped at a shriek noise and ducked as something whooshed above them and out through an opening in the roof where the thatch was missing. Tierrrrumpt!

"What was that?" Ricky yelled.

Dergus glanced back at him as he and Sarah walked towards another door near the base of a wide stairwell. "You've never seen a tierumpt?"

"Uh, we don't have them in the North," Sarah said to Dergus as she cast a look at Ricky.

"Ah, they've been nesting here at the hall more and more. They must feel safer here, less hunted. Everything's grown sparse in the land. People clambering for food," Dergus waved his hand around matter-of-factly.

Sarah cast a sympathetic look in the old man's direction. "I'm so sorry, Dergus. I truly didn't know things were so bad."

"Ah, don't you worry. We've done all right here. It's just me and Netta and the two oafs that Vasimus sends to watch the place so Rathrop's men don't burn it down."

Sarah stopped and looked at Dergus through the dimly lit hall. A single candle burned in a holder by the kitchen doorway and flickered shadows about them. "Ranthrop?" Sarah's voice was meek.

Dergus squeezed her arm gently. "They've been at war ever since the summer Deronda and you... Well, you know what I mean," he patted her hand and continued on to the next doorway.

Ricky looked at his aunt who'd gone pale. "Are you all right?"

"Y...yes. I'm...I'm fine," Sarah smoothed her hands over her dress and started after Dergus.

Ricky stepped through the doorway after Dergus and Sarah. The room was more illuminated than the great room had been, and it felt much more cozy; heat was permeating from somewhere within. Sarah stopped just inside the doorway causing him to almost slam into her. Ricky stepped around her and saw another fireplace, an open stone half-walled pit where some embers burned, along the far wall. A long waist-high table ran the length of the room, and above it hung wooden bowls and rudimentary black pots suspended from the ceiling by long hooks. There were wooden shelves on the wall extending out above the fire pit. Much of the shelf space was empty, but held some brown sacks that slumped in different directions from their contents.

"Netta, where's the beetleburry?" Dergus called and strode past a little white-haired woman, his motions more fluid now that he'd been moving for a while.

Ricky heard Sarah gasp as she stared at the old woman who sat next to the table. The woman's long white hair was pulled back into a bun at the base of her head, several strands hung down in front of her wrinkled, age-spotted face. She sat hunched over, elbows on the table, peeling a brown hull off of some type of vegetable that was bright green once the peel was removed. Her knobby-knuckled hands shook slightly with each graze of the little paring knife.

"Now you stay away from that, Dergus! Unless you start scouring the woods for the berries, I'm not making it anymore at the rate you drink it!" The old woman's crackly high pitched voice chirped after Dergus as he continued past her and into a back room.

"Netta," Sarah whispered more in declaration than question. Ricky looked at his aunt. Her eyes appeared watery against the flickering candlelight in the room, and he wondered who this woman was to her.

The old woman looked up slowly at the doorway where Dergus had disappeared. Then she turned her head in the opposite direction searching for the sound she thought she'd heard. Upon seeing Sarah, the woman brought her posture more erect and narrowed her eyes, the wrinkled skin at their corners constricting even further. Sarah started around the table in small steps over to where she sat. As Netta stared at Sarah, the knife in her hand fell into the metal blow with a clatter. She gasped and held her hand to her heart. "Sss… Sarah?" her voice came out in a whisper.

"Oh, Netta!" Sarah cried and wrapped her arms around the woman's bony shoulders.

"Ohhhh! Sarah! Sarah? Am I dreaming?" Netta's pale blue eyes peered up at Sarah in shock. Sarah bent down so she was eye level with her old friend. Ricky watched in wonder as the two women seemed beside themselves in joy. Netta brought her hands up to cup Sarah's face and touch her hair.

"It's me! It's me, Netta. I'm so sorry I didn't come back," Sarah cried.

"Dergus! Dergus!" Netta squealed. "It's Sarah! You didn't tell me *Sarah* had come!" She hugged Sarah's neck.

Ricky heard a clatter and a grumble from Dergus in the back room. The weathered man then appeared in the doorway with a bulb shaped bottle in each hand and a confounded expression on his face. "Well what did you think I wanted the beetleburry for?"

"Tsk!" Netta shook her head at his words, still taking in the sight of the woman before her. Sarah laughed through her tears as the women continued to embrace each other.

Dergus lumbered up to the other side of the table and pulled out a stool. He looked over at Ricky. "I'm gone for a minute and they're crying," he rolled his eyes. "Come on, son. Sit down and let's get started on this." Dergus slid a bottle to his side in front of another stool.

Ricky obeyed and took a seat next to him. He inspected the dark glass bottle and pulled the cork out after seeing Dergus do the same. This better not be like that tea, Ricky thought.

Ricky watched as Dergus took a long pull from the bottle and eyed it lovingly while he let out a satisfied sound. He raised the bottle and clanked it against Ricky's. "Welcome to Allister Hall of Farwin Wood."

"Thanks," Ricky let out and watched the old man slurp another long draw from the bottle. Ricky sniffed the liquor inside and his senses perked at the hints of watermelon that floated into his nostrils. He hoped it tasted similar to the aroma and took a sip. Ricky's eyebrows perked up at the refreshing flavors of lime, watermelon, and something else he'd never tasted before, as they tingled in his mouth and down his throat.

"Good stuff, huh?" Dergus winked at him.

"Oh, you! Get a goblet! Give me that!" Netta snapped and grabbed the bottle away from Dergus who looked utterly depressed once it was robbed of his grasp.

Sarah settled down onto the stool beside Netta and introduced her to Ricky. He felt awkward as she stared at him and made references of how he looked like his father. Ricky suspected there was very little he knew about his father's past.

As the four laughed and smiled over their exchange of greetings, the mood soon turned somber and then Ricky learned he knew even less about his father than he thought.

"Your father and I both fell in love that summer, Ricky," Sarah told him about the last time she'd been to Farwin Wood.

"Those were happy days," Netta smiled at him with her hands wrapped around her drink. "For a while," her smiled began to fade.

"They were a brother and sister we used to play with when we would visit as children. They're sort of the noble family in the land, the Daundecorts—Vasimus and Deronda. Deronda, however, was engaged to be married to Ranthrop Groslivo, but I didn't learn this until later on in the summer. She must have fallen for your father right away after seeing him again and I suppose the same happened to him," Sarah continued.

"She was the most beautiful girl in the land," Dergus stared into his goblet. Ricky watched them and sipped his beetleburry. He suspected it was alcoholic and hoped it would help jolt him out of this dream.

Sarah stared down at the table with a perplexed look on her face. Netta glanced over at her and then back to Ricky who waited with anxious eyes. "Your aunt came upon them in the woods one day. Your father had *said* he was going hunting," Netta shook her head with a sour chuckle, "the foolish scamp. You see, they had been meeting in secret while Sarah was...," Sarah looked away in shame. Netta patted her hand. "Sarah was engaged to Vasimus...and we thought Richard, you father I mean, was just giving them room to flourish."

"How did you know we were engaged, Netta?"

"Sarah, darling," Netta's wrinkled eyes creased and she smiled. She flicked at the ring on Sarah's bracelet. "I was old then too, but not blind. Besides, Vasimus made it known just what had been taken from him after you were...gone." Sarah turned her eyes away in pain.

"So? What happened?" Ricky didn't like the eerie silence that had fallen over the room.

"We found out later that someone had seen Deronda and your father together, so Ranthrop sent his men out to look for Richard. They found him with her in the woods and the arrow meant for your father, well...it didn't hit who it was intended for," Dergus forced a hard gulp down his throat. "I wish he had come to me, Sarah. I wish he would have told me and we could have gone to Lord Clennon," Dergus' voice became harsh.

"Shh, tsk," Netta chirped at him.

"So someone tried to kill my father because he was chasing after someone else's girl?" Ricky interrupted while he had the chance.

"Yes," Sarah mumbled.

"And then she was killed because of him?"

"She was killed because Ranthrop Groslivo is a jealous, greedy, cold-hearted fool!" Netta barked.

"Yes," Sarah added firmly looking at Ricky. "It was an accident, but it happened because they didn't stay away from each other."

"So what does all of this have to do with Shelby? Is this going to cause problems finding her? I mean, can we show our faces around here? They're mad at my father, not you, right?" Ricky felt himself speaking rapidly from the numbing sensation the beetleburry was giving him.

"Who's Shelby?" Netta looked at him.

"She..." Ricky stopped and looked at Sarah, not knowing what the people *from* the book knew *about* the book, if they knew about the book at all.

"She's a girl from our land, from Blinney. She's...part of my court and she got lost. We think she ventured into Farwin Wood, and as good as it is to see the both of you, I've come to get her out of here…after all that's happened as you can imagine," Sarah spoke carefully to Netta and Dergus.

"I wouldn't come here now if I didn't have to. No offense taken," Dergus held up a hand.

"What was that business about the girl yesterday and the Wortwart brothers, Dergus?" Netta tapped the table in front of him to capture his attention.

"That young girl they found?" He looked at her in thought. Sarah and Ricky locked eyes and then jerked their heads back to Dergus.

"Shelby's sixteen. She's blonde and she…well, she would have been wearing clothes strange to Farwin Wood. She…she looks a lot like Deronda actually," Sarah swallowed.

Dergus stared at Sarah with his mouth open for a moment. He carefully shifted his eyes away from her, but then found Netta's equally anticipatory stare on him. He let out a ragged breath. "Sarah…they've taken her to Ranthrop from what I heard."

"What? Why?" Sarah tried not to panic.

"Sarah, after Vasimus thought you died, he blamed Ranthrop for you and Deronda. They've fought ever since then. Ranthrop would kill any of Vasimus' men or Northern villagers that came to the Southern swamplands and vice versa. They'd ride into the villages that bordered the North, not just Daundecort property, but villages friendly to Daundecorts, and burn and raid everything. We've only managed to keep Allister Hall standing because of the high wall, constantly repairing what we can, and fighting them off between me and the two guards Vasimus continually keeps stationed here," Dergus explained.

Sarah looked horrified by what she heard. "But…but Dergus why would the Wortwarts take Shelby to Ranthrop? This was Daundecort friendly territory and they were friends to my brother."

The old man stared at her for a pause. "I'm afraid no one was a friend to your brother after he disappeared and left us with these two men who've grown so much to hate each other," Dergus spoke in a delicate tone. "The villagers weren't able to hold off Ranthrop's men as well as we have here at the hall. Being a border town between the North and South, they do what they have to do just to get by. The Wortwarts were boasting that they'd found a match to Ranthrop's long lost bride and would bring her to him in the hopes of securing some peace here."

"What? So this sleazeball has my girl?" Ricky blurted out followed by a thunderous hiccup.

Netta canted her head in understanding at the young man's declaration and then looked at Sarah with a grimace. Sarah uttered, "I couldn't leave him behind. I'm sorry. I know I shouldn't have brought him here."

"What's a sleazeball?" Dergus poured himself and Ricky another glass.

Ricky casually tilted his goblet for the pour and rested his chin on his other hand. "Wait, why would this Vaso-max guy think my aunt died?"

"Ranthrop found Sarah when she was trying to hide your father from the search parties that were sent out looking for him. They never found your father. Ranthrop was so enraged that he took your aunt with him to get Richard to show himself, but he never did," Dergus explained.

"Your father had already gone back to Blinney. I made him," Sarah forced that point with Ricky. She didn't want him thinking his father was a coward. "Ranthrop didn't know this though, and held me captive in his stronghold. The only thing it did was send Vasimus after me with his men and even his father, Lord Clennon, came."

"He thought very highly of you and your family. You were like a daughter to him Sarah," Netta nodded. "Rest his poor soul. Things wouldn't be this way if he still lived."

"What? When did he die?" Sarah gasped.

"After Ranthrop forced you into the River Duke and you...well, disappeared I guess, Vasimus ran in after you they say. When he couldn't find you he went after Ranthrop and they fought," Netta spoke uneasily. She looked at Ricky then, "You see, Ranthrop felt he'd been slighted because he loved Deronda, although he didn't seem an openly affectionate man, he must have hid his true feelings for her. When he never found your father, he thought he'd not only lost his love, but his chance to avenge her death. Lord Clennon, so distraught at losing his daughter, and then Sarah, and seeing how it destroyed Vasimus, screamed to them from the shore to stop their quarrel. He suffered an attack and fell from his mount," Netta shook her head.

Sarah gazed at Netta waiting to hear more, but the old woman was done in. She turned to Dergus as he began to finish for the old woman. "Lord Clennon lived but three years after that, weakened by his distress. Vasimus then blamed Ranthrop for the deaths of you, his sister, and his father. There were some troubles in those first years, but not many as Vasimus swore to his father he would keep the peace. After Lord Clennon died, he publicly denounced Ranthrop and...well, it was all vengeance on both sides then."

"Sssoo," Ricky started to slur, "what happened to you? In the river?" He blinked at his aunt.

Sarah saw that both Netta and Dergus waited for her to answer the question, equally interested. "I...I woke up far away, not remembering until later what had happened. Then I went home to make sure Richard had made it there safely and to assure our parents that I was all right."

"Yeah, but you could have come back and seen your boyfriend, right? I mean then maybe he wouldn't have been so pissed off, and who knows, maybe nobody'd be fighting anymore," Ricky scratched at his temple.

"I thought Vasimus and his family had been through enough pain, Ricky. I...I didn't think there was a way to make up for," she glanced at Netta and Dergus, "for what Richard had done. Things would not have been the same." She felt a pang of guilt after seeing the decayed state of Farwin Wood and the life Netta and Dergus now lived. She knew now that she should have come back, no matter how painful it would have been for her or even if Vasimus was not the same after losing his sister.

Ricky shook his head, "this is the most depressing story I've ever heard." He extended his empty goblet to Dergus who started to refill it. Sarah reached over and stopped Dergus.

"No. I think he's had enough. We should get some sleep. From the looks of things, I don't think it would be wise of me to wander into the swamp tonight. I'll go at first light," she looked to Dergus.

"Well, I'm going with you," Dergus slammed the bottle down. Ricky stared stupidly at his empty glass and frowned.

"No, Dergus. I won't put you at risk, not after all that's happened because of me and my family already. No. I need you to stay here and make sure Ricky isn't seen by anyone. He looks too much like Richard, and after what you've told me I don't think it would be wise for him to venture outside of Allister Hall," Sarah commanded.

"Good point," Dergus nodded. "Well, we have one stroomphblutel in the barn. He's the pup of yours and Richard's old rides. He doesn't get out much, but he can take a saddle. Just be careful and stay off the roads or you'll be robbed and walking in no time. Best take a cloak and cover up that face of yours too in case anyone recognizes it. You're worth more than troogies to anyone in these parts now." Dergus' words made her shudder.

Ricky tilted his head back and let the last drops from his glass drip into his mouth. "Well, I'll go as long as there's no wickrits out there." Sarah rolled her eyes.

"Come on, Ricky. I'll help you upstairs." Sarah collected her nephew whose legs had grown limp from over imbibing in the sweet liquor. Upstairs she shoved open the door to Richard's old room and saw that Netta still kept the beds made. She steered him over to it and let him flop down on the blankets.

Ricky winced as his sword jabbed into his side. He started to unfasten it clumsily, but Sarah placed a hand on his wrist. "Ricky, no. Best you leave it on."

"What? Don't tell me something's going to attack me in my sleep now," he groaned.

"No, but you have to leave Farwin Wood with exactly what you brought with you. You can't leave anything behind or the book will pull you back in. Are you listening to me?"

"Yeah, yeah," Ricky yawned and let his head hit the pillow.

"I mean it. Don't lose anything. Not a lace, not a thread. Nothing or you'll end up right back here once we get home," she scolded.

"And how exactly do we get back home? Is there another book here?" Ricky peered up at her with his glazed eyes.

"We drown ourselves," her voice was flat.

"What?" Ricky scoffed. "You're kidding me, right?" Sarah just stared down at him. "I'm not freaking drowning myself! Now you've completely lost it! Either that or you drank more bug juice than I did," Ricky scowled.

"I'll do it for you," she sneered. "I just wanted you to know in case I don't come back with Shelby." Sarah started for the door, but stopped when she heard Ricky mumble.

"I should be the one to go after her. I'm the reason she ended up here. What if they hurt her? Would they hurt her?" He lifted his head up to see his aunt's reaction to the question.

"No. I don't think there would be any benefit in that for him. And Ricky, don't try to follow me, please. You have to stay here and wait for me. I need you here when I come back with Shelby so you can get home and get the book to the hospital. I've never known the book not to be next to someone when they woke up from Farwin Wood. I don't want to take any chances. Besides, it's not safe for you out there. You can't be the one to go to Ranthrop's."

"Because my father was a jerk," Ricky muttered and flopped back down on the pillow.

Sarah grasped the door handle with a pained expression that Ricky could not see. "No. He wasn't. He just fell in love with the wrong girl," she mumbled and walked out of the room.

CHAPTER

TWENTY

JUST BEFORE the morning light, Sarah came downstairs to find Netta already awake and in the kitchen baking bread. Sarah inquired about some of Richard's old clothing, having decided it would be better to dress like a man and give the impression of a peasant or hunter for her trek through the swamp. Netta directed her to some old trunks that used to sit in Richard's room, but had been moved when the raiding started in Farwin Wood. She kept them hidden in the floor under a door that was covered by a woven mat.

Sarah rifled through the clothing and found a pair of pants that would look baggy on her and perhaps give the impression that the muscles in her legs were larger than they actually were. She grabbed one of Richard's old wide-sleeved shirts and a leather vest, and found a thin brown cloak that would cover her head and curves, but not stifle her once the day grew hot.

Sarah took the clothing back upstairs to change and peruse her appearance in the shard of mirror that remained in her old bedroom. She carefully gathered up the clothing she'd worn on her arrival to Farwin Wood and set it on her bed. A last look at her new wardrobe and she was content; until she noticed she still wore her bracelet. Sarah unfastened it and placed it on top of her folded gown. She didn't want to risk losing it in the woods or having it stolen by the robbers Dergus had warned her about. As a child, she had been cautioned by her parents that she might never wake up if she didn't leave Farwin Wood with everything with which she'd arrived.

Content that she'd left all of her Blinney Lane apparel behind, Sarah slung one of her brother's old holsters across her body and loosened it so that it would not press down between her breasts and give her gender away on first glance. She sheathed an old sword into the holster and also took Richard's old bow, which she slung across her back. Sarah then peeked in on Ricky and found him snoring. She shut the door quietly and went back downstairs to the kitchen to say goodbye to Netta before she set out in search of Shelby.

Netta forced Sarah to sit down and eat something before she left, although Sarah was too anxious to have an appetite. She felt horrid for what Richard and Deronda had gotten mixed up in, for what had become of Farwin Wood, and now for Shelby being taken. Even more, she wondered what had happened to Vasimus to become so relentless as Netta claimed, even if he had thought Sarah to be dead. She always knew him to be a kind and loving man. Killing for revenge wouldn't bring her back if she had died as he so thought. He loved his land and his people. Couldn't he see that they were suffering because of this bitter feud? She wanted to know the answers to these questions. Part of her wanted to see him, but mostly she wanted Shelby back safe and to leave Farwin Wood without crossing paths with Vasimus at all.

"Netta? Does Vasimus ever come here?" Sarah inquired nonchalantly.

Netta sipped on some hot tea and wiped her brow. "He used to quite a bit right after you…were gone, but now…only once or twice a year and just asks how we are doing."

"That's kind of him," Sarah added feeling guilty that after all these years he still checked on Allister Hall and its workers.

"Well, I fear the kindness in him is nearly gone these days. He's not the man you once knew him to be, Sarah," Netta nodded for emphasis. "There's a restlessness about him, a deep pain that fuels him."

"Netta…I have to tell you something. I would have told you a long time ago, but…but I didn't want to shock you."

Netta chuckled, "Well, I could do with a little excitement around here. It's been a droll twenty years."

Sarah proceeded to tell Netta about the book and Blinney Lane. She knew she didn't need to, but her guilt over not returning was eating away at her. Netta would never give the impression she begrudged Sarah for not coming back, but Sarah couldn't take the twenty years of Farwin Wood history hitting her all at once, knowing that if she had just returned to soothe Vasimus things might have been different. Sarah carefully told Netta how they got to Farwin Wood and how they returned, how they slept at Blinney Lane while they were also somehow in Farwin Wood. She only left out the detail that the book was written by Durley Allister. She didn't want to insult Netta by saying that she and her world were merely the imagination of one of Sarah's ancestors. That part would be the most unbelievable. She also needed Netta to know how to send Ricky back in case she didn't return.

"So that's why everyone thought you drowned?" Netta gasped.

"I thought Ranthrop would not release me to Vasimus and that would cause more trouble. I thought that if I could become Ranthrop's vengeance then he would not place any demands on the Daundecorts for what Richard and Deronda had done, so I...*went home*...through the water. I didn't know it would make things worse, but now I see it was the cowardly thing to do," Sarah stared at the crumbs on her plate.

"Sarah? How can you think that sacrificing yourself was cowardly? Don't tell me it hasn't hurt you these many years to have given up Vasimus yourself! I see that Richard has a son, but I haven't heard you speak of any children," Netta clasped her hand.

"No. No, I have none. I never married."

"All these years wasted over your guilt, tsk. Sarah you were a lovely girl and you've become a beautiful, intelligent woman who has a lot to offer. Don't be what Vasimus has become," Netta looked at her intently and Sarah countered with an inquisitive expression, "a sad and angry empty shell of a human being, blinded by a love he hasn't felt in years. Was there no one that made you feel again, even through your misery?"

Sarah let a pathetic laugh out and shook her head. "Netta, have you not heard a word I just told you? There's no magic in this world, just as people believe there is none in mine. We have to keep it a secret so people don't think we're insane. Even if I wanted to meet someone new, how could I explain my life to them? There's...Henry," Sarah paused and thought of Henry. "He delivers things to my shop. He's always been so kind to me. It reminds me of how I felt when I was with Vasimus, but I could never tell him about Blinney Lane. He'd never come back and then I would lose the only thing that makes me happy — seeing his face when he walks through the door." Netta harrumphed and shook her head at the complexity of it all. Sarah patted her hand and stood up. "I'd best get going. There's young love that still has a chance," she smiled with reassurance.

Dergus met Sarah in the courtyard and helped her up on the rambunctious stroomphblutel. It shifted under the weight of her and the saddle and shook its head, ears flapping from side to side. "Hey, hey now. What did we talk about?" Dergus pointed a finger to the beast's slobbery snout. The stroomphblutel let out a yowling yawn and snorted, looking away in defiance.

"You'll be fine," Dergus called up to Sarah as he patted her ride. "You remember how to get there?"

"Southeast, due southeast," she nodded.

"Yes, just head out behind the hall and stay in the woods. Once you hit the thick of the swamp you'll know you're close and then cut south to the road."

Sarah looked down at Dergus wondering if it was the last time she would see him. Deronda had proved that people could die in Farwin Wood, violently for that matter. Would it be possible for an outsider, someone from another world, to do the same, Sarah wondered. "You'll make sure Ricky stays here?"

"He won't get past me," Dergus winked up at her.

Sarah managed the stroomphblutel out the gate and along the front wall in the street. She urged him around the corner at the end of the wall where the woods began and they headed into the trees. Sarah scanned through the forest against the dim light of the rising sun that crept into the shaded foggy forest bed. There was no one behind the hall, and she continued on only stopping once to take a last look back at Allister Hall before it was no longer in view.

Occasionally, Sarah would pass some patches of grass that struggled to remain green and vigorous, but those sites were few as she headed towards the swamplands. She could tell by the ravaged appearance of the woods that many parts had been burned, timber had been chopped, or a drought had killed much of the vegetation that she remembered. Dergus had told her that an ample amount of rain had come through over the last few weeks, flooding much of the land. The irony of the murky landscape unsettled Sarah. Not enough nourishment had reached this place when it needed it the most and then too much had come only stifling any potential growth.

As the sun slowly rose and burned off the morning fog, Sarah could see nothing but the black quagmire of forest floor turning to swamp ahead of her. The species of trees changed as she descended to where the woods turned into marsh. The trunks were twisted and black with spiderweb foliage lounging from the limbs creating an eerie mythical view.

Sarah wanted to avoid cutting to the road for as long as possible, but she could feel her stroomphblutel struggle with each step as they traversed further into Ranthrop's land. The ground was saturated, leaving a slimy, black, clay substance under her beast's paws. She nudged the reigns for them to turn off due south to avoid becoming stranded in the middle of the quagmire.

Sarah's stroomphblutel clearly wasn't enjoying the ride. It snorted and shook its head at the numerous reptilian creatures that inhabited the marsh. A foul stench crept into Sarah's nostrils and she discovered its source as they passed by a rotting wickril covered in black gooey mud. The wicked beast had likely ventured too far into the swamp after being chased by hunters, seeking its valuable meat. Once Sarah spotted the road ahead, she halted to survey it for passersby. Two shabby looking women shuffled along and Sarah waited until they were far from hearing distance before she made her approach.

On the road to Ranthrop's stronghold, Sarah lumbered along on her ride for a good half an hour undisturbed. She passed a young boy who didn't pay her much attention as she kept her head down and under the hood of her cloak. A few minutes after passing the boy, Sarah came to a small village called Naublock. She kept her eyes ahead as she rode through the village, but she could hear the few men mingling near the market building whispering about her curiously. Sarah pulled her cloak away from her waist and grasped her hand around the hilt of her sword. Without looking at them, their whispering ceased. After she cleared the village she glanced back down the road and was grateful to see that no one had followed.

Sarah drank some water from a skin flask tied to the stroomphblutel's saddle while she had the chance. She wasn't sure how obliging Ranthrop would be once he discovered who she was. As she neared his stronghold, she assumed the next villagers she encountered would be less intimidated than the last. As the morning sun rose, Sarah began to sweat under the cloak and wiped her brow. The road curved up ahead and she heard the sound of men laughing just in time to re-adjust her hood.

The men quieted as Sarah neared them and she knew they were watching her. She rode on, intent to pass them without a word, her eyes and head fixed downward under her hood.

"What say you there, man?" one called to her. Sarah didn't answer. There were three men and one stroomphblutel hitched to a rickety wagon.

"Ye' deaf old man?"

Sarah was in line with them now, but decided to continue her silence. Just forget about me, you thugs, she thought.

"That's a nice beast you've got there. Don't think I've seen any as good except at Groslivo's stronghold. Where'd you get a mount like that?" Another man called from the road-side. When Sarah still didn't respond she heard the dirt of the road scrape under the man's feet as he approached her. From underneath her hood she saw a filthy hand reach up to grab her stroomphblutel's reins, "Hey! I'm talking to you!" the man growled up at her.

242

With a swift pull, Sarah drew her sword from its holster and brought the tip to the man's throat. She turned her head to glare down at him as his hands went up and freed her reins. "Touch those reins again and I'll cut you another smile," she seethed.

The man gasped upon seeing Sarah was a woman. The other two men came up behind him, but stopped a few feet away as to not encourage Sarah's promise of slicing the man's throat. "She's...a woman," the first man whispered over his shoulder, hands still in the air.

"I see that," the largest of the three said giving Sarah an icy stare. "So what is a woman with a sword, alone, doing on a fine bred stroomphblutel?"

Sarah shifted her eyes to the domineering voice and did her best to maintain a display of courageous determination. "I am delivering a message to Lord Groslivo. Perhaps you will take me there to ensure he gets it," she nudged her sword ever so slightly against the cowering man's throat as she gritted out the words.

The large bossy man took a step forward, but halted at his comrade's plea, "Lunkrot, no! She's serious. I can tell," he whispered as he looked past the blade of Sarah's sword to the scowl on her face.

Lunkrot exhaled angrily and glowered back at Sarah. Apparently courtesy towards women in Farwin Wood has depleted in the last twenty years, Sarah mused as she took in the man's hostility. "And from who is this message that you're so intent on delivering you would slice poor Dony's worthless throat?" Lunkrot crossed his arms over his chest.

"House of Allister," Sarah seethed.

Dony's eyes widened even further and Lunkrot shifted, uncrossing his arms at Sarah's statement. "But...but, no one from House of Allister has been seen in Farwin Wood in nearly twenty years," Dony sputtered from where he stood below her.

Sarah reached up and yanked the hood of her cloak back with her free hand. "They have now," she barked out the words and glared down at the three of them. Dony staggered back, dazed by the affirmation. The other man did the same, retreating closer to the wagon. Lunkrot's once defiant mouth hung agape, his arms limp at his sides by the sight of Sarah's intricately braided hair running down over her shoulder, fierce grey eyes, and noble features in comparison to theirs.

"Shall we go share this news with Ranthrop before any more hooligans like you find out? I don't think he'd take too kindly if something were to happen to me," Sarah arched her brow at Lunkrot, assuming he'd be further convinced by acknowledging him as the men's leader.

Lunkrot's stunned look was depleted by a hint of anger after being sassed by her, yet not near as much hostility appeared as before. He simply waved her on and strode back to the hitched homely looking stroomphblutel by the road side. "Follow us," he grumbled.

Dony backed away slowly still staring at Sarah in awe. Does he know who I am, Sarah wondered? She sheathed her sword and pulled the cloak hood back up onto her head. Dony and the other man got in the back of the wagon that was full of sticks and vines. Lunkrot sat at the front and flicked his reins hastily to move their stroomphblutel forward. Sarah ignored the stares of the two men on the back of the wagon as she followed them into and through the next village. The morning light had found people out and about in the next village who stared at the procession as they passed through town.

As they rode on, Sarah worried less about being vigilant, content that her escort would get her to Ranthrop's stronghold, and more about her impending meeting with the man. She had a plan to get Shelby back and leave with the girl

244

unscathed, but she fumbled through her mind for an alternate solution in case that plan failed. Her display of ferocity had worked on these three bumpkins on the road, but she knew it wouldn't likely cow Ranthrop Groslivo.

Sarah was used to being pleasant, finding people the right book for a lazy afternoon of reading or a research project, not intimidating people. The closest she'd ever come to being intimidating were the icy glares she cast at Reggie Nurscher when he was fool enough to make an unwanted advance towards her. What Sarah worried most as she followed the men in the rickety wagon up to the gates of Groslivo Stronghold, was that if Netta warned the years had made Vasimus become dark and brooding, someone she'd known to be loving and pleasant, what had they done to a man like Ranthrop?

CHAPTER
TWENTY-ONE

RANTHROP GROSLIVO, Lord of the Southland Swamps and Groslivo Stronghold, let out a low growling moan as he slung his bare feet off the fur-pelt covered bed and set them on the cool stone floor of his room. His brains felt as though they were swirling inside of his skull underneath his mop of long light brown curls. He rubbed one of his mighty hands across his massive bare chest and scratched at the thin layer of hair that dusted his pectoral muscles. Even his muscles felt sore this morning after the events of last night. Ranthrop exhaled in disgust at the feel of his aging body and stood up, letting the light breeze from the window flood over his sweaty nakedness in the warm late morning air.

With heavy footsteps, Ranthrop's feet slapped against the floor as he trod over to a water basin at his wardrobe. He splashed several handfuls of the stale water onto his face and brought his head up with a shake. His bloodshot eyes peered into the mirror of his wardrobe as the water dripped from the tendrils of hair at his temples. His jaw, set firmly in its ever unenthused arch beneath the light whiskers of his trimmed beard, remained fixed in frustration as Ranthrop gazed at his rough appearance. When was the last time he'd ever drank that much beetleburry ale, he wondered.

The night before was not as much of a blur as Ranthrop had hoped it would be. He stomped around searching for clothing, recalling what had surpassed. The arrival of a gift from the Wortwart brothers of Oedher Village yesterday had disturbed his entire state. The sight of the angelic wisp of a girl who called herself Shelby had unsettled something within him.

The brothers had brought Shelby there to tempt him, he knew this well enough. Surely she should have (although she was much too young for his tastes), but there was something too hauntingly familiar about her to even think of dreaming about what she would be like when she became a more fitting age for his forty years. Ranthrop had become angered by his feelings upon trying to speak to her as he found the more he looked at her, the more she reminded him of Deronda Daundecort in all her young beauty. The innocence of Shelby's age brought Ranthrop's mind back to a time when everything in his world was pleasant and had promise. After having lived so bitterly the last eighteen years, these feelings did not settle with him naturally.

Just when he'd found his voice would soften to speak to the girl, the anger in Ranthrop would creep up and his next query to Shelby would come out seething with anger, leaving the girl cowering in silence, her big blue eyes staring at him in question. Seeing her fear of him only increased his temper, yet the sight of her at ease reminded him of the face he should have woken up to each morning for the last two decades. Ranthrop hadn't been able to stand it and had Shelby sent away to a locked room until he could compose himself. He'd spent the rest of the evening trying to do so and when he realized composure was not likely to come, he decided for drinking away his agitation to numbness with the company of some of the women who frequented the stronghold for him and his men. When the women left him for the evening he hoped the final descent into a drunken, whoring oblivion would find his mind erased of the new developments come morning. Oh, how wrong he had been.

Ranthrop shoved his massive calves into some boots and thought on the matter in spite of himself. Perhaps he would make this girl his personal servant and she could grow to trust him, while he could grow to disassociate her from his memories of Deronda. Would that be possible on his part, he wondered. She truly could be a gift if it were – if he could grow to find enjoyment in her presence as he had whenever Deronda had simply entered a room.

Ranthrop sighed as the tight leather boots settled around his legs. It was more than that, he knew. His bitterness stretched beyond having Deronda taken from him. She had been incredibly lovely indeed, yet losing the promise of uniting his lands with the North and pulling him up to the heightened level of nobility the Daundecorts enjoyed – that could never be remedied. His people needed full access to the Northern lands to truly prosper. Losing Deronda had not only slighted the possibility of his personal happiness, but also his pride as a leader for what their union would have brought Groslivo lands.

Somehow improving his personal happiness didn't seem all that fulfilling now, Ranthrop thought as he yanked one of his thin black shirts over his head. The Wortwarts were sorely mistaken if they hoped offering Shelby would alleviate the harrowing war between him and Vasimus. Ranthrop sighed and rubbed his puffy eyelids. He resolved that finding a place for Shelby in his household might at least improve his mood if he could learn more about her. If he couldn't learn to disassociate her from his memory of Deronda, however, then he would send her packing far away from Farwin Wood. Lord help him if Vasimus ever saw the girl's face and was reminded of Deronda as well.

A loud rap at the door broke his thoughts and he gladly turned to call over his shoulder. A dark haired man with heavy stubble, clad in Ranthrop's colors strode into the room. "You are awake, my Lord?"

"Hrmph. Yes. I am *alive* Varmeer," Ranthrop ran his hands up his face and through his hair as he stood up.

"Sir, there is a messenger to see you," Varmeer rested a hand on his sword hilt as he looked anxiously at Ranthrop's turned back.

"Well, send them in," Ranthrop grunted and tucked his loose shirt into his snug buckskin colored pants.

"Sir, I've...instructed them to wait in the great room," Varmeer shifted from one foot to the other.

Ranthrop turned around and studied his personal guard and oldest friend with a shrewd eye. Varmeer was not one to worry easily and Ranthrop noticed as the stoic man shifted his weight. Ranthrop would meet a messenger anywhere unless it required a formal setting or extra guards. Those types of messages did not come frequently as they had in the beginning of the war when demands and negotiations had been attempted.

"Where does this message come from?" Ranthrop fastened his belt and holstered his sword.

"The escort said they claimed from...House of Allister," Varmeer watched Ranthrop's expression turn to the same one of bewilderment his own face held.

Next Varmeer heard the swift inhale of air through Ranthrop's flared nostrils. The towering man's chest puffed up under his tunic and any sign of his hangover quickly left his appearance in that moment. Ranthrop's eyes darted back to Varmeer with intensity.

"Has the gate been locked behind them?"

"Yes. I ordered it as soon as I heard where the message was from and they were safely inside." Varmeer's posture straightened slightly, proud of his vigilance.

"Good," Ranthrop grumbled softly and slapped a hand on Varmeer's shoulder as he headed swiftly to the door. He stopped abruptly, wondering what had surpassed to cause a message from House of Allister to come for him after having heard nothing from that family in nearly twenty years. "Where is the girl?"

Varmeer stopped quickly behind Ranthrop so he wouldn't slam into him. "She...she is still in the guest wing. The door is still locked. I checked it this morning."

"Did she tell you where she was from or mention anything of the Allisters?" Ranthrop looked off in thought.

"No, sir. Only the same as she told you—Salem. Some place called Salem, but no one has heard of it from what I've gathered," Varmeer studied Ranthrop's face.

Ranthrop turned and went out the door with a grunt. His conscience didn't need this much frustration in the span of twenty-four hours. Was his paranoia getting the better of him, he wondered, worrying that this girl had something to do with the arrival of a House of Allister messenger. Had this messenger been to Daundecort Hall as well? As far as Ranthrop knew, Vasimus had never heard again from anyone of House of Allister or Ranthrop's spies would have informed him directly.

Varmeer took his place next to the large sculpted wood chair that sat on the stone mezzanine level of the great room. Far down at the end of the great room, the cloaked messenger stood silently waiting. Ranthrop's guards had been summoned and five stood on each side of the great room in the wings that aligned the center. The guards stared out across the room at each other under their own bloodshot eyes that matched their crimson tunics.

Varmeer wished the guard looked a little more awe inspiring this morning, given the origin of the message that would be received, however he was simply grateful they'd roused as quickly as they had after last night's brouhaha with Ranthrop. With a quiet sigh after the silent inspection, Varmeer unsheathed his sword, held it high, and then brought the blade down to the stone floor with a resounding thump. The guards drew their feet together all at once and slammed their own sword tips to the floor in front of them.

"Lord Ranthrop Groslivo, ruler of the free Southlands and all its peoples!" Varmeer bellowed the customary cry he had not called in so long through the high ceilinged room. The messenger stood statuesque, seemingly unaffected by the loud sound.

Ranthrop's feet pounded in from the side entrance, his chest out as he strode to his chair. He stopped before his seat and squinted to spy the messenger at the end of the room. Swiftly brushing the ends of his tunic back, he sat down against the high back of the chair, letting his large arms come down to rest on the thick armrests. "Approach!" Ranthrop barked so his voice would carry down to where the messenger stood.

Sarah walked slowly out of respect as was appropriate, but ensured her steps were purposeful, as her dark cloak swept against the floor around her. She'd taken care to tuck her braid behind her back before Ranthrop entered. She wanted to try and get Shelby without exposing her identity. Whether it would be demanded of her or not, Sarah would reveal herself if necessary, but she was still unsure if doing so would secure her plan. She stopped just below the three steps that led up to the mezzanine where Ranthrop sat mightily on his throne, but kept her head lowered enough that her face was not visible under her hood.

"State your purpose," Ranthrop called down to Sarah, his voice held the same annoyed tone that she remembered from her last meeting with him so many years ago.

"Lord Groslivo, I bring you a message from House of Allister," Sarah spoke loudly to ensure her voice carried up to Ranthrop and to give her house the sound of might a noble family would carry.

"House of Allister?" Ranthrop cooed in thought. "That is a house that has been spoken much of in the lands, yet ironically..." Ranthrop looked around to Varmeer and his men, "no one has near as smelled an Allister in almost twenty years! And now...a woman, I presume, comes to me with a message from these illusive Allisters. What business could an Allister possibly have to honor my stronghold with?" Ranthrop's tone sneered the words. He cast a brief glower at Varmeer for not informing him the messenger was a woman, to which Varmeer let out a minuscule shrug. Ranthrop would know a woman's figure from a mile away and it was not common that a woman brought messages, let alone from high borne households. His curiosity made his breath quicken, but he forced himself to remain firmly seated in a ruse of calm authoritative demeanor against his chair.

"Your Lordship, a young girl was lost from Allister lands and we have learned that she was brought to your stronghold...as a peace offering gift from the Wortwarts of Oedher Village," Sarah's voice trailed up to Ranthrop's ears. His annoyance grew as he tried to view her face from his vantage point and absorbed the claim she made.

Blast it! He knew this girl was not from Farwin Wood. Had he not gone off so quickly to imbibe himself, he might have progressed further into discovering her background. Who was she that House of Allister had suddenly appeared, he wondered.

Ranthrop let out a grunt, "As you say, she was a gift. If she is simply 'of Allister lands' and has entered our *war torn* domain, then her fate will be ours to determine."

Sarah tried not to let her frustrated inhalation show as her chest rose upon hearing his words. "Lord Groslivo, that is why I am here. House of Allister kindly requests that you relinquish her to me so that I may return with her to her homeland."

Ranthrop blinked several times at the request as he leaned forward, then he threw his head back and let out a hearty cynical laugh that echoed through the room. He slapped his hand on his armrest and glanced from Varmeer to his guards. Sarah heard some soft chuckles behind her and knew that the guardsmen were joining in her mockery upon Ranthrop's request, although she still could only view his boots from where he sat perched.

"*Kindly requests*? House of Allister *kindly requests*? Ah! Well, then, kindly take them my answer. No!" Ranthrop let out another chuckle. "Is that all then?"

"No, your lordship," Sarah didn't hide her disdain as she spoke this time. "House of Allister offers this request with the knowledge that House of Daundecort is not yet aware of this situation. Should such news reach Lord Vasimus, that your lordship willingly detained a young lady of the Allister court, he might be inclined to view such an action as an open invitation to retaliate."

Ranthrop's laughter ceased and his fingers dug into the arms of his chair. He leaned forward, eyes glowering and jaw muscles twitching. The audacity, he thought! Ranthrop inhaled to consider his retort, but could not keep his feelings from flowing freely. "Retaliate? Retaliate? Ha! Vasimus has been retaliating for twenty years without provocation! And now, Allisters have the audacity to bring me idle threats over vague claims of some unknown little court mistress! Who is she that it was so worth the trouble of an Allister messenger appearing to request her return? There is only one Allister left that I know of and if he lives, he will get nothing from me! Nothing! I'll have her head before I release her to Richard Allister!"

"She is not of Lord Richard's court, your lordship."

"Ha! Then what care I or Vasimus, for that matter, if a House of Allister request be honored," Ranthrop scoffed. "Even Vasimus wouldn't be fool enough to broaden this feud at the sake of protecting extended Allister cousins he's likely never heard of."

"Because she is from the court of Lady *Sarah* Allister," Sarah's flat words quickly responded.

Ranthrop's throat tightened at the mention of Sarah Allister. He didn't like to be reminded of *her* even more than he did of Deronda Daundecort after the hand he'd played in Lady Sarah's fateful death. The thought of Sarah's hair slipping through his fingers as he forced her head down into the River Duke still haunted him.

Ranthrop didn't know how she'd been lost from his grip that day. He'd only meant, even in his rage, to hold her under the water for a brief moment to taunt Vasimus. The next thing he'd known as he stood glaring at Vasimus across the river bank, was pulling his empty hand up and staring down into the flowing water with no sign of Sarah to be seen. Eighteen years of torment over a woman he hadn't meant to kill who had died as the result of his anguish over another woman who also shouldn't have died. Ranthrop was lucky he hadn't gone insane. Each attack from Vasimus and his men had been enough to harness his guilt into justifiable anger as Ranthrop knew in his heart he hadn't committed murder and thus wasn't deserving of Vasimus' level of wrath.

Pulling his mind back to the cloaked woman before him, Ranthrop narrowed his eyes. He knew just how long it had been since the fateful day that began this war. Whoever had sent this woman to place demands on him clearly didn't, even he could see that despite how much he'd drank the night before. "This mistress Shelby…could not possibly be of Lady Sarah's court, madam," Ranthrop's words came out forcibly calm. "Lady Sarah has been dead nearly twenty years now and this girl…has not even seen her twentieth year. Is this some kind of cowardly ploy by Richard! Does he take me for a fool? Is he such a coward that he would hide behind his sister again?" Ranthrop's voice grew as he stood from his chair, fists clenched at his sides. "Will this disgrace continue while he hides behind her even in death?"

"Your Lord, I assure you…she is from the court…of Lady Sarah," Sarah stated more gently.

"That's not possible!" Ranthrop growled.

Sarah raised a hand slowly to her hood. She saw a glint and the motion of Varmeer take a step closer to Ranthrop as she did. With a swift pull, she drew the cloak back from her head. Sarah shook the loose strands of hair from her eyes and let her braid fall over the front of her shoulder as she raised her head up to look into Ranthrop's dark eyes. "It's actually… quite possible…Ranthrop."

Sarah took in Ranthrop's aged face as she watched him stand before her with his mouth open. She never would have admitted it aloud, but he had always been somewhat ruggedly handsome. Even in her youth, however, he had been the enemy as soon as one of his men's arrows had pierced Deronda's heart. She'd only met him once after he'd found her while looking for Richard. The two days she'd spent in his stronghold had not been pleasant due to her worry over what would transpire once Vasimus learned she'd been taken and come for her, which he had done.

Ranthrop stood before Sarah now much the same in appearance as he had the last time she saw him. He was bigger if that were possible, likely grown in strength from years of doing battle. There were tiny scars on his face and forearms where his sleeves were pulled up to the elbow. His light brown hair seemed shaggier in appearance and there were lines around his eyes that had not been present on his once smooth bronzed skin.

"Varmeer," Ranthrop croaked as he blinked at Sarah.

"Yes...sir," Varmeer stammered still looking at Sarah himself.

"Am I seeing a ghost?"

"Nay, sir. I think not," Varmeer uttered. Varmeer had been a young guard at the time of Sarah's death. Ranthrop's father's old guard had served as the young lord's personal guard at the time, but Varmeer distinctly remembered the beautiful eyes and auburn brown hair of the woman who'd unhappily sat next to Ranthrop at his table for two days before she disappeared under the foam of the River Duke when the Daundecorts had come to retrieve her.

Ranthrop staggered slowly down the steps to Sarah, never taking his eyes from her face. He stopped a foot in front of her and studied her with his eyes — her nose, her chin, her hair.

Sarah looked up the foot that he towered over her and tried to remain calm under his intense observation. "It is I, Ranthrop," Sarah spoke softly. "I...woke up far down the river and then...found my way home. I had to return to make sure my brother made it back to Blinney safely."

Ranthrop's mouth still hung open in disbelief. He reached out one of his rough hands and touched Sarah's jaw line. "I would not have killed you," was all he could manage in a hoarse voice over the shock of feeling her in the flesh — alive.

"I believe you," she reached up to touch his hand with hers, but he quickly pulled his away upon the contact.

"And Vasimus? Has Vasimus known all this time?" Ranthrop's eyes went wild again.

"No! No, he hasn't. He still doesn't," Sarah stepped closer to him as his face changed from tense to confused. "I...knew he would not be the same after Deronda died and I had obligations in my own house after what transpired. I could not come back. However, I did not know that *not* returning would lead to the destruction that has happened here. I swear, I had no idea until recently," Sarah's look was one of pleading now.

Ranthrop relaxed a little and walked back to his chair for a moment to think. "Then your threats before of Vasimus fighting to reclaim your mistress for you...you have no idea if he would do such a thing to simply honor your memory?" Ranthrop arched a brow at her.

"His guards watch House of Allister in Oedher Village. This I'm sure you know." Ranthrop merely nodded once. "Well, I fear my arrival there will have caused them to alert him of my presence. I would not taunt you with empty threats, Ranthrop. I want peace in Farwin Wood more than anyone," Sarah assured him with conviction.

"Fear? How is it that you've come to fear someone you once loved so deeply? Or perhaps you have seen your dear Vasimus already, after all?" Ranthrop let out a chuckle and smirked.

Sarah swallowed at hearing another proclamation of Vasimus' new character she had yet to learn herself. "I have heard...that he has changed. I have heard how this war has changed a lot of people. I am simply asking for you to return Shelby to me before Vasimus learns of it and of me being here. If he should find that I am, indeed, alive...well, I think it would be in your best interest that I am nowhere near your stronghold. The people of Farwin Wood don't need to suffer anymore vengeance."

"I see you don't hesitate to add threats, even if they are not empty," Ranthrop gritted out realizing her declaration held merit. If Vasimus learned that Sarah was alive and she was in Ranthrop's stronghold, he would gather the whole of his army and storm the place at any cost. Good heavens, would Vasimus be crazed enough to think that Ranthrop had somehow kept Sarah there alive all these years, under wraps? Suddenly, Ranthrop was quite furious that Sarah had so boldly come to his stronghold. He knew he'd been outwitted by the predicament she'd put him in. "If you want peace, Sarah, how could you have come here?"

"Ranthrop, Shelby is dear to me. I could not let her be lost forever. I beg you. Let me take her and I will go as quickly and undetected as I came," Sarah pleaded. She didn't want to stay in Farwin Wood any longer than she had to after seeing how the thought of Vasimus learning of her arrival had unsettled Ranthrop. She needed to get back to Allister Hall before his men had time to send word that someone had arrived. In the least, she needed to get as far away from Ranthrop's land without Vasimus ever finding out, in case he was still committed to avenge anything his nemesis did to her.

Ranthrop stood again and began to pace in front of his chair. He knew he needed her gone, and Shelby as well. The new information of Sarah's survival had his mind reeling at what he could benefit from the news for himself or his people. "You have no intention then of seeing Vasimus?"

"I did not come here to see him. My only intention was to help Shelby," Sarah started, realizing she hadn't given the possibility much thought. "Now that I have seen Farwin Wood, I believe if I could see him and speak to him, that if it could help to end this war, I would, but…"

"But you fear your lover may not greet you with open arms after learning you did not return to him?" Ranthrop stopped pacing to give her a pointed look.

"No, it's not that," Sarah wrung her hands. "Richard left Blinney upon our return due to his shame, and he never returned. Vasimus would understand that I had to stay in Blinney."

"What then?" Ranthrop scowled at hearing of more cowardice from Richard, but wanted to let Sarah finish.

"Ranthrop, I have been gone almost twenty years. I don't know all that has happened between the two of you. I cannot ask Vasimus to end a war if I know you have no intention of ending it as well," she held her palms upward with emphasis.

"Me? I wouldn't be in this war if it weren't for Vasimus!" Ranthrop threw his arms up and picked up the speed of his pacing. Sarah's silence after his comment ate away at him, knowing it meant she didn't agree. He stopped pacing and looked at her, "You must know that! If only Vasimus knew I did not want to lose Deronda either. I killed the man who struck that arrow myself!"

Sarah winced upon hearing the violence that had occurred after her departure. She was also shocked to discover that Ranthrop had disposed of the man who killed Deronda. "Ranthrop...do you not think there would have been war if that arrow...had hit its intended target?" Sarah asked softly to remind Ranthrop he'd intended to have Richard killed.

"Your brother deserved to die for coming between the promises of others! Look at what it has done to the people of the Southlands! We could have been united with the North through economies and agriculture. Were there ever an army beyond Farwin Wood to come through now, both of our houses would be wiped out because of what your brother started!" spit flew from Ranthrop's mouth as he ranted.

Sarah glanced to Varmeer who looked painfully from her to Ranthrop. She could tell the man knew she spoke reason, although Ranthrop didn't want to accept it. Sarah remained silent again as he fumed before her, pacing back and forth. Hopefully he would come to his senses. After a few moments his pacing slowed and he stopped. Hands on hips, he inhaled gruffly and looked at her. "I demand you request of your brother to meet me for a public duel. If you promise to honor this request...I will declare peace if Vasimus will."

"Ranthrop...I would gladly honor your request, but I do not see my brother. I did not lie when I told you he has left Blinney. I don't even know where he is," Sarah lied convincingly. That's not entirely true, she thought. He's somewhere in Europe, I know that, but I'm not even going to let on about cell phones to this guy. "If he had stayed in Blinney...I would have returned to Vasimus," Sarah added, admitting that part very well could have been true to a younger version of herself.

After a while of muttering under his breath and shaking his head, Ranthrop spoke. "And now you leave me no choice to see if you are telling the truth, for you know I cannot keep you here. Are all Allisters this conniving?"

"Ranthrop..." Sarah was growing impatient with the slurs of past sins. "I am only telling you what we both know will occur if I do not leave here. As for my brother, I am sorry he came between you and Deronda, but she would not have loved you if you had killed Richard. He is a coward for not facing you, but you are a fool for not allowing Deronda to love whom she wanted. What has become of Farwin Wood is the result of the vengeance of two men who could have altered this history by simply accepting both their losses for their people's sake."

Ranthrop's fists were clenched again as he looked down at Sarah and listened to the insult of his character. "It was my duty to defend my honor. If I had not, how would my people respect me as a leader? Would I not have appeared weak to let the smear of a broken betrothal go without reparation?"

"I will speak to Vasimus as an offer of reparation for you. I will make it known that I am alive, but know this...respect from your people will only come if I carry with me your promise for peace to him as well."

Ranthrop then stepped back down the stairs of the mezzanine and stood before her. "You'd best pray then, that in learning I did not cause your death, your former lover is as reasonable as I. You're lucky the years have been kind to you," Ranthrop eyed her up and down. "Let us hope it sways him in his decision at the sight of you. My men will take you to the edge of Naublock and from there you can return to Oedher alone."

Sarah gazed up at Ranthrop her mouth agape at his submission for her safe release, yet he still had not answered her request. She still had not seen Shelby. She watched him look at her with cold eyes, watching her squirm in worry. "Get the girl," he finally called to Varmeer.

CHAPTER
TWENTY-TWO

RICKY RUBBED his face as he sat on the edge of the bed. His head felt foggy as he looked around the castle-themed room realizing all had not been a dream the night before. Steadying himself, he rose from the bed and swore he didn't look forward to turning twenty-one if this is what a hangover would feel like. "Beetleburry," Ricky muttered aloud. "It better not be made out of beetles," he added as he hobbled towards a dresser with a large bowl on top of it next to a pitcher. He'd vaguely recalled the sound of the woman named Netta come in earlier and inform him that his "wash tub" was set up for him.

Blinking down at the water pitcher, Ricky sighed realizing this would be his shower for the day. If he'd thought Aunt Sarah's store and Blinney Lane were more archaic than his father's flat in New York, then he had no words for what Allister Hall and its accommodations were. Ricky groaned at the ache in his head and poured water from the pitcher into the bowl. He glanced at the cracked mirror to see he still wore his father's old Medieval getup. He was going to have to have a serious talk with old Dad when he got home…well, after he got out of the book and then back home. Ricky splashed some water on his face at the urge to get downstairs and find out if there was news of Shelby and Sarah.

A far off thud resounded somewhere deeper within the hall and Ricky brought his head up to listen. He heard a muffled voice and footsteps coming from the stairwell that led to the hallway outside of his room. Another slam resounded and Ricky jumped as it echoed, knowing his aunt's bedroom door had been thrust open across the hallway. Then he distinctly heard a deep commanding voice yell, "Who is here Dergus? I was told that someone claiming to be Sarah was at Allister Hall!"

"She's not here, Lord Vasimus! She'll be back. I promise you," Dergus' voice could be heard as it neared Ricky's door along with the sound of heavy footsteps. Ricky turned and braced himself against the dresser as he watched the shadows dance in the light under the doorway of his room. The door rocketed open and slammed against the wall.

Ricky caught his breath in his throat at the sight of a giant man who stepped into the room with a glowering intensity in his eyes which fixed on Ricky. The man's hair was long and black, hanging just below his shoulders in waves. It dusted the top of two shiny silver floral epaulets that rested on his wide shoulders, holding a dusky blue cloak that flowed out behind him. The man's matching shirt clung against his arm indicating a bulging bicep. The fabric pressed against his skin where his arm outstretched. A clenched fist held the door open in its place. He looked at Ricky with a tight-lipped expression behind the covering of dark whiskers on his lower jaw; every muscle in his face clenched.

"Holy shit," Ricky whispered.

263

"Lord Vasimus," Dergus' voice came from behind the man. "This is…"

"Richard?" Vasimus uttered in a barely audible tone so different from his last. His face now stunned as he slowly stepped further into the room.

"No," Dergus chuckled. "Thought so myself at first." Finally Dergus came around Vasimus and Ricky could see him smiling at the massive lord's side. "This is Lord Richard's son…Ricky."

"A son?" Vasimus' surprise was evident as he quickly glanced to Dergus for confirmation before looking back at Ricky.

Ricky straightened up hastily from his cowered stance against the dresser as Vasimus stepped lightly towards him. He cleared his throat and tugged his mussed vest down. "How do you do?" Ricky managed, wondering if the greeting was appropriate. He couldn't believe he'd actually used those words for once in his life.

"Your father…married?"

Ricky arched his brow at the question. Well how the hell do you think I got here, Ricky felt like saying. Suddenly he remembered the fairy tale that Netta, Dergus, and Sarah had regaled to him the night before. He glanced down in thought for a moment and then decided upon a simple, "Yes." I bet they don't have divorce in Farwin Wood if dudes go pouting around over lost fiancés for twenty years, Ricky prided himself on his quick thinking.

Vasimus merely gave a curt nod after a pause. Just as he neared Ricky, he diverted his steps and turned to pace around the bed. He looked about the room in thought and then back at Ricky once the boy was in his view again. "You may leave us master Dergus," Vasimus nodded at the old man.

Dergus looked to Ricky for a second with a curt smile meant to be reassuring, then nodded at Vasimus and retreated for the door. He left without another glance and shut the door behind him leaving Ricky aware he was now alone with this herculean man.

"Rick...y," Vasimus muttered. "That's an uncommon name."

"It's Richard...after my father, but everyone calls me Ricky," he followed Vasimus' careful prowling steps from where he stood.

"Best not to be known for your father, I suppose," Vasimus nodded at the thought, hands clasped behind his back as he stared at the floor.

Why I'd pop you if you weren't twice my size, Ricky thought at the rub about his father. Ricky didn't have the best relationship with his dad, but he sure wouldn't let anyone slander him for something Ricky didn't view as harshly as the people here did. This poor Deronda woman must have been miserable if all the men in her life were as gruff and unpleasant as this Vasimus guy, Ricky thought. No wonder she fell for Dad.

"Then I presume you have traveled here with your mother," Vasimus sounded like he sighed out the words.

"Uh...no," Ricky let out. What am I supposed to tell him? I don't know if I want Aunt Sarah running into this guy again, past love or not.

"Don't tell me your father has come? Who is this Lady Sarah that claimed to be so to my guards?" Vasimus snapped his head back around and his sharp words caused Ricky to shudder once more.

"No...my father hasn't been to Blinney in years," Ricky tried to recall the story of what happened in Farwin Wood and relay only information that would benefit everyone's situation.

"And the woman my guards saw here? Do you have a sister?"

Ricky swallowed. What if this guy hung around long enough for Aunt Sarah to return? Lying hadn't done Ricky much good the last time he tried it. Spooky or not, Netta swore this Vasimus guy still treated them well. Here goes nothing, Ricky sighed. "No. I am an only child. I came here with…my aunt. Aunt Sarah."

Ricky didn't think it was possible for such a rigid and ferocious looking man to become so drastically weak and limp in every fiber of his body, but that is just what happened to Vasimus' constitution upon hearing Ricky's words. He staggered a half-step and clasped his iron fist around one of the high bed posts to brace himself.

"Sarah lives?" Vasimus' words came out as a whisper.

Ricky could only nod as he watched Vasimus process the information. The man's free hand came up to his chest and he gripped a handful of his tunic tightly, staring down at the floor with his mouth agape. Crap! What have I done, Ricky wondered. "She…she told me what happened here, but…she had to go back to Blinney to…take care of things there," Ricky offered. If Aunt Sarah was lucky enough to find Shelby, Ricky didn't want her coming back to be thrown in shackles or whatever this guy was capable of doing. Would he be angry that she hadn't returned to Farwin Wood? There's no way Vasimus could understand why she couldn't, and Ricky wasn't about to explain it to him, barely understanding it himself.

"Why? Why did she not send word?" Vasimus looked up at Ricky with hurt in his eyes.

Ricky just shook his head dumbly with his mouth ajar. "I…I don't know. No one ever told me about what happened here until recently. I…I'm sorry. I'm sorry about your sister," Ricky fumbled to find the right words.

Vasimus inhaled and looked away. He let his hands fall to his sides again and began another steady bout of pacing. "Where is she?"

"I don't know. She rode out this morning. I don't know when she'll be back," this much was true, Ricky worried at the possibility.

Vasimus looked at Ricky again and then strode to the door, forgetting the boy. He yanked it back open with ease and walked across the hall. Ricky blinked after him unsure what the man was feeling now. Damn it, why did I tell him? See! Lying isn't always a bad thing, Ricky mentally scoffed as he hurried after Vasimus.

Vasimus walked into Sarah's room and stopped before her bed. He stared down at the pile of clothing she'd left folded there and then sat down next to it, never taking his eyes from it. He lifted a hand to touch the fabric of her dress as Ricky looked on nervously from the doorway. "Did she marry as well? Like your father?" Vasimus spoke without looking at Ricky, his jaw clenched as he barely grazed the dress with a finger tip.

Ricky let out a soft chuckle at the thought of Aunt Sarah being married, but then stifled it with a cough when Vasimus shot his stare at him. "No. There was never anyone." Ricky thought of Henry for a moment and wondered if Vasimus acted towards Sarah the way the delivery man did. Vasimus clearly felt a sense of possession for Sarah that was nothing like how Henry behaved. Truth be told, the level of flirtation between Sarah and Henry was so sad, nothing would likely ever come of it. "She lives alone," Ricky muttered the words as pathetically as his aunt's life truly seemed in his opinion.

The tension drained a little from Vasimus' face as he looked down blankly now at the little pile of clothing. "Is she...happy?"

"Happy?" Ricky sighed at the question. "Well, I don't know really...I don't see her much. I live...far away from Blinney," Ricky cleared his throat.

"You don't know your own aunt?" Vasimus queried, but there didn't appear to be any hostility in his words for once since Ricky had met him. He simply wanted to know something about Sarah. That fact was evident.

Ricky shifted under his weight and picked at a splinter in the door. "She...she always seemed happy to see me," Ricky truly gave the idea thought, recalling the times he had visited her and how she'd laugh and hug him. It made him feel bitter at their much less personal reunion of this summer. "But no... mostly she's always seemed...kind of sad, I guess," Ricky stared at the floor now realizing a little more clearly what his aunt's life had been like. He glanced back up to Vasimus then and saw that the lines around the man's eyes and mouth were drooped in his own expression of sorrow.

"When do you plan to leave Farwin Wood?" Vasimus cleared his throat.

"Hopefully today or tomorrow," Ricky said too quickly and instantly felt embarrassed by his desire to flee the land.

Vasimus simply nodded and took another ragged breath. "Will you leave me for a moment, Lord Ricky?"

The sound of a title before his name and kind tone in Vasimus' voice took Ricky aback. He looked at Vasimus as the man sat with his hands resting on his knees, a look of pain on his dark whisker-covered face. The relief of being dismissed tore Ricky from the man's anguished face and he backed out the door, pulling it closed behind him. Ricky sighed once he was in the hallway. "Man, this place is too intense," he muttered. He spun around and narrowed his eyes, now remembering that Dergus had let Vasimus in for the rude awakening. Ricky hurried down the stairs to give the old man a piece of his mind and find out when his aunt would be back.

Once the door closed, Vasimus let out a long ragged breath to quash the pain in his chest. He'd nearly come undone at hearing the boy confirm Sarah lived. With shaking hands he gathered up her dress and crumpled it against him, bringing his face down into the fabric to stifle an agonizing sound from his lungs. Vasimus felt tears in his eyes against the fabric at the familiar scent of Sarah. Slowly he brought the dress away from his face in his shame. Did she even feel the same about him anymore, he wondered. The boy said she'd never married, that she lived alone, and that she was sad, but were all those indications of her longing for him? Why hadn't she come back or at least sent word that she survived? She had to know the anguish he'd gone through in thinking she'd died in the River Duke that day.

Vasimus lowered the dress to his lap, but still held it firmly in his grip. He didn't want to let it go, as though doing so would allow Sarah to slip away from him again. He growled at the tightness in his throat and blinked through the water stinging his eyes. Something clanked beneath the folds of the dress and he lifted the fabric to see Sarah's bracelet fall into his lap. Vasimus reached out carefully and picked it up to study all of the baubles fastened to it.

She'd kept it, he thought as he rotated the cuff through his fingers. All these years and she still has it. The idea that she still thought of him made him smile. He brushed his hand over a small silver key, and then a little white pearl. Vasimus stopped turning the leather when the small golden ring flopped down over his finger — the ring he had given to Sarah. He stared at it and remembered the day he gave it to her. He recalled the night they'd exchanged their feelings. "Let it serve as a reminder that I am always with you," he had told her upon giving her the ring. The tension in Vasimus' chest came back at the thought of how long it had been since he'd seen Sarah. She'd carried this ring knowing he lived, but he had carried only the memory of her.

Vasimus yanked the ring off the bracelet and stared at it. "No more, Sarah," he whispered. He tossed the clothing back to the bed and set the bracelet onto them. Vasimus stood up and looked down at the ring between his thumb and forefinger. "If you want the promise of my love furthermore, you'll have to face me...just once my dear," Vasimus said to the ring. He tucked it into the pouch on his belt and looked back at the few possessions in the room.

There was nothing there he wanted. There was no Sarah. He wanted physical proof that she was back in Farwin Wood — he wanted to see her face, her eyes, and her hair. He wanted to hear her voice tell him that she had loved him all these years. Mostly, Vasimus felt foolish knowing that she was out in Farwin Wood likely seeing how the years of war had decayed the place she claimed to love so much. What would make her want to stay now? He wasn't the bright-eyed, silky-skinned young man he'd once been. Vasimus swallowed at the thought Sarah would find him too altered, too different from the memory she carried with the ring. He walked swiftly from the room, his hand tightly grasped over the pouch that held their aged promises.

CHAPTER
TWENTY-THREE

SARAH AND Shelby rode in silence on the stroomphblutel between the four man escort Ranthrop had sent to see them safely past Naublock village. Once they reached the end of the village, Varmeer halted the procession and turned on his mount to look at Sarah. Shelby sat astride their beast; her arms wrapped around Sarah's waist and peered over at him from underneath the hood of Sarah's cloak, which she now wore. Shelby wasn't dressed like everyone else in Farwin Wood with her barefoot striped stocking feet and short ruffled skirt. She'd gladly taken the cloak from Sarah upon seeing her to hide from the staring eyes of Ranthrop and his men.

"Lady Sarah, this is where we will leave you," Varmeer called.

"Thank you, Varmeer," Sarah answered flatly. She bore no hostility towards the man, but the anxiety of the morning that was now stretching into the stifling humid early afternoon in the swamp had left her feeling ragged. She would not be at peace until she had Shelby back at Allister Hall and was assured Ricky had stayed clear of any trouble. Sarah turned forward again and reached for the reins, but stopped at the sound of Varmeer's voice.

"Lady Sarah...for what it's worth, you were brave to return to Farwin Wood...no matter when you may have returned," Varmeer called from his mount and added a curt nod to the sentiment. Sarah just eyed him in wonder at the compliment.

"I'm not brave. I just did what I had to do."

"Then do what you said you would and speak to Vasimus. Ranthrop does not want this war any more than the rest of us, whether he will admit to it or not."

Sarah's stroomphblutel shifted its weight underneath her and Shelby, sensing her agitation. She glanced back at Shelby who peered up at her from behind her shoulder and then turned back to Varmeer. "I will send a message to him. If he comes to find me, I will speak with him, on that you have my word."

"My Lady," Varmeer's expression changed to one of coddling, "he will find you, message or not. When you see him, you'll decide how brave you really are." With that Varmeer turned away and signaled to the other guards to follow him. Sarah watched them ride back towards the village with a perplexed look on her face.

"Sarah?" Shelby finally spoke softly once the men were out of sight.

Sarah glanced back and smiled sympathetically at the poor girl whom she'd barely been able to speak a word to since being reunited. Sarah had told her not to speak until they were alone and that she would explain everything later. Luckily Shelby had been wise and complacent enough to comply. She'd sat silently behind Sarah the entire ride from Groslivo Stronghold until now. Sarah reached back and squeezed Shelby's hand. "Yes, dear?"

"We're...we're in that book...the one Ricky gave me. Aren't we?" Shelby spoke hesitantly, afraid Sarah might deny the claim and think her insane.

"Yes," Sarah admitted, still clasping her hand. "I'm so sorry. I told Ricky to never touch that book. At least you're easier to convince of its powers than he was."

"He's here? Ricky's here...in Farwin Wood?"

"Yes. I have a home here. I've left him back there with my house workers and that's where we'll go now and then return to Blinney Lane, to get you back home." Sarah turned back around then and cracked the reins to start them moving down the road.

"Sarah...this place. It's not...exactly like I pictured it would be from what I read in the book," Shelby's voice floated over Sarah's shoulder.

"I know," Sarah mumbled in guilt. "Hopefully, that will change." Sarah explained everything that Shelby needed to know on the long ride back to Allister Hall. The task was much simpler than it had been with Ricky. Shelby didn't stop to question anything Sarah told her, only listened intently and her silence made Sarah glad that the girl trusted her so deeply. How could two teenagers be so different, Sarah wondered. Shelby accepted any reality around her with an imagination as expansive as Farwin Wood, while Ricky scoffed disdain at anything new to his narrow world. One thing Sarah knew, was that sending Shelby home would be easy. Sending Ricky home, on the other hand, well, she just might have to enlist the help of Dergus to accomplish that feat.

Back at Allister Hall, Ricky paced up and down the lengthy expanse of the kitchen. He knew his aunt had told him not to discard any of his possessions, but the heat of day combined with the steam from the pot Netta was stirring over the fire pit had overheated him. Ricky tugged at the loose shirt to fan himself, and when Netta wasn't looking he'd yank the tight fitting pants away from his sweaty groin. He'd sat in the great room for a while, and when Dergus caught him peering out the window to look into the courtyard in hope of catching a glimpse of the village beyond, the old man had barked at him to stay hidden. Ricky went back to the kitchen feeling like a prisoner.

When Ricky had come down the stairs earlier that morning, before Vasimus left, he stormed into the kitchen to find Dergus laboring lazily over a bowl of something Netta had prepared. Without thinking, Ricky had barged up to the old man and lightly backhanded him across the shoulder demanding to know why he'd let Vasimus into his room. The action was deftly halted as Dergus' rough grasp clasped Ricky's wrist, twisted it, and forced him to the floor under his bent arm. "All right! All right!" Ricky whined as the pain shot up his arm and was glad when the old man finally released him.

Ricky had sat pouting on a stool in silence after that until Netta smiled and set a bowl of lumpy, leafy green mush in front of him and some bread. He ate it in spite of its lack of visual appeal and found he felt much better afterwards, the gnawing sickness of the beetleburry ale gone from him. A little while later they all turned as Vasimus' footsteps could be heard through the doorway, walking across the great room and out the door. "Well, so much for saying goodbye," Ricky had muttered. His sarcasm was met only by a "hrmph" from Dergus who'd gotten up and left to go man his post at the gate.

Another hour passed, and then another. Ricky had made about ten laps up and down the stairwell of the upper portion of the hall, coming back down to circle the great room. Finally he returned to the kitchen in the hopes that Netta was still there. He longed to hear a voice, anyone's voice, and the woman seemed to have a comforting pleasantness about her. Ricky sighed as he leaned against the doorway, so his presence would be known.

Netta laughed from where she sat peeling some bright green potato type of vegetable. "You're as patient as your father was," she smiled. Ricky just rolled his eyes, knowing the woman wasn't looking at him. He really didn't want to hear anymore about how much these strangers knew things about his father that he didn't. "Tell me, what is Lord Richard like these days?"

Ricky scoffed under his breath and walked over to take the stool across from Netta. "Lord Richard..." he lingered on the words, "well, he's very serious and short tempered."

"Doesn't sound at all like the Richard I knew," Netta raised a brow. "I guess he grew out of his youthful ways after all."

"I can't imagine him ever being carefree like you've talked about. He's...always mad at me. Nothing I do is right," Ricky grumbled and picked up a knife and a green potato.

"Well," Netta spoke in a soothing sound, "perhaps he just wants to make sure you don't make the mistakes that he did. Life isn't always easy to figure out. You try to guide the people you love as best you know how. Oh, the things I would have told those two if I had known how life would have treated them," Netta sighed referring to Richard and Sarah.

Ricky grimaced under Netta's sensible reasoning. He didn't like to give his father any credit when it was so much easier just to be angry with him. "Well, it'd be nice if he could just be my father instead of guiding me by yelling at me, considering what little I do see of him. He works and then comes home and tells me what I did wrong. How does he know what I do if he's barely ever there?"

"Maybe he's afraid of you, Ricky," Netta let another peeling fall into the bowl.

"Afraid of me? Why would you say that?"

"Maybe he's afraid because he doesn't know you, and the only thing he knows to do is to teach you not to become the kind of man you shouldn't," Netta glanced up briefly.

Ricky just stared at the old woman. Why did he even get into this conversation if he never liked to hear what people had to say about his relationship with his father? Ricky wanted to be a good person, he did. He just wished his father would see that too. "Do they pay you extra for this kind of wisdom?" Ricky arched a brow. Netta just chuckled at him.

The creak of the great room doors echoed into the kitchen. Ricky and Netta looked up at each other. They listened and the sound of voices and footsteps soon followed. Both of them abruptly sidled off of their stools and hurried to the kitchen doorway.

"Ricky?" Ricky heard his aunt's voice and felt anxious to see her face. He rushed to the doorway and walked through into the cool air of the great room, but stopped when the sight of light blonde hair caught his attention.

Ricky held his breath at seeing Shelby, mobile and lifelike. There was color in her cheeks and the light flooding in from the windows glinted in her eyes. She smiled at him and let out a little laugh. Ricky finally exhaled with a relieved laugh of his own. As he started towards Shelby, he gave a look of gratitude to his aunt who stood somberly next to the girl.

"You're all right!" Ricky declared in front of Shelby as he started to bring his arms up to embrace her. Just as he stopped the motion, catching himself gushing over her, Ricky was pulled into her by her own arms about his waist. He sighed and happily let his arms come down around her and rested his chin on her head.

"I'm never borrowing a book from you again," he heard Shelby mumble into his shoulder.

Ricky drew her back from him by the shoulders and looked down into her bright blue eyes. "Shelby, I'm so sorry.

I didn't know! Did they hurt you?" He cast his eyes up and down her, but could see little sign of her flesh underneath the old cloak she wore.

"No. No, don't worry. I'm fine," Shelby smiled reassuringly. "But I'm glad your aunt came for me."

"I would have come for you, I swear, but she wouldn't let me," Ricky spoke rapidly still clasping her shoulders.

Sarah sighed, "Okay Romeo, come on." She started towards the kitchen doorway where Netta stood smiling with arms open wide. Ricky looked back from his aunt to Shelby.

"Really, I would have come for you. This was all my fault," Ricky added softly with sincerity now that it was only he and Shelby.

"I believe you," Shelby smiled. "But your aunt told me about what happened here…with your father. I think it was best she made you stay behind or something could have happened to you. It's…not very nice out there, Ricky."

Dergus strolled through the doorway and shut the massive doors behind him. Ricky stepped back from Shelby letting his hands drop down to his sides until he caught her eyeing his outfit. He tugged at the loose shirt to pull more of the fold out from his pants and heard Shelby chuckle. Ricky smirked and batted her nose. Dergus smiled at them as he approached.

"So little miss, what was our old friend Ranthrop like?"

Shelby turned to the old guard that had helped them down from their mount in the courtyard. "Like a wrestler, big and ornery," she replied with distaste.

"Hrmph, well if he's anything like Vasimus was then I'm surprised you escaped unscathed," Ricky grumbled.

"Vasimus was here?" Both Sarah and Shelby chimed at the same time, Sarah's tone in alarm, Shelby's in excited curiosity.

"You ran in so quickly I didn't get a chance to tell you," Dergus said as he came up to Sarah and Netta. Sarah looked at him, having gone a bit pale.

"What did he…want?"

"Well, to see you of course, but he left after speaking to Lord Ricky here," Dergus looked back to Ricky.

"Lord Ricky?" Shelby whispered at his side. Ricky nudged her with his elbow and swallowed under the stare of his aunt.

"Shut up," he mumbled.

"Are you all right, Ricky?" Sarah neared the distance between them and looked over his figure. "What did he say to you?"

"Nothing. I'm fine," he soothed her with his words. "He thought at first maybe my mother had brought me and I just told him…" Ricky looked at Dergus for a moment, "how she and my father live far beyond Blinney and I only came to visit you." Dergus patted Sarah on the shoulder and left then to return to the gate, slinking away from a conversation he couldn't contribute.

Sarah's shoulders relaxed a bit and she almost managed a smile at Ricky's cleverness. "And?"

"And…he asked if you'd ever married, so I told him you hadn't, but that you had to stay in Blinney…alone," Ricky swallowed hoping his revelations to Vasimus would be acceptable to his aunt. He was so tired of having to make judgments every day only finding out that they were the wrong ones.

Sarah sighed. "Well done, Ricky," she smiled happily against the agonized look on her face. "Now come with me. We've got to get you out of here quickly. Ranthrop said he has spies even at Daundecort Hall. I don't trust them not to inform him that *a Richard Allister* is in Farwin Wood."

Sarah and Netta retreated into the kitchen. Ricky stood for a moment basking in the satisfaction that his aunt was pleased with him for the first time in weeks. He sighed then and looked down at Shelby as he started towards the kitchen. Her brows were canted down at the sides and he wondered why she seemed to look worried all of a sudden. "What?"

"Nothing," she murmured as they walked into the kitchen. "It's just that you have to...go back now."

Ricky stopped in the doorway of the kitchen. Netta was looking on as Sarah leaned over a large wooden tub in the corner of the room. Sarah stretched her arm up to a spigot that stuck out from the wall and turned the knob. Water began to trickle and then flood out from the spout into the over-sized barrel. Ricky looked at Shelby who he found was staring at him with an anxious look on her face. When he glanced back to his aunt and Netta he saw that they had both turned their attention from the filling tub to him. Ricky swallowed. "Right..." he muttered vaguely remembering something his aunt had said about drowning and her recent mention of "going home."

"Don't be afraid, Ricky. When you wake up, you'll be at home," Sarah said softly.

Ricky looked to Netta, "Wait. You know too?" Netta's usually cheerful expression was gone and had now been replaced by the dismal one that colored both Shelby and Sarah's faces. "I thought you said not to tell anyone about this?" Ricky demanded from his aunt, hoping an argument would buy him more time.

"I had to...in case I didn't make it back." Sarah approached him now and he took a step back, but hit the door frame. She grasped his face in her hands and talked to him in a voice like she had when he was a child. "Ricky, you have to go back first so you can take the book to the hospital. It's the only way Shelby will wake up. It's the only way to get home."

"Really? There's not some other way? Some less...violent way?"

Sarah shook her head and dropped her hands from his face. "No. This is the only way I know. I've done it before, you'll be fine. Just hold your breath until you can't stand it and then..."

"Then what?"

"Then just stay under the water, no matter how much your body tells you to come up for air," Sarah spoke in too calm of a voice for the words she was saying. Ricky looked at Netta and then to Shelby.

"I'm afraid too, Ricky. I'm sorry you have to do this," Shelby's voice was meek.

Her sympathetic eyes eroded the defiance and fear in him enough to win him over. From everything he'd seen so far that he didn't want to believe, he knew his aunt wouldn't lead him astray in doing this. He wanted to see Shelby in the flesh again…in a normal world, in their world. Ricky even wanted to go home and work in the book shop of all things! Anything but this creepy land full of angry knight-like men, horned beasts, and devastated woodlands. Realizing that Sarah and Shelby would have to do the same as him, Ricky flushed with color at his cowardice. "What if I do something wrong?" Ricky looked back at his aunt.

"You can't do anything wrong," she smiled. "When you wake up, get to the hospital as soon as you can. I'll give you… five hours," Sarah thought for a moment. It was around two in the afternoon in Farwin Wood, Sarah guessed. Five hours would give Ricky enough time to get back, wake up, and get to the hospital before visiting hours were over for the day.

"Five hours until what?"

Sarah looked at Shelby then, "Until I send Shelby back."

Ricky stared at Shelby who appeared much calmer than him considering the possibilities that were running through his mind. "But…but, what if," Ricky didn't want to say it in front of Shelby and scare her.

"What if I send her before you get the book to her?" Sarah finished the thought for him.

"Yes!" Ricky's eyes bugged open.

"That won't happen. You'll wake up soon after you go. Just get to the hospital and sit by her or...as near to her as you can get, with the book open. Just make sure the book is open," Sarah stressed each word.

"Can't you just wait until tomorrow to send her back? Just give me more time so I know for sure I'll be there," Ricky pleaded.

"Ricky, I don't want to keep her here in Farwin Wood after today. I don't know what Ranthrop or Vasimus might do, or anyone who's heard I'm here for that matter. This is our best chance. You'll be fine. You can do this," Sarah urged him.

Ricky wiped his brow and clutched his stomach. He turned his head at the feel of a small hand around his forearm. "Ricky," Shelby said, "I trust you."

Ricky shook his head at Shelby's sweet smile. How could she have so much faith in him? He knew each minute he wasted worrying was one less minute he had to get the book to the hospital, yet it was also one more minute he at least got to see her in a living state, real or not. "I don't know why," he sighed and looked back to his aunt. "All right, let's do this."

Sarah eyed Ricky up and down. "Where are your things?"

Ricky glanced at his appearance and remembered that he'd discarded his vest and belt at the other end of the kitchen. He walked past the long table to where he'd left them and listened as his aunt call nervously to him.

"Remember what I said, Ricky. Make sure you didn't lose anything you came with or the book can pull you back in."

"No, I remember," Ricky called as he donned his leather vest and replaced the belt that still held the sword in it. Luckily he hadn't needed to use it and find out if the protective dust in the hilt worked. "Shelby? Do you have everything?" Ricky started back towards them after he was satisfied he had all of his apparel from the basement closet of the book shop.

"Yes, your aunt made me check before we left Groslivo Stronghold. No one took anything from me, I'm sure of it," she assured him.

Sarah arched a brow at Ricky's concern over Shelby. It was the first time she'd truly seen him take anything she'd said about the book and Farwin Wood seriously. The water stopped behind her and they all turned to see Netta push the spout knob closed with the end of a broom handle. "It's full," she sighed.

"All right, Ricky. When you wake up, go straight to the hospital with the book," Sarah started again.

"And get as close to her as I can with the book open," he added without his usual sarcasm.

"Yes and just wait. Don't panic, remember I said five hours. Just sit there and wait," Sarah emphasized.

Ricky nodded. "I got it. And you? What about you?" His voice rose at the thought.

"As soon as Shelby is awake, come back to the kitchen where we fell asleep and just leave the book open on the table. I'll come home tomorrow. Just open the shop if you want and tell the others I'll be home soon," Sarah smiled.

Ricky couldn't believe his aunt was already thinking about work again. All he could think about were the next few minutes. Man, she had some brass buns on her, he thought. "Tomorrow?" Ricky nodded as a reminder. "All right, don't worry. It'll be there."

Sarah wanted to smirk at the rising confidence in her nephew, but she thought better of it. She didn't want to tease him when he was doing the most responsible thing she'd seen of him yet.

Ricky exhaled a long breath and walked over to the water barrel. He stepped up on a small stool Netta had pushed over to it for him and swung one leg over the side into the water. Next he dunked the other leg in and paused a moment as his butt careened on the edge of the barrel. He looked at his aunt and then at Shelby who watched him. Ricky turned his head to Netta in thought and said, "Netta, it was nice to meet you."

"You too, Lord Ricky," Netta smiled, her hands clasped together over the mound of her chest waiting to see the phenomenon before her.

Ricky started to bend his knees and lower himself into the barrel, but stopped when Shelby yelled, "Wait!" She leaned over the edge of the barrel, grasping a handful of his shirt, and as he looked up at her in confusion she pressed her lips to his. When their mouths parted, Ricky blinked at her dumbly, but she looked seemingly unaffected from where she stood. Sarah and Netta both held their hands to their mouths and Ricky could see the corners of their smiles. In spite of the cold water, he felt his cheeks burn from their amusement and the rush of his heart from the excitement of what had just occurred. Now was as good of a time as any to drown out of sight, he thought, and let himself fall to a sitting position beneath the water.

Submerged inside the cold water of the barrel, Ricky felt pressure against his head. Drown, he told himself. Drown. How the hell do you drown? Several bubbles crept out of his mouth and trailed upwards to the light. Ricky peered up and saw three warbled faces gazing down at him. He felt the urge to cough and tried to suppress it, the result was the last of his breath forcing its way out of his mouth. He heard the high pitched squeal of his moan echo inside of his skull as he tried to withstand the rising pressure in his chest. Instinctively, when he could bear no more of the lack of air, Ricky started to rise from the water. He pushed when he felt something prevent him from rising, but the force pushed back. Ricky looked up and saw his aunt above him. Her figure then towered over him and she stepped into the tub as she forced her weight down on him, both of her hands on his shoulders.

Ricky tried to shake her off, tried to stretch his neck upwards in the hopes his lips would reach the surface, but a withered hand appeared in the water above him and forced his head back down. Netta! Netta too? Ricky couldn't believe what was happening. This couldn't be happening. His father and aunt couldn't have done *this*! No one could do *this*! His aunt was crazy and now he was going to die like a wet rat in front of Shelby! Ricky flailed against the sides of the tub, but his aunt's legs held firmly against his thighs from where he'd sat at the bottom of the barrel. With his legs bent Indian style there was no way he could push her off of him and he grew weaker with each passing second. His lungs burned, the water stung his nasal passage and the more he willed himself not to, the more he sucked in the water. Just as Ricky thought the pinnacle of the fire in his lungs would climax and burst them, everything went black and he felt nothing.

CHAPTER
TWENTY-FOUR

FARWIN WOOD

SHELBY SAT on the floor against the kitchen wall, her legs pulled up to her chest, weeping uncontrollably with her face in her hands. She jumped at the solid grasp on her shoulder and the feel of cold water dripping down on her. When Shelby looked up and saw Sarah standing over her, soaked from the chest down.

"It's all right, Shelby. He's gone," Sarah whispered.

Shelby batted Sarah's arm away instinctively after seeing how she'd jumped on top of poor Ricky in the water barrel. Shelby quickly got to her feet and ran to the barrel, afraid she would see his lifeless body floating inside. What she saw was simply water — no Ricky.

"It worked, Shelby. It's okay," Sarah soothed behind her. "I'm sorry if it scared you."

Shelby gasped and glanced around the room. She looked at Netta whose eyes were wide as she herself still stared at the tub.

"Miss, he disappeared right before my eyes. I didn't want to believe it myself, but Sarah would never do that if she didn't think it would work," Netta reassured the girl. It had been easier for Netta to accept since she'd long thought Sarah had drowned in the River Duke.

Shelby exhaled and brought her hand to her chest. She wiped her eyes with her damp sleeve and regained her composure. "I'm sorry, Sarah," she finally looked up at her old friend.

"Ha, sweetie. Don't apologize. Believe me, it terrified even myself," Sarah sighed nervously.

Sarah changed into one of her old gowns that Netta had hidden away and returned to the kitchen where she found Shelby curiously listening to Netta explain the recipes she was cooking. Sarah smiled at the sight, but felt the pang of melancholy standing before the scene in the kitchen, wearing a dress she'd worn many times in Farwin Wood. Had she stayed in Farwin Wood, would she have had children? A daughter like Shelby, perhaps? Would she have noticed the new lines on Netta's face each passing year instead of seeing them all at once some twenty years later? And worse yet, it would soon be time to say goodbye to Netta again, forever. She sighed and decided to force a smile through the last dinner she would ever have at Allister Hall.

Dergus joined the women in the great room when the meal was ready. He of course convinced Netta to bring him some beetleburry ale and although she put up a fuss, Sarah imagined it was much less sincere than usual. Shelby seemed to delight in the stories the two old people told and cooed at the tastes of Netta's cooking. Sarah occasionally would glance at the door each time she heard a sound out in the street beyond the courtyard, wondering if it was Vasimus, come to see her. When they'd finished the meal, Dergus left to return to the gate, but not before he gave a knowing look to Sarah. He understood full well that Vasimus might return and he would alert her immediately when and if he did.

Sarah and Shelby helped Netta clear the table and return everything to the kitchen. She tried to scold them, but they ignored her and in no time the table was empty. Shelby helped Sarah wash the dishes and they both looked to the window as the sun set, knowing Shelby's time to go home was soon upon them. Shelby exhaled a long breath now and then, glancing over at the barrel, but she would return a smile to Sarah letting her know that she knew she had to go.

More familiar with the passage of time in Farwin Wood, Netta called to Sarah when she was certain that nearly five hours had passed since Ricky had plunged into the water barrel. The women walked over to the barrel and Netta brushed the girl's light hair from her face with a loving smile. She crushed her with a hug, enormous strength still left in her bony arms. "I'm so glad you made it back here safely, my dear," Netta smiled and patted her cheek.

"Thank you for the lovely dinner," Shelby didn't know what else to say. She looked at Sarah for a moment and then hugged her.

"Oh, well, what is that for? You'll see me soon," Sarah laughed, but hugged her back.

"I know," Shelby acknowledged softly, "but do you remember the first time I met you?"

Sarah looked off in thought trying to recall how old Shelby had been. Not more than ten, she was sure of it. "Yes, I suppose. Why?"

"You told me a book can take you anywhere," Shelby smiled.

Sarah let out a sour chuckle at the thought. "Ha, I did say that, didn't I?"

"Well, I'm glad it was one of your books and that you were here with me," Shelby smiled.

Sarah didn't know whether to revel in the affection that Shelby had conveyed in the compliment or cry over the circumstances that had brought them all there. She chose to smile in spite of herself, knowing that in the next few minutes Shelby at least would be safely back where she belonged. "Up you go, dear," Sarah choked away the tightness in her throat.

Shelby disappeared more easily and quickly in the water than Ricky had, likely because she had seen it done once and because she was much more fearless than Sarah's nephew. Sarah rolled her dress sleeve back down and rung out the portion that had been soaked when she'd helped to hold Shelby beneath the water's surface. Netta remained peering over the edge of the barrel into the dark reflection of the water now that the sun had faded below the horizon.

"She's gone, Netta. I felt her slip away," Sarah said softly as she wrung out her sleeves.

"I know. I was just wondering…do you think that would work on Dergus?" Netta glanced up hopefully at Sarah.

"Netta!" Sarah tried not to laugh, but couldn't help herself.

After another hour of visiting, Sarah bid Netta goodnight. Sarah walked out to the gate and handed a note to one of Vasimus' guards. She'd rather request he come to her than have Vasimus just show up unannounced. Sarah expected the shock might be less injurious to her system if she had it that way. "Please take this to your Lord this evening. I'm sorry it is so late, but I request his presence here tomorrow if he is free," Sarah told the man who'd first tried to stop Dergus when she'd arrived at Allister Hall.

The man took the note with hesitation. "Yes, m'Lady of course, but…" The man looked over at the unmanned tower where his comrade usually stood above the gate.

Sarah glanced in the same direction and realized she had not seen the other guard since she returned from Groslivo's stronghold earlier in the day. "But you've already sent him word that I have returned," she muttered knowingly.

"Yes, m'Lady. It was his wish."

"And will he be here in the morning?" Sarah inquired.

"I suspect he will...but I will send Slaunacht back with your message if he brings other news," the man offered and put her note in his belt pouch.

"Thank you," Sarah grimaced and then returned to the hall. She took a candle up the dark stairwell with her to her room and set it on the bedside table. Falling asleep proved difficult in spite of how exhausted she felt. Every passing second she wondered what Vasimus would look like, what his voice would sound like, and how she would react to him. When she didn't think of him she wondered if Ricky had made it to the hospital with the book and if Shelby had miraculously awoken from her "coma" for her dear parents' sake. Finally able to convince herself the sooner she fell asleep the sooner she would know the answer to these questions, Sarah drifted off.

Without feeling she had slept a wink, Sarah flinched at the sound of rapping on her bedroom door. She opened her eyes to see the morning light creeping over the tree tops and into her bedroom window.

"Lady Sarah!" Dergus called from behind the door.

"Yes?" Sarah's hoarse voice cried out.

The banging stopped and was followed by a pause. "He's here," Dergus' voice came more quietly.

Sarah breathed in quickly and slung her legs over the side of the bed. "All right! Give me a moment!" she called to the door. Her heart began to flutter in her chest and she hurried to tug the dress off that she'd fallen asleep in the night before. She ran her old brush through her hair, still damp from being splashed when she'd sent Shelby and Ricky home. It settled down in long waves over her shoulders. She let out a deep breath as she looked down at herself, secure with the knowledge she had everything she needed in case she needed to flee to water. Sarah gasped at the sight of her bracelet on the floor and rushed over to quickly fasten it to her wrist. "Get a grip, Sarah," she muttered aloud. "Hello, how are you? Sorry I didn't call. And please stop fighting. That's all there is to it," she mumbled and stared at the door. One last soothing exhale and she yanked the door open to go downstairs.

As Sarah quietly descended the stairs, she listened to the sound of firm steps pacing back and forth across the stones of the great room floor. The occasional clank of metal told her that Vasimus wore his sword and metal knee guards as the two clashed together with his movements. He'd been in battle for years, the knee guards she'd only seen him wear during fencing matches as a child had likely become a daily part of his dress.

With only a few steps left until she reached the base of the stairs, Sarah reached to the wall to steady herself as Vasimus' back came into her view. She stopped and held her breath at the sight of him, his long cloak falling behind him over his shoulders. The black hair that she remembered running her fingers through hung a little longer than she'd ever seen it, likely gone uncut in his hasty lifestyle. Sarah knew she had to make it down the last few steps, but didn't think she could move. Her body felt paralyzed as Vasimus turned and she saw his face for the first time.

Sarah brought a hand up to her stomach and forced herself to swallow at the sight of his ragged, but still so handsome face. She wanted to run away in fear of how he would react, in fear of what had happened to him to make him the way everyone claimed him to be. She also wanted to run to him and reclaim the feelings she had so long ago, but she suspected that danger would follow no matter what direction she chose.

The shift of his clothing stopped. The scrape of his sword tip against his leg guards ceased as Vasimus turned sensing something in the room. He looked up at Sarah, his light blue eyes fixed on hers and he froze at the sight of her. "Sarah," his voice eventually came out.

Sarah took a shaking step, guiding herself down with her hand grazing the stone wall. Her knees wobbled and her fingertips began to sweat against the cloth of her gown. Sarah tried to speak, but only her lips moved. She could not make a sound escape them.

Vasimus approached the base of the stairs in what seemed like an eternity for the both of them. Sarah somehow managed one more step, but didn't dare try for the last. The sheer height of Vasimus from where he stood below her was enough to intimidate her already and she briefly remembered the times he would swiftly lift her off her feet and twirl her around like she weighed no more than a feather.

"I cannot believe my eyes," his voice was hoarse as he looked her over.

"Vasimus," Sarah's voice finally came out although no more than a whisper, "you…you look well."

Vasimus watched her every movement as she spoke and a look of pain came over him as he listened to her voice. He never left her gaze as he took the final step between them to stand directly before her. He held up a hand, but left it in the air just before her chin as he studied the very sight of her.

Sarah trembled under the sensation of his breath on her skin. She could smell the sweet scent of herb water that he washed his hair with and the aroma of forest on him. He was still so very real, no matter how long he had labored silently in the closed book she'd kept at the back of her shop. He was as real as the day she left him. He had grown into a middle-aged man no matter that pages weren't added to the book. He was human, very human, with a human life and human feelings. Sarah suddenly was overcome with her guilt for not returning, not sending some kind of word that she lived, not bringing this tired man some peace. She realized she had never found her own peace either. The scent of him and the sight of his chest moving in and out were too much for her to bear and a tear dropped from her eyes. She closed them tightly shut in an effort to block him out from her life again.

The feel of his calloused fingers against her face caused yet another tear to stream down her face. The knowledge that he had swung his sword in violence, partially at her expense, devastated her. She reached up to clasp her fingers around his and leaned her face into his palm. How many times she'd longed for a touch from a loving hand, but there were none at her disposal.

"Sarah, don't cry darling. These hands will not hurt you," Vasimus' husky voice came out and his breath shifted the hair from her eyes. Sarah looked up at his face through her tears.

"I am so sorry I did not return. I couldn't leave Blinney, but I would have had I known what happened here," she sniffled and gazed upon his face.

Vasimus brought his other hand up to cup her face. Without a trace of anger he simply stated, "Just a word, Sarah. A word would have been enough to brighten my door from grieving for you."

"You would have tried to come to me, but wouldn't have been able," she shook her head against his hands. "I couldn't pull you away from your lands to search aimlessly for me. And if I sent word that I lived, but did not return," Sarah stared at him as he listened to her frantic logic, "well...I feared you would grow so bitter that it would destroy you from the man I knew."

"Should you not have left those decisions in part to me?" He offered delicately and stroked one of her tears away with his thumb.

"Vasimus, if I could not be with you, I had rather you thought me dead so you did not go on hoping. I remember how you said you would wait for me. If I were not alive to be waited for, I hoped that it would release you to love again… to find happiness that I could not give you. Can you understand that is why I remained silent all these years? Why would I come back only to tempt you with something we could never have?"

"So you just gave me up? Without any thought of me?" Vasimus' voice rose.

"No…I have thought of you every day," Sarah hated that the words came out blubbered.

"How could you think of me every day, knowing exactly where I was?" He tried to hide his anger, but couldn't help thinking of all the wasted years.

Sarah let out a ragged breath, "Very painfully."

Vasimus drew her in to him then and held her tightly to his chest. Sarah grasped to the sides of his shirt and felt comfort in his arms, yet it was mixed with an awkward foreign feeling after having not been held by him in so long.

After a moment had passed, Vasimus lightened his grip, afraid to let go that she may slip away from him again. He brought her chin up with his fingers and murmured just before her lips. "I think we have both hurt long enough." As the last word left his mouth he brought his lips to hers and his embrace once again pulled her closer to him.

Too weak from her distress and unable to get the words out to stop him, Sarah let herself fall against him as his lips hungrily parted hers. Vasimus' hand came up and dove through her hair where he pulled her closer into his deepening kiss. Sarah's legs went from trembling to a numb weakness at the sensation he still stirred inside of her. She thought she would faint from excitement and lack of air, but his mouth finally released her with his own panting breath. In her daze, Sarah inhaled another scent of his shirt as his kisses moved across her forehead and down to her cheek.

"Come with me. Come back with me to Daundecort Hall," he whispered in the husky tempting voice she remembered from her last summer there.

"No," Sarah muttered as his mouth neared hers again.

"I don't like you being here, so close to Groslivo's lands and the bandits who plague this place. Come back with me, Sarah," Vasimus started for her lips again, but Sarah shook out of her euphoria long enough to push against his chest and look up at him.

"No, I can't. I'm leaving today."

"Today?" Vasimus halted his kiss and looked at her. "When will you be back?"

Sarah said nothing as she looked at him. She swallowed to brace herself for his reaction, knowing no words would assuage him.

"Will you come back?"

Sarah shook her head slowly. "I cannot, Vasimus," she offered as delicately as possible.

Vasimus pushed himself away from her then. He stepped down the stairs to the great room floor and stared down, hands on hips, fuming. He looked back at her, lips parted but said nothing, then turned his gaze out towards the empty room. "Why did you come here, Sarah?"

"A girl...from my court got lost and I learned that she came to Farwin Wood. I came to return her safely home."

"You did not come here to see me, did you?" His face remained turned away from her as he spoke.

294

"No," Sarah spoke the word softly. "I came for the girl. She left last night with my nephew." Sarah thought she heard a scoff as his shoulders raised.

"Yes, I had the pleasure of meeting Lord Ricky. I see your brother has fared well in love," Vasimus' words came out in a sour tone.

"He did not choose well, Vasimus. His wife left him long ago. They...no longer share the same home," Sarah didn't quite know how to explain divorce to him having never heard of it in Farwin Wood. He glanced back at her, his expression annoyed, and raised a brow in thought.

"It wouldn't be the first time," Vasimus muttered at the thought of Richard's poor choices. He had never begrudged Richard of falling in love with his sister. He would have given his sister anything she wanted, had she only asked. Now, however, he felt the need to hurt Sarah, hurt her for leaving again and for not coming to see him.

"His wife...looked very much like Deronda, Vasimus. I believe that was the only attraction. He's never loved again," she offered.

"Then that makes two of us, Sarah. How can you claim I would find happiness again in thinking you were dead if your own beloved brother could not do the same?" Vasimus let his words seethe with the derision Sarah deserved.

"Because the only alternative was to let you know that I lived, but that we could never be together," Sarah found strength in her own voice finally and took the last step down to the great room. He was being unreasonable. He was hurt, she comprehended that, but still he had to see how knowing she lived was not a better solution than thinking her dead.

"I cannot believe that it is impossible as you do. You are *here*. Sarah," Vasimus' hostility turned to a pained pleading again, "you are here! How is it that something so important brought you here, but I am not one of those things? I think, perhaps you just don't want to admit that our precious feelings have died on your part. Is that it? Was that the only death that has occurred?"

"I am here but a day in nearly twenty years! One day in twenty years would have been enough for you? I have to rule Blinney. My parents died and Richard went away. How can I leave my people, just as you can't leave yours?" Sarah felt foolish for claiming to rule a street in Salem, but Vasimus was making her act foolish.

"Will not your nephew inherit your house? Can he not stand up to take your place when he comes of age?"

"No. Since his father left...he must...rule Richard's new house when the time comes," Sarah's anger diminished as she concentrated on the awkward words.

"I see your brother has fared well in other ways," his voice was a sarcastic tone of praise. "My congratulations to his success."

"Vasimus, would you be happy if he were starving and a beggar?"

"Like my people? Is that what you mean? I suppose there is nothing here to tempt you anymore. I am sorry that Farwin Wood is not the idyllic place you remember it to be, Sarah," Vasimus declared his words with evident offense, his arms rising as he gesticulated.

"I never said that. And I sent a message for you, Vasimus. Did not your guard tell you?"

"Ah...yes, to bid me goodbye. One jaunt through Farwin Wood was enough to make that an easier decision for you," Vasimus grumbled in his self-pity. He paced in agitation back and forth at the base of the stairs feeling foolish for the words that were coming out of his mouth, but still unable to hold them back.

"If you are not happy with the state of Farwin Wood then why not end this war?"

"End it? Just like that? And what's to stop Ranthrop's people from burning cottages and timber or from stealing roomples and muckas from the villages. Who will protect my people when his men hide along the roads to rob them of what little they already have?"

"I have seen Ranthrop, Vasimus," Sarah paused until he looked up at her, his eyes widened. "He will gladly end this war if you would do the same. His people suffer the same atrocities," Sarah tried to sound sympathetic, but braced herself for what was to come.

"Ranthrop? Ranthrop?" He took a swift large step and stopped just in front of her. "Is that where you were yesterday? I am given twenty minutes of your time in twenty years, but Ranthrop! The man who would have killed you is given your audience the whole of yesterday?"

"I went to look for the mistress of my court in the swamplands and I inquired of her from Ranthrop, who obliged me. He was civil, Vasimus," Sarah fudged that statement just a little, she knew, but any alternative wouldn't help the case of peace.

"Hrmph, likely afraid of what would happen were he not! And why did you not come to me? Do you not know how dangerous it is for you to go to the Southlands now?" He looked down at her face and in spite of his rage, Sarah could see the concern in his eyes.

"Yes. Yes I do. Which is why you were the last person I would ask for help. I would not let you go there to ride to your death," Sarah tried to reach for the front of his shirt, but he pulled away from her upon noticing the gesture.

"Both Ranthrop and I will die one day, but you can be assured it will be he first," Vasimus grumbled with an icy glare for the sentiment she had just spoken to him. She put herself in harm's way to keep him free of it and Vasimus didn't want to be reminded of her good nature. Sarah had always been kindhearted and caring. He wanted to forget that now that she would leave him again, but no matter what fault he tried to find in each phrase she spoke, he could not. Suddenly, Vasimus was emotionally exhausted from the angry banter that had passed between them. This is not how he'd imagined their reunion. Why was she not still in his arms, smiling and kissing him?

"How do you know that? When you go on so obsessed with this...this wasted vengeance? Do you think Deronda would rejoice in what the two of you have done? Was it worth it? To you...to your people? What has it brought you? All that it will bring you is your death and I cannot bear to leave you knowing that you go to it willingly!"

Vasimus turned away from her then and pinched his eyes shut. He heard her dress rustle as she came up behind him, but he stretched an arm back as a motion for her to halt. "Do not tell me how I should run my affairs, Sarah, when you give me no say in how to run yours," he muttered in a low defeated tone. He let his arm drop by his side and took in a long breath as he straightened his posture. "You must go. I accept this as I once told you I would. But in going, know that if you love me, if you *ever* loved me, you will return. Don't wait another twenty years, Sarah," his voice was almost a whisper just before he started to the door.

Sarah stood looking at his back while he strode in great lengthy steps to the great room door. It seemed he could not leave quickly enough by the effort he placed in his footing. Sarah's lips sat parted and she felt she could almost taste the bitterness of his words, they were so palatable. The slamming of the door sent a shudder down Sarah's spine and she felt fresh tears begin to form in her eyes. Why couldn't he have just said goodbye to me, she wished. What a stubborn fool he's turned into. This isn't how I wanted the last time I saw him to be, she thought. How long would it take her to regain the sense of contentment she had acquired since the last time she'd seen him? Would she grow mad in her bookshop as the years slowly passed by, wondering if he'd ceased his destruction? Sarah didn't want to think of the things that would torment her over the next twenty years or even longer. She buried her face in her hands and tried to keep from sobbing.

The sound of soft footsteps grew at her side and she looked up to see Netta hobble daintily over to her in haste. The sight of the woman's worried face that changed to compassion upon seeing her own, filled Sarah's heart. "Oh, Netta," she cried and threw her arms around the little woman's shoulders.

"Shh...there, there," Netta patted her back. "It's done now. He's gone."

That was just it, Sarah choked back another sob. Whomever she'd just argued with was not the Vasimus she remembered. The Vasimus she knew was gone.

CHAPTER
TWENTY-FIVE

BLINNEY LANE

RICKY SAT groggy-eyed on the couch in his aunt's living room as Reggie Nurscher changed the channel with the TV remote once again. It was too early for Ricky to adjust his eyes to the flashing colors at the speed Reggie clicked the control. Either that or he just hadn't slept well last night. Ricky had continually done impatient laps the night before around the kitchen table where his aunt's body lay face down in front of the infamous open book. When he'd given up on her waking up early, he'd finally walked over to Mary's where he was told he had to sleep for the evening.

The image of a tanned blonde in a French-cut leotard zoomed in on the screen and Ricky rubbed his eyes when he realized what he was staring at. The woman smiled and shifted from one long drawn-out stretch to the other. Ricky slowly turned his head and squinted at Reggie who sat lounging on the other end of the couch, legs wide open, one hand on a biscuit the other on the remote. Reggie chewed and stared, entranced by the woman on the screen. Ricky watched as biscuit crumbs fell from Reggie's mouth and onto his polyester shirt. Ugh, Ricky thought, and tightened his grasp around the bulky pillow he hugged to his chest with his pajama clad legs pushed up on the other side of it.

"You know...Reggie, you can go man," Ricky called groggily to get Reggie's attention away from the blonde.

"Nooo, it's my turn to babysit, remember?" Reggie scoffed and took another bite causing a large biscuit chunk to fall and land on his crotch.

"I'm not a baby," Ricky grumbled, dismayed that his suggestion had fallen on deaf ears.

"I know that," Reggie scoffed, "you think I wanna be here?" Reggie's eyes never left the screen. "I ain't listening to them old goats blab at me if they find out I went off and left you and you got into some kind of trouble," he muttered and dusted the crumbs off his shirt causing them to fall to the floor.

Ricky sighed in disgust and looked back at the TV. The woman's pelvis now undulated up and down as she lay on the floor on her back. "Really?" Ricky guffawed. "Can't you put something else on?"

"It's Sunday morning! There's nothing on!" Reggie shifted on his seat cushion and leaned against the arm of the couch to reach his cigarettes on the table. "Geesh," he muttered as he tucked a cigarette into his lips.

Ricky sighed and buried his face into the pillow on his chest. It blocked out his vision of Reggie's fixation and some of the smell of his putrid cigarette smoke. Come on, Aunt Sarah. Any minute now, Ricky wanted to scream. He hated the waiting. He'd waited for hours next to Shelby's hospital bed yesterday with that heavy book in his lap, waiting for her to wake up. Luckily her parents thought it was cute that he'd come to 'read' to her and let him be. They looked exhausted, probably not having slept since finding Shelby unresponsive in her bed and said they would go home to get some sleep if he would stay with her.

The thought of seeing her eyes open again made Ricky smile against the fluffy pillow. He wondered if that's how parents felt when they first saw their newborn babies. At first he thought he'd imagined it, having stared at her for so long, but finally she blinked and then blinked again. Ricky had rushed to her side and squeezed her hand until he felt hers wriggle under the tension.

"Are you all right?" he gasped.

"I'm...I'm fine," Shelby looked around the room, realizing she was actually in a hospital as Ricky and Sarah had told her. Ricky thought for a moment of returning the kiss she'd planted on him in the water barrel, but as he leaned in her eyes widened and she barked, "Sarah! Go take the book to Sarah!" The brief moment of consolation had been abruptly devastated by yet another long period of waiting.

Now here Ricky sat, still waiting. No wonder his aunt had been so testy about the books in her shop and her rules. Ricky felt awful for all the grief he'd given her, when she'd only been trying to help him—trying to keep him safe. He arched himself up off the couch enough to careen his head over the back and peer into the kitchen. The book still sat open on the table and he could see Sarah's lifeless hand lay stretched out before it on the table. He sighed and settled back on to the cushion, but caught Reggie looking over at him.

"She'll be all right, kid," he muttered and clicked the remote as he looked back to the TV.

Ricky didn't know if Reggie was trying to be comforting or if it was just more of his selfish lack of concern for anything that didn't involve him directly. Ricky leaned into the arm on his side of the couch and stared at the floor. He was tired, but didn't want to shut his eyes for fear he'd end up right back inside the book just as Sarah was leaving. He'd slept across the street at Mary's last night, as she shared the same worries he did. No way did he feel like taking the water plunge home again. Ricky nearly let out a chuckle remembering what had followed that pathetic episode in Netta's kitchen.

Just as everything had gone black, the next thing Ricky knew was that the darkness was only from his closed eyes where he lay with his head rested on the kitchen table in Sarah's flat. When he'd pulled his eyes open and saw that he was back home, without any pain in his chest, without any water in his nostrils or lungs, he'd jolted out of the chair. He'd patted himself up and down to make sure all of his body parts were still intact for some reason. It seemed the logical thing to do after a near death experience.

In his excitement, Ricky nearly forgot the book as he went to the door. He bolted back and retrieved it from the table and then ran downstairs through the empty shop. Outside, Ricky beamed as he took in the sight of Blinney Lane from the top step of the book store. He never imagined how happy he could be to see the place. Book under one arm, sun on his face, normal looking people passing by, he couldn't contain his words and yelled, "I'm alive! I'M ALIVE!" Ricky didn't even notice that the tourists altered their paths to steer clear of him. Franci came out of her shop, startled at first but then waved to him.

"Franci! I'm alive!" He hollered across the street. "I'm going to the hospital now! I'll be back later," Ricky started down the steps, but stopped when Franci called to him.

"Ricky! Maybe you should go change first!" Ricky looked down to see that he was still wearing his tight pants, leather vest, and sword.

"Right," he mumbled to himself and did a quick u-turn back to the store.

Ricky chuckled softly against the pillow at the sight he must have been to those people on Blinney Lane. Perhaps he looked like he just fit right in with the rest of the shop owners, he thought. If Sarah had been there to see it, she surely would have teased him.

Reggie barked out a ragged cough as a smoke plume formed in front of him. Ricky looked over to see the wiry man pound once on his chest and rasp again, his face gone flush under the congestion of phlegm and choking fumes.

"Iluuhhn!" Reggie croaked. His coughing stifled to throat clearing. Ricky heard another cough, but Reggie's mouth did not open, nor did his chest heave again like it had the first time.

Whipping his legs around under him on the couch, Ricky pushed himself up onto his knees and looked into the kitchen. The hand that he had spied earlier from his vantage point was now gone from his view. Ricky jumped over the back of the couch and caught himself from falling where he landed on the living room floor. He ran the few steps into the kitchen. When he turned the corner of the doorway he saw his aunt, sitting up in her chair, rubbing her face.

"Aunt Sarah?" he called softly.

Sarah turned to focus on him with a sleepy look in her eyes. She let out an exhausted sigh and muttered tiredly, "Ricky...you made it. Thank goodness."

Ricky laughed and threw his arms around her. He squeezed her tight and didn't want to let go. "I was worried. Are you all right?"

Sarah brought a feeble hand up to pat her nephew's arm. She let her tired head lean against his shoulder and inhaled the smell of coffee and biscuits. She was home. The nightmare was over. "I'm fine. Shelby?" Sarah lifted her head and opened her eyes to their fullest extent under her grogginess.

Ricky smiled and laughed. "She's fine. She woke up...just like you said."

Sarah relaxed and gave a weak smile. "Good," she croaked.

"Morning, sunshine!" Reggie chirped, leaning against the doorway. He smirked at Sarah behind the vapors that wafted up from his cigarette.

Ugh, maybe the nightmare's not over yet, Sarah scoffed mentally. "Reggie," Sarah's voice was half sleepy, half unenthused. "What are you doing here?"

"Babysittin'," Reggie nodded towards Ricky.

Sarah looked up to see Ricky casting a patient, but annoyed look at her to indicate his emotion for the time he'd spent with Reggie. Sarah stifled her chuckle and leaned back in the chair. "Well, thank you, Reggie, but you can go now."

"You got any more coffee?" Reggie scanned the counter.

"Ricky, why don't you show Reggie out," Sarah's tired words were flat.

Ricky didn't hesitate at the command. He strode to the door, slapping a hand on Reggie's shoulder as he did to steer the man to the exit. "It's been fun, Reg, but I think we should give her some time to wake up. See you around," Ricky forced a smile, but didn't have to force the cheerfulness in his voice.

Once Reggie was out the door, Ricky let out a long sigh and turned back around. He saw Sarah resting her chin in her hand at the table, eyes closed. He dashed over to the table and slammed the book shut. "Hey! Hey! Hey! Wakey wakey!"

"Huh? I'm up," Sarah grumbled and popped her lids back open. "I'm awake," she yawned.

"You'd better be," he grumbled and picked up the book. "Why don't I go put this back?"

Sarah fixed her eyes on the book. He should burn it in hell, Sarah thought for a moment on her words with Vasimus. "Good idea."

Ricky came around and helped Sarah take the bracelet off her wrist and took the leather band in his hand once it was loosened. "Why don't you get up and have some coffee? You look like you need it," he eyed her. Sarah stood up slowly and shuffled her feet over to the counter. "I don't remember being that tired when I woke up," he wondered.

"Hrmph, well...you're younger than I am," she scoffed. "I didn't sleep so well last night," she offered, fumbling with the coffee pot.

Ricky watched her inattentiveness. She sounded more than sleepy. His aunt seemed troubled still by the events of their adventure through the book. "Did you see Vasimus?"

Sarah set a cup down in front of her and stared at it. "Yes."

Ricky smirked in anticipation. "Was it a...romantic reunion?"

"Tsk! Just the opposite," she muttered. "Can we not talk about him...ever?"

Ricky creased his brow wondering what had happened to cause mention of Vasimus to hit one of her nerves. "Yeah," his tone was agreeable. "No problem." He went to the door with the book and bracelet in tow, but stopped to look back at his aunt whose far-off stare was directed down at her coffee cup. "You know, I don't think I would have liked that guy as an uncle anyways," he added to reassure her.

Sarah let out a faint chuckle. "Why? Because I wouldn't be able to send you Christmas presents from Farwin Wood," she joked over her shoulder.

Ricky usually laughed at her jokes, but Sarah didn't hear any laughter from behind her. All she heard was a serious and very mature sounding reply of, "No...because you deserve someone who looks out for your best interests."

Sarah turned around to make sure it was Ricky who had actually spoken those words, but only saw the door as it shut behind him. How had her nephew become so prophetic in the last two days? What had Vasimus said to him to make him say such a thing? Had Vasimus indicated his bitterness over Sarah to him? Sarah was humbled by the protectiveness and concern of Ricky's words, but hated that her nephew might be aware of how she let her feelings and history with Vasimus manipulate her emotions. She sighed, knowing that today started the process of once again trying to forget the man.

CHAPTER
TWENTY-SIX

MONDAY MORNING found the shop full of customers, leaving Ricky and Sarah both occupied. Ricky manned the cash register, and when he had a free moment, he set his mind to the task of creating a computerized version of Sarah's archaic handwritten inventory sheets. How had she gone so long without doing so, he wondered. If he was going to be here for the rest of the summer he was going to do what he could to make her life easier. It was the least he could do to repay her for what he'd put her through.

Ricky noticed his aunt hadn't seemed very perky the whole of the morning. She didn't walk as quickly to each customer as she usually did and her voice was low and forlorn when he heard her speak. Ricky's face brightened upon seeing Henry enter the store for the simple facts that Henry was the only normal adult male he'd met that summer and the possibility that Henry could lighten Sarah's mood.

"Hey, Ricky! Didn't see you Saturday," Henry called as he shoved his hand truck over the threshold.

"Yeah, I'm sorry. I forgot to call," Ricky had forgotten all about Henry and football practice after his aunt had seemingly lost her mind over the book debacle. He thought of how he'd woken up hung-over and met Vasimus Saturday in Farwin Wood, and was overjoyed to see the difference a few days had made. "We, uh...went camping...out of town," Ricky smiled.

"Really? Good. I've never seen her close the store before for anything," Henry chuckled and looked around to locate Sarah.

"Yeah, well, me either. Guess she wanted some quality time with her favorite nephew," Ricky laughed.

Sarah waved to Henry and then left a customer to study the cover of a book she'd just handed them. Ricky got up from the counter and smiled at her as she approached, "I was just telling Henry how we went camping Friday night and forgot all about letting him know I'd miss football practice." Ricky patted his aunt's shoulder as he walked past her to give Sarah and Henry some privacy. Maybe he can take her mind off the angry woodsmen, Ricky thought.

"Oh..." Sarah looked at Ricky as he brushed past her and then back to Henry. "I'm so sorry, Henry," she looked at him guiltily.

"Ah, don't worry about it. I'm glad, though. You need to get out of this place more," he smiled. "Honestly, I don't know that I've ever seen you around town in the five years since I moved back to Salem."

"Well, it's hard for me to get away, but I thought...it was worth it for the one day just to get Ricky away from here," she offered and rested her arms on the counter. "I don't want him going back home saying what a boring summer he had with his aunt."

"I don't think he's bored, Sarah. He looks happy. You two must be getting along a little better than the last time I saw you."

Sarah lifted her head up to look at Henry. The effort drained even more of her energy. She didn't know if she was exhausted or just depressed. Sarah rubbed her hands over her face and spoke lazily through them, "Yeah…yeah, we are actually. What a day in the woods will do, I guess."

"I didn't know you liked the outdoors." He leaned forward on his hand truck to hear her quiet voice and wait for her face to appear from behind her palms.

"There's not much to look at here on Blinney Lane and I barely have a yard to speak of so I've always liked the wilderness…when I was able to see it," Sarah let her hands drop and folded her arms down in front of her.

"Well, I know some great spots around here to go hike or fish if you'd ever like to go," he offered. He couldn't tell if she was disinterested in him today or just tired from her weekend in the woods, but Sarah had barely looked at him since he came in the shop. She looked pale and had the hint of dark circles contrasting under her light grey eyes.

"Oh…well," Sarah looked at the floor and frowned as she brought the back of her palm up to her brow, "I think I've had enough of the wilderness for a little while." She glanced at him meekly from under her hand and gave a weak smile. "But thank you, Henry."

Henry noticed then how her eyes seemed more dull than usual. Her skin glistened with perspiration under the light that flooded through the window. His dismay over her polite refusal was forgotten by these observations and he straightened up. "Are you all right, Sarah," his voice was soft and low. "You look a little pale," Henry's brows came together.

Sarah let her hand drop from her forehead, her bracelet chiming with the motion, and brought it to her stomach. "Oh, I'm fine. Sorry, I'm just a little tired today for some reason," she forced her mouth to curve up at the sides.

The lines in Henry's concerned face remained as he unstacked the boxes and deposited them in a pile next to her. He watched Sarah's back as she remained leaning against the counter, staring blankly out the window, while he continued the task. Henry didn't like to unnerve her, but he had to admit he enjoyed the moments when he fancied she was nervous around him. It gave him hope that she might return his feelings. Today there was no anxiety present in her as he passed by her so closely. Usually she fidgeted between batting glances at him and smiled, but today it was like he wasn't even the room. When Henry finished unloading the boxes he came up next to her and peered down at her face. She didn't even seem to notice as she continued to look out the window, her mouth in a bit of a frown.

"Sarah?" Henry murmured. She shifted her head toward him.

"Hmm?"

"Are you sure...you're all right?" Henry's voice was full concern now.

Sarah set her hand on Henry's forearm without thinking. "I'm sorry, Henry. I'm just not feeling very well, but...I'll be fine. I just feel exhausted."

Henry felt the moisture from Sarah's palm against his arm and reached up to touch her forehead with the back of his hand. She closed her eyes at the gesture without flinching and he noticed her breathing even seemed labored. "Sarah, you're cold...and clammy."

Sarah seemed to process everything slowly that morning, but through her foggy state and a tired breath, she caught the scent of Henry's skin and cologne come through her nostrils. His hand and arm felt comfortingly warm and the mixture of it with his aroma gave her the sensation of feeling some respite. Vasimus' touch and scent had roused a feeling in her, but with his lack of kindness it seemed less pleasing than what she just felt from Henry. Perhaps it was because she truly did not feel very well, she thought. Would Henry react the same had his and Vasimus' situations been reversed, she wondered. Somehow Sarah didn't think Henry ever possible of feeling bitterness or at least showing it so openly if he was even capable of the emotion. Vasimus had an intensity about him that made Sarah think the potential for hostility may have always been there, in spite of how merry the people of Farwin Wood used to be. But Henry... No, Henry had always been consistent in his character—calm, compassionate, and almost too reasonable in his judgments.

Sarah straightened her back and let her hand fall from Henry's arm. The motion brought his hand away from her head and she looked into his eyes, now aware of their true level of worry. "Maybe I'll go lie down after the rush is over and Ricky can watch the shop for a while," she offered.

"Yeah, I think that might be a good idea." Henry lingered for a moment, but then started to leave after Sarah handed over the signed invoice to him. He stopped at the door to look back at her once more.

Sarah noticed his gaze and smiled from where she now sat behind the counter. "It was...good to see you, Henry," she hesitated, not sure if he'd understand why she was saying the words.

"You too, Sarah. Feel better," his face still anguished in concern as he walked out the door.

Sarah ignored the suggestion she'd made to Henry to go rest and mulled her way through the rest of the day. By closing time however, she had donned a sweater and turned the air conditioning down enough that customers started to complain.

The next morning, Sarah awoke to find Ricky nudging her as she lie in her bed. She hadn't even heard the sound of her alarm clock and muttered groggily as she got out of bed. Her arms and legs felt heavy as she moved about the bathroom getting dressed. Sarah blinked at her pale complexion in the mirror and the circles under her eyes. Great, I'm getting sick, she thought. The depressing thoughts of Netta, Dergus, and Vasimus were enough to wear on her already. Battling off a flu bug or whatever was giving her these cold sweats and exhaustion would only be more difficult with a perplexed conscience.

Ricky insisted that Sarah work the register that day after seeing her fumble with some book stacks and walk around dragging her feet. She listened to him without objection and took the opportunity to bask in the warmth of the sunlight as it streamed in through the window by the counter. Her spirits only perked up when Shelby came in later, having been released from the hospital the day before after her mystified doctors could no longer think of any more tests to perform.

Sarah watched as Ricky and Shelby laughed and talked on the old sofa by the window. She was happy to see the familiarity of Shelby sitting in her shop and glad that Ricky was fond of a girl she approved of so highly.

That night, Sarah woke from her sleep to the chattering of her teeth. She was soaked in sweat yet felt like she was freezing to death. Even the thick blanket on her bed was slightly saturated by the sweat she had perspired in the night. She got up and stood under the hot water of her showerhead until her chill was nearly gone, then donned a pair of sweat pants and an old sweatshirt. She tore the blanket off her bed and swaddled herself in a new one as she fell back on to the mattress.

Ricky nudged Sarah again the next morning and stared down at her with bleak expression. "Are you all right?"

Sarah rasped out a cough and felt a rattle in her chest from the endeavor. She quickly noticed the feel of her damp skin against the inside of her sweatshirt and groaned. Sitting up on the bed, Sarah felt dizzy from the motion and breathed in only to cause another bout of coughing to erupt. Her lungs felt full and she shuddered trying to erupt the feeling from her chest.

"Maybe you should go to the doctor," Ricky warned.

Sarah waved a hand at him and pushed the covers back. "I'll be fine. Maybe I'm too old to go jumping into books," she offered.

"Can you contract sickness from anyone in Farwin Wood and...I don't know, bring it back here with you?" Ricky wondered aloud as he watched his aunt slowly rise from her bed. She walked slightly hunched over to the bathroom like an old woman.

"What, like beetleburry disease?" Sarah muttered.

"Seriously?" Ricky's alarm came fast.

Sarah rasped against a laugh and pressed her hand to her chest with the pain it caused her. She scoffed, "No, Ricky. There's no such thing."

"Hilarious," he muttered.

"Just go downstairs. I'll be down in a while," she yawned and shut the bathroom door behind her.

Franci came into the store with some coffee, but returned straight away to her shop upon seeing Sarah's condition. She came back with yet another paper travel cup, this time filled with some Menthalotum scented tea that she swore would alleviate Sarah's congestion. The aromatic beverage warmed Sarah's insides and perked her up for a few hours.

By eleven o'clock, Sarah was miserable again. Ricky came over and slammed a stack of books down on the counter with a thud in front of her. Her drooped eyelids and lowered head bobbed back up at the sound and slowly focused on him. "Huh? What?"

"All right. Get out of here," he grumbled. "I can watch the shop the rest of the day. You're starting to scare the customers away," Ricky half-grinned at her to lift her spirits.

"Ugh, I'm sorry, Ricky," Sarah grabbed a tissue and blew her nose.

"It's fine. Go upstairs and go to bed. I want to work on my inventory spreadsheet anyways."

Sarah sniffed and squinted at him. "Inventory spreadsheet?"

"Yeah," he beamed. "I'm digitizing your entire stock list so you can just search and look up whatever you want instead of flipping through your lists."

"I'll help him watch the shop," Shelby smiled, coming up to lean on the counter next to Ricky.

Sarah looked from Shelby back to her nephew who leaned on the counter looking altogether too content with the project. "Who are you and what have you done to my nephew?" Shelby chuckled, but then peered proudly at Ricky.

"Hey, Lord Ricky can handle this," he whispered to Sarah. "Now go on," he nodded towards the stairs.

"Oh brother," Sarah muttered and peeled herself off the stool.

Ricky watched his aunt trudge up the stairwell, her coughing echoed down as she went. He felt bad that she looked so miserable given what she'd already had to go through in Farwin Wood. Ricky felt better than ever and the difference in their states of health didn't seem fair to him. The marks on his back had begun to fade and hadn't caused him a second of pain since they'd returned from the book. He was grateful it meant he didn't have to worry about not being able to leave Blinney Lane, but ironically now that the marks were diminishing he no longer had a desire to leave. Ricky was actually happy to help his aunt. It gave him a sense of pride working in the shop. He felt productive, and with Shelby back it made the task even more enjoyable and less like actual work.

Ricky had even spoken with his father yesterday on the phone and surprisingly had an actual conversation with him, without either of them yelling. He hadn't mentioned anything about the journey into Farwin Wood to his father, nor did he feel like doing so unless they were face to face. He'd like to learn more about his father's past, but hoped that could happen one day when they were together again so he could truly appreciate the moment.

Shelby helped Ricky man the shop all day and they closed up for the night together. He lingered against the door as she stepped outside to leave. "Thanks for the help," his gratitude was much easier to give since returning from the book. He was no longer embarrassed to express himself around her and found the contentment with that fact suited him just fine.

"No problem. See you tomorrow?" She queried rocking up on her toes slightly in hope.

"You'd better," he smiled.

Shelby smiled at the demand for her presence and took a dainty step towards him, looking at her sneakers with the motion. She brought her head up slowly, her face looking up at him just below his chin and gazed into his eyes.

Ricky brought his hand down from the door frame the second he saw her eyes shift ever so slightly to his mouth and clasped her shoulder gently. He held his breath as he looked at the anxious expression on her face and leaned in slowly until their lips touched. The skin of Shelby's fingers touched his wrist and sent a tingle sensation down Ricky's arm. He drew back after a moment and rested his forehead against hers, both of them smiling shyly.

"Well, goodnight," Shelby's voice was but a joyful whisper.

"Goodnight," Ricky murmured back as she turned and walked down the steps. He watched her go and she looked back to flash a blushing smile at him. The sight made him laugh in delight as he went inside to lock up the book shop.

Ricky bounded up the steps with ease, his pounding heart urged him on effortlessly. He smiled to himself when he shut the door to the flat behind him. "All locked up for the night," Ricky called over his shoulder assuming his aunt would hear him. He turned around the well-lit kitchen and saw an empty coffee cup on the table, surrounded by a clutter of wadded tissues. "Ugh," he grimaced. "Aunt Sarah?" Ricky called, but heard no answer. He walked through the living room to her open bedroom door and saw her face half buried in the pillow.

Ricky stepped into her room and walked over by her nightstand. He looked down at her and heard the faint sound of congested snoring. Her arm hung down off the bed, a wadded tissue dangled from her limp fingers. Ricky shook his head and tugged the blanket up to cover more of her shoulders. He flipped the lamp on the nightstand off and tiptoed to the door. He looked back at her and decided to close it behind him in case she was contagious. I don't want her cooties floating around the entire apartment, he thought.

The next morning, Ricky didn't see his aunt in the kitchen after he came out of his room dressed for the day. He had a feeling she wasn't likely down in the shop yet. "Man, how did I become the responsible one here?" Ricky chuckled to himself as he started towards her room to wake her for the third time that week.

The door to Sarah's bedroom creaked when Ricky pushed it open, but he noticed that the noise had not roused her. Sarah lay curled up under the covers which were pulled up to her neckline. All Ricky could see was the back of her head as he approached, dodging the wads of tissue that littered the floor next to the bed.

"Aunt Sarah?" He called loudly, but she didn't even flinch. Ricky frowned. "Man, forget this," he grumbled. She'll just mope around the shop looking pathetic all day if I wake her up, he told himself. Ricky leaned over to the alarm clock and pressed the buttons until the alarm was set for noon. He'd deal with her later if she was angry about sleeping in so late. He didn't care. She obviously needed the rest. Ricky left the room and went downstairs to open up the shop.

Shelby came in around ten and sidled up next to Ricky for a few moments to inspect his spreadsheets on the computer screen. He nonchalantly placed his arm around her as though it were the only position the limb would be comfortable in given their close proximity. When some customers came, in they parted and Shelby cheerfully greeted the shoppers, happy to offer her knowledge of the books in the store.

Everything went smoothly throughout the morning with Ricky and Shelby taking turns at the register and helping customers. Around noon, Henry walked through the door with a small box and an envelope under his arm. Ricky came over to greet him where he stood speaking to Shelby at the counter.

"No. Sarah's still not feeling well. Ricky let her sleep in late. We've got it covered for her though," Shelby reported to Henry.

"Oh, well she's lucky she's got such good helpers," Henry smiled in spite of his disappointment.

"I'm going to have to dock her pay soon, though," Ricky patted Henry on the shoulder, coming up beside him. "Missing work two days in a row like this, well…that's just unacceptable." Ricky smirked at his own joke.

"*Two* days? Didn't she work yesterday?"

"She tried, but I sent her upstairs when she started nodding off at the register," Ricky said. "It's all right. I figure she never gets a break, so she might as well take advantage of it while I'm here."

It was one thing for Sarah to close the shop once for a trip out of town, but Henry had never seen her miss a day of work in all the time he'd been coming to the store. A week hadn't gone by that he didn't see her in the shop for both of his weekly deliveries. Henry wondered if his dismay at not seeing her now was a bit greedy on his part. Seeing her last Saturday when he'd picked Ricky up for football practice had merely been an added bonus, he knew that. Still, he had the urge to find a reason to see her today and hoped he was familiar enough with her now that checking on her well-being wouldn't seem inappropriate. She didn't have anyone to look out for her other than the rest of the shop keepers on Blinney Lane. However, they were all busy with their own stores, just as Sarah usually was. Henry hated that fact — a beautiful, hardworking woman like Sarah left to do everything on her own.

"Do you mind if I...just go up and check on her," Henry mumbled to Ricky, "and...say hello?"

Ricky suppressed the coy smile that wanted to creep across his face. "No. Not at all. I set her alarm for noon, so hopefully she'll be up by now. Maybe you can calm her down in case she's mad at me for letting her sleep in."

Henry slapped Ricky on the shoulder. "I'll do my best," he smiled.

Henry went up the stairs and felt a little nervous as he stood before the doorway leading into Sarah's apartment. He'd only been as far as that very landing once before when she'd asked him to change the light bulb in the fixture of the high ceiling. As silly as it was for him to remember when he'd changed that light bulb, Henry felt silly now feeling nervous to knock on her door. After five years he should have asked her out to dinner by now and somehow perfected the question so that she wouldn't be able to refuse. He knocked and waited, but didn't hear any footsteps approach from within.

With a sweaty palm, Henry swallowed and slowly opened the door. He winced as it creaked, and called through the narrow opening. "Sarah?" With no sound of a reply, Henry carefully guided the door open. He leaned in as far as he could without actually taking a step. "Sarah? It's Henry!" Feeling uncomfortable in his frozen position, he stepped inside, but left the door open behind him.

319

Henry looked around the empty kitchen and then through the wide archway that revealed the living room. There was no sign of Sarah and the only two rooms left to inspect were likely bedrooms. He heard the faint sound of an alarm clock chirping coming through one of the open doors as he stepped into the living room. Across the living room, Henry could see some men's sneakers and a bookbag with patches sewn to it sitting on the floor of one bedroom. He turned to look at the open door of the other room where the alarm was coming from and called again to the void, "Sarah? Sarah, I just wanted to see how you're doing?"

The sound of the alarm continued with its obnoxious beeping as Henry crept closer to the doorway, feeling like an intruder. He sighed uncomfortably as he approached and wiped his sweaty palms on his jeans. He reached up and rapped lightly on the half-open door and waited. Lord, don't let her be in the bathroom, Henry thought. I'll die of shame.

Inhaling a breath of confidence, Henry pushed the door fully open and stepped inside Sarah's bedroom. A small mound bulged underneath a comforter on the bed and Henry could see the mess of brunette hair on the pillow that poked out from under the blanket. "Sarah?" She didn't even rouse and Henry frowned in sympathy, now less worried over his intrusion. Clearly she was out like a light. He walked over to the nightstand and switched off the alarm and then hesitated to reach for her. Maybe I'll go around the other side of the bed, so I'm not scaring her from behind, he considered.

Henry walked with soft steps around the end of the bed until he stood by its side. All he could see was the top of Sarah's forehead down to the middle of her nose, but he didn't like the look of the view. Her skin was so pale it nearly matched the light cream colored blanket that was pulled up to her face. Henry rested one hand on the mattress and called to her again. "Sarah. Sarah?" He pressed down on the bed and then relieved the pressure to shake the mattress, but she didn't budge. Henry frowned and leaned forward. He grasped the top of the blanket, careful not to snag a strand of her hair and slowly pulled it down from her face. A sharp gasp pierced his lungs and he froze with his mouth open at the sight of her.

On closer look, Sarah's lips were a grayish lavender color, her skin pale to include the tightly clenched fingers pressed in a fist to her chest as though she had been shivering in her sleep. Henry reached down and felt her cheek with his hand. Sarah was ice cold and her skin was damp. Looking down at the bulky New York Giants sweatshirt she wore, Henry could see a ring of sweat had soaked through under her arm. Henry flung the cover aside and kneeled on the bed, clasping her icy fist. He shook it as he spoke, "Sarah? Sarah!"

Henry watched, eyes widened in anticipation and saw her chest slowly rise under the sweatshirt. He moved his hand from her fist to her shoulder and rocked her body several times. "Sarah! Wake up! Can you hear me?" Henry felt helpless and astounded at the same time. "Oh, no. Oh, no," he muttered and pressed his palms to his temples. He bent down and rocked her violently several more times, but her only reaction was her fist falling limply onto the mattress.

Henry dashed out of the room all the way to the open door by the landing. He stopped for a second and took a deep breath to calm himself. He didn't want to cause a scene downstairs, but knew he'd have to tell Ricky to call an ambulance. He took a step out onto the landing and traipsed down enough stairs so he could see Ricky from down below. "Ricky!"

Ricky looked around until he saw Henry up on the stairwell. He arched his brow quizzically.

"Can you come up here?" Henry tried to sound calm. Ricky looked at Henry with a confused look on his face. "Now...please."

"What's the matter?" Ricky panted from his trek up the stairwell.

Henry looked at Ricky intently and grasped onto his shoulders. "Ricky, something's wrong with your aunt," he spoke low and steady, "she's breathing, but she won't wake up. We need to call an ambulance."

Ricky stood with his mouth open and looked from Henry to the open door several times as Henry had spoken. She won't wake up, Ricky thought. That sounded all too familiar and his expression turned as worried as the one Henry was trying to conceal. Ricky pushed past the bulky man and ran into the flat all the way to Sarah's bed.

With a firm grip, Ricky rolled Sarah onto the back by her shoulder and stared as she flopped onto her back without making a sound. Even yesterday, in her weak flu-like state, she'd at least groaned when he nudged her.

"Ricky, do you have a phone up here? We need to call an ambulance," Henry spoke delicately coming up behind him.

"No! Just wait a minute," Ricky studied his aunt's face, his heart beating wildly in his chest.

"Ricky! We can't wait. Look at her!" Henry tried to pull Ricky back away from where he leaned over Sarah, but Ricky pushed his hand away.

"No! She didn't look like this last time," Ricky mumbled more to himself.

"Last time?" Henry looked down at Sarah wondering if this had ever happened before how could he have not learned about it. Her condition looked so fatal. "Has she been like this before?"

Ricky panicked, trying to think of a way to stall Henry and to process the meaning of Sarah's appearance. Would Sarah have been fool enough to go back to Farwin Wood to see Vasimus? She seemed out of spirits after she'd returned and Ricky sensed her lovers' quarrel had worked on her nerves. Then he remembered how agreeable she had been to him locking the book back in its cabinet. She wouldn't go back on purpose, he was sure of that.

"It'll pull you back in," Ricky remembered her saying of the book. Is that what this was? His mind whirred with the possibility. She hadn't looked so pale when he waited for her to awake after they'd brought Shelby back. Was it different if the book pulled you back in? What happened if the book pulled you back in? Could she come back out again or would her body die on Blinney Lane? Damn it, why hadn't she told him more about this stuff? Why hadn't he asked more questions!

"Ricky? Has this happened before?" Henry repeated himself in a louder voice.

"Yeah...yeah, she..." Ricky brought his hand over his mouth in worry.

"She what?" Henry couldn't stand the valuable seconds idly passing by that could save Sarah's life if she were in real danger.

"She...has a condition," Ricky finally blurted out. He needed more time to think without Henry prodding him to call an ambulance.

"A condition? What kind of condition? Does she have medicine we should give her? Ricky, come on. We're going to lose her," Henry's questions came in rapid fire panic.

Lose her, Henry's words jolted Ricky's attention. Ricky remembered his aunt's words just before she'd pounced on him in the water barrel: Make sure you didn't lose anything or the book will pull you back in. The breath caught in his throat upon the realization. She lost something, he thought. Ha! After all that worrying over me and Shelby, she didn't even pay attention to her own advice!

"She lost something!" Ricky declared in excitement at his discovery, sure he was right.

"Lost something?" Henry fidgeted anxiously by Ricky's side.

"Uh...yeah. Her medicine," he blurted out. "She...lost the rest of her medicine, but...Franci has something that will work. I'll be right back. Will you stay with her?" Ricky didn't wait for Henry's answer; he was already out the door.

As he reached the bottom of the stairs, Ricky glanced back up to make sure Henry hadn't followed him. He looked back at Shelby who stared at him from the stool behind the counter. Ricky rushed over to her quickly and whispered.

"Get everyone out of the store and lock up. I think the book pulled Sarah back in."

"Oh, no!" Shelby gasped.

"I'm going to go get Franci, but...Henry's freaking out. He wants to call an ambulance. I think we're going to need help keeping him away from my aunt so he doesn't fold under pressure. Will you call Mary and tell her what's going on? See if she can come over." Ricky saw her nod and reach for the phone. He sighed, grateful they could discuss the subject now without having to dance around explanations. Life on Blinney Lane was so much easier when you were part of the inner circle, Ricky thought as he rushed out the door to Franci's.

CHAPTER
TWENTY-SEVEN

FRANCI REHEARSED the fib that Ricky had told Henry on her way across the street to Sarah's shop. She lifted her gown with one hand to avoid tripping while she carried a bag of tea and her purse in the other. No one knew Sarah better than Franci and she hadn't taken much convincing to believe Ricky's opinion. Sarah had always been in excellent health and as unpredictable as illness could be, it was too ironic that she appeared to be in a coma-like state. Franci also knew the council ledgers by heart, and remembered the descriptions written by Durley Allister of how he was continually pulled back into one of his books no matter what he tried, until he finally remained in Blinney Lane on his last attempt to return. After weeks of thought, he surmised that the shoes he'd set aside in favor of a local pair from the book's world had only been worn on his first trip into the book and his last trip out.

Ricky was grateful to see Mary walking up the stairwell as Shelby let him and Franci into the shop. Shelby stayed behind and relocked the door, having gracefully dismissed any remaining customers. Franci hurried behind Ricky up the stairs and they walked into the kitchen to find Mary clasping a reassuring hand over Henry's.

"Do you have her medicine?" Henry looked to Franci as she came in behind Ricky.

Franci panted in her excitement and the rushed jaunt up the stairs. She gasped for a breath and noticed Mary give her a brief nod with her eyes wide, hidden from Henry's distracted stare. "Oh! Right here!" Franci patted her purse and smiled reassuringly. She followed Ricky into the bedroom and he waited to close the door behind her, but Henry stood in under the frame.

"Henry, dear. Won't you give us some privacy and...wait in the kitchen," Mary smiled in her calm mannerism and gently urged him back so she could step around him. "Go on, dear. We just need a little privacy for...the medicine," Mary tried to smile again with the odd insinuation of a lie she'd just uttered as she shut the door. She locked the door once it was closed and turned around to find Franci leaning over Sarah on the bed. As she approached her and Ricky, she stopped to gasp at the sight of Sarah's face. "My word! Look at her coloring."

"Shh," Ricky scoffed in a quiet tone. "You want Henry to hear?" Mary brought her hand up to her mouth and glanced behind her at the door.

"It think it's exactly as you thought, Ricky," Franci grimaced looking down at her friend's listless body. "I mean, thank goodness that's all it is."

"Thank goodness? Do you know what it's like in there now? Farwin Wood isn't the same wonderland she used to play in as a kid. And how the hell am I supposed to find what she lost? That place is huge," Ricky whispered forcefully.

"You're going back in then?" Mary queried to him across the bed from where she stood next to Franci.

"I have to. What if she needs help? It's not safe for her to wander around there by herself now. There's a war between Ranthrop and Vasimus. The whole land is divided in a feud because of her and my father. Vasimus wasn't very pleasant to be around and it didn't seem like he was any more graceful to my aunt when she saw him, and he was her only real ally there."

"Hmm," Franci sighed in disappointment, "and she made him sound so dreamy when she first told me about him."

"Francis, pull yourself together!" Mary scolded harshly. Franci cleared her throat and adjusted her spectacles. "Ricky, your aunt didn't seem to think it was very safe for you to go to Farwin Wood the last time," Mary pointed out.

"I know, but I'm the only one of us who's been there. She wouldn't want any of you to go. There's no able-bodied men on Blinney Lane except for maybe…"

"No," Mary interrupted him with a firm word.

"No. Absolutely not," Ricky agreed thinking of Reggie Nurscher's unpredictable comments. "If I could just go and search our house there with her, maybe we could find whatever it is she lost and get home."

"Ricky," Franci looked at him, "you said so yourself. Farwin Wood is a big place. What if what Sarah lost isn't in the house? Where else did she go when she was there?"

Ricky paled at the thought and recalled how secretive his aunt had been about sneaking into the swamplands. Shelby had told him how gruff and gnarly the men at Ranthrop's stronghold had been and he couldn't imagine scouring the woods with wickrits running wild.

"Well, I'm not leaving her there alone, but she certainly needs some help."

"What kind of help, Ricky?" Mary grew impatient.

"A small army," Ricky groused in his bitter despair. "Or at least a strong guard that no one would think of messing with."

As Ricky stared at his aunt's face thinking of how she should be protected by people at least as large as Vasimus, he shifted his gaze upwards to Franci and then at the locked door.

Mary followed his line of vision and then gasped, "An outsider? No! It's unheard of."

"Oh! I think it's grand," Franci cooed and gave Ricky's arm a squeeze of congratulations.

"Shelby was an outsider and she's fine."

"Tsk, are we to give away our secrets to all of Salem then?" Mary scoffed.

"Henry's not really an outsider, Mary," Franci soothed. "He's here all the time and...well, if you ask me I think he's had eyes for our Sarah for quite some time. No one would be better suited to watch over her than Henry."

Mary grumbled an unintelligible noise. "That settles it. Henry's going in with me," Ricky stood up from the bed.

"But how?" Mary held her palms out in frustration.

"Tea, anyone?" Franci smiled and held up the small bag she'd brought with her.

Ricky started for the door, but stopped to look down at his blue jeans. "We're going to need to get Henry some clothes," he spun back around to look at the two women. He glanced down at himself again and added, "some bigger clothes than I have."

"And some of those tight pants," Franci murmured more to herself as she stared off at the wall.

"Ew," Ricky muttered.

"Well, run down to the dressmaker's and I'll stay here and try to occupy Henry," Mary finally forgot her disapproval of the plan at the chance to make decisions again.

"No, wait. I have a better idea," Ricky snapped his fingers.

Ricky went into the kitchen and assured Henry that Sarah was coming around. Henry looked near as pale as his aunt did, having worried himself into a tizzy. Ricky coolly changed the subject and unfurled an elaborate lie of what they could do to surprise Sarah once she was feeling better. It was much easier than Ricky had thought it would be, or at least easier than it would have been to convince himself of the charade. Ricky elaborated about a medieval festival that the shop owners on Blinney Lane were going to have and how excited Sarah was about it. He even went as far as to tell Henry how Sarah never thought a man so confident as when he could let loose and dress up in costume without feeling ashamed. Ricky turned to adding a hint of pleading to the request for Henry to attend, so that Ricky wouldn't feel so silly looking like Robin Hood all alone. After about twenty minutes, Ricky had finally convinced Henry to go to the dressmaker's with him to select outfits together. He bragged that they could show them off to Sarah when they came back to give her a good laugh, as Ricky assured him she would be up and about by then.

Henry called his company and told them about the emergency that had come up, although he left out the part about costume shopping so he wouldn't lose his job. He wanted to wait around until he saw with his own eyes that Sarah was okay. If satisfying Ricky's own anxiousness by playing dress-up helped the boy, he'd do it to pass the time. If it did end up impressing Sarah, well, he just prayed that would be an added bonus.

On the way to the dressmaker's, Ricky asked Henry to wait for him while he ran over and spoke to Alexander at the blacksmith shop. He ran back quickly before Henry could change his mind and they continued on to the dressmaker.

Thirty minutes later, Henry hesitated to go out the door of the dressmaker's as he stood with his delivery uniform folded under his arm. He shifted his hips one way and then the other, but the fabric still clung to his legs. Henry looked at the wide-sleeved grey shirt and the dark grey leather vest over top of it that clung to his chest. The clerk had cinched a wide leather holster belt tightly over them around his waist making him feel like the entire get-up fit like a leotard. Below that was form fitting pants that inappropriately accentuated his bulging thighs above the laced up knee-high leather boots that had been difficult to find in his size. Henry sighed wondering how distraught he had been to let Ricky talk him into thinking this was a good idea. She'll never go to dinner with you now, idiot, he thought. Henry turned to look at Ricky who waltzed up proudly beside him.

Ricky wore the same style and color of everything that Henry did. Henry eyed him up and down, unable to discard the thought that he looked like a mini version of his own ridiculous self at the moment. The only difference in their appearance was that Ricky looked way too happy, where as Henry was sure he looked miserable.

"Well, what do you think?" Ricky beamed.

"I think we look ridiculous," Henry muttered.

"Ah," Ricky waved him off with a hand and yanked the door open. "That's just because you don't have your sword yet. You'll get used to it," Ricky strode out the door, but stopped for a second to yank his tight pants out from his butt.

Henry closed his eyes and shook his head as he followed his misguided little friend. "Yeah, nothing says confidence like pulling tights out of your ass," he muttered and slammed the door behind him.

Ricky and Henry walked into the kitchen to find Franci leaning against the counter by the stove. She smiled at them and giggled as Henry's sword clanked against the doorway. Ricky was happy to see the book sitting on the table and smiled at how clever and helpful his little Shelby was.

"How is Sarah?" Henry coughed away the embarrassment that choked his throat as Franci gawked at him.

"Oh, she's doing much better. Why don't you sit down and have some tea while we wait. She'll be out in a little while," Franci pulled a chair out so Henry would feel compelled to sit.

Henry sat down, happy to hide his body from the waist down underneath the table. Franci set a steaming cup down in front of him and patted his shoulder. Ricky eased around behind Henry's chair and peered over his shoulder at the cup. "This stuff is great. Franci's grandmother came up with the recipe," Ricky fibbed, remembering how awful the stuff tasted. Maybe if he gave it a sentimental connection, Henry would feel more compelled to drink it with Franci looking on at him. Ricky took a cup of the brew from Franci and went around to sit in the chair opposite of Henry.

Bringing the cup to his mouth, Ricky tried to hide his grimace at the odor. He took a sip and smiled at Henry who had his own cup up to his mouth. Henry looked into the cup after taking a sip and stared for a moment. Come on, Ricky thought. Drink up, big boy. What the heck am I supposed to do if he won't drink it, Ricky started to worry. Just then Henry took another much longer sip.

"Mmm, tastes like licorice," he turned his head to Franci. Ricky beamed at her while Henry's head was turned, but quashed the excited expression before Henry could see him.

"Told you," Ricky chimed and took another sip, wanting to choke as the strong liquid ran down his throat.

Ricky made idle chitchat with Henry, answering his questions about Sarah's supposed "condition." Luckily Franci chimed in, her knowledge of medical terms more broad than Ricky's lies. Ricky would say something and she would elaborate, somehow making it all seem credible as Henry listened intently. At one point, she gracefully poured more tea into Henry's cup, filling it again.

As the conversation died down and the yawning from Ricky and Henry ensued, Ricky tried to stay conscious long enough to make sure Henry fell asleep before he did. Ricky was happy to see Henry rest his chin on his hand as he had done. Henry queried after Sarah a few more times and Franci in her nervousness left the room to go to Sarah's bedroom. Ricky was grateful for it because the less talking, the less alert Henry might become. Henry's head bobbed a few times and he shook it to revive himself.

"Boy, I'm sorry. I'm getting sleepy sitting here," Henry yawned.

"Ah, take a nap. They'll wake us up when they come in," Ricky tried to sound as coherent as he possibly could. "I'm beat myself," he offered.

Henry leaned back in his chair and sighed. After a few minutes his eyes began to droop and he lowered his head ever so slowly until his chin touched his chest. Ricky blinked under heavy lids to see if Henry's head would rise again, or if his eyes would open. When they didn't he murmured, "Thank goodness." Ricky rested his head down on the table and closed his eyes. Don't worry Aunt Sarah, he thought as he began to nod off, Lord Ricky to the rescue.

CHAPTER
TWENTY-EIGHT

FARWIN WOOD

SARAH GROANED and felt something nudge her arm. "Ricky," she grumbled, "I'll be down in a minute." Sarah breathed in the fresh air and her senses came into focus. The air flowed into her lungs with ease, her congestion having cleared and she sighed at the warmth she felt after shivering for that last few days. Perhaps her fever had finally broken, she thought. She heard a man's voice saying, "Madam. Madam," over and over. Sarah blinked at the sound and opened her eyes slowly to see if she had fallen out of bed onto the floor. There was something hard underneath her, and when her eyes finally focused she stared down at cut grey stone slabs.

Sarah jerked her head up and spied a pair of boots in front of her. She pushed up off her stomach onto her elbows and followed the boots up to see a man in Farwin Wood type apparel crouched down beside her in the darkness. "Madam, are you all right?" he asked.

Flailing back away from him, Sarah turned over to her backside and scooted across the rough stone patio floor. She whipped her head around, still groggy from her sleep, and saw a stone wall of a building in front of her that towered over where she sat on the ground. "Wh...where am I?" she gasped.

"Miss, you are at Daundecort Hall of Farwin Wood," the man spoke softly as he looked at her.

"What? How...how is that possible?" she muttered and looked around, horrified to see that the surroundings were familiar to her. She was on the patio behind Vasimus' home where they'd walked the night of the dance when his family had welcomed her and Richard back to Farwin Wood. Sarah started to bring her feet underneath of her to stand, but the man outstretched his arm.

"Madam...perhaps you should wait to rise. I think you may be unwell."

Sarah quit moving at the sound of footsteps approaching and turned her head towards it. She felt herself go rigid when she saw Vasimus walking towards her, his expression confused and concerned.

"Sarah?" Vasimus paused only briefly upon realizing that she was the woman his guards had informed him was on the patio. He started again more rushed and swooped down to kneel by her side. "Are you all right? Has something happened?"

Sarah was surprised by his concern after their last encounter and could only muster, "N...no, I'm fine."

"But..." Vasimus looked her up and down and found no injury on her person. He was overjoyed to see her again after the way they had parted, but he wanted to know the reason behind her presence at his hall. "But you were leaving?"

"I...I was. I did," Sarah added as she put a hand to her head, "but...I came back."

Vasimus didn't notice the distress in Sarah's expression. All he heard was that she had come back. "You have come back to me," he murmured in overjoyed disbelief and lifted her up to cradle her in his arms as he smiled.

Still in awe over her return to Farwin Wood, Sarah could only gape at Vasimus and her surroundings. She didn't understand if she had sunk into a dream in her fevered delirium or if she truly was back in Farwin Wood. She certainly felt like she was back, but didn't want to believe it. With each step that Vasimus carried her into Daundecort Hall, she felt the pounding of his steps on the ground reverberate up and through her body, leading her farther and farther away from the belief that what was happening wasn't real.

Vasimus carried her through the great room and up the familiar stairs to the hallway of the living quarters. Sarah noticed the great room looked less awe-inspiring than the last time she had seen it, and knew she would not have imagined these changes.

"I knew you would come back to me," Vasimus whispered in a husky voice at the top of the stairs. Sarah shifted her eyes from inspecting the hall to Vasimus' face. He looked at her with a humbled smile, but all she could do was stare at him. He canted his brows when she did not speak. "Sarah, why were you on the ground? Did you fall?"

"I...I don't know. I've," Sarah tried to think of an explanation, but she didn't know the answer to his question, "been a little ill."

"You should not have come in search of this girl by yourself," he scoffed and quickly strode down the hallway with her still in his arms. "You should rest. Now that I have found you again, I do not want to lose you," his voice lessened with anger and rose with concern as he opened the door to the room across from his.

Vasimus set her down on the bed. He eyed the lettering on her sweatshirt in silence. "Is this your mode of dress in Blinney?" his voice was curious. "I will have some clothing brought for you," he offered before she had time to respond. He stared at her a few moments more, but Sarah could still not find any words to fill the silence. Finally, he leaned down and kissed her forehead. "We will speak in the morning. I am glad you have found your way back," he whispered before leaving.

After Vasimus left the room, Sarah let out a long breath. She wanted to scream, "But I didn't mean to find my way back!" She got out of bed and began to pace around the room, accepting that she was back inside the book. Was the book open, she wondered. Sarah knew Ricky wouldn't mess around with the book after what had happened. There was no way he had taken it out of the case. Sarah quashed the idea. She'd seen the book closed and in its place with her own eyes. A knock at the door nearly caused her to jump out of her skin.

Sarah opened the door to find a maid carrying a stack of ladies' clothing. The woman came in and deposited several dresses on top of the wardrobe and Sarah tried to hide her sweat suited self behind the open door until the maid left. She swallowed at seeing several garments to choose from, although she knew the woman had brought her options only to be kind. Sarah didn't want to think of being in Farwin Wood for any longer than the evening.

Against her wishes, Sarah found a chemise to change into. She didn't know how or when it would be appropriate for her to get back home, but she knew traipsing around Daundecort Hall in her New York Giants sweatshirt would make her the recipient of some unusual stares. As she folded up her pajamas and searched for a suitable drawer to put them in, Sarah reminded herself that she would have to take care not to lose the modern garments.

The thought created a sickening feeling in her stomach as Sarah realized the reason she was back in Farwin Wood. She had lost something — it was the only explanation. She flopped onto the bed and tried to think of what it could be, but found the task frustrating since she wasn't at Allister Hall or anywhere near the swamplands. Those had been the only places she visited on her last trip to Farwin Wood. Even more perplexing was why she had woken up, why she had arrived to Farwin Wood on Vasimus' back patio. Never before had she arrived to Farwin Wood in any place other than the glen just beyond Oedher Village. After what seemed like an eternity of scattered and hopeless thoughts, Sarah fell asleep.

THE NEXT morning, Sarah met Vasimus downstairs for breakfast. The silence between them was uncomfortable as they sat and began the meal. Vasimus smiled faintly at her several times, not near as broad as he used to as there was something dark and brooding about him which never seemed to go away. Sarah still expected that his happiness was genuine even if its physical indication was muted from the old Vasimus she remembered. Something felt different and she couldn't tell if it was her worry over what she had lost, the memory of how he spoke to her on their last meeting, or because she had been parted from him for nearly two decades.

Vasimus didn't know what to say to Sarah. The only thing that kept coming to his mind was how long she was staying, but he didn't dare find out the answer to that question, so he remained silent. Perhaps he could skirt around it, he thought. "Your nephew...has he returned to Blinney or... his home?"

"He is...on his way to Blinney, to handle things there until I return," Sarah was glad of her clever thinking. "It will be good experience for him," she added quickly.

"Indeed," Vasimus spoke to avoid another bout of silence. "It is a great opportunity for a young man to learn and prove his responsibility." He took a bite of bread and thought. "You must trust him very much to allow such an opportunity."

Sarah smiled at the thought, "I do...actually." She didn't think she would have responded the same a week ago. "Vasimus, thank you for the clothing. That was thoughtful to have it sent so quickly."

"It was Deronda's. I am sorry it is not so easy to call to a dress maker on short notice anymore with the war."

"No. I understand," Sarah blushed. "I am proud to wear her dresses. It reminds me of happy times."

"I fear I have dwelled more on what came after rather than the happy times," his voice was glum. "Perhaps your perspective in the hall again will do me good," he managed a smile.

"I hope so," Sarah added softly. She thought on the topic and decided to use it to her advantage. "I did not return to Allister Hall on my way back. I should like to go there today and let Netta and Dergus know I have returned. Then I may gather some of my things," she tried to make her words more of a statement than a question.

"Sarah, clearly you were not well last night upon your arrival and it is not safe for you to travel like it was before ...when we were younger. I shouldn't like you to go alone and I am ashamed to admit my men are far stretched as it is. I wouldn't ask them to place others in risk by shorting manpower to offer the level of security you would require venturing to Oedher Village."

Sarah's shoulders slumped. She didn't want to admit she was afraid to travel through Farwin Wood, but she didn't have time to risk being kidnapped or injured by a bandit or worse yet, one of Ranthrop's uninformed men. Not everyone in the land would know who she was and she had to face the fact she wasn't untouchable anymore after being a part of the family who had caused the onset of war. "Would a message be able to be sent at least? I could write to Netta instructing her of what I would like sent to me," Sarah offered.

"This would be wiser," he nodded.

After breakfast, Sarah wrote a letter to Netta trying to explain as vaguely as possible that she had returned without knowing why in the event the letter was abducted. She emphasized that she had lost something and that Netta should search for it in her room where she'd kept the clothing she had arrived in to Farwin Wood on her last trip. Sarah was sure Netta would understand the message, but was vexed that it lengthened her stay in Farwin Wood. She would much rather search for whatever it was she was missing herself, to give the satisfaction that no stone would go unturned. Sarah wanted to retrace every step in the hopes she could remember what it was that had gone missing. She tried not to think of what she would tell Vasimus when she was ready to leave again or what Ricky must be thinking back on Blinney Lane.

Sarah explored Daundecort Hall and its attached patios and courtyards after she turned over her letter to the messenger who had been charged with its delivery. She found the hall to be quiet and dismal with a lack of decorations in public areas, while other rooms were used to hoard and store precious family relics as though they were put there to be safeguarded in the event of a raid. She imagined Vasimus spending his nights here over the many years passed and conceded what a lonely, depressing life it must have been for him. Each day would have served as a constant reminder that the hall was nothing like it had been in his father's day, yet there was nothing there to offer hope for future happiness. Somehow she couldn't blame him for traveling down the more pessimistic road he had chosen as the course of his life. Falling victim to the desires of war and vengeance would have been easier than seeking hope in such haunting surroundings.

Although the grand passion Sarah would instantly feel upon seeing or thinking of Vasimus in her youth was damaged by the awkwardness of absence and pain between the two of them, she found herself worrying the longer he was away from Daundecort Hall after breakfast. He had excused himself directly after, apologizing that he must personally visit the captains of his outposts where the vantage points of Ranthrop's lands were best viewed. She began to wonder if he took the same route each day and if so, how easy it would be for someone to attack him. The more time that passed, the more these silly and terrifying thoughts of Vasimus' well-being began to wear on Sarah's nerves. While time, maturity, and the seriousness of her situation might have diminished her former teenage passions, Sarah could not deny the affection and concern she still felt for him.

When the doors of the great room finally opened, Sarah jumped up from her seat on a bench in the vestibule. She let out a hearty sigh upon seeing Vasimus' face as he walked through the doorway.

"Sarah," he stopped abruptly surprised to find her waiting in the shadows. "Is something the matter?" He approached and brought a hand up to the elbow of her arm that was bent holding her hand to her chest.

"No," she smiled and shook her head. For her own reassurance she brought her own hand up to rest on his other arm. "I was just…worried when you did not return straight away."

The lines in his face relaxed and his entire expression softened. How much more handsome he looked when he let this new guard of his down, Sarah thought seeing the more pleasant and relaxed look of his face. Vasimus took his hand from her elbow and brought it up to her cheek. Her skin tingled at the touch.

"You need not worry. I was in no danger today," he murmured in a gentle tone. The sight of her concern for him warmed Vasimus' heart.

"Today…" Sarah repeated, her sad eyes fixed on his.

Vasimus slid his fingers back through her hair as he lowered his lips to hers. The taste of him was still as sweet as Sarah had remembered as he pulled her close to him. The feel of his strong body against hers wiped away her worries. The solidness of him made her think of invincibility and the great force that would take to smite this man. When the fear of his well-being had left her, another concern arose through the passions that were forming in her. As indestructible as Vasimus seemed, Sarah knew one reality that have never deterred his love for her. She could not allow herself to tempt him if and when she was able to return to Blinney Lane, no matter how delectable the present physical temptations were. Sarah pulled her head away from his so their lips would part.

"No, Vasimus," she whispered. He landed one kiss on her cheek before comprehending her words and then gazed into her eyes. "I can't do this to you."

"Do what? We are older Sarah, but *that* is certainly something I'm sure we both still enjoy doing," he smiled.

"No," she laughed painfully, "that's not what I meant. I can't…ignore that nothing has changed. I still cannot stay here."

"I don't care. You came back. That's all that matters to me, that I know you still love me. If you came back, you will come again. I've thought on it and I prefer that now. You should not be here all the time while it's not safe for you. I will worry about you less knowing you are far away while I fight this war." He grasped his hands about her waist. "We'll enjoy the time we have together, cherish each day. How long will you stay this time?"

Sarah looked at him and felt pain in her entire being. "Until I find what I lost," she uttered.

"Lost? What do you mean?"

Sarah took a long breath and then began to explain what Blinney really was. She told him the version of the story that she had told Netta, hoping he would believe it as willingly as she had. The difficult part came when she had to explain how she'd returned this last time, how it had been unintentional. She ended by explaining that she had to return to Blinney Lane and needed to search for whatever it was she had lost.

"But you are real," Vasimus laughed incredulously and touched her cheek.

"I know," she cried, "and so are you." She smiled and touched his face as well. Vasimus stared at her as he processed her explanations.

After a while, his hands dropped from her and he uttered bitterly, "Would you have come back…had you not lost whatever this is you are searching for?"

Sarah swallowed and slowly shook her head. "I cannot. There is no one to rule my house in Blinney Lane and even if there were, I would not place that burden on them."

"Sarah, I would take a day now and then if you can get away as easily as you say you can. Could you not fall asleep for a day or two with this book now and again? Is our love not worth attempting that for you since it is just a matter of sleeping and not traveling miles as I had previously believed?"

"Vasimus, we are not the same people who fell in love twenty years ago. How could I come here for moments of happiness while other people suffer because of you and…" Sarah was about to say Ranthrop and herself, but the growl of Vasimus' voice cut her off.

"Me? Because of me?"

"And me! And Ranthrop!"

"He got what he deserved! I did my duty! My people will understand that! Have you grown so weak in your world that people do not trust their leaders?" Vasimus flailed his arms in fury.

Sarah trembled at the sight of the rage that had erupted so quickly in him. "It is not our duty to blindly follow an unjust cause," she cried.

"Justice? Justice! What do you think I fight for?" He took a step closer to her.

"It is your justice alone, not theirs. Ranthrop killed the man who shot Deronda. That was enough justice."

Vasimus shot her an unbelieving look at that comment. "That will never be enough for her death or what he intended to do to you! Have you forgotten? You are only lucky you had the power of this…this sorcery to allow you to escape through the water!"

"He would not have killed me! He did that only to taunt you out of his hurt. He told me so," she pleaded nearly as loud as his own ranting. "He loved Deronda."

"Ha! And you believed him? If he loved her he would not have provoked me by *attempting* to kill you!" Vasimus began to pace with his hands on his hips.

"And if you loved me you would not have allowed your people to suffer these past twenty years for your own broken heart. You have lost your compassion!" The tears in Sarah's eyes were close to welling over their lids.

Vasimus stopped pacing and stared at her. His chest rose quickly up and down under raging breaths. "You have made a fool of me, Sarah. If my heart was not broken then, you most certainly have broken it now," his words were slow and unfeeling.

Sarah's lip trembled as she shook her head. "No. We are both fools. You didn't know me at all if you thought vengeance would honor my memory. And I have loved you for

343

twenty years because I never imagined in any lifetime that you would become this selfish and blind." She turned away and started across the great room before Vasimus could see the tears fall from her eyes.

Upstairs in her room, Sarah walked to the balcony doorway and looked out on the desolate land below. She let her tears pour freely from her eyes and wondered if she was doomed to stay in the place she once loved with the remnants of the man she once loved. The breeze from the open doorway wafted in and cooled the hot tears on her clenched face and she wiped at them as they rolled down her cheeks. The door burst open with a thunderous slam and Sarah jumped. She spun around to see Vasimus looking at her with wild anger in his eyes. He breathed in at the sight of her distressed face and she lowered her eyes in her shame.

Vasimus strode across the room and Sarah braced her arms around herself as she looked up to see him approach. Her back tightened as he neared, but his eyes were not on her. He stared out the balcony doorway and strode straight past her out onto the small balustered landing. She watched as he drew his sword and brought it down with all of his might on something around the doorway that she could not see.

Sarah flinched at the sound of a loud thud and then another, which reverberated a hollow plunking sound. She watched as splashes of water flicked up into the air on Vasimus' face while he slung dept blows to the place where Sarah remembered the rain water tub sat on the balcony. She gasped as she heard the cracking sound of the wood and a few seconds later the sound of trickling water was followed by a loud splash. A puddle quickly formed at Vasimus' feet as he sheathed his sword and looked down at the water spilling over the base of the balcony's edge.

Vasimus turned back towards the room and gave her only a cold passing glance as he took great strides out of the room, slamming the door shut behind him. Sarah took gulps of air and brought a shaking hand to her chest as she looked back to the sound of the water spilling off the balcony. She closed her eyes and shook her head that Vasimus had become so incensed he thought to remove the rain water tub from her access. She hoped he would calm down and accept the realities of what she had said down below, but just as the thought crossed her mind she heard a rattle at the door. Sarah walked over to it as the noise continued and caught her breath at a sharp click sound.

He locked it? He locked me in! Sarah rushed to the door and pounded. "Vasimus! Vasimus! You can't lock me in here! What are you thinking?" Sarah silenced herself and pressed an ear to the door. All she heard was the scrape of his feet just before his footsteps departed down the hallway. "No," she moaned and slid down the doorway to crumple on the floor.

CHAPTER
TWENTY-NINE

FARWIN WOOD

H ENRY PEERED around the forest from where he knelt down on one knee. He felt like he was in his high school Algebra class again. That was the last time he could remember feeling there were so many things all at once he didn't understand. Why did he wake up in the woods? Why was Ricky asleep on the ground next to him…in these woods? Why did the woods smell like a mixture of some floral scent he'd never known before and charred wood? How did they get from Sarah's apartment to here without him remembering it? Why in the hell had he let Ricky talk him into wearing tights? When had there been a drought or wildfire in the greater Salem area to cause this much damage to the forest? *Tieeeerrrrumpt!!* What the hell was that sound?

The shrill sound in the air was followed by a groan from Ricky who slowly sat up next to him. Ricky blinked and yawned as he stared calmly across the stream in front of them. Henry breathed quietly, but rapidly as he watched Ricky's reaction to their surroundings. Henry wasn't dreaming this, he knew that. Seeing the boy freak out would just prove as an affirmation for him.

Ricky sighed and looked at Henry. He smiled and slapped Henry on the knee, "We're here." He got up off the ground and looked around, paying special attention to a spot directly across the stream from them.

"Here? Where exactly do you think *here* is, Ricky?" Henry rose from the ground with hesitation as he stared at the back of Ricky's head.

"Farwin Wood," Ricky whispered now.

"Farwin Woods?"

"Farwin Wood...dh." Ricky enunciated the singularity of the last letter.

Henry shifted his eyes back and forth at the woods without moving any other muscle. "And...why would we be there?"

"Because I needed you to come with me to help my Aunt Sarah," Ricky turned around slowly to face Henry.

"Okay, buddy. I put these silly clothes on because you convinced me it would cheer her up, but how does taking me out into the woods...and I'd like to know how you managed that without me remembering it...how does being out here help Sarah?" Henry held his hands out palms to the ground as though the earth would move below him if he didn't maintain his balance.

Ricky walked over to Henry and set his hands on the big man's shoulders. He looked Henry straight in the eyes. "Henry...you're a very sensible man so I understand that you won't believe a thing I'm about to tell you, but the sooner you do...the better you'll feel. Trust me."

Henry stood frozen with his mouth open, "O...kay."

Ricky glanced over his shoulder and then back at Henry. "First off, whisper. There's some scary…animals in this forest that you don't want to mess with. Second off, do you believe in other worlds?" Henry blinked at Ricky, one of his eyebrows arched upwards. Ricky pursed his lips, "Of course you don't. That was a stupid question. Okay. There's a curse on Blinney Lane and it does weird stuff to the shops there. Anybody that…works there is stuck there, sort of. Anyways, there's a few books in my aunt's shop that are cursed…like really cursed. If you fall asleep next to one of these books when it's open, you wake up inside the world of the book. You following so far?"

"Ricky…where are we and is this some kind of game?"

"We're in Farwin Wood…it's a book. It's the book that was on the table in our kitchen. We fell asleep next to the book. That's why we woke up here," Ricky tried to speak slowly like he would to a five year old. "The only way can get out of this world, this book, and back to Blinney Lane is by diving into some water until you feel like you're going to drown. When you wake up though, you're back where you fell asleep by the book. There's a problem though…"

"Yeah…" Henry agreed, his mouth still agape as he listened to the craziness spilling out of Ricky's mouth.

"I'm serious!" Ricky barked in a harsh whisper and tried to shake Henry's shoulders, although he wasn't able to move him much. "If you lose anything you came here with…like your sword or your boots," Ricky gestured at Henry's outfit, "the book will pull you back in like it did to my aunt. That's why she's here. She's not sick, the book got her. She's here and we need to find her and help her get back."

Henry sighed and shook his head uneasily once he realized Ricky was done talking. How could he not have noticed this kid had mental problems before? He seemed so sane every other time he spoke to him. Did Sarah know Ricky had problems? Goodness, what was going on and was Ricky going to hurt them out here in the woods? How had he gotten him past Franci and Mary?

"Ricky? Where did Franci and Mary go?" Henry asked slowly.

Ricky shook his head and scoffed. He glanced around the woods again. He didn't have time to waste explaining this to Henry. He remembered the only way that he truly believed his aunt was when he saw the wickrit and as much as he wanted Henry to believe him, he didn't want to stick around the woods and see another one of those things. "Henry, can we just get out of these creepy woods, please? Then we'll go home, I promise," Ricky fudged a smile.

Henry looked around and winced at another sound of the strange shriek and a flutter as something swooshed past them. "Yeah, let's do that."

Ricky began to head out of the glen through the woods the way his aunt had gone the first time he came there with her. He glanced back, and Henry who still stared at him began to follow. Every twenty or thirty feet, Ricky would stop to listen and scan the perimeter. Henry would stop and do the same, looking from Ricky to the woods in question.

Up ahead, Henry smelled a foul stench of rotten meat and saw something large lumped over in a viny bramble. He watched as Ricky steered clear around the mass and held his hand up to his nose as he passed it. Henry slowed on approach when he saw a horn and a hoof sticking up in the air. With his hand clenched firmly over his nose and mouth, Henry peered down at the rotting carcass of the massive beast. It was nearly twice as large as any cow he had ever seen. It had hooves with spiked claws sticking out of them. The long skull was as large as his torseo and the animal had a snout with a wide horn on the top of it that arched backwards toward its head.

"Ricky!" Henry called.

"Shh!" Ricky spun around a finger to his lips.

"What is that thing?" Henry lowered his voice.

"It's a wickrit. It chased me and Sarah the last time we were here and she tricked it into getting caught in those vines so we could get away," Ricky told him, silently happy that the animal had met a fate as bad as it had planned for them.

"A what? Ricky, *where* are we? Are we still in Salem?" Henry was intent on whispering now without a reminder for reasons he didn't know why. He glanced around in search of other similar beasts.

"We're nowhere near Salem. We're in a land inside of that book I told you about. I know it sounds crazy and I didn't believe it either, but I'm serious. Come on, you'll see," Ricky turned back around and quickened his pace leaving Henry to try and catch up so he couldn't stop to ask any more questions.

Henry came up beside Ricky alongside the dirt road that led into Oedher Village. He grasped Ricky by the shoulder to turn the boy towards him. "Ricky, take me back to your aunt's flat right now. This is no time for messing around. She's sick, okay. You can't ignore that, I'm sorry," Henry breathed quickly in his distress over their location and his concern for Ricky. Was the kid in denial over his aunt's condition? Had she died in the bedroom after they forced him to wait in the kitchen? Why hadn't he called an ambulance? Henry ran a hand through his hair as he looked up and down the road.

"Is that what you think? I'm in denial?" Ricky scoffed. He rolled his eyes knowing there was no point in arguing with Henry. It was like trying to convince a drunken person they were drunk. Ricky started walking again, sure that Henry would follow him.

When the first sight of Oedher Village appeared down the road, Ricky turned back to look at Henry. Ricky gave him a sympathetic smile as Henry looked in awe at the architecture style of the buildings. The large man bounded up quickly to him seeing that Ricky had stopped.

"Ricky? Is this that Medieval festival you were talking about? Is that it?" Henry chuckled, "I thought you said it would be on Blinney Lane."

"There's no festival, buddy. I just told you that to get you to put those clothes on so you'd fit in when we got to Farwin Wood. Sorry," Ricky slapped Henry's arm and continued into the village. He stopped only once more to tell Henry, "If anyone asks, you're from a land called Blinney, got it?"

Henry scowled and raised his brow as he looked around, "Yeah, but if anyone asks what happened to you after I get out of this, I don't know anything."

"That's the meanest thing I've ever heard you say," Ricky almost laughed. He walked with purpose directly to Allister Hall, avoiding the eye contact he'd made the last time with the villagers. When he spied Dergus standing outside the gate he beamed with joy. Finally a friendly face.

"Lord Ricky! We thought you'd gone!" Dergus laughed and slapped the young man's shoulders.

"Yeah, I know you wanted to get rid of me," Ricky smirked.

"Hrmph, you're the first drinking partner I've had in twenty years, don't let me fool you," he scoffed. "Who's the swordsman?"

Ricky's face brightened at the comment and turned to look at Henry who was staring at Dergus' clothing and the wall to Allister Hall. "You really think he looks like a swordsman?"

"Well, isn't he? He's as big as a stroomphblutel," Dergus chuckled.

"*Lord* Ricky?" Henry finally spoke.

Ricky threw a sour look at Henry and then slid his thumbs underneath his belt as he rocked back on his heels. "Henry, may I introduce Dergus, guardsman of Allister Hall and captain of the gate." Dergus chuckled at the title Ricky added due to the addition of Vasimus' men within the courtyard. "Dergus, this is…Master Henry Teager, my…personal guard."

Henry sighed lightly as to not offend the man who looked to be about ten years his senior. He still hadn't figured out this charade Ricky had gotten them into, but one thing was certain, Henry had never been a rude man. "Nice to meet you, Dergus," he said grasping hands with the guardsman.

"Dergus, can we go inside now, please? I'd like to see my aunt."

"Hrmph, well Lord Ricky you don't need to ask me to go inside, this is Allister Hall after all, but if you want to see your aunt you won't find her here." Dergus opened the doors.

"Imagine that," Henry muttered under his breath, his head shifted to observe everything.

"What do you mean she's not here?" Ricky passed through the gate.

"Well, she left. The day after you did, back to Blinney. I thought she would have told you that," Dergus closed the gate.

"She did. But has she returned?" Ricky began to panic.

"No," Dergus was now curious sensing Ricky's alarm. "Will we be expecting her?"

"Yes, I think so, but…I thought she would have been here by now," Ricky rubbed his forehead and looked to the ground in thought. What if something had happened to her when she came back? What if a wickrit had gotten her?

"I hope she hasn't gotten into some kind of trouble with Groslivo over that Shelby situation," Dergus scratched his chin in thought.

"Shelby? You know Shelby?" Henry blurted out.

"Yes, she was here with Lady Sarah and the young lord here just a few days ago," Dergus muttered still perplexed over the new information about Sarah's whereabouts.

"*Lady* Sarah?" Henry looked at Ricky who paid no attention to him.

"Yes, that's what I said," Dergus scoffed and headed across the courtyard to the doors of the hall.

Henry saw a movement in the corner of his eye and peered up into a watchtower on one side of the gate. A bearded man in a pennant style tunic peered down at him. Henry followed the other stone tower up and saw a second man in the same colors as the first guard gaze down at him with a quizzical look on his face. Henry turned back to see Dergus and Ricky enter the two-story stone building at the end of the courtyard. He jogged up following behind them.

Ricky found Netta who, in spite of her apparent surprise and happiness in seeing Ricky again, appeared distressed. She informed him that a letter had just come from Sarah and handed it over so that he could read it.

"Ricky? Are you all right?" Henry took the letter from Ricky once the boy's eyes had dropped away from reading it. The paper slipped out of his lax hand easily. Henry recognized Sarah's handwriting but didn't understand the meaning of her message or why he cared about a letter that had nothing to do with why she had appeared to be in a coma back in her bed. "Who's Vasimus?" Henry felt compelled to ask.

"Dergus? Can we get another stroomphblutel?" Ricky muttered.

Dergus puffed out his cheeks and blew the air out slowly as he thought. "I'll see what I can do, m'Lord." He left them and went back outside.

"What's a stroomphblutel?" Henry looked at Ricky who seemed pale and was staring at the floor again. Henry turned to Netta and gave her a pleading look.

"Are you not from Farwin Wood, dear?" Netta asked.

"Farwin Wood..." Henry repeated the name after her for the simple fact that he didn't know why so many people seemed to think it a commonly known place. "No...I'm from...

Blinney," Henry looked back to Ricky who finally sighed and looked up at Netta.

"He doesn't know anything about all of this. He still doesn't believe we came here through the book," Ricky explained to Netta as though Henry wasn't even there.

"Ohhh," Netta's face lit up in understanding. She gave a kind smile to Henry then. "I'm Netta, housekeeper and cook of Allister Hall. I've served the Allister family for years." Henry glanced around the dusty tomblike stone room. "And you are?"

"Uh...Henry. I...deliver things to Sarah's store," he stumbled over his words not knowing why his explanation felt like it would be foreign to the woman. Her face lit up after he spoke and she reached out and clasped his hand.

"You're Henry?"

"Y...yes."

"Oh, Sarah told me about you! What a handsome man you are, I must say. She's certainly chosen well," the old woman smiled so widely her eyes crinkled at the corners.

"*Chosen* well? She...she told you about me?" Henry staggered, dumbfounded by the feeling it gave him that Sarah had ever spoken about him to anyone. He backed up and took a seat on the bench by Ricky. Sarah never went anywhere, he thought. Who are these people that all seem to be so familiar with her? And *where* the hell are we? It's starting to sound like she has an entire life I don't even know about. Henry realized he was gawking like a fool in his bewilderment. "I'm sorry. I don't even know where we are. This is all a little too much for me. Can someone please tell me what's going on?"

"You poor thing," Netta patted him on the shoulder. "Ricky's telling the truth. There are two worlds, yours and ours. And this...this book, for whatever reason, has the power to bring you to our world. I've never been to your world, but Sarah would never lie to me and she told me all about it. She

354

even told me about you. She fancies you, you know," Netta leaned to peer into his face a bit more.

Henry caught his breath from the shock, "She...she does?"

"Oh, she wouldn't have told me if she didn't, but she never had the heart to tell you about the strange things that happen, like with the book. She imagined you'd...well, react as you are now and think she was crazy." Henry let out a soft laugh of disbelief on multiple counts.

"Is that all I had to do to get you to believe me, Henry? Is tell you that my aunt goes gaga whenever you're around?" Ricky finally spoke and looked over at the two of them.

Henry grimaced, "I...never said I believed all this...yet."

"Well, you'd better start believing because she's here and she's in trouble! If we can't find a way to help her she might never be able to get back to Blinney Lane," Ricky's expression was sour. "I...I am sorry though that I dragged you into this. I didn't know who else to ask for help." Ricky then gave Henry a look of earnest guilt.

Henry looked from Ricky to Netta and back out into the great room. Candles flickered on the walls. There was no electricity in the building, he noticed. He hadn't seen any cars on the road—a *dirt* road. "What kind of trouble?" he finally asked.

"Remember how I said if you don't leave here with everything you came with, the book can pull you back in?"

"Uh...vaguely," Henry muttered.

"Well, the book was locked up. It wasn't even open. There's no way she would have gone in just by falling asleep. It pulled her back in, back here to Farwin Wood! She lost something when we came here over the weekend and doesn't know what it is. Netta said she can't find anything that Sarah would have brought with her when we came here. I didn't know about the book and loaned it to Shelby. Shelby woke up in the book so we had to come in and help her get back

355

out, since she was like you and didn't know what the hell was going on. While we were here, Sarah must have lost something." Ricky spoke quickly in his anxiety.

"Well...then we just look for it. What would it be?" Henry swallowed at his words. He was in a book? How long did the air last in a book? How had Ricky said you get out of the book?

"I...I don't know. She doesn't even know according to that letter," Ricky stood up and began to pace. He leaned his head back and folded his fingers together on the top of it as he walked.

Henry looked down at the rugged parchment paper and read the words again. "Who is this Vasimus guy and why is she at Daun...Daundecort Hall?"

"Vasimus...was her first love. Her only love...well, maybe that has changed," Netta squeezed his hand and smiled meekly. She began to tell him the story of Richard and Deronda and all that had passed. Ricky disappeared upstairs as Henry sat listening to Netta. He came back down a while later and went into the kitchen, but Henry barely noticed as he was absorbed in the old woman's story.

If all of this was true, Henry thought, how could Sarah, or anyone for that matter, have gone on and functioned in a normal life afterwards? The whole thing was too much to take in all at once. Henry felt mentally exhausted. Most of the time, he prided himself on being calm and content. He wasn't quick to get a rise out of and rarely was he ever depressed. Henry thought of himself as a happy guy whom nothing bothered. Now, however, he sat with a storm of emotions. He felt empathy for Sarah for losing a friend, her childhood innocence of the world, her close relationship with her brother, and even losing love. He had to admit that he also felt jealousy towards this Vasimus character, especially if he distressed Sarah now after all these years. She was too fragile and kind to combat any manipulative ploys of guilt. The burden she must have felt all these years worrying about others and neglecting her own happiness, Henry bemoaned silently. Most of all Henry mulled over what Netta had said about Sarah's feelings for him. Sarah cared for him but felt she had to hide it?

"I can't find anything, Netta!" Ricky whined when he came back into the great room. "Did she leave any strange looking clothes when we left? Something that might not be familiar to you?"

"No, Ricky. I'm sorry. I couldn't find anything either and I sewed every dress she ever wore in Farwin Wood with my own hands so I'd recognize anything foreign," Netta sighed.

"What I don't understand is why she didn't wake up *here*," Ricky folded his arms over his chest. "Why did she wake up at Vasimus' place? When we arrived we woke up in the same place me and Henry just did." The three of them were silent, each lost in their own assumptions. Ricky paced in front of them.

"You said the book *pulled* her back in?" Henry finally broke the silence.

"That's what she warned me about," Ricky grumbled.

"Well...if it's a pulling force because she lost something...would the force be from the thing she lost?" Henry felt his cheeks go flush as Netta and Ricky stared at him. "I'm sorry, I know that sounds stupid," he sighed. "I don't know how this works."

"No..." Netta smiled and looked at Ricky.

"Yeah, that might make sense," Ricky rubbed his thumb against his index finger held out before him. "If that's what caused the pull to come back and she woke up at Daundecort Hall then...then maybe what she lost is there!"

"My goodness, I wouldn't have thought of that," Netta exclaimed. "Ricky...Dergus and I will keep looking here even in the courtyard, just in case. Do you think you could go to

Daundecort Hall to your aunt? I don't like the thought of her being there alone with Lord Vasimus after the way he spoke to her."

"What did he do to her?" Henry snapped without thinking.

"His words were not pleasant. They did not part well," Netta grimaced.

Henry stood up off the bench abruptly and pinned his stare on Ricky. "Let's go. Where does this guy live?"

CHAPTER

THIRTY

EVERY SINGLE patron in Oedher Tavern stopped speaking and stared at the odd pair of men who had just walked through the door. The room was dark and smelled of dank beetleburry ale and sweat. Several women sat in the laps of some filthy-haired men at the round wooden tables which littered the tavern hall.

Ricky swallowed a tight gulp in his throat as the eyes scanned over him and Henry. Most of the expressions he was met with were of awe, likely at Henry's size. Some were curious as they fixated on their much cleaner clothing, but others just seemed annoyed as they stared at Ricky's face. He felt like he'd just farted and robbed their bank. Do they have banks here?

Clearing his throat, Ricky called out, "I am looking for the brothers Wortwart."

After a pause, a chair in the back of the room creaked as a wild looking red-haired man stood up from his seat. "We are Wortwart," the man drawled out, hands on hips. A man in the seat next to his slowly turned and peered over his shoulder at Ricky. His square jaw and thick bridged nose made his face look exactly like the first man's, with matching red hair.

"I was told you have a stroomphblutel. I would like to hire it from you," Ricky stood firmly, trying not to lower his chin as he spoke.

"It's not for sale...or hire," the man scoffed and walked up to the middle of the room.

Ricky grabbed a small leather pouch from his belt that he'd found in the chest where the troogies were stored at Allister Hall. He tossed the pouch so it landed on the table next to where the first brother Wortwart stood. "I'll pay you a hundred troogies for two days."

Several people let out quiet gasps and stared at the coin purse on the table. The man looked down at the pouch and Ricky thought he saw the man's eyebrows rise at the sight of it. The other brother came up beside the first to also ogle down at the bulky pouch and then gawked at Ricky and Henry.

"Another fifty to take me to Daundecort Hall."

"And who are *you* to be throwing around troogies like that? Not that there's much to buy with them in case you haven't noticed, *fancy lad*," the Wortwart crossed his arms across his chest and smirked as he canted his head to the side.

"Lord Richard Allister the Second, of Allister Hall and Blinney," Ricky brought his own hands to his hips.

More gasps throughout the tavern sounded, a little louder this time. "I thought you looked like Richard," the first brother sneered.

Henry shifted beside Ricky noticing the reactions of the patrons. Some got up and walked out the back door. He didn't like the look of this. No one seemed to want to have anything to do with them.

"I need to leave immediately. Are you going to help or not?" Ricky spoke more firmly this time.

"Tsk, and why should we be helping you?" the other brother sneered.

"You kidnapped a mistress of the Allister court the other day and gave her to Lord Groslivo. Lady Sarah was not very happy that she had to travel from Blinney and fetch the girl back from Ranthrop, nor was he too happy to learn you'd put him in such a position that could fuel the fire between he and Lord Vasimus." Ricky impressed even himself with that warning as he watched the Wortwart brothers go pale.

"Lady Sarah? But she's…"

"Alive. Very much alive. As we speak, she is at Daundecort Hall trying to seek peace on behalf of Lord Ranthrop. Now…are you going to take me and my man there or not? You're lucky I'm offering you something for your services instead of seeking reparations for the girl you stole," Ricky didn't have to fake his anger thinking of Shelby being duped by these two country bumpkins.

The brothers looked at each other, both met by the other's worried expression. "We meant no offense, Lord…Richard," the second man said. "We didn't know that Sarah…Lady Sarah lived or that the girl was from her court. We'll take you to the road that leads into Daundecort Hall."

A half hour later, Ricky and Henry met the Wortwart brothers in front of Allister Hall and saddled up on their stroomphblutels. Ricky chose the one from his family's hall, while Henry was left to ride a more scraggly looking one supplied by the Wortwart brothers. The brothers, Deacon and Baisley, shared a stroomphblutel. Deacon, the one Ricky had first spoken with, rode the beast while Baisley sat in a small wagon pulled behind it.

Henry had barely gotten over the shock of seeing a stroomphblutel for the first time as Dergus led Ricky's over to them, when it was time for him to saddle his own. Luckily he'd let his wild comments fly before the Wortwart brothers had arrived, asking Ricky again if they truly were in a strange land within a book. As Henry mounted the beast, he grimaced and scowled at Ricky. "I feel like I'm riding a giant dog."

Henry's stroomphblutel took off in a hyper lumbering run on the road out of the village as Henry hung onto the saddle horn tightly. He hollered over to Deacon, "Is this thing trained?"

Deacon smirked, "Aye, but he's not had so much weight on him in a while. Probably just trying to bounce you off." The brothers laughed at the sight, both of them quite large men in their village, but nowhere near the mass of Henry.

Henry's ride slowed down gradually and let its tongue hang out to catch its breath. Henry patted its back hesitantly; grateful it decided he was staying on top of it. Ricky and the Wortwart brothers caught up with him and they road in silence down the roadway for a while with the brothers casting the occasional glance at the two men.

"It's not far now. Just about another twenty minutes and then we turn on the road to Daundecort Town," Deacon spoke to Ricky as he rode along next to him.

"How will I know it?" Ricky inquired.

"You can't miss it. It's the tallest building on the hill," Baisley spoke lazily where he lounged in the wagon and wiped the sweat from his brow. Baisley rubbed his eyes and peered down the road in the direction they had come from. "Someone's coming."

The men all turned around to spy three figures mounted on stroomphblutels. Ricky arched a brow as he stared. Stroomphblutels lumbered along lazily or they trotted awkwardly when they ran, just as Henry's had when they started out. From the look of it these men had their beasts stretched to a pace just between those two speeds. "They're moving with a purpose I think," Ricky muttered offhandedly.

"What's wrong with you," Henry asked Deacon sourly, noticing the man's face had gone pale.

Deacon turned to look at Ricky and Henry, his mouth flapping open. "It's Groslivo's colors. I'm sorry," he whispered and yanked on the reins of his beast to turn it off the roadway.

"Where are you going?" Ricky called as Deacon steered the stroomphblutel and wagon into the tree line along the road. The wagon arched up on one side as Baisley hung on tightly, his eyes affixed to the approaching men.

"Halt!" one of the approaching riders called.

"Ricky, what's going on?" Henry muttered as his beast shifted underneath him.

"I don't know. Maybe someone in town ratted us out," he whispered.

The riders stopped several feet away from Henry and Ricky. The lead guard stared at Ricky. "Lord Richard?" the man called inquiringly.

Henry and Ricky glanced at each other. "Yes?" Ricky finally responded.

"Lord Richard Allister?" the man clarified.

"The second," Ricky added, worried he'd be confused with his father.

"The second?" the man urged his beast to walk slowly to Ricky's side.

"My father was Lord Richard. I am named after him," Ricky tried to sound proud of the name.

"Tsk," the man chuckled sourly. "Lord Richard the second," he spoke sarcastically, "I think you should come with us. Lord Groslivo will like to meet you personally," his words were cold.

The other two men started to approach the other side of Henry and Ricky. Ricky gaped at Henry, who eyed the movement as well and placed a firm grip on the hilt of his sword as he looked back to the lead man. "I think not," Henry warned.

"And who...might *you* be?" Groslivo's man spoke in a snotty tone.

"He's my..." Ricky started, but was cut off by Henry.

"Personal guard Henry, master of combat," Henry gritted between his teeth. There was no way he was going to let Ricky refer to him as "my man" again, even if the self-proclaimed title Henry'd just given himself was a fib. Football was a form of combat, right?

The man swallowed and looked over Henry's large muscular arms, wondering if he should doubt his words. Meanwhile, Henry drew his sword and pointed it at the two men who'd come up near him. Ricky took the cue and drew his own as quickly as he could, holding the tip out in the direction of the snarky one who'd done all the talking.

The men by Henry started for their swords upon hearing Ricky's, and Henry swiftly brought his blade down to slice the reins of one of the man's beast so he could not steer it. Henry yanked up on the reins of his own beast and dug his feet into its sides. The stroomphblutel reared up with Henry still on top of it, and he pulled the reins to the side so the beast would be forced to turn as it came down. He elbowed the first man in the face, knocking him off his ride and then swung his blade as his mount came down to paw the other man's in the face. The force caused the man and his beast to jolt to the side. Henry swung his sword so the flat portion of the blade came up and cracked the man alongside the head.

Meanwhile, Ricky had begun to swing his own blade, meeting the blows of the lead rider. He worried that the man's advantage of strength would knock the sword from his hand, but just as the blade would touch his own, it seemed to bounce back off of his own like the opposing ends of magnets. Ricky hoped the phenomenon would continue as he didn't think he was causing the force to knock the man's blade away. It must be the stuff Franci and Alexander poured in there, he thought as he wielded the weapon. When Henry came around to his side, the man quickly yanked the reins of his stroomphblutel to flee back the way he had come.

Henry and Ricky quickly did the same but took off galloping on their stroomphblutels in the opposite direction. They slowed the beasts down as they came to the turn in the road where the Wortwarts said they would need to go. They let the beasts pant for a while as they bounded down a small incline in the road and around a curve.

"I was worried about you," Henry looked over at Ricky.

"Me?" Ricky scoffed. "Franci and Alexander did something to my sword to keep me safe. How the hell did you fight off two guys, when I could barely take care of one?"

"Franci and Alexander?" Henry shook his head at how many people lived so commonplace with the supernatural while he was still trying to accept it. "Well, back in my day they actually did fencing in gym class, but I just outwitted them so luckily I didn't have to see how little I remember."

"I hope we don't see any more of them. I don't want to get into or cause any more trouble here," Ricky grumbled. "Henry?"

"Yeah?"

"I meant it…when I said I was sorry for dragging you in here with me. I'm sorry I didn't know what to do."

Henry felt himself smile, "It's all right. Apart from the clothes," he looked down at himself, "and the weirdness of it all. I'm guessing you've given me something to remember for a very long time. Besides…if Sarah's in the trouble you say she's in, then I'm glad you brought me. Your aunt's a good woman. I'd do anything to help her. She wouldn't want you to go through this all by yourself."

"Yeah," Ricky's sigh was forlorn, "but she's going to shit when she sees that I brought you here."

Henry laughed, but stopped when he saw the hilltop fortress in front of the setting sun up ahead of them. "Wow," he muttered. A large stone wall ran all the way around the top of the hill with rooftops sticking up over it. At the highest point of the hill was a breathtakingly majestic imposing stone building with squared towers at each corner.

"That must be it," Ricky murmured.

They travelled up the winding road through some lower otlying villages and under a great archway that led into the walled hilltop fortress. People looked on at them as they passed, but didn't gawk like those in Oedher Village had. These people seemed well-dressed, but Ricky could tell their clothes were dated from the wear of them. The war had even hurt the upper crust of Farwin Wood. Ricky and Henry followed the winding road through the town, keeping their eyes on the great hall as it grew larger in size with each passing step.

At the gate, the guards inquired of them and Ricky announced himself as he had been getting used to doing. They were let inside the courtyard, but told to wait. Some stable boys came out and escorted their stroomphblutels away. Henry felt compelled to pat his beast goodbye for not throwing him off and for the deft blow it had delivered during the roadway fight.

The doors to the hall were opened and a guard motioned for Ricky and Henry to enter. They looked at each other, both surprised it had all gone so easily. Ricky shrugged, "I guess my family still has some pull here."

Henry didn't want to think of why the Allisters would be so easily welcomed into Vasimus' home. He couldn't imagine Sarah in this enormous ominous place. He'd only ever seen her in her quaint little book shop. Henry's own home wasn't even comparable in size to Sarah's two story building. How was he supposed to compete with mythical animals and a massive castle, he wondered. The thought didn't sit well with him as he realized too potently that he was about to enter the home of his possible competition and her former love interest. He sighed and walked up the stairs next to Ricky. Thinking about his little one-story ranch house and glancing down at his outfit, feeling like one of Robin Hood's "merry men", Henry groaned inwardly. "He just had to have a castle, didn't he?" He muttered under his breath.

CHAPTER

THIRTY-ONE

IT HAD to be close to five o'clock from the look of the lowering sun in the sky, Sarah thought as she moved away from the balcony and back into her room—now her prison. She walked over to the door and listened as she had several times in the last few hours, but heard nothing. A maid had brought some food up for her on a tray around lunch time and a guard stood by the doorway as the woman silently deposited it on a small table in the corner before she left. Neither person had said two words to Sarah before the door was closed and the sound of the lock clicked again.

As she paced away from the door again, she jumped at the sound of a rattling noise on the other side. She turned around as the door opened to see Vasimus standing there. His face was somber. It held no joy or anger, just a blank look as their eyes met.

"You have visitors," he looked away. "Your nephew is here."

Sarah felt her heart skip a beat. Ricky! Ricky had come for her! What a clever boy, she thought. Still, her joy over being freed from the room was mottled by the anxiety of Ricky being back in Farwin Wood. He shouldn't be here, she thought. Not with that face of his father's he carries around. She held her hand to her chest and walked carefully towards the door, wondering if Vasimus had only come to inform her of the news. She watched as he stepped away from the door and into the hallway, leaving it open as he did.

Stepping daintily out into the hallway, Sarah glanced up at Vasimus. His gaze was directed towards a place on the wall beyond her shoulder so that he didn't have to meet her eyes.

"Your nephew may stay here. It is too late to travel back out on the road tonight." The key ring in Vasimus' hand rattled as he looked down at it. He clasped his fingers around it to silence the noise and walked towards the door of his room. "Your door will remain unlocked," he muttered over his shoulder before he went inside his room.

Sarah hurried down the stairwell with excited steps. She wondered how Ricky had found his way to Daundecort Hall, having never before been there. She hoped he had seen Netta at Allister Hall before coming. With any luck, Netta would have turned up something that Sarah left behind and sent it along with Ricky.

As she reached the bottom step and looked across the great room between the wide stone pillars that lined the room to support the ceiling, she saw Ricky gawking at the vastness of the room. Her heart jumped and for the first time since before Vasimus had shattered the rain barrel on her balcony, she smiled. Sarah grasped a handful of her gown and raced over to her nephew.

"Ricky! Oh, Ricky!" she cried. She wanted to weep at the sight of him, but settled for throwing her arms around him and squeezing him tight.

"Oh, thank goodness. Are you all right?" Ricky grasped her elbows and looked her over.

"Yes. Yes, I'm fine, but you shouldn't have come here," she scolded him softly as their voices carried throughout the high ceilinged room.

"Yeah, yeah. Save it. You didn't look so hot back at home. Once we figured it out I wasn't about to let you stay here by yourself with your crazy boyfriend."

Sarah scoffed, "He's *not* my boyfriend, Ricky." She let her scowl fade and smiled at him again. "But how did you get here?"

"I...had a little help," Ricky glanced over his shoulder.

Sarah was startled by the sound of a scrape against the stone floor. She scanned the room and gasped when she saw Henry next to one of the wide pillars. She blinked and looked him up and down as he walked slowly over to her. "Henry?" she gasped, still taking in the sight of him in his Farwin Wood clothing.

Henry felt like he couldn't breathe. He knew he shouldn't doubt Ricky's story about the book anymore, but it still didn't change the fact that his mind wanted to find fault in the idea. Gazing at Sarah however, in her long smoky blue gown with her shiny hair wound into a mound of intricate braids at the back of her head, left him stunned. She looked gloriously beautiful. She looked like she should be called Lady Sarah and nothing else in her royal appearance. More importantly she looked alive and tangible. Henry was grateful for the color in her cheeks and the vibrancy in her eyes, but he wanted to touch her, just to prove he wasn't dreaming.

"Henry...I...I can't believe you're here," she whispered. She cast a quick look of disbelief at Ricky, who squirmed in place.

"I figured I'd better not come here alone," Ricky whined.

"Is it you? How can it be you?" Henry gasped. "You were...you were so pale and...cold," his eyes traveled up and down her with each tiny movement she made.

Sarah brought her palms to her mouth and winced. "You… you saw me like that? I'm sorry, Henry. I hope this…this whole thing hasn't scared you or…made you lose your mind."

Henry let out a weak laugh, "I'll be careful who I call crazy after this, that's for sure."

Sarah chuckled at the look on Henry's face. He did believe. She could see it. She was glad that she wasn't the one who had to tell him all he needed to know to get to this state of acceptance. She didn't think she could have bore seeing how he must have reacted on waking up in Farwin Wood. Oh brother, Franci probably had a hoot of a time serving him tea. And those clothes, she thought as she looked over his formfitting appearance.

Henry reached out hesitantly to touch Sarah's arm, but she just looked up at him with kind eyes, letting him know she understood why. He grasped her arm with a light squeeze and she laid a hand on his chest so he could finish the epiphany that she was real and they were both *here*. Henry let out a soft laugh and exhaled.

"It's really me, Henry," she felt like blushing now and smiled. "I'm all right."

Henry wrapped his arms around her and pulled her to his chest. He closed his eyes and sighed, resting his face against her hair. "Lord, I thought you were going to die," he whispered.

Sarah gingerly rested her hands on the backs of his firm triceps and squeezed. She closed her eyes as her head was pressed against the leather vest on his solid front. The comforting feeling of being in his arms for the first time in her life was like a dream, especially after what she had gone through that day. Sarah didn't think herself fragile, but she couldn't help notice the way Henry held her so delicately. If this was how he held her during a near death experience, it was nothing compared to the way Vasimus would have reacted in his all-consuming possessive manner. She pulled her head away to look up at Henry's face, their arms still about each other. His expression appeared concerned and pained, but was nothing like the dark and intense look she was used to from Vasimus.

"Aunt Sarah?" Ricky chimed in causing her to break away from Henry's gaze. "We couldn't find anything at Allister Hall...that you might have lost."

"No," Sarah cried softly. "Ricky, what am I going to do? I can't stay here. You have to go back and look again."

"No. That's just it. I don't think it's at Allister Hall. Henry had an idea," Ricky looked to Henry. Sarah turned her head, confused as to why Henry of all people would have an idea about the matter.

"Sarah...you woke up here?" Henry's brow was furrowed in concentrated worry.

"Yes."

"Well, then wouldn't that mean that what you lost... might be here?"

"Huh," Sarah looked off at nothing in particular. "Well, yes. I suppose it could, but I never came here last time."

"Well you said yourself that people had been robbing and looting," Ricky chirped. "What if someone got into the hall and took something of yours or what if you dropped something and the person who picked it up is here?"

Sarah chewed on her thumbnail and began to pace. "Can you search the hall and the grounds tonight?" she whispered looking over her shoulder to make sure they were alone. "I think Vasimus would be afraid I was trying to leave if he sees me wandering around," she looked to both Ricky and Henry.

"He can't force you to stay here, Sarah," Henry grumbled. Sarah blushed in shame.

Ricky brought up a hand to silence Henry, "What would we be looking for?"

"I don't know!" She threw her hands up. "I had my shoes and dress when I woke up and my bracelet. Maybe I lost a ribbon or a tie from the dress. I'm not sure."

"Great, we have to go around peeping at all the women and look like perverts," Ricky grumbled.

Sarah grasped her nephew's arm. "Ricky, please. I don't know what else to do."

They all froze and turned at the sound of footsteps from the other end of the great room. Vasimus descended the last step and walked in his lengthy strides over to them.

"Lord Ricky, welcome to my home," Vasimus gave him a curt nod. He looked then to Henry with a stern eye.

"This is...Master Henry, my...personal guard," Ricky blurted. Henry's usually pleasant face seemed to match the scowl on Vasimus' as the two men gave each other a vague nod.

"You are welcome as my guests. Let me show you to your rooms. I have had the cook prepare a meal for you, but I am sorry I will not be able to join you this evening," Vasimus glanced at Sarah for a second to see her reaction before he continued. "I will join you in the morning for breakfast though, if you will excuse me."

"Thank you," Ricky nodded. "That is most kind." Ricky cast a glance with a helpless look at Sarah as he started to follow Vasimus.

Henry lingered a second until both men's backs were turned to him. He leaned and whispered to Sarah. "We will look tonight. Don't worry." They then started after Ricky and Vasimus up the stairs to the living quarters.

After dinner, Ricky and Henry explored as much of Daundecort Hall as they could without drawing notice to themselves. Sarah walked out to the courtyard and made an excuse to see her stroomphblutel that Ricky had rode from Oedher Village. When the stable boy disappeared she inspected the stalls and the ground in the building, but didn't see anything that looked like a feminine adornment which she might have lost. What if whoever brought her lost object to Daundecort Hall had left already and taken it with them? She sighed dismally at the thought, but didn't want to lose all hope just yet.

Sarah left the stable and walked to the patio where she had woken up the other day, in the hopes she might find something at the site. She stepped carefully, bent over, and squinted through the darkness at the ground. Her exploration was interrupted by the sound of a voice.

"You should not be out alone at night," Vasimus called in a calm voice as he approached.

Sarah straightened up quickly and looked around to see if she was in danger. After finding they were alone and the concern was merely a result of his protective nature, Sarah offered a smile, "But I am at Daundecort Hall. Surely, no one would harm me here."

Vasimus glanced around as she spoke, "I do not trust the security of this place as I used to. Better that you use caution and stay indoors at night." He stopped a few feet from her, "lest I have to worry for you."

Sarah couldn't tell if his tone sounded annoyed or if it was the unenthused manner he had adopted from years of war. She took the few steps to the patio wall and sighed. "I'm sorry. I didn't mean to burden your thoughts."

Vasimus felt the pang of guilt over her remark for the way he acted that morning and also her current compassion in not wanting to vex him. He hadn't liked hearing what she said to him about how he had changed, but he knew some of it was true. She would never understand why he had become so gruff, not having lived through the war herself. Still he hoped the feelings between the two of them were strong enough to repair what had been broken. "You do not burden my thoughts," he murmured as he came up beside her. "Nor do

I wish to burden yours. I only want you safe...safe from this war. I know I have...changed, but I do not want to see this war change you as well."

"Vasimus, then why don't you end it? Why do this to yourself?"

"Sarah, there are so many slights that have occurred over the years it is not as simple a task as you think. There is no trust between the North and South. What good is a declaration of peace until trust is earned?"

"But how can it be earned without it?" Sarah countered looking up at him.

Vasimus stared into her eyes and sighed. They were on course for another disagreement, he could see that. The sight of her not hiding her beautiful eyes from him was enough to make him discard the topic. "Were you looking for something out here?" he nodded.

She glanced to the side and admitted quietly, "Yes. I thought perhaps since I woke up here maybe what I lost would be around here."

Vasimus swallowed, knowing he had been standing out on the patio not much before Sarah had arrived. The ring he had taken from her bracelet still hung on a chain around his neck where he had placed it upon his return from Allister Hall several days ago. It was safely tucked away underneath his shirt, but he rubbed at his chest to make sure he could still feel it there. The acknowledgement that she truly was bound to stay in Farwin Wood as long as she didn't find the ring put him at ease, in spite of him knowing it was wrong. Her main argument had always been that she had to return to Blinney, but if she could not, he wondered if she might grow to view things differently knowing she now *had* to stay in Farwin Wood.

"Sarah? What if...you never find what you lost? What would happen then?" Vasimus spoke carefully.

"Then...then I would have to stay in Farwin Wood," she looked off wide eyed.

Vasimus reached down to clasp her hand. "Sarah, if that is to be, I would like very much if we could cease our quarreling. I would make sure you lived well here."

"Vasimus, I don't want to quarrel with you, but...how could I live well when the people here still suffer because of me?"

"Sarah? Is everything all right?" Henry's voice came from the side door of the hall and broke the silence in the air. Sarah quickly pulled her hand from Vasimus' and looked at him, mouth open for a second before she turned and walked towards Henry.

"Yes. I was just saying goodnight," she forced a nervous smile at Henry and then walked past him through the doorway.

Henry and Vasimus stared at each other both erect and rigid in their postures. Henry didn't know if that's how wide and tall Vasimus truly was or if he imagined the man had postured his chest up and out further as he cast a cold glare at Henry. Henry gave a half bow with his head, his eyes never leaving Vasimus, before he too turned and went inside the hall. Sarah was already hurrying up the stairs across the great room and he watched her go, knowing he wouldn't get a chance to speak to her until morning.

Outside, Vasimus stewed, half angry that what could have been an intimate moment with Sarah was interrupted. Who was this guard that Sarah retreated from Vasimus at the mere sight of him? Most infuriating was that Vasimus realized he had not heard the familiar jingle of the trinkets from Sarah's bracelet as her hand had fallen away — no, was pulled away from his! She no longer wore the bracelet he had given her and while he shouldn't let such a small gesture disturb him, it did greatly.

CHAPTER
THIRTY-TWO

THE SILENCE at the breakfast table was painfully awkward the next morning. Vasimus sat at the head of the table while Sarah and Ricky sat on either side of him, facing each other. There had been a slight insinuation that a guard had no place to dine with the lords of a house, but Ricky had piped in and said it was common practice in Blinney. Vasimus said nothing as Henry took a place next to Ricky where he could view Sarah's face.

"What skills do you possess, Master Henry, to have been afforded the position of the young lord's personal guard?" Vasimus finally broke the silence in a dry tone.

The three foreigners glanced at each other with the question. "I…believe it was my strength and judgment that figured into Ricky's selection of me," Henry muttered as he cast a glance at Ricky.

"Hrmph," Vasimus grunted, "judgment I understand, although that should be left to the lord. Strength is all very well and good, but not if the bearer cannot apply it to a useful form of combat." Vasimus flung a bone down onto his plate.

"Henry is...a master of hand-to-hand combat," Ricky spoke excitedly. "And he is an expert swordsman," he smiled proudly. Under the table Ricky felt his toes smash together as Henry's boot came down on them. "Ah," he gasped quietly.

"The young lord exaggerates," Henry glared at Ricky with a pointed look.

Vasimus eyed Henry's broad shoulders again, his disdain only minimally diminished. "Well, the personal guard of a lord *should be* an expert swordsman. Lord Ricky would no doubt then benefit from your teachings."

Ricky cleared his throat under Henry's dark look, "Indeed, I have." Couldn't Henry see that he wasn't completely making this stuff up? What about the scuffle on the road the other day? The irony of the thought was compounded when the doors to the great room burst open and one of Vasimus' guards took several steps into the room.

"Lord Vasimus...a messenger from Groslivo Stronghold!" he called across the room.

Vasimus gave one of his lazy nods and his guard nodded to another beyond the doorway outside. The sound of footsteps and sword clanking against metal shin guards echoed through the hall. The bright crimson color of Ranthrop Groslivo's house could be seen on the tunic of the man who descended the few stairs by the doorway and walked towards the table.

Sarah watched as Varmeer, Ranthrop's personal guard who had escorted her and Shelby from Ranthrop's stronghold, walked proudly towards them. He held one arm bent across his middle for stately appearances only, while the other remained down to his side.

Varmeer halted several feet away from the end of the table. He gave a half bow to Vasimus. "Lord Daundecort," he stated. Then Varmeer did a half turn and looked at Sarah, "Lady Sarah," he nodded.

Vasimus' nostrils flared at the apparent familiarity between the two of them as he saw Sarah nod her head in acknowledgment of Varmeer's greeting. He didn't want to be reminded of the recent trip she'd taken into Ranthrop's lands.

"Well, what is it Varmeer," Vasimus growled.

"Your lordship, I come here assuming you have heard of the encounter Lord Ranthrop's men had with Lord Richard the Second and his man on the roadway the other day," Varmeer spoke flatly, his eyes fixed on the wall just above Vasimus' head.

Vasimus shot a look at Ricky, his eyebrow raised only to find Ricky's eyes avoiding his own. Sarah gasped, "Ricky! Why didn't you tell me?"

"The young lord was requested to come to Groslivo Stronghold with this escort to meet with Lord Ranthrop, but denied the invitation."

"Escort?" Vasimus scoffed. "The young man is less in age than us, but I assume he knows the difference between an escort and a kidnapping party when he sees one." Varmeer did not answer, only stood like a statue, eyes fixed waiting to finish his duty. "Go on, then," Vasimus sighed.

"In consideration of this refusal of a peaceful meeting," Varmeer hesitated at the sound of Vasimus' sour chuckle, but continued, "and now knowing that the young lord is a guest of Daundecort Hall, Lord Ranthrop kindly requests your approval for a duel between himself and the young lord."

"What?" Sarah gasped and looked from Varmeer to Ricky's worried face to Vasimus' brooding expression. "He can't! Why would he want to fight Ricky? He is not my brother. This is ridiculous!"

"Lady Sarah forgets this request entreats *me*, but she does raise a point. Why would Lord Ranthrop want to duel a young man he has never met?" Vasimus warned. He cast a glance at Sarah and she blushed in spite of herself.

This was more her place than his, she wanted to scream. How crafty of Ranthrop to make the request to Vasimus and not her own family.

"Your lordship, as you well know, Lord Ranthrop does not expect he will ever have the opportunity to see Lord Richard again. In light of that matter, and given that the young lord so hastily refused to meet him as to insult him in doing so, Lord Ranthrop proposes this... Give your consent to a duel with your guest, in the name of both Allister and Daundecort family honor, and Lord Ranthrop will make a public declaration of peace on said day."

Vasimus straightened up in his chair and stared at Varmeer. He was only shaken from the shock of the words and not the feel of Sarah grasping his forearm tightly.

"Vasimus! You can't allow this! He's twice the size of Ricky!"

"What of the peace you have so boldly demanded of me these past days? Do you no longer feel the people deserve peace?" he said in an eerily calm voice.

"Of course I want peace," her whisper was harsh, "but... but not..." she couldn't say it.

"Not at the hands of your own family?" Vasimus glowered at her and raised his brows. He tugged his arm out from her grasp. "You claimed yourself that Ranthrop killed the man who shot Deronda. Clearly her death was not a result of his orders. How can I deny this request?"

Sarah's mouth hung open and she gave a defeated look of pain to her nephew. Ricky had gone pale where he sat and met her eyes with a blank look. Henry sat uncomfortably out of place next to him, his fists clenched on the table.

"And where and when does Lord Ranthrop propose to hold this duel?" Vasimus turned his eyes back to Varmeer.

"He offers you the arena, your lordship. He suggests it be done as soon as possible," Varmeer cleared his throat with his final words.

Vasimus nodded in thought, surprised that Ranthrop would give him the honor of trusting him to hold the duel in his own lands. He must truly be dedicated to this declaration of peace, he thought. "You may tell Ranthrop that I consent. Lord Ricky will be present at the Daundecort arena just after noon...tomorrow."

Varmeer let out a soft sigh of relief and bowed graciously. "Thank you, m'Lord. I will deliver your answer directly." When he stood he looked hesitantly at Lady Sarah who sat with her eyes down dejectedly and thought he could see them glisten with tears. He turned quickly away and strode out of the hall before anyone could change their mind. Clearly the young man's size was no match for his bitter lord, but if this is what it would take for there to be peace in the land, Varmeer didn't care.

"Lord Ricky, you and your man are welcome to take advantage of my training area in the wing behind the great room while you prepare," Vasimus offered pleasantly while he took another bite of his breakfast. He stopped chewing at the sound of Sarah's chair scraping against the floor as she stood. He looked up to see her glower down at him before she turned and walked to the stairwell.

"Excuse me, please," Ricky muttered and shakily stood as well. He hurried out the side door to the patio, likely to vomit.

Vasimus looked over one shoulder and then back over the other until he could see neither Allister any longer. He exhaled and set his fork down, dropping both clenched fists to the table as he leaned back in his chair. He looked over at Henry and saw that the man sat with his bulky arms crossed over his chest, glaring at Vasimus. "What? This is the first offer of peace Ranthrop has ever offered me! She *wanted* peace!" Vasimus said waving an arm in the direction Sarah had gone.

"Peace," Henry repeated. "Not murder."

Vasimus' mouth turned down in a sour expression and he picked up his fork again. "Then perhaps his expert swords-man should see that he is well-prepared," he shot a taunting look back up at Henry.

Henry shoved away from the table and walked out of the room through the doorway that Ricky had gone. Vasimus threw his fork down again and slumped back in his chair, no longer having an appetite.

Outside, Henry found Ricky leaning against the patio wall, looking down into the garden grounds below. He walked up beside him and grasped Ricky's shoulder with a tight grip of reassurance. "Are you all right?"

"Yeah...I think. I just..."

"What?"

"If I'm going to have to die...I just wish it meant Sarah could go back home. I mean, what's the point if she's still stuck here," Ricky looked up at Henry.

"You're not going to die," Henry shook him as he empha-sized each word. "And we'll get Sarah home."

"Tsk," Ricky shook his head. "Now *you're* the one who's living in the fantasy Henry."

"Come on," Henry tugged at Ricky's shoulder and started walking down the stretch of patio that curved around the hall. "We'll practice a little and then we'll search again for what-ever it is she lost." If Henry didn't keep himself busy, he might lose it, he thought as he looked for the training area.

Once they found the open air patio with the wooden train-ing dummies and fencing equipment, Henry quickly came up with a game plan in his head that would best suit his young friend. Ricky drew his sword and sighed at the sight of it as he watched Henry, deep in thought and pacing back and forth in front of him.

"He's probably the same size as Vasimus, I'd guess," Henry started, "so just imagine that when we're practicing here."

"Is that supposed to make me feel better?" Ricky yelped.

"Just focus on me. I'm a few inches shorter than Vasimus, but I've got him on muscle mass at least," Henry scoffed with worry. "You're strong for your age and size, Ricky. It's not hand-to-hand combat so your speed will work to your advantage."

"I hope so," Ricky sighed. "I hope this protection stuff they put in here still works," he inspected the hilt of his sword. "I could feel it push that guy's blade away from mine when we fought on the road."

Henry spent the next half an hour showing Ricky how to block. He gave him the basics of what he remembered from fencing, but knew that was a gentleman's sport and not likely how the duel would play out so he improvised after that. The best bet they had was that Ricky learn how to fight off Henry, since he would be comparable in size to Ranthrop.

Sarah walked out of a side door from the hall and approached a bench to watch them. She sat in silence, hands in her lap as she looked on in worry. When they noticed her they both stopped clanking swords and looked in her direction.

"Ricky," Sarah glanced around to make sure they were alone. "I think you should go home."

"No. I can't. Not while I know you're still stuck here," he barked defiantly.

"I'll be safe," she insisted walking over to him. "This is stupid. It's not worth you getting hurt or..." she didn't want to say the words.

"Look, my father started this mess, whether he meant to or not. If I leave, I can't imagine the family name will keep you safe in Farwin Wood if you're still stuck here. I don't have a choice."

Henry came up beside Ricky. "He's got a point Sarah. It's not safe for him to fight, but if he doesn't, you won't be safe."

"I'd rather take my chances then let you go through with this," she barked. "I won't let you go through with this!"

Ricky inhaled and pursed his lips. "Well, I'm going to go through with it, no matter what you say. Best just let me make sure I'm prepared."

Sarah's body shook with the urge to cry. "I can't bear this. What would your father say?"

"I think he'd actually understand," Ricky offered delicately.

Sarah shook her head and looked away. She'd cried enough in the last week, she couldn't bear the shame of it anymore. There had to be something she could do to stop Ricky from so nobly going to his death. "I'm going to search every inch of this place again and again until I find what I lost," she came back with more fortitude. "Don't wear yourself out," she scolded before she left them.

Vasimus returned to the hall at lunchtime after seeing to the arena preparations. No one met him at the table and he finally commenced eating after waiting for a while impatiently. His staff informed him that the men were practicing and Lady Sarah did not have an appetite. Satisfied with this report, knowing none of them had fled, he brooded over the silent treatment he was receiving by their absence. After he finished eating, Vasimus left again to continue the duel arrangements and did not return again until dinnertime.

When everyone arrived to the dinner table and stood behind their chairs as Vasimus walked up, he thought he saw Sarah shake her head while looking across the table to her nephew. Her expression looked bleak and her eyes sad as he neared his chair. "I see you have all decided to join me this time," Vasimus spoke as they took their seats.

No one responded as the servers brought more food to the table. Vasimus looked over at Sarah who stared blankly down at her plate. The only one who looked at him was Henry on occasion, but he didn't like the look in the man's eyes and couldn't help but notice Henry's lip seemed to curl up to the side each time their eyes met. They ate in silence and Vasimus couldn't think of anything to offer to the group as he chewed, sensing they all held bitterness towards him and worry over the impending duel. Finally, he settled on that as a topic since it was likely what occupied all of their minds.

"My guards said you took the liberty of the training area today," he offered cordially. "Ranthrop's thrusts are clumsy and often from a downward angle, but his strength is great enough that he can fight so precariously and still come out successful."

After a pause, Ricky muttered, "Thank you for the insight." He truly was grateful to know that extra little bit about his unknown opponent, but thanking Vasimus sickened him. He wouldn't be in this mess if it weren't for him.

"The talk in the town is that people from all over Farwin Wood are expected to attend tomorrow," Vasimus almost smiled at the declaration.

"Does that make you happy, Lord Vasimus?" Sarah muttered and set her spoon back down.

"It makes me happy that the people unanimously approve of peace and will be mixed together in one place so freely to witness it, without fear of repercussion or mistrust."

"Imagine that...a promise between two men was all it took to allow them to do so," she added bitterly.

Vasimus shot her a look realizing her implication. He looked back to Ricky and Henry who eyed him with flat disdain. Vasimus set his fork down on the table. Just as the metal rattled on the wood of the table, Sarah stood up.

"You'll excuse me, please," her voice nearly a whisper as she turned and walked towards the door to the patio.

Vasimus pressed his palms on the table to stand, but stopped when he saw Henry quickly rise from his own chair. The annoyed look that Vasimus had cast in the direction of Sarah while she departed turned on Henry now, realizing he intended to follow her.

"I'll see after your aunt, Ricky," Henry said to him, but kept a shrewd look trained on Vasimus as he came around the table.

Vasimus leaned back in his chair and exhaled in frustration. "Your aunt's every opinion perplexes me these days," he rubbed a hand down his face. "She was much easier to speak to when we were younger."

"Well, good looks only get you so far with women as they get older," Ricky offered dryly.

"Hrmph," Vasimus grunted at the sense the boy made. "You understand why I felt compelled to commit to this duel, do you not?"

Ricky sighed and dropped his fork. He couldn't muster swallowing the food even though he had something of an appetite. "I understand, even though agreements like this can be reached by peaceful negotiations. I think if my father had any idea things had gotten this out of hand he might have come back."

"Are men so weak in your world that they cower away from fighting when there is no other alternative?"

Now he's really starting to piss me off, Ricky thought. "I'm not going to be a coward, even if I know I will likely die. It's just that we don't give way to violence as easily as you seem to do here in Farwin Wood. It's not weak to debate with your enemy, to speak like men and compromise. That takes more strength in character than...than any display of force," Ricky couldn't believe what a statesman he sounded like.

"I would like to see this take place in your land, so I could understand it, if it's even possible. You are young. What can you know of war?"

"We have our history and we teach our children the importance of it so we don't make the same mistakes again for their future," Ricky began. He segued into a version of World War II for Vasimus to prove his point, ad-libbing countries and Adolf Hitler for terms like "houses" and "lords" so that he would understand. If anything, the tale would keep him from chasing after his aunt and Henry out on the patio.

OUTSIDE IN the cool night air, Sarah hugged herself and looked out beyond the patio wall. Tomorrow her nephew could die. If that happened, she couldn't even go home to explain to Richard what a terrible chaperone she'd been to his only son. Tomorrow could also mark the beginning of her dismal future in Farwin Wood. Would Ranthrop keep his promise of peace regardless of the outcome of the duel? She could scarcely keep the happy thought of what that meant for the people of Farwin Wood, when she knew she wouldn't be able to rejoice with them. At least she would have Netta and Dergus to spend her glum days with after she buried Ricky.

Sarah wanted to have faith in Ricky, even with the sword she'd given him, but she kept thinking of Ranthrop's size and his temper when he had asked about her brother. And Henry...this was not the way she wanted to say goodbye to Henry. She'd never see him again once she sent him back. She knew Franci and Mary would know better than to allow him to return to Farwin Wood.

"Sarah?" Henry's voice interrupted her thoughts.

"Henry," she sighed on seeing him walk towards her, his gait much less intimidating than the stomping steps of Vasimus, who she had worried would follow her.

"Are you okay?" Henry gently grasped her shoulder as he came up to stand next to her.

"Henry, I found nothing today. I thought...maybe I could save him from this...this foolish duel...I," Sarah stammered for words to express her feelings, but sighed when she looked at Henry's expression of sympathy. She'd never opened up to Henry about anything, and now as she confessed her deepest anguish, she was met with nothing but kindness from him.

"Just don't think so hard. Keep looking tonight. And Sarah...I can't imagine this Ranthrop would...truly want to harm a teenage boy. Maybe he'll settle for just humiliating him tomorrow," he offered with hope.

Sarah shook her head. "No. I told him I had no contact with Richard. When he learned that Ricky was here, that likely enraged him and led him to believe I had lied to protect Richard. No, he'll want his duel and probably thinks it's a way to draw Richard out by challenging his son. To these people a family member stands to honor their house, regardless of who it is. Ricky's barely a man, but to them he's old enough to duel."

"Sarah," Henry let out a rattled breath, "I will do whatever I can to keep him safe tomorrow. I promise you that."

"No, Henry! I don't want to lose my nephew, but if you interfere and keep them from their fight, they'll kill the both of you for sure," Sarah grasped his hand and kept her eyes fixed on his. "I wish the stupid kid would just go home! He's so stubborn!"

"Sarah..." Henry brought her eyes back to his by gently turning her head with his hand under her jaw. "If your roles were reversed, would you leave Ricky stranded here?"

"That's not fair, Henry," her lip quivered and she pinched her eyes shut.

"I know it's not fair. None of this is fair, but it's true isn't it? I know you can't right now, but you should be proud of him for being so responsible and for…loving you so much. You've seen what broken hearts have done to people here. Would you want Ricky to live like that knowing you were trapped here, surrounded by the wrath of an entire kingdom he could have prevented? That's a lot to ask of a young man."

"Ugh," Sarah let out a painful sob. She brought her hand up and clasped it around Henry's wrist that held her chin. "Henry, I know I can't stop him and I know…you won't drown him for me either…you stupid stubborn men," she paused for a breath, "but promise me something."

Henry took a step closer to close the little distance that remained between them. "What?" his words a delicate whisper as his pained face watched her teary eyes look up at him.

"No matter what happens tomorrow…promise me that you will leave immediately and never come back."

"Sarah," Henry scoffed.

"I mean it, Henry! If I have to stay here the rest of my life…I don't want to see your face reminding me of what I…"

"What?"

"Of everything I truly lost," Sarah settled on the words.

"Sarah…" Henry whispered and brushed the hair from her face. "I will leave when you find what you're looking for and not a minute sooner."

"Henry, promise me!" she glared at him.

Henry let his hand slide down from her head to the base of her neck. He pursed his lips tightly together as their eyes remained locked, but Sarah's angry expression did not change. Did she still love this Vasimus character? How could she ask this of him? Didn't she know leaving her here would torture him? He couldn't stand thinking of her living in miserable depression all alone here or, worse yet, with Vasimus and the cruel authoritative way he seemed to treat her. Every fiber in his body wanted to refuse her request, but it was the only thing she'd ever asked of him, even if he didn't think it was good for her. Henry clasped his fingers about the back of her neck and squeezed when he gritted out his reply, "I promise." He looked away as he said it, disgusted with himself.

"Thank you," Sarah let out a long breath and grasped the front of his vest with both her hands. She tugged on the fabric once hoping it would bring his eyes back to hers and remove the bitter look from his face.

"And will you promise me that you'll never give up looking for what you lost?" Henry finally spoke and pinned his stormy green eyes on her.

"I promise," she whispered with conviction.

Henry suddenly had the instinct to pull away from her. If the possibility of never seeing her again was real, he didn't want the smallest touch to remember her by. He already had five wasted years of passing glances and hands brushing past each other that clouded his every waking thought. Henry took a step back, but Sarah caught one of his hands and squeezed it. She looked at him in questioning wonder.

"I'm not a noble man, Sarah, but I'd do anything to rescue you, if you'd let me," he muttered.

"Henry, you don't owe me anything. Don't dwell on me, please. Look what it's done to Vasimus after all these years. He never stopped loving me even after he thought I was dead and it's twisted him into something bitter and hateful."

"Love shouldn't do that to a man," Henry shook his head and spoke low. He let Sarah's fingers fall from his hand. "If you were mine...I would try to make the world the kind of place it was when you were in it." Henry turned swiftly then and walked back into the great room.

Sarah watched him go and felt like something had just kicked her in the heart. She braced herself tightly with her arms and squeezed her fingers into a fist on the hand that had just left his. She wanted to savor the feel of that touch—the brief touch of a man who'd just spoken a credo she'd been longing to hear.

CHAPTER
THIRTY-THREE

DAUNDECORT ARENA

SARAH WATCHED Vasimus' back shift up and down with each step of his stroomphblutel as she and Ricky rode behind him out the gates of Daundecort Hall. There was a light breeze in the warm air that fluttered the shimmery light grey fabric of her dress skirt. To her surprise, Netta and Dergus had arrived that morning, bringing with them the finest clothing of House of Allister's colors for her and Ricky. Sarah glanced over at her nephew on the beast next to hers and felt a sense of pride in his appearance. Dergus had brought a shined shirt of chainmail for him, which he wore under a finely stitched tunic to represent their colors. If they were going to be on display for this atrocious moment in Farwin Wood history, at least they looked dignified, Sarah consoled herself. She cast her head slightly backwards, knowing Henry was riding just behind them, but gave herself the reassurance by glimpsing the nose of his stroomphblutel.

Ricky could hear the hum of voices when they neared the edge of the arena. He let out a long breath and tried to peer around the dilapidated wooden beams of the awning that poked up from the high stone walls around it. What he did notice out of the corner of his eye, was the bright flash of red approaching from the opposite side of the arena's exterior. Ricky swallowed at the sight of the man he assumed was Ranthrop Groslivo.

Vasimus held out a hand for them to stay behind and he rode up to the outer gates where Ranthrop met him on his own mount. Their faces both retained grumpy expressions for a moment as the two men eyed each other, but then Ricky saw their mouths move. He couldn't hear what they were saying against the noise coming from inside the arena. He took the time to study his opponent undetected. Ranthrop wore a similar shirt of mail under his own tunic and Ricky scoffed when he noticed this. "Like he needs chainmail," he grumbled at the size of the man's arms, nearly as big around as Henry's tree trunk biceps.

Sarah reached out and grasped Ricky's hand. "Be fast. And if he fights dirty, then don't be afraid to do the same. Make yourself smaller every chance you can," she offered as she started to dismount.

"That won't be hard to do," he grumbled and got down.

Sarah came around her stroomphblutel and hugged Ricky tightly. She clasped his face with both of her hands. "Ricky...I hate this and wish you were more of a coward, but...I'm proud of you and your father would be proud of you too," she smiled painfully at him, her grey eyes sparkling with the hint of tears that had welled up in them.

The words made a genuine smile form on Ricky's face. "So you forgive me...for being a pain in the ass?"

A ragged laugh came from Sarah's throat and she pulled him to her tightly. She pinched her eyes shut and pressed her head against his while she held him.

"I love you, Aunt Sarah. Try to be happy after all of this, okay?"

"I love you too," she whispered and scoffed at his request.

"May you fight well, Lord Ricky," Vasimus' voice came and he stood with a hand outstretched to Ricky. Ricky went to shake it, but Vasimus clasped it in his and pumped their united hands slightly downward and back up before releasing. He gestured with an outstretched arm to two of his guards for Ricky and Henry to follow.

Sarah watched them go. Both gave her a last glance. She turned to see Vasimus watching her curiously with his hand outstretched to a wooden doorway in the arena wall. A Daundecort guard bowed to her and opened the door as she approached.

Vasimus waited for Sarah to stand beside him on the stairs under the arena seats that led up to the honored seating box. Once Sarah was in place he reached down and grabbed her hand. She did not look at him as he placed her palm in the crook of his arm. Vasimus watched her face as she stared blankly up the stairs, her chin raised and her mouth set in a vacant unfeeling position.

"He will fight well, I am sure, Sarah. Do not hate me for allowing this. Your family will be honored today by the peace that Ricky will bring to the land."

Eyes still fixed ahead of her, Sarah spoke evenly, "I'm already honored. There's a boy out there willing to do what a man had twenty years to accomplish."

Vasimus looked at Sarah's cold profile while she spoke. Her words hit him with a pain in his chest and tightness in his throat. He let out a breath and began to lead them up the stairs into the abyss of the cheering crowd.

They took their seats in two high-backed chairs which sat just behind the stone wall that overlooked the dirt arena some ten feet below. Behind them, the wooden bleachers were filled to the brim with people from Daundecort's lands. Sarah caught a glimpse of the smiling and cheering faces as she'd gone around the low wall behind the chairs into the honored seating box. People waved and watched as she and Vasimus took their seats. Across the vast arena was yet another stadium section of seating. It was was also filled from one end to the other. Amongst the crowd there, Sarah saw villagers, but there were also many guards and foot soldiers wearing red tunics and she knew that the opposite section was full of people from Ranthrop's lands. As they waved and cheered towards her and Vasimus, they threw flowers out into the fighting area in their direction, although none of them would have made it across the expanse to where they sat.

Even Ranthrop's people were ecstatic and approving of the peace that was about to be declared. Sarah took a small comfort in the deafening noise all about her, knowing that it was the sound of joy, yet she still couldn't help feeling the opposite. If Ricky's impending demise and her pain were worth anything, she knew the memory of these overjoyed people would be her only comfort in the years to come, she tried to remind herself.

A guard came and whispered to Vasimus, then departed. Vasimus stood from his seat and didn't even have to raise a hand for silence. The roar of the crowd instantly ceased in anticipation upon seeing him rise.

"Good people of Farwin Wood! We have lived some twenty years embroiled in war and death throughout these lands, but today…marks the end to the suffering of the good people of the North…," behind Vasimus a loud roar came from the crowd, "and to…our brothers in the South!" Another blast of cheering then came from across the arena. "With the happy return of Lady Sarah Allister to Farwin Wood, she has seen what has become of our land since her untimely departure and has offered in tribute, the hand of her nephew, Lord Ricky Allister, in duel against Lord Ranthrop Groslivo! Lord Ranthrop, do you accept this honor in the name of peace?"

The gate at the end of the arena opposite where they had arrived opened and Lord Ranthrop rode in on a stroomphblutel guided by Varmeer. The crowd went wild again on both sides with their eagerness for the words he would speak. Flowers were flung again into the arena from both sides as Ranthrop's beast strode to the center of the pit, while Ranthrop held a hand up and turned slowly from side to side with a stately wave. When Varmeer stopped the beast just in front of Sarah and Vasimus, Ranthrop dismounted and stood before them. He drew his sword and held it high above his head.

"I, Lord Ranthrop Groslivo! Leader of the Southlands and all its peoples...accept this honor in the name of peace!" The second his sword tip stuck into the ground in front of him, the screams and shouts of everyone but three in the arena resounded.

Sarah closed her eyes as the deafening cries rattled her eardrums. She gripped her fingers tightly around the handles of her chair and took bated breaths. When the cries died down, Vasimus spoke again.

"Without further delay...Lord Richard Allister the Second of Oedher Village and Blinney of the North!"

Sarah opened her eyes to watch Ricky ride in as Henry led the stroomphblutel her nephew rode on. Ricky met her eyes instantly and just gave her a nod with a faint half smile before he looked back to the general madness about him. Henry, however, looked around for Sarah until he caught her gaze and held it as the audience went wild again while he led Ricky to the center of the arena. Ricky dismounted when Henry stopped several feet away from Ranthrop. Ricky gazed upon the sight of the crowd before him while they wept and waved and smiled. They carried on this bout longer than they had previously and Ricky felt humbled by the display even when they continued in spite of Vasimus holding a hand up for silence.

Two men ran out from either side of the arena to fetch the stroomphblutels and led them lumbering away back out the gate. Varmeer inspected Ranthrop's chain mail, shin guards, and helped him to remove his sword holster. Henry came over to Ricky and did the same.

"Remember," Henry whispered as he unfastened the belt from Ricky, "use your speed and keep your balance."

Henry handed the sword to Ricky once he saw Varmeer waiting to leave the two fighters in the arena. "Henry...thanks for everything," Ricky smiled and took the sword from him.

Varmeer walked towards the wall of the arena in front of where Sarah and Vasimus sat. Henry turned and walked towards the wall in front of the Southlands crowd. Both men stood against the wall and looked out into the arena at their respective lords.

Ranthrop stared at Ricky with an unenthused look on his face. He looked the young man up and down, unsatisfied by the size of him. He felt like somewhat of a fool with their size on display for comparison, but he pushed the thought from his mind and reminded himself of the gleeful uproar the crowd had sent them. They were satisfied with the sacrifice for peace, so he would be too if it suited them.

Ricky and Ranthrop turned to look at the honor box. Ricky watched as one of Vasimus' footmen handed a daphne flower on a platter to Sarah. She took it hesitantly and then stood to meet Ricky's eyes. She turned her gaze on Ranthrop then for a moment and let it linger as if to say, "Please don't do this." Ricky followed her gaze in time to see Ranthrop cant his head in what appeared to be a feigned stretch, likely an excuse to avoid her eyes. Sarah took the step closer to the stone wall that formed a balcony rail in front of her where it rose from the arena. She stretched her arm out over the wall, flower in hand, and tossed it to the dirt.

Ricky turned on his heel to face his opponent and slowly raised his sword tip off the ground. He watched as Ranthrop held his own weapon out to his side with only one arm and stepped to the left as he approached Ricky. The young Allister wanted to take a step backwards, but he chose to shift to the left as well as they circled each other. He kept both hands on the hilt and raised the blade up so that it was parallel to knee-height.

A sharp swoosh sound came with the flash of Ranthrop's blade when he twisted his upper body to swing at Ricky's head. Ricky pivoted and leaned back, sensing the tip of the sword mere inches from his face as it swung away from him. As the crowd went wild, Ricky could feel his heart pounding against his chest. And as deafening as the cries of the audience were, he could hear the whooshing pulse of his blood deep in his ear drums.

Ranthrop growled and took a lunging step towards Ricky as he swung the blade back at a downward angle. Ricky instinctively brought his sword up this time, no longer paralyzed in fear but rather spurred on by his panic. He arched back as he swung upward to deflect the blade from reaching his skull. The metal of the swords clashed together with a piercing clatter and Ricky felt that force reverberate through his arms. The blow worked, deflecting Ranthrop's steel up into the air and back over to the side.

As they circled one another, Ricky kept his eyes on the angry look of the man. He watched for minuscule signs of movement from the man that would indicate a sudden change in footwork or stance. When he saw Ranthrop's wielding arm move back, he sensed he was in for a jabbing blow and twisted his wrists around to prepare himself to butt it, counter-clock-wise. Ricky smote the blade with all his might and deflected it barely in time to miss his cheek. He was fast, he thought, but Ranthrop was strong. Again, Ricky had felt the impact jolt his forearms into his ribs. Was the protection remedy no longer working or was Ranthrop's might just too much for what little Ricky and the hidden powder could muster?

Ranthrop's steps were forced to the side and when his torso leaned with it to follow the force of his deflected sword, Ricky gaped at the opening it created for him. Quickly Ricky remembered the fluid motion in which Henry had told him to fight, not wasting time to reposition his weapon. He swung his blade downward, back in the other direction and aimed for the place just above Ranthrop's shin guards. Ricky felt the tip slice through the cloth and even the skin on Ranthrop's leg and allowed himself to spin with the motion so he would be prepared for any angry retaliation from Ranthrop's blade. As Ricky spun he heard a growling snarl from Ranthrop. Ricky turned around to see a wild-eyed Ranthrop thrusting his blade down towards the side of Ricky's neck. He ducked and brought his blade up, diverting Ranthrop's to the space above his head.

The crowd oohed and aahed with each motion and Ricky was able to catch his breath when Ranthrop did not retaliate straight away. Ranthrop turned his chest back towards Ricky slowly as he grunted with each breath, holding Ricky's face in his gaze.

"And I thought for a moment, boy," Ranthrop sneered, "that I might have to take it easy on you." Any worry over their size difference was now gone from Ranthrop's mind. He wasn't about to let himself bleed anymore in front of the whole of Farwin Wood.

Henry watched with bated breath from where he stood some thirty feet away from the battling men. Ricky had started out well. Henry wondered how much of it was Ricky's quick adeptness to sword fighting mixed with adrenaline and how much was Franci's doctored sword working its magic. He didn't care as long as it continued that way, but after the brief pause when Ranthrop had likely uttered a taunt at Henry's young friend, things turned in a different direction.

Henry gripped his own sword hilt tightly in anxiety as he watched Ranthrop's blows increase in speed and onslaught. Ricky did his best to deflect them, but had little chance to deliver any of his own. If he didn't get one of his own in soon, the boy would wither his endurance to nothing. "Come on, Ricky," Henry muttered. Henry caught his breath then as Ricky stumbled backwards after leaning too far and fell to the ground.

The crowd moaned at the sight and Henry watched as Ricky quickly rolled in the direction he fell. Ricky shot up onto his feet just in time to stay off the running blow that Ranthrop charged at him. Luckily, Ricky's defensive swing had enough momentum to deter the growling man's swooping blade.

"I can't take this anymore," Sarah muttered loud enough for Vasimus to hear her. She leaned forward so she was on the edge of her seat after watching Ricky rise up off the ground. Vasimus moved his hand off of his own armrest and down onto Sarah's, clasping his fingers down over top of her hand. "Sarah, be patient."

Sarah yanked her hand out from under his and clenched her fists together in her lap. She gritted her teeth as she watched the sight below her. Ricky deflected several more blows, but not nearly as fast as Sarah thought he should have. The blood that trickled down the golden colored shin guard on Ranthrop's leg matched the color of his tunic as he stomped steadily with each step towards Ricky when he swung. An angry growl came from Ranthrop and he made a spin of his own to mimic those that Ricky had undertaken several times. When Ranthrop came around, Sarah caught the startled look on Ricky's face as he waited with his sword to the opposite side ready to swing, but he started too late. The tip of Ranthrop's blade grazed across the side of Ricky's ribs where he had left himself exposed for too long.

Sarah gasped as she stood and slapped her hand to her mouth seeing Ricky take a tumbling step backwards. The collective gasps of the crowd were audible along with the one to her side where Vasimus himself had also risen at the sight in the arena.

Ricky clutched his side where the burning sensation instantly began to throb. He'd felt the pressure of the sword push the chainmail against his ribs hard enough that a section broke, allowing the sharp tip of the blade to pierce his skin. He suspected it wasn't a fatal gash, but merely an awful pressure burn that would make his ribs ache for weeks, yet the small portion of his flesh that had been sliced was enough for his hand to come away from the spot covered in blood.

Ranthrop lumbered slower from side to side as Ricky did the same across from him. The older man was growing tired from all the hefty blows he'd wheeled at Ricky. Ricky, however, didn't know if he could get the upper hand again feeling the exhaustion from the heat, the weight of the mail, and the numbness his tiring arms were causing his body.

When Vasimus saw Ricky's hand come away from his side, covered in blood, he inhaled a thick breathe. The sound of Sarah's whimper behind her hands where she stood beside him contributed to his agitation at the scene. "I'm sorry, Sarah," he whispered to her with a painfulness in his voice.

Sarah closed her eyes not wanting to hear the conviction behind his words. It was too late for apologies with Ricky bleeding before her eyes. The apology only distressed her more knowing it meant that Vasimus didn't hold much hope for the outcome to end in Ricky's favor. Vasimus dropped back to his seat with a thud, and the finality of the sound left Sarah to think it further signified his opinion on the hopelessness of the situation. When Sarah opened her eyes again she saw Ranthop swing his blade low and then lean far into the thrust. Ricky stepped backwards with one leg as far as he could and leaned, but before he could pull his front leg away with the rest of his body, Ranthrop's sword tore across Ricky's thigh.

Ricky's cry echoed throughout the arena while he staggered back and Ranthrop stumbled to the side catching himself as the bloody tip of his sword stuck into the ground. No one cheered this time. The arena was silent enough to hear not only Ricky's yowl resonate through it, but also the cry that came from Sarah's throat when she saw Ranthrop righten himself before her nephew had even gathered his footing. "Nooo!!"

As the call escaped from Sarah, she stepped up onto the top of the inner wall that separated her from the arena. Just as she started to leap down to the dirt far below her, Vasimus lunged forward and grasped at the back of her gown. The force against her momentum caused her remaining foot to slip from its place on the wall top back towards the honor box. In a split second, her toe scraped over the wall and Vasimus was left with just a scrap of her gown in his hand as it tore away from her dress.

"Sarah!" Vasimus cried as he watched her foot follow her down headfirst along with the scream that erupted from her lungs. He threw himself onto the wall in time to see her come down on her head in the dirt next to Varmeer as her scream ceased. The thud of her body slamming hard onto the ground was the last sound he heard in the silent arena as all eyes turned to view the spectacle.

Henry stood breathless for a second after the flash of grey caught his eye at the wall on the far side of the arena. When he did not see Sarah's body move, his legs pushed mightily at the dirt beneath him as he raced between Ranthrop and Ricky standing in awe, to the wilted pile of grey fabric. Henry collapsed down on his knees by Sarah's side where Varmeer himself had also done.

"Aunt Sarah," Ricky uttered breathlessly giving a brief glance of question to Ranthrop who stood with a pained expression, mouth open staring at him. Ranthrop turned and took a step towards the place where Sarah lie and Ricky did the same, then hobbled as quickly as he could in the direction of his aunt.

Sarah lay as lifeless as she had when Henry had found her in her bed. He grasped one of her hands and reached his other out to her dusty face where he saw a trickle of blood drip from her mouth. He touched his fingers there to press at the skin just below her lips and doing so easily parted her limp jaw, revealing her bloodied teeth.

"Her teeth may have hit against her lips," Varmeer spoke softly looking up to Henry. "I think she landed more face first."

Henry moved his hand up to the darkest spot of dirt that clung to Sarah's face on her forehead and saw little clumps of dirt in her bound back hair. He dusted the dirt away gently and could feel the warmth of her skin there. The skin was red underneath where he removed the dirt and already clearly swollen. He slipped his fingers behind her soft neck and grazed the vertebrae there, but felt nothing jagged or bulging.

Vasimus lay half-slumped over the wall top looking down at Sarah's motionless condition when he heard the sound of footsteps. At the sight of Ranthrop approaching, the man's sword still in hand, Vasimus let out a low growl, "You!"

Ranthrop stopped his hurried steps and pulled his eyes away from where Sarah lay, up toward the sound. He saw Vasimus leap down from the wall top and land with a harsh thump just beyond Sarah's feet. As Vasimus peered up from his crouched stance, his teeth showed between his lips, eyes fixed on Ranthrop.

"This is your fault!" Vasimus drew his sword. "You and your vengeful duel! I'll give you your duel!" He snarled and charged towards Ranthrop with wild eyes.

Ranthrop braced his stance to receive a wicked blow, but tore his eyes away from the raging predator before him when Ricky stepped into his line of vision. Ranthrop reached a hand up to push the boy out of the way and in doing so he saw that Varmeer had jumped on Vasimus' back. Henry clasped a fist around Vasimus' wrist of the arm that wielded the sword.

Vasimus tried to shake Varmeer off and push Henry away with his free hand, but Henry grabbed a fistful of Vasimus' shirt and twisted the man's wrist to loosen his sword grip. "No! No more of this!" Henry barked. He shoved Vasimus back once he'd finally caused the sword to fall to the ground.

Ranthrop and Ricky stood side by side panting from their bout and the excitement. They gave each other a quick glance of wonder and then looked back to Henry who'd widened his stance between the men.

"Enough!" Henry glared back and forth at both Vasimus and Ranthrop. "Enough!" he called out to the crowd.

Vasimus huffed where he stood, both of his arms hung outward from his sides, fists clenched. He pointed a finger at Ranthrop, "I suppose now you will renege your peace!" The sounds of women softly weeping pierced eerily though the stagnant air.

"I have had my duel, Vasimus," Ranthrop panted and glanced at Ricky. "Take my peace as a blessing to Lady Sarah's health."

"If she dies I will kill you, Groslivo!" Vasimus snarled.

Henry grabbed another handful of Vasimus' tunic and glared at him. "If she dies…" he muttered lowly, "*I* will kill *you!*"

Vasimus felt his chest rise with wild breathes and rub against the tight fist that Henry had pressed to him. He tore his eyes from the man and looked back to where Sarah lay oblivious to the world around her. With another growl, he brought his hands up and ripped free from Henry's grasp. Vasimus rushed down to Sarah and carefully swept her up in his arms. He carried her to where his footmen waited with a rider on a stroomphblutel pulling a long narrow wagon, and sat down on the back of it still holding her in his arms. The man flicked the reins like his own life depended upon it and turned to race them out the arena gates and back up to Daundecort Hall.

Henry took a step forward watching them go. He turned back to Ricky and eyed the boy's bloodstained tunic and the trail that ran down his gaping leg. "You need a doctor too, Ricky," he walked towards him.

"I have one in my party. Let me escort you both back to Daundecort Hall and he can tend us together and perhaps help Vasimus' own healer with Lady Sarah," Ranthrop spoke with sincerity.

"Thank you," Ricky eyed Ranthrop up and down with a curious look. Even more astounding than the verbal gesture was the physical one Ranthrop did next: he offered one of his thick rough hands out to Ricky.

"You fought well, young lord," Ranthrop nodded.

Ricky scoffed lightly in disbelief and glanced at Henry whose brow had lifted at the scene. Ricky reached out and clasped hands with the man, "You too."

As they walked to the edge of the arena where a team of Ranthrop's men waited with rides, they heard several claps. The clapping increased in number and sound as they mounted stroomphblutels and both tired warriors looked up to either side of the arena at the sea of somber-faced onlookers.

"Imagine that...a war started because of a woman was ended by a woman," Ranthrop said under his breath to Ricky as they gave unified waves to the people on their way out of the arena.

CHAPTER

THIRTY-FOUR

H ENRY RACED up the stairwell as soon as he and Ranthrop's doctor had cleaned and dressed both of the men's wounds. He saw Varmeer pacing back and forth outside of Vasimus' bedroom door. Henry strode up to him with a questioning look on his face, palms upwards.

Varmeer shook his head slowly. "The doctor is in there with them now. No change as of yet."

Henry inhaled sharply and pursed his lips. He looked to the door and walked towards it, fully intent on bursting in. Varmeer reached up a hand and pressed it against Henry's chest to block his path. "I tried that already...Vasimus slammed it in my face as soon as the doctor went in and I heard the lock click behind him."

"That man," Henry grumbled and glared at the doorway. He turned and brushed his fingers through his hair at the thought of Vasimus' brutish ways around Sarah in her most delicate of conditions. He took up pacing in the opposite direction of Varmeer and they began to cross paths with the ritual.

After a while, when Henry had calmed himself, he stopped and rested his hands on his hips. "You can go if you'd like. I won't break the door down and start another war," he added for good measure. "Ranthrop's down below with Ricky."

Varmeer managed a smile. "Well, only because you're not from the South. Let us know how she does," he finished more seriously and then went down the stairs.

Down in the great room, Ricky and Ranthrop sat leaning back in two chairs by an open window in the corner nearest the bottom of the stairwell. The cool afternoon air wafted in over their sweaty skin while each of them sat holding a goblet of beetleburry ale.

A plate of fruit and cheeses had been brought out by the kitchen staff and placed on the small table that sat between them. Several of Ranthrop's guards along with some of Vasimus' lingered together at a similarly dressed table in the corner of the room, speaking lowly over their goblets to avoid disrespect for the current situation.

Bandaged leg outstretched before him, much like Ricky's, Ranthrop glanced over at the men when he heard a quiet gaggle of laughter. The sound was quickly followed by a silence, when they saw the lord looking in their direction, but Ranthrop let his head turn back to stare at the floor in front of him with a thoughtful smile. "So this is what peace sounds like," he muttered and took a drink of his ale.

"It sounds good," Ricky winced as he shifted in his seat and brought his free hand down to his ribs.

Ranthrop looked over and saw that a spot of blood crept through the bandage the doctor had wrapped around Ricky's middle. He reached over to the bottle on the table and tugged the cork out with his teeth. "Here," he gestured for Ricky's goblet, "this'll take the sting away."

"The leg is worse, but any time I move, this darn side stabs me," Ricky brought the goblet back up to take a drink once it was refilled.

"Hrmph," Ranthrop scoffed as he refilled his own drink. "You sliced me deeper above the knee, you little half pint," he jested. "Plus…I'm old enough to be your father."

"So?"

"So, I've earned the right to complain more than you," he raised his glass.

"Fair enough," Ricky toasted his former opponent, grateful the man had decided to let him live.

Upstairs, Henry racked his mind with worry during the two hours that had passed since he'd been pacing outside Vasimus' chamber door. He'd walked up and down the entire expanse of the lengthy hallway several times and then he sat on the bench outside the door until he could stand the immobility no longer. He whirled around at the creaking sound of the door and saw an old man in a long dark robe walk out, whom he figured must be the doctor. The door closed behind him and latched again, infuriating Henry with the sound.

Henry stepped closer to the doctor who walked towards the stairwell. "How is she? Will she be all right?"

The doctor sighed and started down the stairs, Henry right alongside him with each step. "She had a mighty fall. It's hard to say."

"Did she break anything?" Henry uttered.

"There's no sign of a break from what I saw. Her compression is minimal…considering how high she fell from and how she landed, but only time will tell. If her brain swells too much, well, there's no telling if the body will recover from that on its own. I have given her a remedy to prevent it, but we'll have to wait and see."

Henry grimaced at the glum diagnosis. Clearly this man wasn't used to giving the most hopeful version of a story like the medical professionals in Henry's world did. He continued to walk down the stairs with the doctor to create some distance between himself and the dismal hallway where he'd been pacing. He found Ricky lazily leaning his head back against a chair. Ranthrop sat in a similar manner in a chair next to him. The two of them chuckled about something and then stopped when they saw Henry approach.

Ricky sat forward quickly and winced from the endeavor. "How is Aunt Sarah?" His question was followed by a loud hiccup, which was followed by a slap when Ricky brought his hand up too quickly to cover his mouth.

"She's still the same," Henry sighed and eyed the glasses in Ricky and Ranthrop's hands. He didn't mind the apparent intoxication settling into the two of them and preferred there was something to distract Ricky from Sarah's condition. "We just have to wait and see if she wakes up."

"Wakes up? *Hiccup!* Wakes up? I'm sick of waiting for her to wake up! That's why we came here," Ricky pounded a fist on the arm of his chair. Ranthrop cast the boy a confused look but then looked back to his goblet.

"I know, Ricky," Henry muttered.

"What if she never wakes up?"

"Don't think like that," Henry bit a little too harshly.

Ricky sobered his thoughts for a moment and sat back again. "Even if she does wake up...she's still stuck here," he muttered dejectedly. "She's stuck searching for some stupid ribbon...or worse yet one of those tiny little charms from that crazy bracelet she always wears," Ricky peered through the tiny space he'd formed by holding his thumb and index finger close together before his eye. When he dropped his hand due to the blurred vision it cause him, Henry was gone. "Hey... where'd he go? *Hiccup!*"

Henry dashed up the stairs all the way into Sarah's empty room. If he found her bracelet he could examine it. He'd eyed every little bauble on that leather cuff over the last five years. If he found what was missing, could he send her home in her current state? Better she was in a coma in Salem than in Farwin Wood. At least there were doctors with access to electricity in Salem!

Through the soft orange light that flooded in from the balcony doorway of Sarah's room, Henry opened anything with a drawer or door. He caught his breath when he saw a New York Giants sweatshirt folded up in the bottom drawer of a clothing bureau. Henry lifted it out carefully and heard a scrape underneath the clothing as he did. He stared down at the leather cuff where it sat in the drawer and set the clothing off to his side.

Picking up the bracelet with his thumb and index finger, Henry looked at the dangling charms. He saw several tiny pearls that he recognized and flicked them aside. The little silver key that he'd seen so many times before was also there. Henry slowly rotated the bracelet and mentally discarded each charm and trinket as he recognized them. When he came to the end of the leather, he closed his eyes. Something was missing. He was sure of it. He tried to picture Sarah in her shop, when her hand would reach out to sign his invoices. Henry knew it wasn't just wishful thinking at the remark Ricky had made, something wasn't there.

Henry carried the bracelet with him out into the hallway and took a seat back on the bench. Under the dim candlelight he turned over the bracelet again and watched each of the trinkets fall onto one another with the motion. There was nothing gold in the mix, Henry thought. "The ring," he muttered. Henry stared at the bracelet and saw where a tiny piece of the leather braiding was broken. He laughed softly. "The ring." He remembered it clearly now. How many times he'd wanted to ask Sarah if it held significance, but had thought better of the inquiry.

As the minutes passed with no sound coming from within Vasimus' room, Henry consoled himself that if Sarah did awake at least he could tell her what she needed to look for to go home. He hated that Vasimus so presumptuously locked himself in his bedroom with Sarah, while he was left to sit like an outcast in the hallway. Henry thought about who would take a ring or whom he'd seen wearing a ring in Farwin Wood to take his mind off his stewing and worry. Sarah never wore a ring. Why did she even have a ring? Was it a family heirloom? Who else would give a woman a ring if not family? Henry stopped fidgeting with the bracelet and looked up at the wall across from him. A man would give a woman a ring, he thought. And a bitter man might take one back!

Henry bolted off the bench and pounded on the door to Vasimus' room. When it didn't swiftly open he began to beat even harder on the solid wood. "Vasimus, you open this damned door now! I want to see her!"

The door jerked open and just as Henry latched eyes with Vasimus, a strong hand reached out and tightly grasped the front of his shirt about the neck. Vasimus pushed Henry back as he clenched the fabric tighter, but Henry pushed the floor with his feet to keep from losing any ground.

"Why are you here?" Vasimus growled and shook the place where he held Henry.

Henry instinctively lowered his head and dropped the bracelet. He gathered his own handfuls of Vasimus' shirt and charged the most forceful defensive push back he could remember since his college days, sending the towering man back into the room.

As the two men clawed and grasped at each other, Henry's forceful push sent them crashing into a table. The table rocked and tipped over with a crash to the floor. The force of the impact halted Vasimus, sending Henry forward. Vasimus took the advantage and swung Henry off of him. Still grasping at Henry's neck, Vasimus held him down by the neck with a firm grip allowing him to lock his elbow in place so he could hold Henry out at arm's breadth.

"You impetuous man! Who are you? A guard or a lover?" Vasimus snarled and wrestled with all his might and weight to keep Henry hunched over while he tried to choke him.

Henry twisted beneath Vasimus' grip and swung with ironlike fists to land them wherever he could on Vasimus' body. "Give it back to her! Give us back the ring!" Henry choked out as he continued to pummel and writhe.

"Arrrrgh!" Vasimus growled at Henry's discovery and slipped him into a headlock. He dragged him with all his might kicking and swinging out onto the balcony. "Leave us alone! Just go home! Go back where you came from!" Vasimus slammed Henry's ribs into the edge of the rain barrel on his balcony.

Henry moaned at the cracking sound his bones made when he impacted the wooden barrel. The jarring motion was enough for him to break free from Vasimus' headlock and he drove a tightly clenched fist into the man's nose. Henry winced at the pain in his side as he tried to take another swing and couldn't, but reveled in the victorious sound of Vasimus' broken nose and growl of pain. "You can't keep her here!" Henry leaned against the barrel, trying for a second of reason. "Give it back to her!"

Vasimus spat the dripping blood away from his lips and lunged again at Henry. He pushed his hands onto Henry's face and pressed his chest down against where Henry held his arm across his broken ribs to trap it there. Vasimus forced Henry's head back towards the water and leaned all of this weight onto him. Henry lost his footing and arched back causing his head to dunk into the water. "Go home!!" Vasimus screamed as bubbles formed at the water's surface.

Henry scraped and grasped at Vasimus' chest to try and pull himself upwards. He managed to pull Vasimus in enough that the man had to take a step back. Henry's hold was tight enough that it brought him up out of the barrel with Vasimus' retreat. They scuffled a few seconds more and Henry looked to his hand when something sharp entangled his fingers as he tried to grab for Vasimus' neck. In his grasp, Henry saw Sarah's small gold ring laced through a thin chain around Vasimus' neck.

Vasimus had ceased his onslaught at the feel of the tension about his neck and now looked down at Henry's discovery. He let go of Henry's collar to knock his hand away from the necklace, but Henry tightened his grip on the chain.

"Let her go home," Henry pleaded to the man's eyes.

"Then I will never see her again," Vasimus gritted the words between breaths.

"If you love her…you'll let her go, not hold her prisoner," Henry shook the chain.

Vasimus stared at Henry in silence as the two men panted for air, still braced in their standoff. After a moment he looked away out into the landscape beyond the balcony. With a frustrated grunt, Vasimus pushed hard off of Henry's chest, releasing him from his grasp. The force brought Vasimus back so abruptly the chain snapped from behind his neck as though he'd intended it. He inhaled and glanced down at the ring that dangled in Henry's grasp. After a pause he cast a blank look up at Henry before he walked dejectedly from the balcony and out of the bedroom.

Henry watched Vasimus go and then looked to where Sarah lay as though she were peacefully sleeping on the bed. He walked out into the hallway and picked up the discarded bracelet, then across the hall into Sarah's room. He came back across the hall with Sarah's sweat suit in his hands and shut the door to Vasimus' room behind him. Henry locked the door without second guessing himself and then came to a chair next to the bed. He dropped the clothing down on the seat and then sat on top of it. Someone would have to pry those clothes from his dead, lifeless fingers if they wanted them, Henry swore. He fastened the ring back onto the bracelet and then fixed it onto Sarah's limp wrist.

Henry sighed and looked at her. He grasped her cold life-less hand and watched as her chest rose slightly up and down under the blanket. "I promised you that I'd go home...now wake up so you can come with me," Henry whispered.

CHAPTER
THIRTY-FIVE

THE WEIGHTY feel of Ricky's head intensified as he gradually woke from his deep sleep. Somewhere near him the sound of a chainsaw stung his sensitive eardrums. There aren't any chainsaws in Farwin Wood, he thought. Ricky swallowed the dryness in his mouth and tasted the remnants of beetleburry ale in his saliva. He peeled his eyes open to see the ceiling of the great room come into focus above him while the reverberating snarly snorting sound beside him grew louder. There was only one thing in Farwin Wood that made that awful sound, Ricky's mind raced as it sobered. "Wickrits!" he jolted upright in his chair as he screamed, but stopped to clasp his hands to his head.

"Wha...huh? Wickrit? Where?" Ranthrop broke from his deep snoring and shot his head up. He too ceased his rapid movements and put a hand to his head, the other he brought to his nose and wondered why it hurt so painfully as though he had snorted in all the dirt in the north land.

"Uhhh," Ricky moaned while every sensation of the previous day's injuries awoke in his body. "Ugh...beetle..."

"...burry," Ranthrop grumbled after him. "I'm getting too old for this dung."

Upstairs, two other people were also waking. Sarah moaned and turned her head on the pillow feeling the sensation of its plushness behind her aching skull. She opened her eyes lazily and blinked at the rays of light cascading above her. She felt the urge to touch the place on her forehead that throbbed, but something held her hand in place. When she glanced down to where it lie by her side she saw Henry stirring from his sleep, the side of his face on the blanket and his hand clasped around hers. Sarah squeezed his fingers and smiled.

"Henry?"

Henry lifted his head after a moment and then jerked his line of sight to her face. "Sarah! You're awake!"

"Mmm," she moaned and feeling her hand freed brought it up to her hairline. "Oooh," she winced on finding a sizable lump there.

"What happened?"

"You...climbed over the wall to stop the duel...and fell."

Sarah sat up quickly, but slowed on the pain it brought her aching head. "Ricky? Is...what happened to Ricky?"

"He's fine. They stopped the duel when you fell," Henry stood now and helped to guide Sarah back against the headboard.

"And will they fight again?" her worried eyes tried to focus.

"No. No, don't worry. I don't think Ranthrop's heart was in it any longer and...he's even upheld his declaration of peace," Henry smiled.

Sarah gasped in awe and stared down at the bed. "I never would have imagined it could turn out so fortunate," she muttered.

"Well, don't go doing anything crazy like that again, but...I think you might have had a hand in it."

Sarah laughed weakly and gazed out the balcony doors. Ricky was alive. Thank heavens. Her next thought was that today started the rest of her life in Farwin Wood, and then she noticed where she was. "Henry?" Sarah gazed across the room as she turned back to look at him. "Why am I in Vasimus' room?" She thought to blush on admitting to him she was familiar with the room, but when she looked up and saw the marks on his neck, she gasped. "What happened to you?"

"Vasimus carried you from the arena and brought you here," he muttered. He ran a hand across the front of his neck gently. The skin there felt raw and swollen. "I ran out of patience when he kept you locked in here half the day. He wasn't too happy when I finally beat on the door."

"Oh...I'm sorry," Sarah muttered. "But...he did that to you?"

"Sarah," Henry leaned in. "I provoked it, in a way. I... found out what you lost...and who had it," he hesitated and held up her bracelet. Henry grasped onto the ring on the cuff and held it up to her.

Sarah stared at it for a moment with a hint of pain in her expression. She reached for it slowly and grasped the bracelet, rather than the ring when she took it from Henry. In her hand she brought it to her lap and then stared down at it, still silent.

"You can go home now," Henry whispered and stood up feeling a bit awkward amidst her silence. He picked up her sweat suit and set it next to her on the bed.

"Yes," she finally whispered. Vasimus had her ring. He'd had it all along, even after she told him she couldn't go home until she found what she'd lost. The realization left her speechless in a sea of emotions. She wanted to pity him, wanted to hit him, and wanted to scream at him for nearly getting her nephew killed when they could have gone home. They could go home now, though.

"Henry?"

"Yes?"

"Get Ricky, please. We're going home," she called without taking her eyes off her bracelet.

CHAPTER
THIRTY-SIX

RICKY AWOKE first and winced when he brought his head up off the kitchen table. He reached down and was unhappy to feel the pain in his side and leg was still there. Aunt Sarah! Would she make it through without any residual problems from her head injury? He got up and noticed Henry still lay motionless on the opposite side of the table. Ricky hobbled into the living room and turned to see Mary knitting on the couch. She roused when Ricky opened the door to Sarah's room with a creak.

"Oh, my word! You need to go to the hospital!" she called seeing the blood seeping through his pant leg.

"Aunt Sarah might need to go too," Ricky called as he hopped over to the bed.

"Oh, no! What on earth happened?" Mary brushed at her hair and ran into Sarah's bedroom.

"Mmm, I'm okay Ricky. I'm fine," Sarah murmured under her blankets and brought a hand to the knob on her forehead.

"Oh! What a goose egg you have, Sarah," Mary gasped. "Come on. You're going to the hospital immediately."

"Mary," Sarah protested groggily, "take Ricky. You can just rub some of your salves on me." She slung her feet over the edge of the bed at Mary and Ricky's insistence.

"Oh, no. I make a mean healing salve, but nothing that can relieve a swollen brain as yours most likely is with a bump like that!" Mary tugged her young friend out the door. "And Henry? Did Henry get hurt also?"

"No. Well, someone tried to choke him, but he's fine," Ricky held Sarah's other arm over the back of his shoulders.

Just as Mary was shoving Ricky and Sarah out the door, Sarah held out a hand to stop her. "No. Mary, stay with Henry please. I don't want him waking up alone. He wouldn't go until I came back. Stay and make sure he wakes up, will you?"

"Oh, all right," Mary wrung her hands and watched them leave. "I'll call for a taxi to meet you out on the street!"

When Henry awoke a few minutes later. He nearly sprung out of his chair. He caught himself against the counter when he realized his head was not ready to balance the rest of his body. He'd watched Ricky and Sarah essentially drown before his eyes, but he didn't realize just how awful the sensation would feel.

"It's all right, Henry. You're all right. Just take your time," Mary came over to help steady the giant of a man who towered over her by a foot.

"Sarah? Ricky?" He murmured.

"They're fine. They woke up already. I sent them to the hospital to get looked at."

Henry let out a ragged sigh and sat down again. "Oh. Thank goodness. It's over."

"Yes," Mary frowned and shut the book with force. "I certainly hope it is."

Mary reminded Henry to change into his normal clothing before he left. She also urged him to go home and just try to forget about everything that had happened. The poor man. What a shock to the system it must have been for him, Mary pitied to herself. She had a hard time convincing him not to go to the hospital to check on Ricky and Sarah, but in the end her stern demeanor won and she sent a frazzled Henry on his way.

"Well, this will certainly make delivery day awkward from now on," Mary shook her head when she watched him walk dazed slowly out of the apartment.

SARAH WAS grateful that she was able to sleep in her own bed that night, having assured the doctors she was fine. Luckily Blinney Lane was only three blocks away from the nearest hospital, which was close enough that Sarah could go there without much adverse reaction to the Blinney curse. Ricky received several stitches in his leg and three along his ribs. He had some fine bruises forming on his rib cage, but fortunately nothing was broken. The uncomfortable moment came when Sarah had to call Richard for medical consent to Ricky's treatment. Finding the privacy to tell him a brief version of what had happened hadn't proved easy. Richard had wanted to fly straight there, go into the book and kill Vasimus and Ranthrop himself. Sarah swore she would have rendered him immobile before she would have let him do that after all they'd gone through. When she finally got him calmed down, she promised him that Ricky would call once they were home and away from normal society.

In the morning, Ricky was surprised to find his aunt up and awake before he was. It was the first time that had happened in nearly a week. He walked stiffly into the kitchen and stopped when he saw that she had the book sitting in front of her on the table.

"I thought Mary put that away yesterday," Ricky eyed it in fear.

"She did. I just went down and got it," Sarah got up and reached for the boiling pot of water on the stove.

"Whyyyy?"

"Because I'm going back in," she called matter-of-factly without turning around to look at him.

"Back in? We just got the hell out of there! Are you crazy?"

"Ricky, there's something I have to do," she answered in a calm voice and turned to look at him.

Ricky dropped his shoulders. "What? What now?"

"I have to say goodbye."

"What?" Ricky didn't hide his bewilderment. "To Vasimus? After what he did? Uh, uh. No way," Ricky waved his arms.

"And to Dergus and Netta," Sarah was annoyed now. "I don't plan to ever go back, but I'm not abandoning all of them again without a word."

"But you are...going to see Vasimus, aren't you?" Ricky gave her a pointed look and crossed his arms.

"Yes," she sat down with a cup of tea next to the book and gave him a defiant look.

Ricky sighed and shook his head. "I don't understand women."

Sarah laughed. "You're not supposed to, Ricky."

"And do you think I'm in any condition to come rescue you again? What if he kidnaps you again and then I have to come duel him? Have you even thought about your poor nephew?"

Sarah scoffed. "I think about you more than you know, Ricky. Trust me. Everything will be fine. I'll be in and then out. Now go on and open the store," she waved him off.

"Just like that? You know when I came here I was the irresponsible one, but now I think it rubbed off on you!"

Sarah chuckled and opened the book. "Come on. I bet there's going to be a pretty little blonde coming in today just dying to see you."

"Oh, no! No, you don't!" Ricky hobbled a step closer to the table and shook a finger at her. "You can't distract me. I'm not the same self-serving kid who came here at the beginning of the summer."

Sarah looked up and stared at him for a moment with a genuinely loving smile on her face. "I know you aren't, Ricky," she said softly. "And I'm so very proud of you. I trust you. Now...trust me, please."

Ricky really hated what she just did. Sneaky women! He let out a long sigh as he watched her face and tried not to glance at the stupid book and tea. He hobbled around and looked at the clock on the wall. "Okay. Fine! But you have... five hours! You hear me? Five hours and then I'm coming in for you," he turned back around and flashed a warning finger at her.

"All right," she smiled.

Ricky sighed again and then finally turned to leave. He grumbled to himself on the way to the door. "This is ridiculous. 'Don't touch the book,' she said. Now she's going in. Nearly got sliced to death and this is the thanks I get."

CHAPTER
THIRTY-SEVEN

FARWIN WOOD

SARAH WAVED to Dergus and Netta where they stood smiling at the gate to Allister Hall. Netta wiped a tear from her eye with a corner of her apron. It had been a bittersweet parting, but Sarah felt much better having done it than if she'd never returned. Dergus and Netta had swore they would stay at Allister Hall until the day they died, just in case an Allister ever wanted to return. It was their home too after all, and no other place in the land would feel the same.

The guard outside of Daundecort Hall recognized Sarah immediately when she approached on her stroomphblutel. Everyone in town did too for that matter. Never in her life did Sarah ever remember being greeted by so many people in such a short time. Everyone waved and smiled at her and many even bowed or curtsied. Sarah tried not to blush, but couldn't help it. She felt foolish that falling on her head had sealed the deal for peace throughout the land, but if they were happy she was happy for them.

The guard let her in and just as she reached the center of the Daundecort courtyard, Vasimus appeared out the doorway of the hall. He walked slowly over to her with his lips parted in thought, but his eyes didn't remain on her as they usually did. He looked down as he approached, like a man who felt ashamed. When he reached where she sat on her ride, he looked up at her in question and held a hand out for her to dismount.

"We...didn't get to say goodbye," Sarah called softly. "Would you take one last ride with me?"

Vasimus lowered his hand and let out a quiet sigh. He was so happy to see her face again, just as he was each time he saw it. He was greatly heartbroken to hear that she had come only to say goodbye, yet equally overjoyed that she didn't seem to be angry with him. "Gladly," he managed a smile and waved for his footman to get him a mount.

They rode out through the town again, greeted by the milling onlookers. Neither of them spoke for a while, each busy waving and casting head bows at the townsfolk.

"Everyone is so happy," Sarah remarked. "Will you keep the peace?" she hesitated and looked over at him as they neared the edge of town.

"Of course," he returned quickly. Vasimus cleared his throat in his eagerness. He didn't want his tone to be misconstrued as bitterness. "Ranthrop just left, actually."

Sarah arched a brow at that comment. Ranthrop had stayed another day in Daundecort Hall? Even after she, Ricky, and Henry had left? She was surprised the two men could stand each other's company that long so shortly after declaring the peace.

"Really?"

Vasimus looked ahead then and as he spoke a slight smirk formed on his lips. "He nearly drank me out of Beetleburry ale, but yes he stayed on another night. Seemed to think I could use the company."

"I'm sorry I left so quickly, but...I was mad at you for..."

"I know, Sarah." Vasimus looked back at her now, his voice pained. "What I did was wrong. I didn't know taking your ring would bring you back here, but I must admit... once I found out that it did, I couldn't bear to give it back if it meant I might keep you a little longer. I thought it meant... there could be another chance for us." He cleared his throat and looked away. "I...know it was wrong of me to force you to stay. I've never listened to you, have I?"

"Vasimus..." Sarah smiled although he couldn't see it. "You gave it back. That's all that matters. A truly selfish man wouldn't do something like that."

They remained silent as they wound down the road from the hilltop town. Sarah guided them in the direction of the River Duke. They said nothing for a while, both knowing what was coming.

As they sat on their rides by the river's edge and stared at the flowing water, Vasimus said, "I will never understand why this book was created...allowing us to meet if we could never be together."

"Me either," Sarah looked at him with sad eyes. "But I'm glad that it was."

Vasimus looked at her with pain in his entire expression. Through the sad lines in his face a smile broke through and he whispered, "Me too."

Vasimus dismounted his stroomphblutel and came over to help Sarah down. Their hands remained joined after she descended and all the fear and bitterness was gone on either's part. Vasimus promised to look after Dergus and Netta as well as continue to restore Allister Hall in her memory. Sarah tried to object, but he assured her that it was non-negotiable.

"Perhaps when I am old and grey, I may yet see you once more or…your children. If I have to think of you in another world, promise me that you won't waste all you have to offer living alone," Vasimus looked at her intently.

Sarah stared with her mouth open. She never could have imagined such a wish coming from his mouth. She even felt a little jealous that he was freeing her from him, although she knew she had no right to such feelings anymore. "You know I wish the same for you…since I won't be here to see it," she added a smile.

Vasimus squeezed her hand at that affectionate remark and brushed the hair away from her face. "This…Henry fellow, well, he…would seem suitable if we had met under different circumstances. There is love there, I'm sure…if you're ready to look for it again."

"I have the rest of my life to think about that, Vasimus, but I only have a few moment to be with the first man I ever loved," she rested her face in his palm.

"I only wish I'd carried that love with me all these years. I see now it was something dark and bitter that I took with me each day instead. You made me a better person then, Sarah, and I should have kept trying to be so even after you were gone."

"You did, Vasimus. I did too, I hope," she mumbled in her forlorn emotions. Sarah glanced at the water with sadness in her eyes. "I hate this. I always have."

Vasimus looked at the river rushing by them. He brought his hand down to grasp Sarah's. "Here, I'll be with you." He led them into the water and carefully guided Sarah until they were waist deep and chanced losing their footing.

They looked at each other and both brought their hands up to trace the curves of each other's faces one last time.

Each smiled under the other's fingertips. Sarah ran her fingers through Vasimus' hair and felt tears well up in her eyes. She felt like she was saying goodbye to the last memories of her childhood.

"Don't cry, my little sweet," Vasimus murmured and brought his lips to hers. They held and tasted each other without thought of anything other than that moment, nothing of the past or yet to come worried them anymore. When their lips finally parted they held each other for several moments, until finally loosening their grasp on the other.

"The water's cold today. You're going to catch a cold because of me, now," Sarah sniffled and wiped at her eyes.

Vasimus smiled and clasped her hand. He looked down at her bracelet and held it up between them. "When you want to think of me," he brought his other hand down over the cuff to feel the ring attached to it, "I'll be here."

"No," she whispered and held her other hand to her chest, "you'll be here."

"Goodbye, my Sarah," he smiled with pure affection.

She smiled with nothing but love in her heart as she stood before him in the water. Just before their hands parted and she slipped down into the water she replied, "Goodbye, my Vasimus."

CHAPTER
THIRTY-EIGHT

BLINNEY LANE

SARAH CHANGED her clothes quickly once she awoke in her kitchen. She felt horridly empty inside, yet relieved and at peace. How could such vastly different emotions be vexed on a person all at once, she wondered. It truly wasn't fair. The next sensation she felt, realizing she was back in the present, was guilt. Poor Ricky. She'd put him through more than any young man should ever have to bear.

Farwin Wood and the curse of Agatha Blinney had come to Sarah and Richard's knowledge slowly. It hadn't been sprung upon them all at once as it had with Ricky or Henry for that matter. Henry! How would her relationship with Henry be affected by all of this? Relationship? Now there's a joke, she thought. Yet somehow they had a deeper relationship now after all of this. Didn't they?

Sarah shut the book and thought of the irony of what Vasimus had said. How had she just said goodbye to one man and was now thinking of what life would be like with another, yet if in a much less intimate way? Intimacy? Ha! Henry won't even be able to look at me now, Sarah rubbed her temples. I just want my old Henry back, she hugged the book to her chest. *My Henry.* The flush that usually formed in her cheeks when she thought of him didn't even rise now on the possibility of those words. Who else's Henry should he be, she wondered. Well, I don't like the sound of that! Suddenly, Sarah wanted to get downstairs as quickly as possible.

Sarah raced down the stairs to find Shelby clasping one of Ricky's arms and leaning into the stool where he sat behind the shop counter. Ricky smiled at the girl until he heard his aunt's footsteps and then both of the teenagers' heads turned to look at Sarah.

"You're," Ricky glanced around the store at the customers, "awake! Man, I was getting worried."

Sarah smiled as she reached the bottom of the stairs. "Yeah, you look real worried. Hi, Shelby." Sarah walked over and hugged her little friend.

"Oh, I'm so glad you're okay," Shelby beamed up at her.

"Want to go lock this thing back up for me?" Sarah hefted up the big book from underneath her arm.

"Gladly," Shelby grimaced and waited for Sarah to hand over her bracelet.

"Thanks," Sarah took the cuff off and gave it to Shelby. Then she turned to inspect Ricky, who sat with his leg propped up on the recycling crate. "How's the leg?"

"A little sore, but I'm fine," he smiled. "I can't imagine what my dad thought when you told him."

"Well...given the trouble he caused when we were kids, he was surprisingly calm...after he freaked out initially of course," she raised her eyebrows.

"Well, I think he and I are going to have a lot more to talk about than usual next time I see him, so it wasn't for nothing I guess. Imagine that…steal one little car and he freaks out. Get into a sword fight and he's all concerned for my well-being. Tsk, parents," Ricky smirked.

Sarah rolled her eyes and then saw the stack of boxes that were next to her. "Did Henry come in already?"

"Yeah. Poor Henry. Looks like he didn't even sleep. Your boy's meat hooks left some mighty fine bruises too."

Sarah stared at Ricky with her mouth flapping open. She knew Henry was gone, but she instinctively looked at the door anyways. "He…didn't wait?"

"No. He…" Ricky grimaced then and looked down at his leg.

"What?"

"Well…he wanted to know where you were and…"

"And what?" Sarah didn't mean to snap.

"And so I told him! It's Henry. Come on. I can't lie to Henry," Ricky shrugged.

Sarah's shoulders slumped instantly. She felt like someone kicked her in the stomach and brought her hand there to quell the feeling. "Was he…did he look angry?" she whispered and waited with an intent gaze on Ricky.

"He…didn't look happy. More like…disappointed, I think," Ricky hesitated. "Come on, now. I didn't want you to go back in there. What do you expect? You went back to see some guy that tried to kill him. How's a guy supposed to feel?"

"You told him I went to see Vasimus?" Sarah didn't realize she'd done it, but had reached over and grasped a fist full of Ricky's t-shirt.

Ricky arched a brow at her and sighed. He ignored her intent look and focused on the fingers gripping his t-shirt as he slowly pried each one open while he spoke. "Nooo. He probably figured that out on his own," Ricky spoke slowly and unclenched one of Sarah's fingers, then started on the next. "Just tell him," he freed the next one.

"Tell him what?" Sarah barked.

Ricky peeled another finger open, but didn't have to free the rest after he enunciated, "Tell…him…that you love him." Sarah's hand fell from his shirt.

"I never said…what makes you think…" her eyes widened and she threw her arms up in the air.

"Like…love. Whatever it is, just tell him. I'm sure you'll feel better afterwards," Ricky frowned and smoothed out the wrinkles in his shirt. Shelby came up to stand by them and looked to Ricky in question. He just rolled his eyes at her, and then looked back at his aunt.

The sickening feeling in Sarah's gut grew worse at the feeling of loss. How could she feel like she lost Henry if she'd never even told him how she felt? How she felt? This was worse than drowning. It was like slamming into a brick wall. She may have just crushed him by appearing to have gallivanted back to Vasimus, when Henry was the one who'd gotten the ring back for her. He tracked her down and found her at Daundecort Hall. He went into a book to save her! He did all that, yet she had no idea how to tell him the way she felt.

"How?" she uttered and looked at Ricky, knowing he'd found out the secret she finally had learned herself.

"Finally! Thank you!" Ricky held up a hand.

"How, what?" Shelby looked from one of them to the other.

"How do I…tell Henry…" Sarah blushed now.

"Oh! That you love him?" Shelby beamed.

"Ugh," Sarah clasped onto the counter and dropped her head in between her arms to hide her shame. "Does everyone know?"

"Well, not Henry, at least," Shelby offered and patted Sarah on the back.

"Here." Sarah felt something hard hit her arm. "Write him a letter."

Sarah looked up to see one of the journals she kept for sale in a stack by the register resting on her arm. She squinted and looked over it at her nephew.

"You want me to write him a letter?" she quipped sourly. "What are you? A teenager?"

"Oh...that's romantic," Shelby sighed.

The rest of the day, Sarah spent scribbling lines onto pages of the journal. The loud sound of ripping paper would pierce the air followed by a crumpling noise. By the end of the day, the recycle basket and garbage can were full.

Ricky came over at one point and reached down into the basket to pick up a wad of paper. When Sarah noticed that he was about to uncrumple one of her failed attempts at declaring her affections, she shot her hand out and clasped it around Ricky's wrist.

"Touch any of those and I'll send you back into the book!" she glared.

"O...kay! Just trying to help," Ricky turned and hobbled away.

CHAPTER
THIRTY-NINE

TUESDAY AND Wednesday dragged on tediously. Sarah felt like she would never see Henry again and began to think pessimistically. What if the ordeal was too much for him and he resigned? What if I never see him again? Learning to live without Vasimus had been miserable, but nothing like this! Sarah truly did care for Vasimus, even now, but for some reason this felt different. She couldn't imagine staying out of the book if Henry were the one trapped inside of it. She'd close the shop for good and stay asleep the rest of her life if that's what it took to see him again. How could that be? Was this the difference between youthful love and adult love? How come it hadn't gotten any easier? This was simply cruel. Worst off, she still didn't know what she would say to him when she did see him again.

Thursday morning came and Sarah was up well before her alarm clock. She tried to busy herself, taking extra care over her appearance, which wasn't difficult to do considering the bags under her eyes. When she couldn't do anything more to make herself look desirable and calm she made breakfast. Ricky came out complaining after the racket of pots and pans woke him up.

Later, down in the shop, Ricky steered clear of his aunt. She was like the Energizer Bunny zooming around and fidgeting with everything. Lord, this better go over well, he mentally grimaced. He didn't want to see what she'd be like if something were to go wrong with the whole Henry debacle. Luckily Shelby came in and gave him someone to commiserate with while his aunt seemingly lost her mind with worry.

After popping her head up to look at the door each time the chimes rang, Sarah had given herself a sore neck. She leaned on the counter, exhausted by her own silliness and rubbed the base of her skull as she tried to relax. The chimes sounded again and when Sarah glanced up, she caught the breath in her throat. Henry. Did he look more gorgeous than ever today or was the light playing tricks on her?

Henry let out his own anxious breath at the sight of Sarah, looking tired and leaning against the counter. That guy better not have upset her again, he thought with a frown and slowly rolled his hand truck over to where she stood. "Hello," he mumbled.

He mumbled. What does that mean? He didn't smile! Was that a frown? Ah! Sarah panicked and studied every motion of Henry's as he approached, all the while staring at him with her lips parted in fear.

"Uh, hey Henry!" Ricky called as he and Shelby walked to the door.

"Hey, guys, sorry. Didn't see you there," Henry smiled then.

"We're going to lunch," Ricky raised his eyebrows as he glanced at Sarah. "We'll see you later?"

"Yeah. Yeah, sure. Enjoy yourselves."

Sarah swallowed when Henry turned back around and they were left face to face. She waited a few seconds, but his usual chitchat didn't come. How were they going to do this now? Would everything be awkward now that he'd seen that strange part of her life?

"How...how are you, Henry?"

"I'm well," he spoke softly. "And...and you? That lump looks like it's gone down."

Sarah chuckled and was sure her face turned red. She pulled at her hair to try and cover the bump at her hairline, but let her hand drop when she realized she was fidgeting. "Yeah. I think it's just about gone. And you? Are you...okay?"

"Yeah," Henry managed a smile.

Henry watched Sarah's eyes shift away from him. She couldn't look at him. He could sense it. It wasn't like her usual shyness. She seemed to be deliberately avoiding eye contact with him. The thought made Henry's lunch sink further into his stomach if that was possible. Had she forgiven Vasimus for taking her ring? Is that why she had gone back into the book—to let him know she forgave him? To let him know she still loved him? Was she going to keep going back there? Henry couldn't bear the thought. He took his eyes from her and pushed the cart around behind her to drop off the boxes he had for the store.

Sarah turned and watched Henry unload the boxes. He didn't look up at her when he started to roll the cart back in front of the counter. The door creaked open and Sarah watched as the only customer in the shop exited. She turned back to look at Henry who now was fidgeting with his clipboard, eyes down looking at the paper. You never look at the clipboard, she thought. Look at me. "Henry? I'm sorry...about everything that happened. You shouldn't have had to see all that," she offered humbly.

Henry managed another weak smile and looked up at her. "It's all right. I...uh...was happy to help. I'm just glad you're okay. I was worried when Ricky said you went back,"

Henry quickly looked back at the clipboard and held it out to Sarah.

He was worried? That's a good thing, right? Or was he just worried because he thinks I'm an idiot for going back? Sarah's hand shook as she scribbled her name on the invoice. When she had finished writing, she held onto the clipboard. If she handed it back, he would leave. "Henry?" She looked up at him again and found his eyes were on her now. "I have to thank you...for what you did for Ricky...and for me."

Henry sighed raggedly. "Sarah," he muttered, "I meant it when I said I'd rescue you...if you ever needed it." He hoped he never had to again if she was going back to that undeserving blockhead, but he knew he would if she needed to be saved. "You don't have to thank me for that," his voice almost seemed a little sour as he took the clipboard from her.

Sarah panicked when she saw him walk around behind his handtruck again. "Wait, Henry!" She grabbed a leather bound book from behind the counter that she had made the night before. He said he meant it, she thought as she looked at the book. He'd rescue me. "I *want* to thank you. It meant a lot to me because...you didn't have to rescue me."

Henry watched Sarah as she came around the counter. She held a leather bound book in her hand. The cover and binding were blank. Sarah walked up next to him and looked down at the book, grasping it with both hands. Then she looked up at him nervously and handed it to him.

"Here. This is for you," she smiled meekly and wrapped her arms around her waist.

Henry stared at her dumbly with the book in his hand. "Oh...thank you." He tried to smile. He didn't want to appear rude or unenthused, but the agony was killing him. He felt like he was holding the consolation prize for losing the love of his life. Couldn't it have been anything else, but a book? Really? Now every time he'd look at it, he'd not only think how he hadn't been the one to win her, but how his foolish attempt at heroics had only served to push her closer to Vasimus. He had to clear his throat in order to speak. "Well, I hope it's nothing like your magical book. I don't know if I feel like going on any more adventures anytime soon...even...even if you are."

Sarah let out a nervous laugh, "Oh, no. No, it's not. And I'm...I'm not going back there."

Henry's gaze shot to her. "You're not? But...I thought. Ricky said you..."

"No! No. *Never*," she smiled and shook her head. "I...I had to say goodbye to Netta and Dergus and... Well, I said goodbye to Vasimus too. I hope you understand. I felt I owed him that much."

Henry let out the breath that he'd been holding in his throat. He looked down in embarrassment now. "Sarah," he said tenderly, "you don't owe me any explanations. I'm sorry. I know you had a life before I met you. I...I just didn't know it was so...far away," he smiled.

"How could you?" she shrugged.

"So..." Henry inhaled to break the awkward silence that followed. "I'm glad I'll have some reading to do after a weekend of sword fights and riding stroomphblutels." Henry clasped the book and raised it as he smiled.

"Yeah," she laughed.

Henry was relieved, but still couldn't help feeling confused. She said goodbye to Vasimus? Was she heartbroken over it? And what about her feelings for himself? Ricky and Netta had given him the impression that she cared for him. Had their ordeal in Farwin Wood caused her feelings to change? Henry felt more perplexed as he noticed Sarah's worried and nervous mannerisms. *She'd* never actually said she cared for him. The book in his hand felt even more like a consolation now and he wondered if she appeared so out of sorts because she wanted him to leave. His stomach turned at the thought. It felt like they were back at square one again, after all these years of bashful flirtations. He turned to leave before he made her any more uncomfortable or himself for that matter.

Sarah watched Henry go. Her breath caught in her throat and her palms began to sweat. She felt like she would never see him again. He stopped in the doorway and let it rest against his back to guide his handtruck outside. He looked back at her and raised the book up again.

"So...what kind of book is it?"

Sarah's mouth opened, but the words didn't come out right away. "It's...a love story," she smiled.

"Oh," Henry couldn't hide the look of surprise on his face. "Any good?"

"I hope so," she murmured.

Henry managed a smile in spite of his puzzlement. "Good-bye, Sarah."

When the door clanked shut behind him, Sarah let out a long breath and a groan. She slapped her face into her hands. "I'm an idiot!"

Sarah turned her back away from the door so she wouldn't have to see Henry leave through the window. She tugged at her blouse, bringing it in and out to fan herself. Her entire torso felt like it was covered in sweat. This is what happens when you're an idiot and you die alone...menopause sets in early, she chided herself.

The chimes on the door clanked again and Sarah stopped fanning herself. She straightened her shirt front and sighed before turning around to greet the customer. Standing in front of the door, however, was Henry without his handcart. All he held was the book open in his widespread hand. Sarah swallowed and was sure he could hear the loud gulp sound it made.

"Excuse me, ma'am..."

"Yes?" Why is he calling me "ma'am"? It sounded so damningly informal. She felt like she was going to have a heart attack.

"There's a problem with this book," Henry stared at her, but Sarah couldn't discern his blank expression.

"Oh...what's that?"

Henry looked down and read the inscription that Sarah had written on the first page—the only words in the entire book. *"The Story of Henry and Sarah. Five long wasted years of passing looks and one bizarre adventure, the noble delivery man rescued the damsel...and they lived happily ever after..."* Henry cleared his throat after reading the inscription and slapped the book closed with one hand. He took two long, quick steps to close the space between them. His breathing was ragged and he felt like his blood was pulsing rapidly through him.

"So..." Sarah's knees trembled as Henry's intent gaze looked down into her eyes. Just inches away from her, she couldn't tell if the heat she felt was from him, her, or something created by the two of them being so close. "What's... what's the problem?"

Henry cupped the side of her face and grazed his thumb across the curve of her cheekbone. In a soft, husky voice he murmured, just before capturing her lips with his, "None of it was a waste."

DEAR READER

I hope you enjoyed *The Weeping Books of Blinney Lane*. If you could please take a moment to leave a review on Amazon, Goodreads, or even your blog, it would mean so much to me. Reviews truly do help.

If you would like to know more about me and my stories, please visit my blog at:

www.dreadamara.wordpress.com/tag/drea-damara

Thanks!
Drea Damara

ACKNOWLEDGMENTS

Sarah Logan Loomis thank you for editing on a deadline, your faithful support, and friendship. Thank you to Dona Buckman and Shawn Petsch for your critiquing and proofreading contributions. And to that English professor years ago, who told me no matter what I did in life that I needed to become a writer, thank you for lighting the fire and allowing me to think it possible.

ABOUT THE AUTHOR

Drea Damara was born in Illinois where she grew up working on her family's farm. Raised in a home of seven with one television, she spent much of her time in the fifty acres of woods on her family's property or reading. Damara began to write poetry in her early teens and saw her first works published at nineteen. She put writing aside to join the Army and later returned to the Middle East conducting similar work as a civilian. She currently splits her time between Illinois and Europe to balance her needs for hibernation and exploring, and lives with her Corgi, "Murphy," who thinks he runs the place.

The Weeping Books of Blinney Lane is Damara's first novel. She is currently working on The Trinity Missions, a spy thriller series.